FIRST A SYMPTOM, THEN A CORPSE—AND HARDLY EVER A CLUE

"This case, it doesn't fit anything I've seen before," the assistant prosecutor said. Plato thought it over. "It sounds kind of like something we've seen in medicine: Fever of Unknown Origin. Somebody comes in with a temp and no obvious symptoms, you work them up for all the normal things—drug reactions, hidden infections, gland problems like thyroid, different kinds of arthritis. And nothing fits. So you start worrying about cancer, but you can't find that, either. So maybe you sent them home. It's a classic story—a week later, or a month, or even a year, they come back. This time, they've got the symptoms. Usually it's something very bad."

"Yeah. Sometimes really bad." The assistant prosecutor nodded. "Except with this, I'm not worried about some patient dying of cancer. This time, the fever's catching. The patient's already dead, and the doctor might be next."

Plato took a swallow of beer to hide ___ shiver. "I see."

"I want you and Cal ___ selves, understand. ___ Chances are, you ask ___ stepping on someone's ___ has killed once already. S___ who doesn't have anything to lose by killing again."

THE ANATOMY OF MURDER

Bill Pomidor

A Cal & Plato Marley Mystery

A SIGNET BOOK

SIGNET
Published by the Penguin Group
Penguin Books USA Inc., 375 Hudson Street,
New York, New York 10014, U.S.A.
Penguin Books Ltd, 27 Wrights Lane,
London W8 5TZ, England
Penguin Books Australia Ltd, Ringwood,
Victoria, Australia
Penguin Books Canada Ltd, 10 Alcorn Avenue,
Toronto, Ontario, Canada M4V 3B2
Penguin Books (N.Z.) Ltd, 182–190 Wairau Road,
Auckland 10, New Zealand

Penguin Books Ltd, Registered Offices:
Harmondsworth, Middlesex, England

First published by Signet, an imprint of Dutton Signet,
a division of Penguin Books USA Inc.

First Printing, June, 1996
10 9 8 7 6 5 4 3 2 1

 REGISTERED TRADEMARK—MARCA REGISTRADA

Printed in the United States of America

PUBLISHER'S NOTE
This is a work of fiction. Names, characters, places, and incidents either are the product of the author's imagination or are used fictitiously, and any resemblance to actual persons, living or dead, events, or locales is entirely coincidental.

To Karen and Leonard Blake
with love and admiration

Acknowledgments

Like pregnancy and delivery, I suppose, the memories of medical school tend to fade with time. But I have been fortunate to continue my association with the Northeastern Ohio Universities College of Medicine—my alma mater—by teaching and continuing old friendships there. Joseph C. Bernard, lab manager and assistant to the chairman of anatomy, has been a good friend and has been instrumental in helping me verify the behind-the-scenes information on the running of a typical anatomy lab. Likewise, Martin Schechter, Ph.D., chairman of the pharmacology department at NEOUCOM, has been an encouraging listener and reader and has provided valuable insight into drug research, the pharmaceutical industry, and academic pharmacology. Finally, Delese Wear, Ph.D. and Marty Kohn, Ph.D., codirectors of the Human Values in Medicine department at NEOUCOM, have fostered my continued relationship with the college and medical students through my faculty position there.

Thanks also to Stuart Krichevsky and Danielle Perez, my agent and my editor, for all their advice and support. And, as always, thanks to Alice—and Benny and Wendy and Danny—for being there for me.

The student must always remember that former living persons have donated their bodies for medical students benevolently and in good faith. Therefore, the cadaver must be treated with respect and dignity.

—From the Introduction to
Grant's Dissector, 10th Edition

Chapter 1

"I hated my cadaver," Plato told his wife.

They were on their way down to the anatomy lab. Twenty-four granite steps worn smooth by the passage of generations of medical students. A stairwell ripe with the fruity smell of embalming fluid, soap, and rubber gloves. The lab was two stories below the main level of Siegel Medical College, and fifteen degrees colder. The lights were dimmer, too. By the time they reached the bottom, it was as quiet and chilly as an abandoned mine shaft, and almost as dark. The cold air helped keep the bodies fresh.

They were moving so quietly, so furtively, Plato felt like a grave robber.

Cal stopped and fumbled for the hallway lights. Fluorescents whined to life, casting a greenish glow across polished tile, washtubs, and banks of lockers. She turned to Plato and frowned. "What are you muttering about now?"

"I said, I hated my cadaver." Down there, beside the lab where the bodies were waiting, it sounded like sacrilege.

Cal seemed to agree. "That's not funny, Plato. It's a *terrible* thing to say."

"It's true." He followed her over to a locker. She pulled out a tiny blue smock for herself and a large one for Plato. They were already clad in their grubbiest jeans and T-shirts, their most ancient tennis shoes. The pocket of Cal's smock featured some fancy embroidery: "Cal Marley, M.D.: Forensic Pathologist, Cleveland Riverside General Hospital." She was a regular guest lecturer for the anatomy department at Siegel Medical College. Plato's borrowed smock didn't say anything; he was a geriatrician at Riverside and hadn't visited the anatomy lab since his sophomore year in medical school. Cal had volunteered to tutor some failing medical students down in Siegel's anatomy lab, and she'd talked Plato into coming along and helping out tonight.

Her shoulder-length blond hair was pulled up in a bun. She grabbed a bathing cap from the locker, pulled it over her head, and explained. "Keeps the smell from getting in my hair. It takes *days* to wash it out."

They moved across the corridor to the sink and donned two pairs of extra-thick surgical gloves apiece. Time to enter the lab.

"I was very fond of Harriet," Cal mused. "She taught me an awful lot."

Harriett was Cal's cadaver back at Northwestern, but she might as well have been a friend. Some of Plato's fellow students had felt that way about their cadavers, too. Usually the nerdy ones who spent hundreds of hours meticulously tracing every artery and vein and nerve and putting little flags in them so the instructors would use *their* cadavers for most of the practical exam questions. A lot of them had ended up as surgeons. Or forensic pathologists.

"That's how I thought I'd feel about mine," Plato replied. "But it didn't turn out that way."

They entered the anatomy lab, and Plato was lost in a fog of memories. Freshman year: the first day with the cadavers, listening to the instructor's benediction, the ritual cutting of the plastic and the shroud, coming face-to-face with death for the very first time. Long days and nights in the lab, going home smelling like a cadaver and usually feeling like one, too. Counting the days before the practical exams, a thousand Latin names swirling through his head like dead autumn leaves. Failure. "My cadaver had something against me, I swear to God."

"What do you mean?" Cal led him past dozens of stainless steel coffins to a niche near the front of the darkened room. Each coffin rested on a gurney parked near the walls. Four medical students per cadaver, so each gurney was surrounded by four dissecting manuals propped open on music stands. Chamber music for a grisly quartet.

"He must have weighed over four hundred pounds." Plato watched her flick on the lights over one of the tables. They eased the steel doors down and furled the plastic, folded back the oily shroud. She grabbed a spray bottle and anointed the body with a fresh layer of embalming fluid.

"Our group was always the last to leave the lab, Cally. It took us half an hour just to bundle him in and get the lid closed."

This woman didn't have a weight problem, Plato saw. Five-three, maybe five-four, but people always look taller when they're lying down. Gray hair, thin as a rail, but with overdeveloped arms and shoulders. Wasting of the legs, with that oddly smooth skin you see on paralyzed limbs—atrophic changes. Probably used a wheelchair. Her hands were big and callused and vaguely familiar. But it was hard to tell what she looked like, since the skin of the face on Plato's side had been carefully peeled back to show the lacework of facial muscles and nerves. Someone had done a good job with the dissection. Facial skin is quite thin, and the muscles beneath are as many and varied as the expressions they make.

"Poor you," his wife clucked, sarcasm dripping from her voice. "Your cadaver donated his body so you could get a medical education."

"I bet your Harriett was young and slim—an exercise fanatic, probably." Not that Harriet was her real name, of course. Cadavers are generally anonymous; the door of this one's coffin was labeled with a simple blue tag: "65 y.o. female, cardiopulmonary failure." But a lot of students named their cadavers. To Plato, it seemed a little too cute, too possessive. As though the body never had an identity of its own.

"Slim, yes. But Harriet was pretty old. I had trouble finding some of her muscles." Cal stared down at the body, reminiscing over an absent friend. "Sometimes I wondered what Harriet was like, when she was alive. I pictured a very gentle lady. Maybe a music teacher. Her fingers were long and delicate, like she played the piano."

She patted this cadaver's gnarled, ropy hand. Beside it, Cal's gloved hand looked small and smooth as a child's.

"Most of the time, I was wondering how my cadaver had managed to live so long," Plato griped. "Everything was either broken or an anatomic variant. He had a horseshoe kidney and three ureters, and half his arteries started in the wrong places."

"Then you'll make an *excellent* tutor, since you're familiar with all the normal variants." She swung her brown eyes up at him and smiled tightly. "You didn't *really* hate your cadaver, did you?"

"No. I hated anatomy class. I was a terrible dissector." Reluctantly, Plato was doing a litte reminiscing of his own.

"I was always cutting through nerves and arteries. My lab partner, Jerry Flint, got pretty good at sewing them back up."

"Jerry's a vascular surgeon now, isn't he?"

"Yeah. I gave him lots of practice."

She turned to the cadaver's head, retracted the gray scalp flaps and lifted the cranial cap, the bony lid of the skull. "Good. The surgery students started the head for me."

"I thought you were teaching the thorax today."

"We are." She replaced the lid and smoothed the flaps back down. The way the gray hair hung like ivy over the vacant blue eyes reminded Plato of one of his patients. "We'll concentrate on the thorax today. But these kids had a lot of trouble with the skull practical. So we're going to drill them on it every evening."

Her repetitive "we" had Plato worried. "Listen, Cal. I didn't mind coming tonight and helping out. But it's just this once, okay? January is a bad month at the office; all my patient are getting the flu. I don't have enough time, and I've forgotten half the stuff, and anatomy was my worst subject anyway."

"You don't have to be a genius just to tutor some medical students." She folded her arms and glared at him. "You told me you didn't mind. 'No problem,' you said. Last week, you were griping about how we need to get out more."

"Get *out* more? You call *this* getting out?" Plato slapped his hand against the steel table. The loud -clang- shattered the stillness of the room. Thirty-six cadavers stirred in their cold and oily sleep. "Other people go to movies, or see a show. My wife, the forensic pathologist, likes to slice up dead people in her spare time." He flapped his arms. "Maybe I should get some candles and wine."

"That's not fair, Plato. I'm just trying to help these kids—" Her voice broke off, and she stared at the floor.

She was right; it wasn't fair. Plato took a deep breath and decided on the truth.

"Cally. I was *really* bad at anatomy."

"How bad?" She sniffed, and wiped her eyes against the shoulder of her smock.

He glanced down at the cadaver. It was discreetly looking the other way, pretending not to hear. "Bad enough to flunk."

Cal shrugged. "*Lots* of people flunk a class or two. It's no big—"

"I flunked all three quarters. I had to take the entire *year* of anatomy over again with the freshmen, while I kept up with all my sophomore classes."

"Oh, Plato." She reached across and squeezed his shoulder. "That must have been *awful.*"

He stared at the cadaver's face, admiring the tidy dissection once again. "I wanted to be a plastic surgeon."

A quiver started at the corner of Cal's mouth. "Really? You never told me that."

"Yeah. But flunking anatomy ruined my chances of landing a residency spot."

"You're kidding me, aren't you?" The quiver turned into a smirk.

"What? What's wrong? Just because I'm lousy at anatomy—"

"It's got nothing to do with anatomy, Plato. It's your *hands.*"

"What about them?" He plucked nervously at his gloves. "With enough practice, I could have—"

"Practice? Pah-*hah!*" The laugh burst out like a shotgun blast. "Put a scalpel in your hands, and you'd be worse than Jack the Ripper. Whenever you get hold of something sharp, your hand shakes like a jackhammer."

He held up his hands and glared at them. "A little tremor."

"Tremor, huh? You were practically *anemic* until you grew that beard. And look what you did to the Christmas turkey."

"Thanks, Cal. You're all heart."

"You're much better at talking than cutting—that's why you're such a good geriatrician." She smiled and patted his arm.

"Flattery won't help. I think my little ego is bruised beyond repair."

"*Little* ego?"

Plato shrugged. "Anyway, you see why I can't tutor these kids. They probably know more than me already."

"I doubt it, I really do." She stared up at him and her eyebrows met. "You passed anatomy the second time, right?"

"I *had* to."

"Some of these students may not be so lucky. All four of them have been bombing anatomy all year—and not for lack of trying."

Cal served on the Academic Advisory Board at Siegel— the medical school's version of Mount Olympus. Years ago, Plato had appeared before the board, when he flunked anatomy. It was the worst experience of his life; he'd gone into the meeting fully expecting to be kicked out of medical school. His stomach had tied itself in knots, his voice had tightened up until he squeaked like a cartoon mouse, and his wits had taken a leave of absence. But still the gods had smiled on him, given him another chance.

"They all flunked their final exams last month—just before Christmas," Cal continued. "Randolph Smythe the Third was ready to can all four of them."

She always called the board chairman "Randolph Smythe the Third," even though "Dean Smythe," or "Randolph," or just "God" would have been so much shorter. But it wouldn't have been nearly so accurate. Smythe was the crown prince in the Siegel aristocracy. Dean of research, chairman of several boards and committees, and probably the next provost of the medical college—once Dean Fairfax retired. Most of the faculty already saw him as the power behind the throne.

"Smythe agreed to let them take a makeup exam in two weeks," Cal said. "Provided that I tutor them, *personally*. They're good students—I know all of them from my lectures here. Maybe if someone had put some time in to tutor *you* when you failed anatomy, it might have made a difference."

"Well—" Maybe a couple of tutoring sessions wouldn't be so bad after all.

"Besides, I made a little bet with him."

"You made a bet with Randolph Smythe the Third?" Plato's jaw dropped.

"It was the only way he would give these kids a second chance."

"So what's the bet?"

"I told him they were all smart enough to pass their anatomy finals." She smiled and shook her head at the memory. "He said if they did—all four of them—he'd nominate me for the chairmanship of the Academic Advisory Board. He's stepping down anyway, and he said I would deserve it. All the other members agreed. Of course they think it's impossible—they think these kids are hopeless."

A board chairmanship would be a real feather in Cal's cap, Plato knew. She would have the power to soften things up at Siegel, and cut down on some of the pressure. Make the college a little more humane.

But Smythe was a hard bargainer—and he certainly didn't plan on losing. The alternative had to be something truly awful. "And if they don't all pass?"

"They flunk out, I'm off the Academic Advisory Board, and we both have to tend bar at Smythe's next fund-raiser. He's running for Congress, you know."

"I know." Plato groaned. Randolph Smythe the Third wasn't just running. He was already favored to win, before the primaries had even been held. Like many successful maverick politicians, he had a unique administrative style— a cross between Machiavelli and a Kirby vacuum cleaner salesman.

"I can't believe you told him—" Plato began, but he was cut off by the squeak of tennis shoes on the linoleum in the hall.

"Hello?" A woman's voice sounded in the doorway, low and husky, more like a whisper.

Cal peered off into the darkness and smiled warmly. "Hi, Samantha. Come on in."

Samantha hurried through the darkened lab to their circle of light. She was one of Siegel's older medical students—early forties, Plato guessed. Dark eyes, long dark hair with a hint of gray that shimmered in the eerie light. Standing near the feet, she smiled at Cal and shot an inquisitive glance at Plato.

"Samantha Ricci, meet my husband. Doctor Plato Marley." Cal gestured with a scalpel. "He's a family doctor and geriatrician at Riverside General, and he's pretty good with anatomy. He's going to help out with the tutoring."

"Pleased to meet you, Doctor Marley." Samantha was dressed like her tutors—tattered jeans and sneakers, a faded Cleveland Indians T-shirt, and the standard blue smock. And a pair of yellow Playtex kitchen gloves—the kind used for cleaning ovens. Plato had worn the same kind when he was a student; they kept the smell off his hands better than the disposable latex gloves.

"Just 'Plato' is fine," he told her. "Otherwise, we won't know which Doctor Marley you're talking to."

Before she could respond, they heard the clatter of lockers out in the hall. A rumbling voice was met by a high-pitched laugh like shattering crystal. Two more students straggled over to join the group, and Cal made more introductions. The laugh belonged to Tiffany Cramer, a tall, willowy blonde with eyes like blue half-dollars. A rich kid, obviously—dressed in ballerina flats, jabot blouse, and a pleated skirt that matched perfectly with the blue dissecting smock. A small diamond solitaire ring dangled from her gold rope necklace. A rhinestone hair clip and a pair of pearl earrings completed the ensemble. Plato had someone like her in his anatomy lab back when he was a student—dressed to kill for every class. At the end of freshman year, she had her wardrobe dry-cleaned and donated it to Goodwill. Daddy probably took it as a tax write-off.

Raj Prasad didn't look old enough for medical school; he hardly looked old enough to vote. He was even shorter than Cal, with coal-black hair and thick glasses like a pair of fishbowls perched on his nose. He shook Plato's hand and grinned. "Pleased to meet you, I'm sure."

His sonorous baritone was way too big for his body. Talking with Raj gave Plato a queasy little feeling, like talking with a disk jockey, or a politician.

Cal glanced at her watch. "Has anyone heard from Blair Phillips today?"

"I saw him in the library this morning," Samantha replied. The others just shrugged.

"We'll go ahead and start without him." Cal folded her hands in front of her and gazed around at the students. "I understand that you folks all did pretty poorly on the head and neck practical."

"I passed all the other parts," Raj rumbled.

Tiffany nudged him and grinned. "There was only *one* other part, silly."

The others laughed. Because the head and neck were so complex, most of the fall quarter had been spent dissecting and reviewing those structures. The thorax had been the only other area covered on the exam; it was quite easy to learn.

"This time, all of you are going to pass the entire exam, *including* the head and neck practical. And we'll review the abdomen while we're at it, since this quarter's first practical will focus on that area. But I want you folks to study the skull every day. It's by far the hardest area to learn." She reached down to a shelf below the body and retrieved a rubber model of the head. It opened in the midline to show the sinuses, oral cavity, and cranial vault. The brain and most of the other soft parts were removable. Tiny hinges swung open to reveal all the little outlets and inlets, nooks and crannies, the beehive that houses the human soul. Like a Chinese puzzle box, but even harder to fathom. "Today and every day, I'm going to drill you on this model as well as the real thing."

She tapped the model and gazed at each of them in turn, her voice rising and falling like a revival's preacher's. "You'll never graduate if you don't pass anatomy. And you'll never pass anatomy without knowing the skull. Tape a drawing of the facial muscles to the back of your cereal box so you see it at breakfast. Hide your television in the closet for a few weeks and put a model of the skull on the television stand instead. Buy some review tapes and listen to them in the car. You'll be able to name these fossa and foramina with your eyes closed."

"That's what I was doing before the exam," Samantha complained. "My roommate said I was speaking Latin in my sleep."

"Good—then we'll start with you." Cal swung the roof of the skull open and held it up for Samantha to see. "My fingers are in the middle cranial fossa, aren't they?"

"I guess so," Samantha replied doubtfully.

"Here, in the middle, we have a bone with a funny shape, don't you think?"

"That's the sphenoid bone."

"Exactly. Do you know what 'sphenoid' means?"

"Umm."

"Wedge," Raj intoned. "Sphenoid means wedge-shaped."

"That's right, Raj. Looking at the bone, you can see how it got its name. But most people think the sphenoid bone looks more like a bat in flight." She traced the edges of the bone and looked up at Samantha again. "Can you see the shape?"

"Yeah—except it has four wings."

"That's right." Cal's voice was soothing, encouraging. "Which are bigger?"

"These, down here." She pointed at the lower pair of wings.

"Excellent—you've just identified the greater wings of the sphenoid."

Samantha gawked. She held up her index finger and stared at it. "Why, that was so *easy*."

"Not all of it will be this simple," Cal warned. But she had won their attention, and at least a little of their respect. She passed the skull around the circle, touring them across shelves and plates, piloting around tubercles, navigating through canals, trolling and cajoling for answers or guesses. By the time she put the skull down again, Plato's head was whirling with names and terms he thought he'd forgotten, like fluttering snow in a Christmas paperweight.

"Any questions?" Cal asked. The students shook their heads. Already, Plato could sense a change in them—dejection and cynicism brightened by a glint of hope. "All right. For the rest of this session, my husband will work with you on the thorax while I finish dissecting the neck."

Last night, after Cal had asked for his help, Plato had dusted off his old dissecting manual and reviewed the chapter on the thorax. It's a simple area to learn—far fewer muscles and nerves than the arm or leg, no three-dimensional confusion like the skull, and the structures are much easier to find than those of the pelvis. Luckily, most of the dissection had already been done during Christmas break by junior medical students who were taking surgical anatomy and vying for residency positions. Cal had used her influence as a part-time instructor to have a fresh cadaver prepared for the tutoring sessions. Otherwise, it could have taken months to simply complete the dissection.

Blair Phillips finally showed up just as Plato began his lecture. A tall, lanky kid with long hair and bleary green eyes. He came in panting, like someone had just called a code on the cadaver. Plato half expected him to start compressions. But he just mumbled an apology and muttered something about car trouble.

After that, everything went pretty well; even *Plato*'s confidence grew. They worked through the muscles, focused on the relationships of veins, arteries, and nerves at the ribs, and finally entered the pleural cavity. Samantha had trouble mobilizing the left lung, so Plato stepped around to the other side of the table. He slipped his gloved finger down into the space between the lung and ribs and stripped the adhesions away with a feel like popping Velcro.

Meanwhile, he mulled over how the poor woman must have felt when she was alive. Ordinarily, the pleura lining the lungs and rib cage are slippery and smooth as greased Teflon; the lungs expand and contract eighteen times a minute over an entire lifetime with less friction than any piston. But the whole base of the woman's left lung was scarred down like it had been rubbed with sandpaper. Pleurisy is extremely painful; each breath must have been agony.

Sliding his finger down farther still, Plato thought about Marilyn Abel, one of his patients. Before she died, Marilyn had pleurisy like this, down at the base of her left lung. Except hers had been caused by an old Vietcong sniper round planted back in the sixties, when she was an army nurse. The bullet showed up on all her chest X rays; Marilyn was rather proud of it.

And then Plato felt it, a tight little knob lodged at the bottom of the costodiaphragmatic recess, like a marble wrapped in cotton. And everything rushed together to make a horrible sort of sense—the familiar callused hands, the gray hair, the pleurisy, Marilyn's death last December.

Plato glanced up at the face. The disectors had left this side untouched; the skin was a smooth and sallow gray. He saw Marilyn's high cheekbones, Marilyn's wide smile, even Marilyn's *wink*—one deep blue eye closed, the other dissected and lidless.

Plato pulled his hand from Marilyn's rib cage and staggered away, stumbling into the wall and knocking a reading stand to the floor. Across the body, Tiffany Cramer glanced up at him with concern. Samantha mined her hand deep into the chest again, excavating with the oven cleaning glove, her face a mask of concentration. She felt it, jerked her head, and gestured for Raj to hand her a scalpel.

The others craned their necks to peer into the the thorax and help mobilize the lung as Samantha wrestled with her prize. Finally, the long yellow kitchen glove emerged triumphant. Marilyn was already dead, but she was free of the bullet at last. Samantha held the object up to the dissecting light—a tiny pellet wrapped in scar tissue. Cal grabbed a

tray and they hacked away to discover the secret of the
pearl.

"It looks like a bullet!" Raj exclaimed.

"Oh, my God!" Tiffany Cramer had forgotten her
clothes for the moment; her oily glove was pressed to the
neck of her jabot blouse. "Do you mean she was—she
was—*murdered*?"

"It doesn't make sense," Blair Phillips was saying. He
stared back at the body. "There should have been blood—
a big clot or something, right?"

Samantha turned the body slightly. She explored the
landscape of Marilyn's back and found the scar just where
Plato knew it would be—one centimeter below the tip of
the scapula. When she was shot, Marily had been bent over,
examining a wounded soldier. Miraculously, the bullet had
threaded the gap between ribs 7 and 8, just clipping the
intercostal nerve but leaving the vein and artery intact. An
excellent demonstration of clinical anatomy. The bullet had
probably been fired from quite a distance, Marilyn had explained. So instead of hurtling on through, it had nestled
in near the apex of the heart. The doctors hadn't wanted
to risk removing it.

"This is an old wound, Tiffany. She wasn't murdered."
Samantha pointed to the scar. "Right, Doctor Marley?"

Cal looked at the bullet again and peered down at the
scar.

"You're only half right, Samantha. That looks like an old
entrance wound." Being a forensic pathologist, Cal had
seen a lot of entrance wounds, both new and old. "Small-
caliber rifle bullet, probably an old war injury."

Plato nodded, impressed but not surprised. His wife was
an expert in her field. But then she said something that
made him wonder.

"I'm afraid you're wrong about the other part, though."
Cal glanced at the neck again; her dissection there was
almost complete. She raised the shroud, folded the plastic
over the body, and gazed around the group. "This woman
was almost certainly murdered. I'll need to take her body
down to the morgue for an autopsy."

Chapter 2

"You sure have a flair for the dramatic, Cal." Plato piloted their rusty Volkswagen Rabbit up the curving freeway off-ramp. It was a typical Ohio January. The mercury hadn't cleared zero in over a week, and the exit from Interstate 77 was a glazed ribbon of ice. Too much speed and you slipped across the curb into the oncoming lane. Too little and you slid down the banked curve into the snow-covered guardrail. "I expected you to announce that it was Colonel Mustard, in the drawing room, with a candlestick."

"I wasn't trying to be dramatic. I was just as surprised as you were." Cal's face loomed white and faded away beneath the beam of a passing streetlight. Lips drawn tight, she was gazing fixedly on the road ahead, leaning into the curve as if to urge the Rabbit away from the guardrail. "Anyway, it wasn't a candlestick. That woman was strangled, or suffocated—or maybe a little of both."

The Rabbit sidled up to the intersection and skated through just as the light turned green. They both breathed easier.

"How could you tell?" Plato asked.

"The first thing I noticed was her eyes—I saw the scleral petechiae right when we pulled down the shroud." Cal shuddered. "Little tiny hemorrhages in the whites of her eyes. From increased blood pressure in the head."

"Lots of things cause scleral petechiae," Plato muttered. "I see them in my patients all the time. Maybe she had a bad cold and did a lot of coughing. Could have been anything."

"I know. It just made me suspicious, that's all." She glanced out the window at the rolling snow-covered hills of Summit county, and held her breath as they crossed the rusting iron bridge over the Cuyahoga River. Beyond the guardrail, the waters swirled dark and cold, a trail of black ink spilled across the paper-white landscape. "So I went ahead and started the neck dissection. The surgery students hadn't gotten that far, so it had to be done anyway."

"Any marks on the neck?"

"Not on the outside." Cal took a deep breath. "But her thyroid cartilage had been fractured."

Plato whistled. From his anatomy days, he remembered that the thyroid cartilage rests in front of the windpipe, forming part of the voicebox. The cartilage is quite delicate; with increasing age, it becomes calcified, brittle, and more prone to breakage. But even in older people, a good deal of force is needed to fracture it. The kind of force used for strangling someone.

Even when no marks are found on the outside of the neck, a cracked thryoid cartilage is a classic sign of foul play. Cal had once told him that she always checked the area closely, especially in older people.

A "Low Bridge" sign bloomed in the Rabbit's dim headlights. Their turnoff was just ahead, past a stand of tall fir trees. Plato skidded past the intersection and backed up again to make the turn. Their street didn't even have a name, just County Road 142. A string of farmhouses and barns and old country estates weaving along the Cuyahoga River in the northeast part of Sagamore Hills. A narrow road winding through trees and foothills, skirting cliffs and ravines, salted once every year around Christmas, and paved every decade or two.

"Maybe the cartilage was cracked *after* she died." Plato mused. "Could have happened when her body came to the lab for embalming."

Cal frowned. "Not likely. There's some bleeding in the area, so the fracture almost certainly happened premortem—before she died. Besides, to make that kind of fracture, you'd have to be pretty clumsy embalmer."

"The embalmer at Siegel is anything but clumsy," Plato assured her. "Sergei Malenkov was there when I was a student. He's about a hundred years old now, but he's still sharp as a tack."

"I've heard about him. But everyone makes mistakes."

"Not Sergei." Plato shook his head firmly. The old embalmer and lab director knew everything there was to know about anatomy. Just *standing* next to him was intimidating.

"The guy's a walking textbook—*Gray's Anatomy* with legs."

"Then she was murdered."

Plato almost skidded past their driveway, but fishtailed in at the last moment. The long gravel driveway was knee-deep in snow; he kept the speed up and piloted the Rabbit through the trees like a twenty-foot Chris-Craft cutting through a crowded harbor. Ahead, their sprawling century-old home was hunkered down in the snow, peeking between the trees with blind windows and a swaybacked roof. They coasted over the stone bridge spanning the ravine, slalomed up the hill with wheels spinning, and finally slid to rest at the door of the carriage house.

They hiked through the snow to the front porch and mounted the stairs with studied care, avoiding the cracked planks and rotting floorboards.

It was a beautiful place, the realtor had promised two summers ago. A classic Victorian home, one with character and charm. She was right; they'd fallen in love with it on their first visit. Cookie-cutter latticework, balconies and turrets, half-moon windows, and a low-slung country porch circling the front and sides. Like a giant dollhouse, Cal had said. They'd stopped looking after that, worked out the arithmetic of student loans, credit card and car payments, and found that they could just squeeze into a mortgage if they ate nothing but peanut butter for the next fifteen years or so.

The giant dollhouse had fooled the appraiser from the bank, too. Despite the size of their mortgage, the place was three shingles away from being condemned. It was their curse.

The lock was jammed; Plato's key wouldn't fit. He took off his gloves, promptly dropped the key ring, and fumbled around in the snow with his bare fingers. He swore loudly, his words freezing in the still winter air.

Cal poked the drift with her boot, retrieved the keys, and nonchalantly slipped one into the lock. Plato glared at her as she swung the door open and stepped inside.

They stood in the doorway stamping their feet, slipping off their boots, and shrugging off the cold. Foley, their blind old Australian shepherd, padding up to lick Plato's hand.

"Why are you so interested in this case, anyway?" she

asked him, soft brown eyes mildly curious. "I thought you didn't like talking shop at home."

Plato sighed. "I just can't believe anyone would want to kill Marilyn."

Cal tossed her coat onto the ornate walnut banister, slid into her slippers and frowned. "Who's Marilyn?"

"Marilyn Abel—the cadaver," Plato replied. He slipped his boots off and followed her down the long bare hallway into the kitchen. "She was a patient of mine—I told you about her when the county guys were getting the body ready for transport."

"I guess I wasn't really listening." She flicked on the lights and shivered. The sight was enough to frighten anyone: countertops littered with open cereal boxes, moldly loaves of bread, and a couple of dirty mixing bowls; the ancient gas stove cluttered with pots and pans from yesterday's Prego feast, the sink piled deep and tall with dirty dishes. Dante, their cat, was curled up on top of the stove like a huge orange oven mitt. "We need a housekeeper."

"We need a *house,* that's what we need," Plato corrected. "A real one, with a dishwaster, a stove that works more than half the time—"

"Tap water that doesn't look like watered-down coffee," Cal added dreamily.

"A furnace that works in the winter instead of the summer," Plato concluded. He rubbed his hands together. "Speaking of which—is it just me, or is it kind of cold in here?"

Cal made an O with her mouth and blew. A lazy puff of fog floated from her lips. "I think we can afford to turn the thermostat up a little."

"Maybe." Plato turned the dial up in the hall, then walked over to the refrigerator.

"So that cadaver was a patient of yours, huh?" Cal asked. "I guess that's why you were so surprised when—"

"When I found the bullet. Yeah—that's when I realized who it was." He closed his eyes, made a wish, and pulled the refrigerator door open. Dante sprang up, tightwired through the piles of dishes, and peered around the corner hopefully. Foley somehow materialized beside Plato's knee.

"I thought maybe you were sick or something," Cal said. "You haven't had any dinner." Behind him, she was frowning at the moldly bread and tossing it into the trash. "How can anything grow in here when it's so cold?"

"Beats me." Plato scowled at the empty refrigerator, then his face brightened. "Hey—we still have one more stuffed pizza left in the freezer downstairs. How about it?"

"Great." Cal shivered again. "And maybe while you're down there, you can check the furnace."

"I don't know if it'll get much warmer tonight," he warned. "It's seventeen below outside, the furnace is fifty years old, and this house has less insulation than a pup tent."

"Maybe we can light a fire tonight—that would be romantic." She turned a knob on the stove, lit a match, and touched it to a hole in the floor of the oven. The gas roared to life. "Then you can tell me all about Marilyn."

"Sure." Plato walked down the long hallway to the basement door and flicked the light switch. Nothing happened. The bulb was burned out again. No point bothering with a flashlight, though; the freezer stood just at the foot of the stairway.

Cal's voice echoed to him from the kitchen. "The water isn't working. Check the well pump, will you?"

"Okay." He shrugged and threaded his way down into the blackness, vaguely curious about the strange rushing noise coming from one corner of the basement. Behind him at the top of the stairs, Foley growled a warning into the darkness.

"It's all right," Plato called over his shoulder. "It's okay, boy."

Three steps, two steps, one.

"Aaaghh!" Plato fell to his hands and knees on the basement floor—or what had been the basement floor. Sometime today, their basement had been magically transformed into a half-frozen skating rink. The water was about a foot deep, with a skin of ice on top. The shock stole Plato's breath away. He choked and gagged, gasping for air.

The cold water had instantly sucked all the heat from his body. The gears in his brain slowed and ground to a halt. He crouched there in the slush, frozen in place, the product of some demented ice sculptor's nightmare. His breaths came in quick hiccupy little heaves. After a few seconds, or a minute, or five, he finally willed his legs into action, staggered to his feet, and stumbled back to the stairs.

"Plato? Are you all right?" From the top of the stairs, Cal was frowning into the darkness and flicking the light switch on and off. "It doesn't work."

"I kn-kn-know." His tongue was stiff with cold.

"What's wrong?" Her voice wavered with sudden concern. She squinted harder into the darkness. "Are you hurt?"

"Not h-h-hurt." His lips felt like setting cement. He forced his frozen legs to move, climbed the first step, then the second. Water trickled from his hair, T-shirt, jeans, and tennis shoes, down to the pond in their basement. It made a pretty sound. "Just—surprised. Would you mind . . . getting a flashlight . . . please?"

She disappeared. He heard her footfalls on the floor upstairs, crossing and recrossing the kitchen, sifting through drawer after drawer, checking the utility closet, the coat closet, the cupboard under the kitchen sink. Plato's shivers were out of control now, like an epileptic seizure. His breaths came in quick puffs, making faint little clouds that danced before his face. He pictured the water rising slowly, slowly, lifting the house off its foundation and floating it over to the Cuyahoga, while Cal carried on her hopeless search for the flashlight.

The problem was obvious—the well pump and rusting water pipes were tacked to the outer wall of the basement. The cold was just too much for them. Probably the furnace had gone out first; that's why the house was so cold. Then the pipes had frozen and split open. But the well pump had kept right on working, even after the outlet pipes broke—that rushing sound confirmed it. Plato guessed it must have happened sometime this morning; with the floor drain taking some of the flow away, it would have taken all day for a foot of water to build up. If he could just make it over to the pump and switch it off, before the water reached any electrical outlets—

Plato stepped down into the water again, and felt a faint popping as his foot split the ice. It really wasn't so bad, now that his feet were numb. Handling the shivers was tricky, though; he almost fell twice during his thirty-foot voyage to the opposite wall of the basement. He plunged his hands into the water and fell the round bomblike shape of the pump thrumming happily away.

"Plato?"

Behind him, a beam of light split the darkness, blinding him for a moment. But his hands had already found the switch. He flicked it off and the pump sputtered and died. He pulled the plug from the outlet, then stood and faced the beam of light, his face frozen into a crazy grin.

"*Plato,* what are you *doing*?" Cal rushed into the water and sloshed over to his side.

His mouth moved with effort. "Shi-shi-shivering."

He slumped onto her shoulder, let her drag him to the stair, then stopped at the freezer to force the words through chattering teeth. "Don't forget the pizza."

She groaned and turned to tug him up the steps.

Two hours later, they were nestled beside a roaring fire in the cavernous living room, tangled up together under a heavy knitted afghan. Tucked under his arm, Cal felt the last of Plato's shivers dying away.

Dragging him upstairs had been the worst part, Cal reflected. His quivering legs had wanted to fall out from under him, leaving Cal's shoulders to support the load. His quick, labored breathing and the bluish pallor of his face had frightened her almost as much as the icicles that had formed in his beard.

She had peeled his wet clothes off and toweled him dry while pots of ice and snow melted on the stove. Filling the huge old bathtub upstairs took almost an hour, but it was worth it. Plato's ruddy color had returned. He'd perked up enough to wolf down half of a spinach- and sausage-stuffed Chicago pizza, stoking his own furnace back to life. Beneath the blanket, his naked body was warm and cozy, his breathing steady and slow.

Dante and Foley were curled up at opposite corners of the hearth, a pair of fuzzy andirons.

Cal nestled in closer, pressed her head beneath Plato's beard and sighed. She could almost forget that the repairmen weren't coming until morning.

"So what about Marilyn?" She kissed his chest and slid her bare leg over his hip.

"What about her?" Plato's voice was furry with sleep.

"How did she die?"

"Hmm." He sighed. "Heart attack, I think. The card on her box said cardiopulmonary failure."

"Nothing unusual?" She propped herself up on her

elbow and stared down at him. In the firelight, Plato's heavy-lidded eyes glittered green like a cat's.

"Not really." But his tall forehead wrinkled a little.

"Did she die at home?" Cal asked.

"No." He sounded a little puzzled. "She died at the medical school."

"At *Siegel*?" Cal sat up and let the blanket fall away. The fire's warmth washed over her skin. "What was she doing there?"

"She worked there." Plato's eyes opened a little wider. He reached for her. "You'd better get back under the covers—I'm catching another chill."

"Hmm. Feels like you're getting better, somehow." Cal slipped away and smiled. "What kind of work did she do?"

He shrugged. "Marilyn Abel was a Ph.D.—a star researcher in the pharmacology department. And a real workaholic. Lots of late nighters; she used to sleep there on the couch sometimes." He smiled faintly. "Marilyn's brother Jonathan is one of my patients, too. He used to tell me that Marilyn would work herself to death—and I guess that's what she did. One morning last December, Marilyn's assistant found her dead in the pharmacology lounge. She must have died in her sleep."

Cal stared at the fire thoughtfully. "There should have been a post."

"There was—Weber did it." Plato yawned. "I think he said it was a myocardial infarction."

"Weber thinks *everything's* a myocardial infarction." She grimaced. Dr. Matthew Weber was a hospital pathologist at Riverside General, but he occasionally handled autopsies that weren't obvious coroner's cases. He was incompetent, but he had connections with Riverside's board of trustees. "Why didn't you tell me about it?"

"What's there to tell? Anyway, I wasn't even on call— Dan Homewood made the decision." Plato and his partner took call on alternate weekends. "I doubt I'd have called in the coroner either. Marilyn was a diabetic with some nasty heart problems. Besides, she was donating her body to the lab—Weber probably didn't want to mess it up too much."

"That's another thing I don't understand." Cal frowned. "If she worked at Siegel, why did they keep her body there instead of donating it to another lab?"

"What's wrong with using her body at Siegel?"

"There's a good chance it would have been recognized, maybe even by the students who were performing the dissection. Freshman medical students are squeamish enough, without having someone they know as their cadaver."

"Marilyn spent most of her time on research—I don't think she did many lectures. Besides, she's only been there a couple of years." Plato sat up and tossed another log on the fire. A shower of sparks took flight and disappeared into the darkness. The damp maple hissed and crackled and finally burst into flame. He settled down again and pulled the blanket up to his chin. "She retired from a drug company and came to work at the medical college. She wanted to slow down, work at a more relaxed pace. Do some teaching."

"And she was still a workaholic? I'd hate to have seen what she was like *before*." Still sitting up, Cal glanced down at her husband. He'd turned toward her, laid his head against her bare thigh, draped his arm across her lap. His eyes were closed, his breath warm, against her side. His heavy black beard tickled her leg. She squirmed. "I'm still surprised no one recognized her."

"The junior surgery students did most of the dissection, remember?" Plato sighed. "They all took pharmacology last year, just after she joined the faculty. She didn't give many lectures. And once her face was half dissected, I doubt *anyone* would have recognized her. I certainly didn't."

"Not until you found the bullet."

"Mmm-hmm."

"She was a paraplegic?"

"Not quite. You noticed her legs too, huh?" He looked up at her. Shadows flickered and danced across his jagged features and deep-set eyes. "Marilyn had multiple sclerosis. Atypical distribution—pretty much restricted to her legs. Her arms were healthy and strong, except during flare-ups."

"Huh." She shook her head. "That doesn't make any sense."

"Why not?"

"I checked her arms over carefully, looked at her hands, her neck, her face." Cal was puzzled, remembering. "There weren't any bruises, no signs of a struggle at all."

"So what? You said someone might have held a pillow over her head. Maybe she was sleeping."

"Even so, she should have woken up. With arms as strong as hers, she could have put up quite a struggle." Cal pressed a finger to her lips. "Unless . . ."

"Unless what?"

"Unless she couldn't use her arms. Maybe they were paralyzed, too."

"How?" Plato asked. The drowsiness had disappeared from his voice. "Marilyn's last flare-up was over a year ago. I saw her the week before she died, and she was fine. Her multiple sclerosis was stable; it even seemed to be improving a bit."

"I'm not talking about multiple sclerosis," she replied. To Cal, the answer seemed obvious. "Maybe she was drugged."

"Mabye." Plato touched her arm gently, gave that patronizing little smile of his. "But, Cally, I think you're taking this thing a little too far. All you have so far is a cracked thyroid cartilage that might have come from rough handling of the body."

"It wouldn't explain the hemorrhage at the site." She pulled her arm away, thought a minute, then smiled. "But you're right—I need to talk to Sergei Malenkov as soon as possible—find out if there were any accidents. Maybe tomorrow."

"Maybe so." He slid away, rolled onto his back, and closed his eyes.

"I haven't met him yet," Cal hinted. She gave her anatomy lectures in the auditorium upstairs; she had never visited the lab during the day. "I wish I knew him. He might get offended, or think I'm questioning his abilities."

"Mmff."

"You're *asleep,* aren't you?" she accused.

"Almost." Plato's eyes blinked open again.

She smiled slowly. "He'd remember you, wouldn't he?"

"Who?"

"Sergei Malenkov."

Plato sighed. "Sure he would. I spent more time in the anatomy lab than just about any other student in Siegel's history." He grinned. "Sergei took me out for a beer on the day I passed the final."

"Great." Cal sidled close again, slid the sole of her foot

along the inside of his leg, slipped her hand down to his hips. "Maybe you could set it up for me, hmm? Maybe you could come along."

"I doubt it, Cally. I'm booked with patients all morning, and I've got a pile of charts to dictate." He combed his fingers through his thinning black hair and smiled apologetically. "Plus I'm giving a lecture on hypertension Wednesday morning. Sorry."

Cal frowned down at her husband. This Malenkov fellow sounded pretty imposing. She had to get in to see him, and it would be a lot easier with Plato's help. But she could feel the door closing. "I'll help you with your lecture."

"What do you know about hypertension? None of your patients *have* any blood pressure." He closed his eyes and buried his head in the pillow.

"I know a lot about hypertension. Especially how to prevent it." Cal reached for his hands, pulled them slowly up to her, and placed them there, and there. She shook her blond hair over her shoulders, leaned down to kiss his nose, and whispered in his ear. "They say daily exercise is extremely important."

"Extremely." Plato's eyes fluttered open.

She slid up a little and slipped her fingers into his hair, pulling his head closer. "And a healthy diet."

"Mmm-hmm."

"And stress-relaxation therapy. Like this—" She demonstrated. "But you don't believe in that sort of thing, do you?"

"Actually, I do." His voice shook a little. "There was an article in the *New England Jour*—"

She covered his mouth with hers, and waited for the right moment to ask again. "So you'll set it up for me tomorrow? And come along?"

"Mmm. You've convinced me." He gazed up at her with a languid smile. "But I might need some more help with my lecture."

"You're doing just fine."

Chapter 3

"It makes *perfect* sense to me, Doctor Marley." Eunice Wisniewski sat on the examining table and glared at Plato through a thick pair of blue-framed cataract glasses. Her arms were crossed, her wrinkles were set into a stern frown, and her yellow wig was slightly askew. "I take the blue pills in the morning with breakfast, the round yellow pills at lunch and dinner, the square pills with my snack, the purple pills when I wake up at night, the red capsules when I have back pain, the green capsules—"

Plato let her drone on while he contemplated the sack of medicines in his lap. A brown grocery bag half filled with no less than forty different bottles of pills. Some of the prescriptions dated back twenty years, their labels a hit parade of golden oldies—drugs that were outdated or dangerous, prescribed by doctors who had long since retired or died.

She was taking a grand total of forty-two pills a day— more, if you counted the as-needed drugs. No wonder she was losing weight; half of her diet consisted of pills. Luckily, Eunice was a retired accountant, and very intelligent. A demented patient might have made any number of dangerous mistakes. The grocery bag held a hundred different ways to die.

"The point is that you don't *need* all these drugs, Eunice." Plato dragged the garbage can over with his foot. He brandished a handful of pill bottles. "These, for instance. You're on four heart medications that do exactly the same thing." He held up one of the bottles. "This one is the best, so we'll keep it. The other three"—Plato dropped them into the trash—"we'll throw away."

Eunice held out her hand for the remaining bottle. "Let me see that one. Oh, yes—Tenormin. Doctor Stevens prescribed that for me. He was very good."

"Yes, he was," Plato agreed. He plunged his hand back into the bag. Four down, thirty-six to go.

"Doctor Stevens died just last year." Her blue eyes were huge and sad behind the thick glasses. "Such a shame. I went to his funeral, you know. We all did. My friend Helen Maschevitz was a patient of his—did you know her?"

Plato looked up and shook his head.

"Well, you wouldn't. She died, let's see, it was four years ago now. She was my neighbor on Ansel Road, back before I moved to Glenwood Acres." Eunice glanced at the little mirror over the sink across the room. She straightened her wig and smiled wistfully. "We both loved Doctor Stevens. All his patients did."

"Mmm-hmm."

"At least *he* didn't make his patients throw good medicine away." She crossed her arms again and harrumphed.

Eunice was in a bad mood today. Her daughter had returned to Chicago with the grandchildren after spending a week with Grandma. Looking forward to her daughter's visit had cheered Eunice through the fall and winter. The post-holiday blues would hit her harder than ever.

The fact that Plato was running nearly an hour behind this morning didn't make Eunice any happier. But the plumber had shown up late, the furnace man never came at all, and then the Rabbit refused to start. Plato had showered in the residents' on-call quarters over at the hospital, then rushed across the street to his office. After just three minutes outside, his wet hair and beard had frozen stiff.

"I'm sorry you feel that way, Mrs. Wisniewski." He sneezed. "But having this many pills around is dangerous. I'm worried about your—"

His pager buzzed. He flicked the switch to acknowledge, then checked the number. The county morgue.

"And Doctor Stevens never wore one of *those*." Eunice pointed at his pager. "He said they were just status symbols, that doctors didn't really need them."

"Most of my patients like being able to reach me during emergencies," Plato countered, trying to hide his irritation. "I'll be back in a minute. How about having a seat on one of the chairs; you'll be more comfortable."

He helped Eunice down from the table, then snuck back to his office to answer the page.

"What's up, Cal?"

"You wanted me to page you when I got started, remember?" Her voice frizzled through a shower of static; the morgue's phone had a bad connection.

"Yeah. I'm just finishing up with my last morning patient." He glanced down the hall to make sure Eunice was staying in her room. "Give me about half an hour, okay?"

"You don't sound very curious."

"I am, Cally." He sneezed, sifting through the piles of charts and bills and memos and insurance forms for a box of Kleenex. He settled for a napkin left over from yesterday's takeout lunch. It felt like coarse grit sandpaper. "Marilyn was my patient, remember?"

"Are you okay? You sound like you're getting a cold."

"I'b fide." Honk. "Just a sniffle. I'll be over in an hour."

"You said *half* an hour."

"Did I? Make it three-quarters, then."

An hour later, Plato finally arrived at the county morgue. Eunice hadn't wanted to surrender several of her drugs, especially those prescribed by Dr. Stevens. Sacred relics from a departed saint. Plato had figured she'd be fine with four medications, but Eunice wanted twelve. They finally compromised at seven.

The autopsy room at the Cuyahoga County Morgue was huge—about thirty by thirty, with brightly painted walls, a ceilingful of fluorescent lights, and a few cheery windows high up in the far end. Chalkboards scattered along the walls advertised organ weights, meeting dates and times, and a pair of extra tickets to next weekend's show at the State Theatre. The room held two tables, each topped by four perforated steel shelves, with sinks at the near ends, and an array of hoses, knobs, and drains leading down into the linoleum floor. The counters lining the walls housed sinks, cabinets, and dissecting instruments. A small nook in the corner held racks and racks of glass specimen jars—a pantry of people parts, a morbid museum of the anatomically bizarre, collected over the decades by the coroner's staff.

Pathologists were a strange breed, Plato knew. He was married to one.

Marilyn Abel's body rested on the L-shaped autopsy table near the center of the room, with only the intact side of her face visible. Seeing her that way, right after leaving his office, brought back a rush of memories. With her multiple sclerosis, Marilyn had been one of his regulars—the core group of patients he saw at least every month. Most of the regulars had chronic diseases, though some suffered from depression or personal problems or just plain loneliness. But with Marilyn, it was strictly business. She had a nasty illness and she was counting on Plato to help slow it down, to keep it under control so she could finish her research.

But over the three years Plato knew her, Marilyn began to let down her guard. She'd put up with MS for three decades, but her last flare-up, a year ago Christmas, had struck especially hard. It crippled her further, slowed her speech, even left her half blind for a while, and scared her out of her wits. The neurologists weren't sure whether she'd get any of it back, or how much. Marilyn wondered whether she'd ever work again, and worried that this might be the beginning of the end. Plato told her the truth, that they didn't know, that they could only wait and hope and work at the rehab.

Three months passed before Marilyn finally returned to her work at Siegel. Three months of strenuous rehabilitation, regaining her arm strength and coordination, learning to survive in a wheelchair, and training her mouth to speak clearly again despite frayed nerves and muscles weak from disuse. She shared her ordeal with Plato, and let herself lean on her doctor just a little bit. She told him stories about her life as a nurse in Vietnam. She opened up about her stormy divorce, her concern for her brother Jonathan, and her sometimes volatile relationship with her daughter Tricia.

Marilyn Abel had tremendous inner strength. At the worst of times, when she had a major setback, when even Plato got discouraged, she would hit him with that little wink of hers. The one that said, *It's okay, it's no big deal, I know I'm going to beat this thing.* With her weakness, winking was such a strain that her face scrunched up horribly, and Plato couldn't help laughing. And then Marilyn would laugh, too.

She tried to explain how it felt to have multiple sclerosis—the anger, the frustration, the depression. As a scientist, she understood the disease intellectually, understood that the insulation sheathing her neural circuits had broken down and that the nerve impulses traveled more slowly, or were short-circuited or garbled, or never arrived at all. But to Marilyn, intellectual explanations didn't help. She told Plato she felt *rusty*. Like the Tin Man in *The Wizard of Oz*. A quick, active mind trapped inside a clumsy, immobile body. The only difference was, no one had found the right oil for her yet.

And no one ever would—not for Marilyn, at least. Lying in the center of the huge room atop the stainless steel autopsy table, her body looked even smaller than ever. Plato tried to imagine how or why someone would strangle a harmless crippled researcher, but he couldn't. It just didn't make any sense. Maybe Cal was wrong.

Standing on a stepstool beside the body, Cal was nearly invisible in her coveralls, mask, and surgical cap. No blood this time; the coveralls were still a spotless white. The faucets at the end of the table weren't even running. A surprisingly neat procedure.

"Maybe you should do all of your autopsies this way," Plato said.

"Very funny." Cal squinted up at him through a pair of loupes. The special glasses had strong magnifying lenses mounted at their centers. Eye surgeons often used them for close work, but Cal employed them to search for tiny bits of evidence during autopsies. The loupes were very expensive; they were a gift from Cal's fellowship director in Chicago.

Using a pair of forceps, she retrieved a tiny object from the chest, peered at it through the loupes, and placed it into a plastic evidence bag. "All done."

Plato slipped on a pair of gloves and stepped over to Marilyn's body. It hadn't changed much since he'd seen it down in the anatomy lab. "So what did you find?"

"I flipped through Weber's report before I even started." Cal stripped her gloves off and tossed them into the hazardous waste bin. "He doesn't say anything about a heart attack—he just lists the cause of death as 'cardiopulmonary arrest.' " She rolled her eyes. "What an idiot. I haven't met a dead person yet whose heart and lungs hadn't stopped. Coronary atherosclerosis is a cause of death. A stab wound to the chest is a cause of death. Cardiopulmonary arrest is a *synonym* for death."

"Down, girl." Plato stepped back a few paces and raised

his hands. At the same time, he was quietly pleased that for once, Cal's rage wasn't being vented at *him.*

"Weber's report says, in writing, that he thoroughly examined the neck," she continued. "When I called him this morning, he just chuckled, like he'd made a trivial mistake." She tore her paper coveralls in two and tossed them into the trash. "I have no patience with idiots, Plato."

"I'm aware of that. Believe me." He grinned, stepped over and squeezed her shoulder. "But Weber's not a forensic pathologist, remember."

"That's just what *he* said. As though that was an excuse for stupidity." She stomped to the sink and scrubbed her hands viciously. "I know plenty of good general pathologists."

If Cal had her way, all cases like Marilyn's would be referred to the county coroner for determination of the cause of death. But the rules for coroner's referrals were a little vague. Homicides, suicides, car crashes, and custodial cases were clearly reportable. Likewise, deaths happening under suspicious circumstances were investigated. On the other side of the spectrum, patients who died after 24 hours in-hospital were generally not reported, if the cause of death was apparent. Marilyn's case fell somewhere in the middle. Reporting to the coroner wasn't required when a patient was under the care of a physician for a disease which could be expected to cause death—even when the situation was a little unusual, like Marilyn Abel's. The decision to report was left to the attending physician's judgment. So Dan Homewood had hedged his bets and had one of the hospital's pathologists perform a limited autopsy.

Unfortunately, Matthew Weber had handled the case.

"Maybe you should talk to Jensson," Plato suggested. Dr. Ralph Jensson, the Cuyahoga County coroner, was a board-certified forensic pathologist like Cal. Not that he had to be; Ohio laws only required that the coroner be a physician, and be elected. Jensson was the best of both worlds—competent in the lab and popular with the voters. He'd won every election in the past ten years by wide margins.

"That's not a bad idea," Cal agreed. She dried her hands and sat at the counter to scribble some notes. "I haven't had a good chat with Ralph in a while. It might be nice to see what he thinks."

Cal respected his opinion. After all, Jensson was a pioneer in the field of forensic pathology, and one of its most respected practitioners. When Cal had come to the Cleveland area, Jensson had offered her a half-time position as deputy county coroner. She spent half her time at the county morgue or in court, and the rest of her time at Riverside General.

Cal was chief of pathology at Riverside General—largely by default, since the position featured no pay increase, and none of the other pathologists in the department were interested. But when Weber had hinted that he might try for the retiring chief's post, Cal had rushed to apply and was quickly approved. As she had told Plato, working *with* an ignoramus was simply irritating and annoying. Working *for* one would have been intolerable.

"I should have left my gloves on." Cal donned a fresh pair and walked back to the autopsy table. "I wanted to show you a few things."

Plato stepped over. "You found something new?"

"I think so." She climbed up on the stool, adjusted a light, and retracted Marilyn's remaining eyelid. "First take a look at what I saw last night."

Plato squinted at Marilyn's face. Death had changed her eyes somehow—they were smaller and less round, and slightly deflated, like week-old toy balloons. Even so, peering into the open eyes of a dead body was always a little unsettling for Plato. After a year of marriage to a forensic pathologist, he was no longer very squeamish about autopsies or cadavers. But Marilyn's deep blue eyes seemed to be staring through Plato, past him, at something he couldn't see. Or didn't want to.

"See the hemorrhages?" Cal asked. Her gloved fingers had spread the left eyelid wide open. The medical students had already removed the right eyelid.

"Yeah." They weren't typical scleral hemorrhages, bright red marks on a field of white. The embalming fluid and the passage of time had turned the sclera a grayish-yellow color, and the hemorrhages—dark brown pinpoints—were barely visible. If the cadaver had been stored for another month or two, the marks would have disappeared completely. "You've got pretty good eyesight, Cal, even without the loupes. If you hadn't pointed them out, I don't think I'd have seen them at all."

"I just know what to look for." She pointed to the conjunctivae—the inner lining of the eyelids. "You can also see some hemorrhages here, and a few along the bridge of the nose. They're very tiny, aren't they?"

"Yes. Is that important?"

"It fits with my drug theory. If Marilyn had struggled, the hemorrhages would have been larger." She glanced up at Plato. "They can also develop naturally, if the body is lying facedown. But Weber's report says she was found faceup."

She reached down and peeled back the skin and muscles of Marilyn's neck to reveal the thyroid cartilage, or "Adam's apple." The cartilage always reminded Plato of the bow of a ship, with a notch at the center and horns extending from the two sides. It forms part of the voicebox, and is much smaller and flatter in women than in men.

Cal pointed to the horns of the cartilage. The right horn stretched back and sideways in a smooth line from the edge of the cartilage. On the left, though, the fingerlike structure took a sharp angle inward. Looking closer, Plato could see that the horn was broken neatly in two. The surrounding tissues were discolored with a brownish-purple stain.

"The hemorrhage is very important—it almost certainly proves that it was an antemortem injury. If the cartilage had cracked because of rough handling of the body, we probably wouldn't see any blood." Cal folded the flaps back again.

"So what do you think?" Plato asked.

"I think someone smothered her with a black or gray pillow, and leaned a little too hard." She pointed down at the neck. "They pressed on her neck, too. From her left side, since that's where the fracture is. Part suffocation and part strangulation."

"How can you be sure she was suffocated at all? Maybe they just strangled her without leaving any marks." Plato frowned. "And what's this about a black pillow?"

"Take a look." Above the paper mask, her brown eyes glittered. She retrieved the evidence bag from a rack beneath the table and showed it to Plato.

It seemed empty at first, but a closer look revealed several tiny blue-black filaments, smaller than human hairs, in the corner of the bag.

"Pieces of thread?"

"Polyester fibers." She took the bag again and placed it on the counter. "Guess where I found them."

"Is that what you were pulling out of her lungs?"

"Yeah. I found them in her nose, her mouth, and deep down in her airways." She crossed her arms. "I've spent all morning tracing the pulmonary tree. She must have sucked them in with her last breaths."

Plato shuddered. "That's a nasty way to kill someone, Cal."

"There aren't very many nice ways."

"Sure there are." He nodded. "A big shot of morphine in my sleep when I'm seventy-five. That's a nice way."

"You wouldn't think so if you were seventy-five."

"Maybe not." Plato stared at the body and mulled over Cal's findings. The evidence still seemed a little flimsy. And he still had trouble believing anyone would want to kill Marilyn Abel. "Have you told Homer about this yet?"

Plato's cousin was an assistant prosecutor for Cuyahoga County. In most cases, the coroner's office dealt with the prosecutor's staff rather than directly with the police. And as Cal's cousin-in-law, Homer was a perfect contact between the prosecutor's office and the county morgue.

Cal shook her head. "I still want to talk to Sergei Malenkov first."

"I thought you were sure that her thyroid cartilage was broken before she died."

"I am. But Weber's report says that the medical school transported her body here when she died—Malenkov probably handled that. And a *severe* blow to the neck, within a few hours after death, could cause some oozing of blood in the area. I need to trace the body and make sure nothing like that happened." She sighed. "I also want to get a feel for how the body looked before it was transported here. Whether there were any bruises that might have faded during the embalming process. I don't trust Weber's report."

"You still haven't found any signs of a struggle?"

Cal shook her head. "I still think she may have been drugged, but Weber didn't save any blood samples or run a tox screen. The idiot."

"I guess you'll never know, then."

She glanced down at Marilyn's half-dissected face. "I suppose we could try the vitreous. With a body this fresh—"

"The vitreous?"

"Vitreous humor," Cal explained. "The fluid inside the eye. Even after embalming, drugs or toxins can still be present and detectable. Here, turn the head this way. You can help me."

Plato watched her gather a syringe and specimen tube from one of the cabinets. They turned Marilyn's head to the side and Cal flipped the plastic cap off of the needle. Marilyn's blue eyes were staring at Plato's right ear as Cal inserted the needle into the white of her left eye, poked around a bit, and finally drew a teaspoonful of clear fluid into the barrel of the syringe. Marilyn's left iris sank a little then, its gaze turning slightly askew to lock with Plato's.

His stomach gave a little lurch. He swayed beside the table.

Cal looked up at him with alarm. "You okay?"

"Fine. Just my cold, I guess." He turned away and sniffed loudly. His paper mask was wet.

"Poor dear. We're almost done." She stepped over to the counter and squirted the fluid into a rubber-topped specimen tube. "Did you get a chance to call Sergei Malenkov this morning?"

"Yeah." He turned Marilyn's head upright again, forcing her gaze away from him and back to the ceiling. He closed her eyes—her left eye, anyway. "He said we could come anytime after three."

"Great—then we have plenty of time for lunch." Cal glanced at her watch. "How about helping me get her into the fridge?"

They pulled the sheet back up, slid the body onto a gurney, and rolled the cart down the hallway and into the cool room. Plato didn't stop it fast enough; the cart bumped the back wall and the sheet slid away from her face.

Marilyn was winking at him again. *It's okay. It's no big deal.*

But it wasn't okay. He smiled sadly at her and shook his head as he pulled the sheet back up and tucked it gently beneath her body.

Chapter 4

"It is a pleasure to finally make your acquaintance, Mrs. Doctor Marley." Sergei Malenkov bowed low and kissed her hand. "I've heard good things about your lectures upstairs. I look forward to working with you down here in the lab."

"Thank you." Cal's eyebrows fluttered with surprise, though Plato had warned her about the formality. On the drive over from the hospital, he had told her all he knew about Sergei. The lab director's family had fled Russia during the Revolution; they supposedly had blood ties with the czar. Sergei still referred to the communists as Bolsheviks.

As he stood, Sergei winced and rubbed his back gingerly. "Please to forgive me—the sunburn, it is terrible. We have just returned from Barbados. Snorkeling and sailing."

"I understand perfectly," Cal replied with a smile. "Plato and I spent our honeymoon in Antigua."

"A beautiful place, Antigua is. Very quiet, very private." His eyes glistened with memory. "Mrs. Malenkov and I spent many summers there. Dickenson Bay, the small town of Saint John, all very simple. Of course, that was many years ago."

"It hasn't changed much," Plato noted.

Neither had Sergei Malenkov, Cal thought. Plato hadn't seen him in the ten years since early medical school, but during the drive he had described Sergei perfectly for Cal. The lab director's long, brooding face was seamed and leathery, his shock of white hair was thinning at the top, and his tall, gaunt body was slump-shouldered and stooped.

Sergei Malenkov had been an institution in the cadaver rooms for generations. He had been old when most the faculty were students at Siegel, and those who could remember said he hadn't changed a bit. An aged, ageless specimen, a living dinosaur untouched by the hand of time—or handled so roughly that a little more wear and tear hardly mattered anymore.

Not that he really looked like a dinosaur. With his height, his prominent yellow teeth, and his long, thin neck, medical students had affectionately nicknamed him The Giraffe. Probably sometime in the forties, Cal mused.

The name suited him well, Plato had told her. During anatomy lab sessions he would trot from group to group, poking his head into clumps of students, asking questions, worrying away at the scanty answers, patiently grazing on scattered bits of knowledge. But he always passed on more information than he received. Though he had no formal degree other than a bachelor's in biology and a funeral director's certificate, the decades he had spent in the anatomy lab had given him an encyclopedic knowledge of human anatomy. First-year medical students would point to a tattered nerve, a bony tubercle, an obscure branch of a misplaced artery, and Sergei provided the name as well as a reference in Gray's anatomy or Grant's atlas.

They were sitting in Sergei's office now, a dusty old room hardly larger than a broom closet, filled with charts and maps and models, a skeleton or two, ancient tomes as old as Leeuwenhoek's microscope, and anatomy journals filled with the latest findings in neuroanatomy and biomechanics.

Sergei stood beside his desk and tugged at his ear. "I am faced with a dilemma, Doctor Marley."

"Please call me Cal." She smiled, charmed by the old lab director. She was looking forward to teaching in his lab.

"Certainly. And I am Sergei." He nodded, then frowned. "When Plato called this morning, I neglected to mention that a body was being shipped to our lab today. The body arrived late, but I would like to complete its preparation while the fluids are still fresh. Would it be too rude if I answered your questions while I work?"

"Not at all." Cal shrugged. This was far easier than she had expected. On the drive over from the hospital, Plato had made the lab director sound like an old dragon. But he seemed like a dear.

They followed him through a connecting doorway into the embalming room, a square chamber much smaller than the autopsy suite at Riverside General, but similarly equipped. A gurney in the corner held a freshly prepared specimen, wrapped in a shroud and a clear plastic bag. And

on the single table in the center of the room lay the naked
body of an obese middle-aged man. His arms were outstretched and his eyes and mouth were open in an attitude
of astonishment. His face, the fronts of his legs, and his
enormous belly were a fishy white, while the backs of his
legs and his flanks were stained a dusky purple.

The Giraffe whirled on Plato. "Why the discoloration,
Doctor?"

"Livor m-m-mortis," Plato stammered. "It's caused by
blood settling into the dependent areas."

Cal smiled proudly.

"Very good." Sergei glanced at Cal and grinned. "I see
you have taught him well. Can I offer you some tea or
coffee while we talk?"

They politely declined. Sergei adjusted the position of
the cadaver on the gurney and wheeled it over to another
corner. Then he donned a pair of gloves and a mask and
approached the fresh body. He slowly folded the arms back
onto the chest and closed the eyelids. Sergei handled his
bodies gently, almost reverently, Cal observed. As though
his charges were still alive. And in some way, for the old
lab director, perhaps they were.

"This poor gentleman suffered a heart attack at home,"
he explained. "He was rushed to the hospital in a state of
ventricular fibrillation. Although the paramedics started his
heart again, he arrested very quickly and died in Riverside
General's emergency room. He had generously specified a
wish to donate his body to our medical school, and his
family complied. And so, he arrives here."

Sergei carved an incision at the base of the neck, probed
for the carotid artery and jugular vein, and looped heavy
black suture around them. His long fingers were deft and
amazingly quick. In seconds, he clamped off the upper portion of the carotid artery, threaded a plastic catheter down
into the aorta, then threaded another catheter into the jugular vein. He attached the arterial catheter to the pump
and switched it on, then explained, "Just a saline preparation. We flush out as much blood as we can before infusing
the embalming fluid."

Purple-brown fluid spurted from the veins into clear plastic tubes leading down to a sink beside the table. While the
pump was running, Sergei led them to a quiet corner of
the room. He dragged some chairs over and seated Cal in

the most comfortable one. "I understand that you took one of our cadavers away for an autopsy last night."

She nodded. "Marilyn Abel. We're investigating her death."

"Such a tragedy." Sergei's gaze grew distant. "So unexpected. Her research was taking some very promising turns."

"Did you know Marilyn?" Plato asked.

"Oh, yes." He bobbed his head quickly and flashed his yellow teeth. "We often had lunch together. A truly dedicated scientist—very rare, these days. But I am puzzled why you ask the questions now. After all, Marilyn died several weeks ago. Has not an autopsy been performed?"

"Yes and no." Cal explained how she had discovered the scleral hemorrhages during their tutoring session last night, then described the cracked thyroid cartilage, the hemorrhage in the surrounding tissues. "So we're pretty sure her death wasn't natural," she concluded. "But as you say, it happened six weeks ago. I was hoping you might fill in some of the details, tell us how it happened and what you observed."

During Cal's narrative, Sergei's face had grown ever longer and sadder. He shook his head. "*Bozhe moi!* What you say, it is unbelievable. Not that I doubt your findings, you understand. It's just that Marilyn Abel, she was so dedicated. Something of a—how do you say?—*fanatic*. Her work was everything to her."

"I was just as surprised," Plato agreed. "She was a patient of mine."

"Perhaps you could help us make sense of this," Cal suggested. "I understand that you transported her body to Riverside General?"

"Yes, yes." The Giraffe chewed his lower lip, remembering. "The police came, of course. And an ambulance was sent from the hospital. But you'll remember that we had a terrible snowstorm here in December. The hospital's ambulance ended up in a snowdrift." He turned a hand palm-up. "I own a four-wheel drive vehicle that is very handy in the snow; I have used it for transports on other occasions. Some of the funeral homes here are not very reliable, you understand. The bodies must be *fresh* when I receive them."

"Marilyn's body was discovered in the morning?" Plato asked.

"Yes—by her assistant. A medical student. She had apparently been dead for some time—she was as cold as this man here, livor mortis had already set in, and no efforts were made to resuscitate her." His huge eyebrows drew together. "It was all a very bad circumstance. Final exam week, the students were upset by the commotion and the police, and I did not want to wait for another ambulance from the hospital. And of course, she was a friend."

Cal touched his arm sympathetically. "That must have been very difficult for you."

The old anatomist tossed his head. "I was happy to help. But this which you tell me, it is still a shock. You are certain she was murdered?"

"Almost certain," she replied. "But we were curious about the handling of the body, the position it was in when she was found, whether the injury might have been produced after death."

"Of course, of course. All this now becomes very important." He glanced over at the body. The pump had completed its work; clear fluid was now returning from the venous catheter. He walked over and switched off the pump, changed the tubes to clear the cranial arteries, then finally ran a length of tubing to a different container and started the pump once more. "My own special formulation. Very little formalin odor; a cleaner and more pleasant smell that washes quickly from the hands. You have noticed it, yes?"

Cal and Plato exchanged dubious glances but nodded enthusiastically. Their hands still reeked of embalming fluid from yesterday's dissection. They had worn surgical gloves during last night's dinner and this afternoon's lunch.

Sergei returned and sat. "It was Friday of final exam week, Friday morning. I learned of Marilyn's death from my assistant. I was busy preparing an examination for some of my graduate students; the medical students had taken their practical test earlier in the week. Of course, I quickly rushed upstairs to learn if it was true.

"Sadly, it was so. Our security guards were already there, turning people away. Doctor Albright, the chairman of the pharmacology department, allowed me to enter the room and see her." He closed his eyes, knuckled his forehead and rocked slowly. "I have seen death many times, as you can imagine. But Marilyn's face, I will never forget. Her mouth open, as if to scream. The tongue protruding slightly. All consistent with a cardiac arrest, perhaps."

He gnawed his lip again, and his voice hoarsened. "But her eyes. In them was written a fear that even now I can see. Stark, overwhelming terror. The kind that drives all reason from the mind."

Sergei shuddered and turned away. He stood quickly and paced over to the body, examined the connections, and fiddled with the flow adjustments on the pump. He rubbed his eyes on the sleeve of his lab coat.

Finally, he returned and sat down again. "The police arrived and took a report. I stayed with her through much of the morning, until we learned that the ambulance was not to arrive."

"You're pretty sure no one mishandled the body?" Cal asked. "Is there any possibility that the blow to Marilyn's neck might have occurred *after* death?"

"I think not. I understand that she was found early in the morning, shortly before I was called. My assistant and I took the utmost precautions in transporting the body."

"What position was the body in when you arrived?" Plato asked.

"Faceup. That was how she was found."

"Did you speak to Doctor Weber at the hospital?"

"Yes, yes. Of course, I mentioned Marilyn's wish to donate her body to the laboratory. He promised to be careful. Perhaps he was a little *too* careful."

"Yes, he was," Cal replied.

"Even with the limited nature of Doctor Weber's examination, the embalming process was somewhat difficult." Sergei stared at his hands sadly, and Cal realized that he wasn't just talking about technical problems. "Marilyn had asked me about the donation process. I helped her with the papers last summer—she was very specific about keeping her body at Siegel. But I had no idea she would arrive here so *soon*."

"I'm surprised her body was used so quickly," Cal said. "I thought the embalming process took longer."

"Yes and no." Sergei shrugged. "With the fluids we use these days, six or eight weeks—even four weeks—is sufficient, though not ideal. We prefer to keep the bodies for up to a year before using them."

Plato sounded surprised. "Why so long?"

"Partially to allow time for the embalming fluid to do its work. As you know, a cadaver must last an entire school year. If the body has not been adequately treated, the tissues tend to dry and decay." He trotted back to the body and switched off the pump again, then tied off the artery and vein and replaced them beneath the skin. Quickly, he sutured the incision closed again. "There is another important reason for holding the bodies, though. Once in a great while, a family's lawyer needs forensic evidence—for issues like black lung disease or other legal matters. Even more rarely, a family cannot cope with the idea of dissection, or the absence of the dead relative's body. And so it is returned."

"You made an exception in Marilyn's case, then," Cal noted.

"My *assistant* did." Sergei shrugged. "I was in Barbados at the time. It seemed a reasonable choice, for the surgical anatomy students. My assistant knew that I had talked with Marilyn personally, and the documents had been signed by her daughter and brother, so everyone was comfortable with her decision."

"But why wasn't an older body used?"

"Ah. Perhaps I have failed to make myself clear." Sergei smiled. "You have both taken anatomy—you understand the different between living tissue and that of a cadaver, yes?"

They nodded.

"The junior medical students, those taking surgical anatomy, required the use of a body for their class. For the study of surgery, a fresher specimen is generally preferable. One that more closely resembles the living body." He made a cutting gesture with his hands. "The tissues of a cadaver are tough, unyielding, while those of a fresher body are softer and more pliable. A fresh body's response to the scalpel is much more like that of living flesh. While we had several fresh bodies available, Marilyn's was the only intact specimen. The other fresh bodies had all undergone major surgeries, procedures that dramatically altered their anatomy." He reached under the table for a shroud, slid it under the cadaver, and tied it shut. He gently bound the head in plastic wrap. Finally, he drew a large plastic bag over the body and sealed it closed. "My assistant saw the opportunity to meet two goals at once—to use a fresh specimen for surgical anatomy, and to provide a partially dissected body for your tutoring purposes. Unfortunately, he made a critical error, one which I deeply regret."

"And what was that?" Cal asked. She and Plato exchanged confused looks.

"You did not realize? My assistant failed to check whether any of your students had known Doctor Abel."

"Had they?"

"Yes, of course. Tiffany Cramer—she was working part-time as Marilyn's lab assistant. She's the poor soul who discovered Marilyn's body on the day of her death." He sat down and shook his head ruefully. "As I said, an oversight on our part. I had just discovered the problem when you pulled the body for a second autopsy."

Cal was shocked. Why hadn't Tiffany said anything? But then she remembered that Plato hadn't recognized Marilyn, either. The surgery students had performed most of the initial dissection, including the face.

"It is fortunate that matters worked out this way," Sergei noted, "although your discovery is a very disturbing one."

"I'm sorry," Cal said. "The death of a friend is always disturbing. And then to learn that it was murder—"

"Yes, yes, of course." Sergei impatiently waved her sympathy away. "But I refer to the larger picture. Marilyn was alive and well on the day of her death—I chatted with her on my way out late that afternoon. And after five o'clock, the outer doors are sealed to visitors." On his knees, his enormous hands fluttered like butterflies. "So the obvious implication is that we have a killer in our midst, somewhere here in the medical school. A brutal murderer, one who inspires fear and terror. The kind of terror I read in poor Marilyn's eyes."

Chapter 5

By the time they arrived home, darkness had fallen, along with another few inches of powdery snow. The Rabbit nearly bottomed out several times on the long driveway, tires spinning and whining, spitting gravel and snow. Plato let out a horrible sneeze, lost hold of the steering wheel, and almost plowed into a tree before getting it under control again. Maybe he really was sick.

Tonight's tutoring session had been canceled for lack of a cadaver, thank goodness; Marilyn's body was still at the county morgue. Earlier that afternoon, Cal had called the four students and promised them that the sessions would resume tomorrow evening. They'd have the cadaver back by then. And it wouldn't do Plato any harm to get some extra rest.

As they crested the last hill, the Rabbit's headlights picked out a huge shadowy figure in a black leather jacket, pacing up and down the long low porch.

"Looks like we'll be feeding Homer again tonight," Plato mused as he pulled the car to a stop beside his cousin's battered Chevy Caprice. Every week or two, Homer ran out of microwave meals and turned up on their doorstep.

The assistant prosecutor grinned at Plato and Cal as they climbed the steps to the porch. "Home late today, huh?"

"Doctors don't work in shifts," Plato replied sourly. "I keep telling you that."

"Yeah, yeah. Neither do lawyers." He stood aside to let Cal unlock the door, then followed them into the house. He shrugged off his jacket and tossed it onto the banister. "Colder than hell out there. Ten below again tonight."

"Why didn't you wait in your car?" Cal asked. "Is your heater broken again?"

"Nope." Homer shook his enormous head. "Know what

it is, Cally? It's *claustrophobia*. That damned car makes me feel like a cork in a champagne bottle."

Plato wasn't surprised. If his cousin ever tired of legal work, he could always turn to pro wrestling. Plato was over six feet tall, but his cousin stood a full head higher and had the rough proportions of a champion Saint Bernard. Homer had been a brilliant short-yardage fullback at Willoughby South, but competition at Ohio State had been a little more fierce. After getting his law degree, he'd come back to Cleveland to join the prosecutor's office.

He coached high school football in Shaker Heights now, so he had free access to some of the best weight-lifting equipment in town. He bench pressed 400 pounds; he could lift Plato over his head with one hand.

His appetite was even more impressive.

"It's Tuesday," Homer pointed out helpfully. "Chicken paprikash tonight, right?"

"Maybe." Cal reached out to poke his stomach with her index finger. It sank past her first knuckle. "Putting on a little weight, are we?"

"Muscle, Cally. Muscle. Plato tells me it's heavier than fat." He followed them into the kitchen and watched anxiously as Plato surveyed the contents of the refrigerator.

"I think we *might* have enough chicken and sour cream," Plato announced. He sneezed again, twice. "I just don't know whether it's worth the time." He sneezed once more. "I thig my code is gettig worse."

"Funny thing." Homer frowned. "My buddy on the force just happened to get me an extra pair of tickets to the Cavs game next month. Cops' night. I'd be willing to trade them for a good dinner. Of course, if Plato's too sick to cook—"

Cal's eyes flashed. "Where are the seats?"

"Lower level, near half court."

"He's fine," Cal said confidently. She squeezed her husband's arm. "Aren't you, Plato."

"Sure." He shrugged. "It's just a touch of pneumonia. I'll probably live. Why don't you two sit down and make yourselves comfortable while I slave away at dinner?"

Behind him, Homer grinned and tumbled into a battered vinyl chair, dragging another one over for his legs. Cal sat across from him at the weathered oak table and rested her chin in her hands. They watched as Plato dragged chicken, margarine, eggs, and sour cream from the refrigerator.

"He's pretty good, isn't he?" Homer asked.

"Yeah." Cal sighed and rested her head on the table. "Just *looking* at him makes me tired."

"Wait till you catch my cold," Plato warned. "Then you'll really be tired."

"Speaking of cold," Homer began, blowing into his hands, "Is your furnace broken or something? It's *freezing* in here."

When Cal explained last night's disaster, Homer frowned and hurried off to the living room. In five minutes, he had built a roaring fire in the fireplace. He returned again and sat down, hands in his pockets.

"Did you leave a message at work for me, Cally?" he asked. "They've got a new system at the office. Voice mail, they call it." He grimaced. "Crappy little machine ate my tape—you sounded like a cross between Donald Duck and Columbo."

"It wasn't the machine," Plato said. "She always sounds like that."

Cal kicked him.

"Something about a murder?" Homer asked. "I haven't heard about any new cases—it's been a pretty quiet week."

Plato mulched a couple of onions in the chopper and listened as Cal recounted her discoveries in the anatomy lab, the results of the second autopsy, and their interview with Sergei Malenkov. He sautéed the onions and margarine, then cleaned the chicken and added it to the pot. Cal explained that she was still waiting for toxicology results from the vitreous humor.

"Vitreous humor?" Homer frowned. He'd listened to several of Cal's autopsy reports before, but the term was new to him. "What's that?"

As Cal explained, the lawyer's broad face wrinkled into an attitude of disgust. He shook his head at Plato. "That's a sick wife you've got, buddy. Sucking juice out of people's eyes. Sounds like a horror movie."

"You should see what she does with the brains." He doused the chicken with paprika, replaced the lid, and started boiling water for the dumplings while the chicken simmered.

It was looking more and more like Marilyn Abel had been murdered, Plato knew. But finding the killer seemed like an almost impossible task. Plato couldn't imagine a reason why anyone would wish to kill an elderly researcher at an obscure medical college—especially in such a cold-blooded, premeditated way. Her family life had seemed stable enough, and he knew of no problems at Siegel. Marilyn was reasonably well liked at the medical school, a quiet type who did very little teaching, kept to herself, and spent most of her time in the research lab.

He spooned the dumpling batter into the boiling water and thought about Marilyn's research. Sergei had hinted that she was on the verge of an important new discovery. The rights to a successful new drug could mean millions of dollars to the patent holder. But researchers were *always* excited about something—was she really that close to a big break? And even if she were, how would her death have benefited anyone?

"So there we are," Cal was saying. "It looks like murder, but we don't have a whole lot to go on."

"It sounds good enough to me," Homer said confidently. Over the past couple of years, he had developed a lot of trust in Cal's judgment. She was hardly ever wrong. "Just revise the death certificate and we'll have the cops open up a file and get started on it."

He stood and fished three Dos Equis from the fridge and handed them around. He lifted the lid from the pot and squinted at the chicken critically. "How much longer, chef?"

Plato forked a pile of cooked chicken parts onto a plate and handed it to Homer. "As soon as you and Cal debone this, we'll be set."

Homer groaned and slumped over to the table. Dante and Foley trailed behind hopefully and parked themselves beside his ankles.

"I don't want any bones or gristle this time," Plato warned. He stirred some flour and sour cream into the broth and watched his cousin nimbly stripping chicken from the bones. Homer's hands were awfully small for his size; his weakness for fumbles had kept him from making the last cut at Ohio State. But his fingers were amazingly deft; he played clarinet with a jazz quartet every Friday night.

Homer finished a thigh and snagged a breast from the pile. "It's going to be tricky, no doubt about it. There won't be much of a crime scene to investigate; most of the evidence is probably gone. If there was any to begin with.

Fishing for alibis'll be like trying to find your lost contact lens in Lake Erie. You know it's in there somewhere, but finding it is another story."

"At least it was final exam week," Plato pointed out.

The lawyer tossed some scraps into the animals' food bowls and frowned. "What difference does that make?"

"At Siegel, the final exams make up most of your grades. And all the finals are given in just a few days." Once in a while, Plato still was haunted by a horrible recurring dream: he was reliving final exam week at Siegel, but he'd lost the textbooks, missed all the classes, and didn't know any of the other students. He filed into the auditorium with a trusty Number 2 pencil, a blank answer sheet and examination book, and a mind every bit as empty. The first question invariably dealt with gross anatomy.

"The medical students treat final exam week like a shuttle liftoff at Cape Kennedy," he continued. "Most of them plot out their study time down to the hour, minute, and second. It's an unusual week for the faculty, too. I bet most of them will be able to remember where they were, and what they were doing."

"Huh." Homer thought it over. "See, Plato? That's the kind of thing you folks could help me with."

"What do you mean?"

"I mean, I'm going to need some advice." He set his feet on the floor and swiveled to face Cal. "This is your baby, kiddo. It sounds like you made a good pickup, but I bet the cops won't have a clue where to start. Give them a dead pusher or a stickup at a Seven-Eleven, and they'll get the job done. But Siegel Medical College might as well be the moon for them—and for me, too."

"So how can we help?" Cal asked.

Homer frowned at the last drumstick and stripped the meat away. "I'll try to get the sheriff's office to handle the case. That way, Jeremy Ames can take statements and handle all the official questioning. He's pretty sharp. But you two know most of the people out at the medical school, right?"

"Right," Plato agreed. Since graduating from Siegel, he had precepted medical students, served on a few committees, and kept up friendships with many of his former teachers. Cal had also spent a lot of time at Siegel, teaching anatomy and setting up a pathology elective for interested students. "I even know Marilyn's family. Her brother is a patient of mine and I've met her daughter a couple of times. Marilyn was my patient, too."

"Damn." Homer sobered, looked at Plato thoughtfully. "So you've got a personal stake in this?"

"Yeah." He remembered Marilyn Abel winking at him from the gurney in Riverside General's morgue. As Marilyn's physician, maybe Plato could do one last service for her. "I suppose I do."

"You won't mind helping out?"

"I *want* to help." Plato leaned on the stove and glanced over at Cal. She looked surprised. Usually, he hated it when she got too involved in a case, dragging both of them into an investigation. This time, maybe he would do the dragging. "I really do."

"So you two could talk to her friends at Siegel, and talk to her family without raising much of a fuss."

"I did a summer fellowship with her boss when I was a medical student," Plato said. "Chuck Albright. He's an okay guy."

Homer nodded. "Maybe you could fill me and Jeremy in on how things work out there, too. Point us in the right direction."

Unlike some lawyers, Homer knew when to ask for help. He'd gone a long way in his five years with the prosecutors' office.

"No problem." Plato took the bowl of chicken from Cal and stirred it in with the sauce and dumplings. He didn't have much free time this week, but at least he wasn't on call. This morning, Plato had felt so terrible he'd wished he could take the day off. Why couldn't he ever get sick when he was on vacation?

"I'll talk it over with Jeremy Ames tomorrow," Homer said. "Where's a good place for us to start?"

"Right here." Plato slopped some chicken paprikash into a bowl for his cousin and ladled out smaller portions for himself and Cal. "Let's eat."

After dinner, Plato took Homer down into the basement to show him the mess. The sump had drained most of the lake away, but the walls bore a high-water mark about two cinderblocks up from the floor. Boxes, newspapers, books, and linens were scattered around like debris from a tiny hurricane.

Homer whistled. "Good thing you guys came back when you did."

"Why's that?"

"If the water had frozen, it could have ruined your foundation big time—seeped into the masonry and busted it to bits. Your whole house could have collapsed."

"You're kidding."

"Nope." He stepped across the floor and dragged a box from one of the puddles. "I saw it happen in one of those old dumps on Fifty-fifth. Same thing—old-fashioned basement, furnace went out and the pipes froze. They got a lake in their basement and the water cracked the foundation. House looked like somebody stepped on it."

Plato swallowed hard and wondered whether insurance would cover something like that. He guessed it would fall under the "Acts of God" clause.

They got a mop and bucket and started working on the mess. Feeding Homer was usually a good investment. Back in college, he had spent his summers working with a general contractor, so lately he'd taught Plato how to shingle a roof, lay brick, and do some rough carpentry. Just last month, he and Plato had refaced the crumbling brick fireplace in the living room.

Homer was one of the fastest workers Plato had ever seen, a brilliant legal mind wrapped up in the body of a stevedore. After especially long days in court, he often came by to mow their huge lawn or work their half-acre "garden," or pitch in on some other chore. Homer called it his occupational therapy, but Plato sometimes felt guilty about it. Especially tonight—he barely managed to plod along after his cousin, coughing and sneezing and sorting through the trash while Homer did the heavy work. Still, it only took a couple of hours. When they finally finished, Plato grabbed another pair of Dos Equis from the refrigerator and sat with Homer on the steps to survey their work.

"It's cleaner than it ever was before," Plato observed.

"I know." Homer tipped his head back, drained half the bottle, and wiped foam from his lips. He glanced up the stairs to make sure Cal wasn't nearby, then lowered his voice. "I've been thinking about the case some more, Plato."

"Yeah? Me too."

"I'm a little worried about getting you and Cally involved."

"You're not getting us involved, remember? We're getting ourselves involved." Plato glanced at his cousin. Homer's hooded brown eyes looked troubled. "Are you afraid Jeremy Ames will get ticked off?"

"Nah." He swatted the air with his hand. "Cal has helped both of us on cases before, and so have you."

"Then what is it?"

"I don't *know.*" Homer closed his eyes, shook his head, and sighed. "It's just a feeling, I guess. You spend a lot of time in court, talking to killers and rapists and drug pushers, and you get a feeling about things."

"Yeah?" Plato waited patiently for his cousin to explain.

"This case, it doesn't fit anything I've seen before. I close my eyes, and I don't get any picture at all. Like it never happened, except it did. The lady's dead, and Cal thinks she was murdered. Okay, I trust her. But it just doesn't fit."

Plato thought it over. "It sounds kind of like something we see in medicine. 'F.U.O.', they call it. Fever of Unknown Origin. Somebody comes in with a temp and no obvious symptoms, you work them up for all the normal things—drug reactions, hidden infections, gland problems like thyroid, different kinds of arthritis. And nothing fits. So you start worrying about cancer, but you can't find that, either. So maybe you send them home. It's a classic story—a week later, or a month, or even a year, they come back. This time, they've got symptoms. Usually it's something really bad, like leukemia or lung cancer."

"Yeah. Something really bad," Homer nodded. "Except with this, I'm not worried about some patient dying of cancer." He set his bottle on the step and rested his arm across Plato's shoulder. It felt like a steel girder. "This time, the fever's catching. The patient's already dead, and the doctor might be next."

Plato took a swallow of beer to hide a slight shiver. "I see."

"I want you and Cal to watch out for yourselves, understand? This guy killed once, and from what I can see, Marilyn Abel wasn't much of a threat. Maybe it was some drug she'd come up with, or maybe she knew something about somebody. Or maybe the killer has a loose screw, deep inside his brain. But chances are, you ask questions and you'll be stepping on someone's toes. Someone who's killed once already. Someone who doesn't have anything to lose by killing again."

Chapter 6

"There was spiders all over that wall there last night. Hundreds of them, thousands. Furry green, with big white teeth." The toothless old woman pointed past the privacy curtain to the wall behind Plato. Mrs. Cummings's dentures were resting on the bedside table. She complained that they didn't fit right, so she usually carried them in her purse and stuck them in her mouth for meals.

Of course the spiders had big white teeth. Mrs. Cummings probably envied them. Plato wondered what Freud would have made of her symptoms.

Dutifully, he turned and inspected the wall. It was painted hospital-issue blue, that dull sickly shade that covered the walls of patient rooms throughout the old west wing of Riverside General. Aside from a bulletin board covered with Get Well cards, a television up near the ceiling, and a shaft of morning sunlight, the wall was completely blank.

"They're gone now," Mrs. Cummings pointed out. She sounded disappointed.

"I think you've had a little drug reaction, Beulah." In simple terms, Plato tried to explain what had happened.

It was a typical case of sundowning, handled in the typical fashion, with the typical disastrous results. Mrs. Cummings was a 78-year-old woman admitted to the hospital two days ago for diverticulitis—an infection of the colon. She had responded well to treatment and was slated to return home this afternoon. But last night, shortly after dark, the nurses had found her wandering in the halls, agitated and confused.

They called the intern, who recognized her symptoms as "sundown syndrome." It was a common problem in elderly patients torn from the familiar surroundings of home and placed in a hospital bed with little sensory or social stimulation. During daylight hours, older patients are usually able to cope with the change. But by evening, the mixture of fatigue, isolation, strange surroundings, and darkness can lead to symptoms appropriately called "sundowning."

Unfortunately, the intern had zapped her with a heavy dose of haloperidol, a strong tranquilizer and antipsychotic drug. The dose young Dr. Miles had ordered would have knocked a water buffalo off its feet. And since drug breakdown is much slower and less efficient in elderly patients, experienced doctors generally stay away from the stronger tranquilizers.

The intern had treated Mrs. Cummings's mild confusion by replacing it with terrifying hallucinations reminiscent of a bad LSD trip. Plato had already had a little chat with Dr. Miles this morning. Dr. Miles admitted that he hadn't reviewed the entry for haloperidol in the *Physician's Desk Reference,* nor had he adjusted the dose for Mrs. Cummings's age or small size.

Dr. Miles confessed that he had never received haloperidol at any dosage, and he declined Plato's kind offer to let him try it. He had promised it would never happen again.

"Everything should be fine when you go home," Plato assured his patient.

"Praise the Lord!" She held a hand to her chest. "Last night was so scary, I was like to have *died* if they hadn't gone and called you. I remember hearing that other young doctor say he'd have to call Doctor Marley, and just knowing you was there made some of them spiders go away, I know it did."

"I'm glad." He patted Beulah's hand and stifled a yawn. The senior resident had called Plato at 3 A.M. and apologized for Dr. Miles's error. Plato's cold had kept him awake the rest of the night. "You'll be going home this afternoon, but a visiting nurse will come every day to make sure you're all right. I'll see you at my office next week."

Mrs. Cummings's visiting nurse was waiting for Plato at the nursing station. Barbara Melnick owned the most successful home nursing service in town, but she still cared for some of the patients herself. Usually the older ones, like Mrs. Cummings, whom Barbara had cared for in the early days before her agency took off.

She had platinum blond hair, deep violet eyes, and a round dumpling face. She wasn't a day over fifty. She had a crush on Plato, and tried hard not to hide it. Barbara had been a floor nurse eight years ago, when Plato was just an intern. She'd helped him through some tough problems, steered him clear of a few bad mistakes during some brutal call nights, and salvaged his dignity in the meantime. Her voice still reminded him of phone calls in the middle of the night, the grubby little on-call room in the hospital basement.

"Are you sure you want four hundred milligrams, Doctor Marley? Maybe you meant forty."

"Sure, Barbara, sure. That's what I meant."

As Plato sat down with his chart, the nurse touched his arm and grinned. "Hello, gorgeous. You come here often?"

"I bet you try that line on the interns, too, don't you?"

"Only the handsome ones, Plato. Only the handsome ones."

"How about young Doctor Miles?" He scribbled a short note in Mrs. Cummings's chart and turned to face Barbara.

"That was a stupid mistake, but I've seen it happen a dozen times before." She shook her head. "I saw him out here, reading over the chart while you were in with Beulah. He looked like he'd just seen a ghost."

"I threatened to give him a taste of his own medicine. A little shot of IM haloperidol."

She tossed her head and let out a high-pitched chitter. "He's a good kid, Plato. I bet it won't happen again."

"Not if he doesn't want to see fuzzy green spiders with teeth." He stood to leave, but Barbara touched his arm again.

"You got a minute to talk?" She gestured at the closed door of the physician's conference room.

He followed her to the room. "No pinching this time."

She chittered again, but sobered the instant he closed the door.

"Something wrong, Barbara?"

Slowly, the nurse took a seat at the table. She stared at her hands for a minute or two and shook her head. Her face seemed suddenly older, and the pancake makeup looked like a crude disguise. A tear found its way through the powder. Finally, she looked up at him.

"I know it's none of my business," she began. "But Marilyn Abel was a friend of mine—a good friend."

Plato reached across the table and patted her hand. "I'm sorry."

"I didn't mean to cry like this, I really didn't." She sniffed, and pulled a tissue from her pocket. She glanced at her face in a hand mirror. "Oh, look at me! A few little tears and I'm a mess."

"You and Marilyn were close?"

She nodded and began rearranging her face. "I was her visiting nurse a while back—remember?"

Plato shook his head.

"Oh, that's right. You weren't taking care of her then." She snapped her compact shut. "It must have been, oh, five years ago. Her first really bad attack. After she got out of the hospital, I helped take care of her at home. I worked there for a month or so, and we got to be good buddies. She loved classical music, just like me. All day, we'd play Mozart, Tchaikovsky, Strauss. She did her therapy to Pachelbel; she liked the slow, plodding tempo. She loved Aaron Copland, and she hated Debussy. We've gone to the Cleveland Orchestra concerts together every Friday night for years now."

"Her death must have been quite a shock."

"It was." She dabbed at her eyes with a tissue. "Of course, I haven't been to the orchestra since. She'd gotten me some CDs for Christmas—the complete set of Szell doing Beethoven with the Cleveland Orchestra. Her brother wrapped it up and sent it to me after the funeral."

Plato wondered where all this was leading. Barbara must have known that he was Marilyn's physician, but why was she dredging all this up now? Unless—

"Tricia told me your wife did another autopsy on Marilyn."

"Tricia?" Plato was surprised—the story hadn't been made public yet. Tricia—the name sounded familiar . . .

"Marilyn's daughter." Barbara sighed. "She and I still keep in touch. Tricia called me yesterday evening, told me about the autopsy. She sounded upset, and a little worried. I promised her I'd pin you down, try to find out what was going on. I'm sorry."

"That's all right, Barbara. I owe you a few favors." If Plato didn't tell her, Tricia would find out soon enough anyway. And as Marilyn's friend, Barbara might have some useful information. Slowly and carefully, Plato told her about their findings: the scleral hemorrhages, the broken thyroid cartilage, the fibers in the lungs. He drew tighter circles around the truth and their conclusions, finally breaking it to her as gently as he could. To his surprise, Barbara took it in stride.

"It's not *how* she died that bothers me. I just miss her, Plato." She shrugged. "And maybe I'm a little stunned. That someone could have killed Marilyn—I can't really believe it right now."

"That's how I felt."

"We were close—really close. We used to joke that we were twins, separated at birth. Even though she was fifteen years older than me." Barbara frowned. "She and her second husband got divorced nine years ago, same year Jack left me. The little twerp. He calls a lot now, like we're old pals or something. I think he wants my money."

"Did her ex-husband ever harass her, or threaten her?"

"Hardly." Barbara laughed. "He was a researcher, too. I met him once—a real nerd. White coat, pocket protector, calculator on his belt, the whole bit. Arnold Welkins, I think that's his name. Marilyn's first husband—Tricia's father—died in some sort of accident years and years ago. Anyway, Welkins owns part of Chadwick Medicon, the drug company where Marilyn used to work. She left two years ago for a research post at Siegel. She had a big falling out with the management—with Arnold, really—something about patent rights."

"Does her ex still work for Chadwick?"

"Yeah, the little ferret. Owns half the company now." Her jowls twisted into a grimace. "Men can be such idiots, you know?"

"Right." Plato grinned. "When was the last time you saw her?"

"She died on a Friday morning. I saw her the Friday before—Symphony night. We had dinner before the concert, just like we usually did. She told me about the CD collection—" Barbara dabbed at her eyes again. "Marilyn never could keep a secret. Then we went to Severance. The orchestra did a couple of Brahms pieces, and something by Chopin, I think."

"That was a week before she died. Did she seem worried, or upset about anything?"

She took a deep breath and considered. "Not that I could

see. If anything, she was kind of excited. She'd gotten a big break at Siegel."

Plato leaned forward. "What kind of break?"

"Marilyn called me Thursday night and told me she'd made dinner reservations at Sammy's." She shook her head. "I was stunned. I said, 'Who's going to pay for this?' And she laughed and said *she* was. Said she had some big news for me, that she'd hit the pharmaceutical jackpot. Those were her exact words—'pharmaceutical jackpot.' She took her work seriously, but she always talked like it was a crap shoot. Just pull the handle and see what pops up—an extra carboxyl group, a methoxy group here or there, maybe an amino acid, and *presto*! You've made a bazillion dollars. She used to talk like that. It made my head spin."

"But she hadn't hit the jackpot before, had she?" Plato had been to Marilyn's house on a few home visits. She lived with her brother in an older colonial out in the eastern suburbs. A nice enough place, but not exactly a bazillionaire's home.

"Now, there's where you're wrong." Barbara shook her head knowingly. "When she was working for Chadwick Medicon, she oversaw the development of two or three big-name drugs. Things you've probably heard of. She worked with antibiotics. Cephalosporins, mostly."

Barbara was probably right; Plato did prescribe a lot of cephalosporins. The group of drugs was derived from penicillin, and dozens of them existed. Over several years, bacteria developed immunity to certain antibiotics. So newer—and more expensive—drugs were always being developed to replace the older ones. The cephalosporins were now in their third generation: penicillin begat cephalexin, cephalexin begat cefaclor, and cefaclor began moxalactam.

Plato had a hard time keeping the names straight anymore.

"Marilyn didn't get much credit, and she didn't make any money from the patent rights." She spread her hands. "Not that money was an issue. But it really galled Marilyn to see Arnold announcing development of all the new products, accepting industry awards, robbing Marilyn and her staff of all the credit."

"So she went to Siegel to work by herself."

"Took an early retirement. A couple of her assistants

came along, too—they were young and rebellious and didn't give a damn about Chadwick's pension plan. What are their names, now? Robert and Therese, I think. The girl is German, or Austrian, or something."

Plato gently guided her back on track. "That night, at dinner, did Marilyn talk about her new drug?"

"She sure did. I couldn't shut her up. I kept telling her there might be industry spies lurking at the next table, taking notes. Microphones hidden in the salt shaker, that sort of thing." She chittered. "But Marilyn told me I shouldn't joke about it. She said she was worried about the patent rights. I guess some of the staff was already squabbling about who would take the credit."

"Wasn't that a little premature?" Plato knew that even if a drug worked safely, the FDA required years of testing and masses of paperwork and documentation before it could be introduced to the market.

"It sounded like a *really* big break. You know how the newer strains of TB are getting tougher to treat?"

He nodded. Resistant strains of TB were popping up everywhere—in AIDS clinics, hospitals, nursing homes—Plato had seen a few of them himself.

"Well, she'd developed a powerful new drug that worked with even the worst strains of TB. She called it the magic bullet." Barbara leaned forward and lowered her voice. "But like I said, she was worried. The people at Chadwick Medicon—Arnold, especially—claimed she had performed most of the research while she was still working for them. Nonsense, of course, but they were threatening her with a lawsuit. Only that wasn't the worst of her problems."

"Really?"

She nodded vigorously. "I guess some guy she worked with at Siegel was trying to pull the same thing. He said he wanted his name as primary investigator on all the documentation and patent applications. Told her it was standard protocol, but she wasn't buying it."

"Did she mention his name?"

Barbara closed her eyes and searched her memory. "Allman? Albert?"

"Albright?" Plato suggested.

"That's it! Doctor Albright. She was pretty steamed about the whole thing. She talked about him the same way she talked about her ex-husband."

Chuck Albright. Director of the pharmacology department at Siegel Medical College. Plato nodded. He and Cal had an appointment to see him this afternoon. It promised to be an interesting interview.

Chapter 7

Driving through downtown Cleveland that afternoon, Cal Marley watched the blocky granite and brick structures of Riverside General Hospital and Siegel Medical College heave themselves over a jagged horizon of vacant warehouses and abandoned steel mills. It was a dismal, dreary day. Leaden clouds the color of artillery shells lofted over the frozen wastes of Lake Erie. Halfhearted flurries powdered the air and road; a bitter wind whipped the snow into frilly white snakes that writhed and danced on the icy streets. Crossing the Detriot-Superior Bridge, Cal glanced down into the oily darkness of the Cuyahoga River and wished she were back home in Chicago.

She was only too aware of the vast distance between Siegel Medical College and Northwestern University, her alma mater. Geographically, academically, philosophically, and a dozen other ways. Northwestern was vibrant, intellectually stimulating, and well-funded—at the forefront of medical research and education. Its medical college and hospitals were enshrined on Chicago's north side and lakefront, in one of the wealthiest areas of the city. Just a few blocks away were the glitz and glitter of Water Tower Place, the Drake Hotel, the John Hancock Building, and a mile or two farther down the shore lay the planetarium and museums.

Siegel Medical College and Riverside General Hospital, by contrast, squatted on the west banks of Cleveland's Cuyahoga River. Downstream lay the neon nightlife of the Flats, hip and trendy after dark, a little seedy in the harsh light of a winter's day. Upriver lay the warehouses and smokestacks of the industrial district that had set fire to the Cuyahoga River twenty years ago and now clung to life by the slimmest of threads. Farther west were the atom-

bombed ruins of some of Cleveland's poorest neighbor-
hoods.

It was a working-class medical school and hospital, with
a lot of working-class students and hard-working instructors. But places like Siegel had trouble attracting the shining lights of medicine. The college would never share the
limelight with Northwestern or Harvard or Case Western
in the big league of academia and research. Its faculty
might never be interviewed on CNN, and its research was
almost never featured in the *New England Journal of Medicine.* But Siegel and Riverside did a decent job teaching
the basics of clinical care and graduating competent doctors, while serving more than their share of the working-
class poor.

Cal parked the Rabbit in the instructors' lot and glanced
up at the crumbling granite of the medical college. From
her vantage near the rear of the Depression-era building,
she could see the east wall tilting out just a bit over the
river and the spiderweb of cracks lacing their way up the
back quarter of the structure. A matter of just a few inches
or so, but the repairs would cost hundreds of thousands of
dollars. Siegel's Development Foundation had been trying
to raise the repair money for years. Each month the cracks
grew, along with the costs.

The college was nominally affiliated with the University
of Cleveland. But UC was across the river, across the town.
And the private school's financial position wasn't much better than Siegel's. Board meetings between the two sites
usually focused on efforts by one school to cannibalize the
other. No help there.

Hurrying up the sidewalk to the main building, Cal
smiled wryly. If this kind of thing had happened back at
Northwestern, some plastic mogul's wife would have raised
the money in a week or two, and gotten a new wing named
after her husband or her great-aunt.

Her smile melted as she scanned the directory in the
main reception area. Coincidentally, Randolph Smythe's
name was listed just after the pharmacology department.
No room number for Dean Smythe—the listening just said
"A Wing."

She was supposed to meet with Smythe on Friday morning to discuss the students' progress. Maybe she could talk
him into offering odds. Or a win, place, or show arrange-

ment. Cal shuddered to think what Plato would do if they didn't win her bet.

She signed in at security and hurried down the main corridor. The pharmacology department was on the first floor near the back of the building, just above the anatomy lab. She passed down a musty marble hallway lined with old steam radiators. Dim lights hung in aluminum sconces on the walls—art-deco with a medieval twist. Halfway back, she stepped over a crack in the floor and uttered a silent prayer that the college wouldn't fall into the river this afternoon.

The heavy oak door to the pharmacology office was open. If it weren't for the computer and bookcases, Cal might have thought she had stumbled into a rain forest. The fluorescent light fixtures were festooned with hanging baskets of ivy and spider plants and bleeding hearts. A double line of cactus rested on the windowsill. Potted palms dozed in the corners.

A plump secretary camouflaged in a flowered dress was huddled over the computer. She looked up at her visitor and gave a tight smile. "Can I help you?"

"I'm here to see Doctor Albright," Cal explained. She glanced at the placard on the woman's desk—June Fitzgibbons. "He's expecting me."

June glanced over at the bank of lights on her phone. "Sorry, he's on a call right now. He should be done shortly."

Cal shrugged her coat off and found a place to sit between a giant cactus and a bushy flowering thing that looked like a white hibiscus with measles. Her sweater and wool skirt felt hot and scratchy. She was already breaking into a sweat. "Sure is warm in here."

June was wearing a sleeveless summerweight dress, Cal saw. Beneath the desk, her shoes were off. A purse, scarf, hat, sweatshirt and pants, and a heavy stadium jacket hung from a clothes tree in the corner.

The secretary smiled apologetically. "For the plants. And Doctor Albright likes it kind of warm anyway." She rolled her chair toward the window, emptied a carafe of water onto a foil pan resting on the radiator, and watched approvingly as it bubbled and steamed. "The palms hate the dry weather," she explained over her shoulder. "And the cactus really don't mind the extra moisture."

Just then, one of the doors flew open and a lanky beach bum stepped into the waiting area. Sandy brown hair thinning at the top, faded bell-bottom jeans and a denim workshirt with the flaps hanging out, and a deep suntan that matched the old leather sandals on his otherwise bare feet. He stepped over to Cal and stuck his hand out. "Doctor Marley? Hi—I'm Chuck Albright. Glad to meet you."

He had the brisk, vigorous handshake of a door-to-door salesman, but his smile was wide and honest.

"Just call me Cal," she replied. "I really appreciate your taking the time for this."

"No problem at all."

She followed him back into his office, a long, narrow room full of windows peering out over the Cuyahoga. They stood in the doorway for a moment while Cal took it all in. Sand-colored carpet covered the floor, East Indian prints and tapestries hung on the textured walls, and track lights in the ceiling poured enough imitation sunlight to warm the top of her head. She blinked in the glare like a mole trapped in a tanning parlor.

"Phototherapy," Albright explained. "I grew up in Arizona and lived in Hawaii for a while before I moved here. I used to get terribly down this time of year until I read this article in *JAMA*. Seasonal affective disorder—has to do with sunlight. Every October now, I tune in to about ten thousand lux until spring, and I'm just fine. And I hit the tanning booths twice a week for good measure."

"We could use a room like this in our house." Cal sighed, thinking of the furnace and the water pipes and another night spent huddling by the fire.

"This place used to be the histology lab." The department chairman smiled proudly. "They were going to turn it into a storage closet or some such thing, and stick the whole pharmacology department in the basement. Next to the cadaver lab."

He wrinkled his nose in disgust. Cal had to agree—the view here was wonderful. Outside the bank of windows, a flurry swirled over the river. Cleveland's entire skyline drifted in and out of existence on the whims of the wind.

"Can I get you anything? Coffee, tea, some Pepsi?" He walked across to a compact refrigerator tucked beneath some bookshelves. Beside it, a long black workbench was covered with texts and syllabus materials and organizer charts and scented candles—the whole room smelled like a flower shop.

"Coffee would be great. Cream, no sugar." While her host poured coffee and snapped open a Pepsi for himself, Cal studied the decor again. Albright's office could have been a time capsule from the seventies. Macramé tapestries, a pair of wicker basket chairs, a carved wooden "etc" hanging on the wall. Beside the door hung a lacquered copy of the Desiderata. Cal glanced over at Albright's hands, half expecting to see a mood ring. But he wasn't wearing any jewelry at all, other than the small wooden ankh dangling from a leather strap inside his shirt.

The department chairman led her across the room to a king-size futon and sat opposite her with legs crossed and feet tucked under his hips. He took a sip of his Pepsi. "Is your husband still coming?"

"He was going to meet me here," Cal explained. "He probably got tied up at Riverside."

"Not surprising." Albright grinned. "He's a geriatrician, right?"

Cal nodded and sipped her coffee. It tasted like Sergei's embalming fluid, with a little water mixed in. She smiled weakly.

"Like it?" he asked. "It's one hundred percent Colombian decaf—the fellows over in biochem made it." He grinned happily. "They have some kind of extracting agent that takes out practically every molecule of caffeine. And it tastes better than regular decaf."

"How nice for them." Cal swallowed painfully and set her cup on the lacquered table beside the couch.

Albright tipped his head back and downed half of his Pepsi. "So what can I help you with? You told June you need some information about Marilyn Abel?"

"Yes." While he finished his soda, Cal explained her findings. She stressed the fact that they had no definitive proof, but that the circumstances were a bit unusual. She tried to make it sound routine.

Even so, Albright seemed disturbed. His pale gray eyes clouded and he turned to stare out the window. "I'm not sure I'm following all this." His voice seemed to come from somewhere far away. "Are you saying Marilyn might have been *killed*?"

"We don't know yet," Cal repeated. "Like I said, it could

have been a natural death with some postmortem trauma. Or it could have been something that happened during her heart attack—perhaps the pain led her to have some kind of accident and injure herself."

And perhaps pigs could fly over the Cuyahoga, Cal thought quietly.

"I see." Albright sat back and took a deep breath, let it out slowly.

"Right now, we're just asking around a little," Cal explained. "Looking into Marilyn's situation. And we're running some further tests that might give us a more definitive answer."

Albright sat up, his eyes flicking back at Cal like a pair of searchlights. He leaned forward and licked his lips. "What kind of tests?"

A brisk knock at the door startled both of them. Plato poked his head in and grinned sheepishly, then stepped inside. "Sorry I'm late."

He had given a lecture at Family Practice Grand Rounds this morning, so he was dressed to kill. Double-breasted navy blazer, taupe pleated trousers, and a French cuff shirt. Last Christmas's gold tie chain over a red paisley tie. He looked stylish, handsome, professional, and thoroughly uncomfortable. Like a small boy in Sunday school on a hot summer day. He kept squirming, shrugging his shoulders, and pulling on his tie.

Plato only wore a suit every few months, and Cal could see why. Though his hands were a pale winter white, his neck and face were a deep crimson. He looked like he was being slowly strangled.

"No problem, Plato." Albright gestured to one of the wicker basket chairs. "Come on over and have a seat."

Plato hiked up his pantlegs and sat down, nearly toppling the chair over. He made little choking sounds like a dog on a tight leash. Cal fought the urge to reach out and loosen his tie.

"Now, where were we?" Albright asked.

"Marilyn Abel," Cal prompted.

"Oh, yes." He turned his eyes to the windows again, his gaze distant and sad. "We were all very sorry about Marilyn's death. She was a terrific lady."

"It must have been quite a shock," Plato wheezed.

"It was." The department chairman ran a hand through

his thinning hair. His boyish face seemed to age suddenly; smile crinkles turned to wrinkles and the deepwater tan faded to gray. "Finding her that morning was very distressing for all of us. June was terribly upset. Of course, we all knew Marilyn wasn't in the best of health." He glanced over at Plato. "I understand you were her physician?"

Plato nodded.

"Then I'm sure you knew that Marilyn's MS was getting worse. Not that she was ready to die or anything." Albright shook his head. "It's hard to imagine Marilyn ever giving in or giving up on anything. Especially her life, her work." He chuckled. "I imagine the Grim Reaper had to do a lot of pushing and tugging to get Marilyn to come along."

I imagine the Grim Reaper had a little help, Cal thought. "How did Marilyn get along with the other folks in the department? What sort of a worker was she?"

The department chairman sighed. "Marilyn was a very . . . *complex* person." He hiked his feet closer beneath him and hugged his knees. "As Plato probably knows, she was an army surgical nurse in Vietnam. During her tour, she witnessed the emergence of the first resistant bacteria— superbugs that our best drugs couldn't cure."

He leaned back and closed his eyes, a skinny beach Buddha in blue jeans. "That was modern medicine's first wake-up call. Our first lesson that science can't cure everything, that Mother Nature is cannier than we could ever imagine."

He was right, Cal knew. Plain old penicillin once cured most infections. Tuberculosis had become a disease for the history books. In the sixties, AIDS hadn't even been described yet. But nowadays, a lot of the latest so-called advances in medicine were just new ways to fight emerging resistant infections. Ways to tread water and keep from getting dragged under by the latest wave of superbugs.

"Vietnam made a great impression on her," Albright continued. "It changed her life. She talked to me about it once—how she had to sit by and watch helplessly while one of her patients died from an untreatable staph infection." He waved his hand absently, as though the rest was obvious. "So she went to school again after she came back, and got a doctorate in pharmacology. Marilyn had a brilliant career at Chadwick Medicon. Headed their antibacterial wing. She was in on the ground floor developing some of their cephalosporin antibiotics. Did some very important work for them—ground-breaking work."

"So how did she end up at Siegel?" Plato asked. Magically, he had removed his tie and stuffed it into one of his pockets. His face had faded from crimson to pink.

"That's what I asked myself, the first time I heard from her." Albright leaned forward to rest his elbows on his knobby knees. "Oh, we had bumped into each other at local meetings before that. I always had tremendous respect for Marilyn—I certainly never expected to be her boss." He sighed and shook his head. "But she'd decided to bail out of her job and take an early retirement. She'd gotten squashed under the administrative thumb too many times at Chadwick."

"How so?" Cal asked.

"Marilyn had a national reputation as a research chemist. She put in twenty years for Chadwick, but, as far as I could tell, they treated her like dirt." He rolled his eyes. "Her last three drug projects all had promising results in animal studies, but some pinhead marketing analyst decided the drugs didn't have enough profit potential. So they killed them."

"Antibiotics?" Plato asked. He sounded surprised.

"Probably." Albright shrugged. "I assume so, since that was her specialty. But she never talked much about what went on at Chadwick. Drug company people tend to be pretty tight-lipped about their work. Even after they quit."

"What sort of work did she do here at Siegel?" Cal asked.

"Some teaching." He had a funny trick of hunching his head down between his bony shoulders, like a turtle. "She was planning to take over the section on antibiotic therapy."

"Was Marilyn involved with any research?" Cal wondered why Albright was suddenly acting so tentative. She wondered if he was holding something back.

"A little bit." His head hunched lower. "She was helping the other two faculty—Bob and Therese—with a little project. Clinical trials for one of the affiliated labs. Checking out drug clearance rates, dosing schedules. Pretty routine stuff, really."

Plato scratched his beard and frowned. "Surely she had some projects of her own?"

Albright shrugged and yawned. "Only one. I think it was an agent to treat tuberculosis."

Plato sat up suddenly, nearly toppling the basket chair over again. "That could be important."

"I doubt it." The department chairman gave a patronizing smile. "The drug was in very rough, preliminary stages—she was just running her first animal tests when she died."

"How did the tests come out?" Plato pressed. "Was the drug successful?"

Cal glanced over at her husband, puzzled by Plato's sudden interest. And curious why the pharmacologist couldn't seem to give them a straight answer. Surely he knew more about what was going on in his department.

"You have to understand, Plato—drug research is a very hit-or-miss thing. It still involves a lot of trial and error. Especially the way Marilyn did things." Albright uncurled his legs and set his feet on the floor. A hint of irritation had crept into his voice. Even Buddhas have bad days once in a while. "Tell you what. I'll look over Marilyn's work and see if she was on to anything important. Would that satisfy you?"

"Of course," Plato replied.

"We'd really appreciate it," Cal added.

Albright stood. Apparently, the interview was over.

On their way back to the main entrance, Plato apologized. "Chuck Albright's always been a laid-back sort of guy. I never expected him to get so huffy. I hope you hadn't planned to ask anything else."

"Don't worry about it." Cal signed them out at the security desk. "But I *was* curious why you were so interested in Marilyn's research."

Plato grabbed her arm and grinned. "Let's head over to the Flat Iron for supper and I'll tell you all about it."

"Great." She glanced at her watch as they stepped through the revolving door and back into the winter chill. It was already dark outside, and bitterly cold. The kind of cold that freezes the tears in your eyes and parches your throat. She hoped the Rabbit would start. "After dinner, we can see if Tiffany Cramer has any ideas."

"Tiffany Cramer?" Beneath the streetlights, Plato's face was blank. "Why would she know anything?"

"She was helping Marilyn in the lab—-remember?"

"Oh. But she's probably gone home by now. How are we going to talk to her tonight?"

"At the anatomy lab, silly!" Cal poked his ribs. "Or did you already forget?"

He groaned. The furnace man had finally come today; Plato was apparently hoping to spend the evening cuddled up to a warm heating vent. "This cold has really got me down, Cally. I think it's a sinus infection. Maybe I'll sit this session out tonight and take a cab home."

"And maybe our students will fail the exam." She glanced around the parking lot. Several of the cars bore a familiar bumper sticker. She'd seen it on Mercedes and Accuras and Lexuses all over town. "Look, Plato. '*Randolph Smythe for Congress.*' Just think—we'll probably be tending bar at his next fund-raiser. Won't that be fun?"

Plato groaned again.

"See?" she chided. "Feeling better already, aren't we?"

He sneezed, and blew his nose into a tattered Kleenex. "Jusd wudderful."

Chapter 8

By the time Cal and Plato had finished dinner and headed back to the anatomy lab, the students were ready and waiting. They were gloved and gowned, huddling in the small circle of light around Marilyn Abel's body like the grave-robbing anatomists from medicine's dim past. Furtive whispers floated to Cal across the darkened room: *"Did you hear— Killed somehow— Could it be this— How did she know?"*

Cal coughed discreetly, and four heads rose as one. Staring, hushed, expectant. Hoping for some detail, some snippet about her autopsy findings. Ghoulishly fascinated with the apparent murder of their cadaver.

She smiled to herself. At least she had piqued their interest in anatomy.

The students shuffled to make room for them around the table. The heavy steel case was open, the plastic wrapping and oily shroud were pulled down and draped over Marilyn's wasted legs.

Sergei Malenkov had done a good job with her. Even after two autopsies and a thorough dissection by the junior surgery students, Marilyn's tissues were still fresh and moist.

"Today we're going to work on the abdomen," Cal announced briskly. "Plato will tour you through the abdominal wall and major organs while I have a word with Tiffany."

Tiffany Cramer jumped at the mention of her name. Her pale blue eyes fixed on Cal with surprise.

"By the way," Cal added, glancing at the others. "Did anyone else here happen to know Marilyn Abel? She was a researcher in the pharmacology department."

Samantha, Raj, and Blair shook their heads. Cal gestured to Tiffany, led her to a nook in the far corner of the lab, and switched on a reading light. They were standing in one of the skeletal exhibit areas. Countertops and tables were littered with an assortment of bones. A set of acrylic cases held three skulls cut in coronal, sagittal, and transverse planes. A complete human skeleton was laid out on a large table before them like the harvest of a dinosaur dig. An assembled skeleton dangled beside Cal's elbow, grinning conspiratorially.

Tiffany was underdressed today—loose knit sweater, black stirrup pants, and plain gold stud earrings. She was staring at the floor, blond hair waving forward to frame her face. Cal suddenly felt a wave of pity for her.

She climbed onto one of the tall dissecting stools in the corner and Tiffany did the same.

"You were Marilyn's lab assistant?" Cal asked softly.

Tiffany gave a quick nod and bit her lip.

Cal reached out to pat the girl's gloved hand. "Did you realize that was Marilyn's body?"

"Yes." Her mouth formed the word without a sound.

"I'm sorry." She squeezed Tiffany's hand. Their gloves squeaked. "We didn't know—"

"Neither did I," the student interrupted quickly. "Not at first, anyway." Her voice quivered. "I didn't get a good look at her Monday night. I was on the other side of the body, where her face is already dissected." She swallowed heavily. "But tonight . . ."

"I had hoped to talk to you before we got started," Cal explained. "There was a mix-up when the bodies were being prepared. The lab director didn't realize you were assigned to Marilyn's group."

From across the room, Plato's voice echoed in the stillness. "Now, who can name the five muscles of the anterior and lateral abdominal wall?"

It all suddenly seemed very trivial.

"If it's a problem for you, we can try to work with another body," Cal offered.

"No, Doctor Marley." Tiffany shook her head and lifted her gaze to meet Cal's. "It's okay. It was sort of a big shock. But I still want to go ahead with it."

Cal sighed with relief. Arranging to use another cadaver would have been tricky. She knew of no other display or tutoring specimens, and performing a new dissection would take weeks. The only alternative was to borrow a body from one of the groups. Unfortunately, each of these four students were from different groups. And freshman medical students tended to be pretty poor dissectors anyway, even the ones that didn't have hand tremors. "You're sure?"

"Yes." Tiffany was looking back at the body lying in a pool of light. "Yes. I think Marilyn would have wanted it that way."

Cal smiled. "Were you and Marilyn very close?"

"We had our ups and downs." She shrugged. "Marilyn was very good, very smart. She helped me study for my biochemistry final—it was the only test I did really well on."

Cal slid down from her stool. "I wish I had known her."

Tiffany sat staring at her gloves. "Funny thing—she used to say she saw a lot of herself in me." She sighed. "Maybe that's why she sometimes acted like she was my mother."

Cal stepped closer and asked quietly. "You found her that morning, didn't you?" She hated to bring it up, but Tiffany would need to be questioned about it eventually.

The medical student was silent for a long moment.

"Yes," she finally replied. "I went in early that day; I needed to talk with Marilyn about one of the experiments. I thought she was just sleeping there overnight—she used to do that a lot." Tiffany hugged herself and rocked back and forth on her chair. "And then I saw her face."

She picked at her gloves without looking up. "I *screamed,* Doctor Marley. I shouldn't have, but I did." She shook her head, still embarrassed. "Doctors aren't supposed to do that, are they? I mean, you get used to dead bodies, right?"

"Not really," Cal replied. *Not even me.* She squeezed Tiffany's arm. Beneath the smock, it felt as frail and gaunt as the skeleton dangling beside her. "Doctors are people, just like everyone else."

"I was so happy that morning," she murmured. "The Patracin testing was going really well."

"Patracin?"

"Marilyn's new anti-TB drug," Tiffany explained. "She named it after her daughter. Of course, Doctor Albright is handling the development now, but he kept the name. In honor of Marilyn, I guess."

Cal frowned. Doctor Albright? At dinner tonight, Plato had explained his curiosity about the new drug. Marilyn Abel had been excited about her discovery, while Chuck

Albright had acted like he knew little about her research. But now Tiffany claimed that the department chairman was in charge of the drug's development.

Why the secrecy?

Across the room, Plato was staring back at them curiously. He had probably finished his tour of the abdomen and was running out of things to say.

Tiffany stirred. "Doctor Marley? Do you really think someone killed her?"

Cal shook her head. "I'm not really sure yet."

But she was getting more certain every minute. She smiled reassuringly. "Come on—let's get back to work. I don't think Marilyn would be too thrilled if we let you flunk the exam again."

Tiffany slid down from her chair and grinned. "Don't worry. I'm going to ace it this time."

Back at the table, Plato had the abdomen splayed open, the long fatty sail of the greater omentum blanketing the coils and loops of intestines beneath, the dark lobes of the liver huddled under the red-gray muscle of the diaphragm, the gall bladder and stomach peeking out from beneath the liver like children hiding behind their mother's skirt.

"We covered all the organs and put everything back," he explained proudly. "I wasn't sure where you wanted to begin."

"Well." She glanced around the group. "Let's talk about blood supply first, and then try to locate some arteries. The blood supply to the digestive organs is pretty complicated, partly because of the way the gut grows during fetal development."

Cal described the embryology of the stomach and intestines, the way everything starts as one long tube dangling down from the aorta, but then through a series of twistings and turnings and loopings, grows into the complex and confusing digestive system. The students listened respectfully, or *seemed* to—Samantha Ricci was busy fitting a new blade on her scalpel, Tiffany and Raj kept trading furtive glances and smiles, and Blair Phillips just stared off into space with those bleary green eyes.

They all looked pretty bored.

"So," Cal finally concluded. "Who can name the three major arterial branches supplying the digestive system?"

Her question was met with a circle of blank stairs. Samantha nudged Raj and whispered something to him. He caught a grin in his glove. Behind the thick glasses, his eyes met Cal's and slid quickly away.

"Anyone?" Cal sighed. "How about you, Blair? Can you name *one* of them?"

"I read over the material," he replied, reluctantly focusing on Cal. He sniffed. "But I don't believe in memorization."

Cal fought back the urge to smack him. She glanced across the table at Plato. His face was red, his eyes bulging. He made strangling motions with his hands.

"Umm," said Samantha. Her dark eyebrows drew together. "Umm. Is one of them the, umm, *celiac*? Umm, then again—"

"That's *right*, Samantha! Excellent!" She looked around the table again. "How about the other two? Tiffany? Raj?"

They both shook their heads.

"Sorry," Raj said in his sonorous baritone. He was standing on a stepstool in order to see over the sides of the table. "I work on it, but the names don't want to stick in my head."

Tiffany patted his arm consolingly.

"Listen up, guys," Plato said suddenly. "I don't think you realize how serious this is." He had raised his voice; he sounded like the losing coach at half-time during the Super Bowl. "Cal had to twist some arms to get you folks another shot at this exam. If you don't pass it, you're finished."

Samantha, Tiffany, and Raj exchanged sheepish looks. But Blair Phillips just shrugged and snorted derisively. "I appreciate that, I really do. But what's the point? Even if I'm able to memorize all this stuff, will I still remember it by the time I'm an intern? Or have any use for it?"

"Believe it or not, you will," Cal assured him. "Not all of it, but—"

"How about Plato?" Blair challenged. "He's a family doc and a geriatrician and that's what I want to be. Can he name the three major arteries supplying the gut? Can he name *any* of them?"

He had her. Cal didn't know what to say. It didn't matter that Blair was being a disrespectful, ungrateful little snot. If she tried to deflect the question, it would be an admission that Blair was right, that most practicing clinicians *did* have trouble remembering all the minutiae they learned in medical school. But there was a point in learning it at least once, committing it to memory, and then later consulting a reference text if needed. Cal fervently believed that. But she didn't know how to explain it to Blair.

"Of course he can," Cal finally replied, hoping to buy some time for her husband. Maybe she could slip him a note. Maybe he could peek at the atlas lying open on the music stand beside him.

Except he probably wouldn't get away with it. All four students were watching Plato, enthralled by the specter of an Attending Physician being suddenly dropped into the mud with the rest of the commoners. Role reversal.

No, he'd never get away with it. And anyway, he wasn't looking anywhere near the atlas. His gaze was fixed on the ceiling, his face turned to the incandescent spots like a flower searching for the sun. Below Plato's beard, his Adam's apple bobbed as he swallowed a couple of times.

"Let's see," he began.

He's going to try to wing it, Cal thought. So much for credibility. She wanted to reach out to Plato across Marilyn's body, to *will* the answer to him.

Beneath his balding scalp, wheels were turning. His ears always turned red when he was thinking hard; Cal had often teased him about it. Right now, they were glowing like twin beacons on the side of his head.

Come on, Plato! You can do it!

"Let's see," he began again. Finally, he turned his gaze to the group. "Now, the trick is to remember that the abdominal aorta has four sets of branches—the anterior visceral, the lateral visceral, the lateral abdominal wall, and the terminal branches."

Cal blinked. This was *Plato*?

He smiled a knowing smile. "The blood supply for the gut comes from the anterior visceral branches. Makes sense, since the gut is in front of—anterior to—the aorta. Right, Blair?"

The medical student blinked back his surprise and then nodded.

"Anyway, that's how I remembered it." Plato smiled again. Wistfully, as though he was dredging up some of his fondest memories. "And the three anterior visceral branches are the ones we're talking about, right? The Ce-

liac, Superior mesenteric, and Inferior mesenteric. *SICK*—
that's how I remember it—the initials SIC, though that isn't
in the right order, and there isn't a K on the end. But how
would you feel if you didn't have any blood in your gut?
Pretty sick—right, Blair?"

Blair swallowed, and nodded again. He gazed at Plato in
awe, like a supplicant at the oracle of Delphi.

"Now, take the celiac artery," Plato continued. "*That* has
three branches, too—the left gastric, splenic, and hepatic
arteries . . ."

He went on like that for another five minutes before Cal
finally cut him off.

"Thank you, Plato," she concluded.

The stunned students were frozen in place, slack-
mouthed and glassy-eyed. Like four dead carp.

"I-I'm sorry, Plato," Blair said meekly. He combed his
fingers through his straggly brown hair, forgetting that he
had his dissecting gloves on. "I guess I should memorize
these things, huh?"

"Like I said, Blair. It's important, even in the clinical
years." He waved a hand carelessly, a magician conjuring
respect from thin air. "I had a patient with a mesenteric
embolism just last month. You can read the location just
from the symptoms, if you know your anatomy." He shot
Cal a meaningful look. "Not to mention that fact that you'll
flunk out of medical school if you don't pass this course."

"Uh—yeah." Blair's head bobbed quickly, plump lips
pursing with determination. "I'll try to work a little harder
on the memorization."

The others nodded their agreement.

After that, the session went pretty smoothly. The students were attentive and appreciative. They answered all
the questions, rightly or wrongly, and did their best to find
the landmarks and commit them to memory.

But now Cal was distracted. She kept stealing glances at
her husband, wondering how Plato had done it, half expecting to find arterial trees drawn on the backs of his
gloves, crib notes stuffed in his sleeves. But she didn't.

Finally, the session was over. They had reviewed the abdomen and moved on to another lecture on the head and
neck, as she had promised. Together, they raised the shroud
and plastic, swung the metal lids closed and said good-bye
to Marilyn once again.

Tiffany Cramer lingered in the darkness beside the casket a moment, then rejoined them all at the washtubs.

Samantha Ricci shared a sink with Cal, scraping her hands vigorously with a surgical scrub brush, stealing furtive glances at Cal, and not saying a word. Finally, she took a deep breath and spoke.

"Doctor Marley?" Samantha asked, studying the soap dispenser. "What made you think our cadaver had been murdered?"

From her tone of voice, she might have been asking about the weather. But the rush of water from the other sinks suddenly ceased. All eyes focused on Cal.

She shrugged. Why not tell them?

While they dried their hands and donned jackets and hats, Cal told the students what she had found Monday night, and described Marilyn's autopsy findings. She didn't mention that the cadaver had been a faculty member at Siegel. Tiffany already knew, and the others would find out soon enough.

"Of course, the fact that there were no signs of a struggle makes it something of a puzzle," Cal concluded.

"Maybe she was drugged," Raj suggested brightly. The furry hood of his jacket was already pulled up over his head. His voice was muffled; he looked like an Ewok with glasses.

"The drug screen was negative," Cal answered, pulling on her coat. "Besides, it doesn't make sense—the fibers were deep inside her lungs, as though she were conscious and gasping for air. But she had no bruises on her arms, no signs that she had tried to defend herself."

As they finished pulling on their coats and headed toward the stairs, the students considered and rejected a dozen possible explanations. All the while, Blair Phillips stood quietly, zipping and unzipping his backpack and staring at the bank of lockers along the wall. Finally, he shifted his gaze to Cal.

"What about a differential drug effect?" He waited for the others' attention and then continued. "Something that works on the smaller muscles but leaves the bigger muscles like the diaphragm intact so she could breathe."

Cal froze, stunned, with only one sleeve of her coat on. *From the mouths of babes . . .*

"Of course, there probably aren't any drugs like that,"

Blair added. He shrugged his backpack on and stepped toward the stairway. "Or if there are, you've probably already tested for them."

He was gone before Cal could reply. She watched the other students head up the stairs, her mind whirling with possibilities. Blair's idea had a lot of merit. The neuromuscular blockers—drugs like curare and succinylcholine—act on the smaller, quicker muscles first and paralyze the larger muscles later, or at higher dosages. The diaphragm, the principal muscle used for breathing, is usually the last to be paralyzed and the first to start working again as the drug wears off. A small dose could have paralyzed Marilyn's arms and legs and left her diaphragm working. Even with the rest of her muscles paralyzed, Marilyn might have had enough strength left in her diaphragm to suck those fibers down into her lungs.

And the routine tox screen wouldn't have picked up that class of drugs.

She'd have to order follow-up studies on the sample of vitreous humor from Marilyn's eye. She hoped the lab had enough fluid to run the tests.

Across the hall, Plato was shrugging on his coat and frowning curiously. "What are you staring at?"

Cal grinned back. "*Gray's Anatomy* with legs, I think." She walked over and slid under his arm. "You were pretty impressive tonight."

"Aw, shucks." He waved a hand. "It was nothing."

Cal cocked her head and squinted up at him. "You were putting me on the other night, weren't you? You really *do* know anatomy."

He considered for a long moment, then sighed. "Actually, no. I got up at five o'clock this morning and studied." He closed his eyes and rubbed his tall forehead. "*Studied!* God—I haven't done that in years. Pulled out my anatomy books, my notecards, the old syllabi. Everything I had on the digestive system."

Cal stared at him, wide-eyed. "And you memorized *all* of it? That's still pretty impressive."

"Not exactly." He blushed. "I got through the blood supply part, and then I feel asleep again."

That sounded more like Plato. "You were pretty lucky Blair didn't ask you about something else."

He grinned. "You're not kidding. But I bluff pretty well, don't I?"

They climbed the twenty-four granite steps and emerged in the hallway outside the pharmacology department. Cal stopped at the fountain nearby for a drink of water, staring at the closed door and wishing she could have gotten more information out of Albright. It would have been nice to get a look at Marilyn's office, or talk to her two coworkers. Bob and Therese, wasn't it?

Maybe later, after the case was officially opened. Of course, talking with them on an informal basis would have been much easier. People tend to clam up once an official investigation starts, once the police start asking questions. Theories and ideas, chance observations and tidbits of gossip stop being mentioned, and people only talk about things they're sure of. Which is usually pretty damn little.

She was waiting for Plato to get a drink when two people emerged from the pharmacology office—a tall, rawboned black man with a droopy mustache, and a trim, red-haired girl with a mask of freckles and a garish orange coat. The tall man glanced at Cal, gave a double-take, and quickly strode over to them.

"Doctor Marley?" he asked her.

"Yes."

"I'm Bob Stahl, and this is Therese Vogel." He gestured to his companion. "We were friends of Marilyn Abel. Can we talk with you a few minutes?"

Cal smiled. Luck was certainly on their side today.

Chapter 9

"Chuck Albright talked to us this evening, after you left," Bob explained. "He said you folks were looking into Marilyn's death."

Cal nodded slowly. She and Plato were sitting on the couch in the pharmacology lounge. There weren't any signs, no engraved plaque saying that Marilyn Abel had slept—and died—here. But the blue-black color and coarse polyester weave of the sofa and pillows matched the fibers Cal had taken from Marilyn's lungs. She glanced over at the two color-coordinated pillows tucked into the corners of the couch. One of them was probably the murder weapon.

Standing near the lounge's single window, Bob shifted his weight from one foot to the other. He was tall and rangy as a pro basketball player, but some problem with his spine had twisted his chest and back so his shoulders listed like the deck of a sinking ship. Even his *mustache* was crooked—a fuzzy gray caterpillar of a thing, teetering over one corner of his mouth like it was about to crawl off his lip. Bob was hunched over a little, too, as though the ceiling was too low for him, the room too cramped.

And maybe it was. The pharmacology lounge was small and close, and crammed with furniture. The fifteen by fifteen room held a round conference table and chairs, a kitchenette area with cabinets, stove, sink and refrigerator, Marilyn's sofa, and about five thousand pharmacology and toxicology textbooks and journals. The window behind Bob's lower shoulder was dark except for a single security light spilling its orange glow down the moldering brick of a vacant warehouse next door.

Bob coughed and smiled apologetically. "Chuck said you might contact us for some information. We'd like to help any way we can."

Therese was sitting in front of him, in a swivel chair at

the conference table. She had draped her garish orange coat over the back of her chair. Her hair was orange, her lipstick was orange, and the freckles sprinkled across her long hooked nose were orange. Her paisley blouse was lemon yellow and lime green. A pair of rhinestone-studded reading glasses hung from a gold chair around her neck, sparkling in tropical colors. Therese looked like a cross between a school librarian and a toucan. She leaned forward and half whispered, "But also we had the hopes that—"

"That you might tell us what this is all about," Bob finished.

"You see, we were Marilyn's very good friends." Therese's English was clear, though halting. Cal couldn't quite place her accent. On the Formica tabletop, Therese made knitting motions with her hands. She looked to be in her midthirties at most, but her ropy, gnarled fingers looked ancient. The freckles around her mouth crinkled into a frown.

"*Very* good friends," Bob added. He patted her shoulder. "Therese lived at Marilyn's house for a while, when she first came to the States."

"To come from East Berlin to Cleveland was *ein ungeheuer Schock* for me," she explained. "But also it was a good change. For three years after I got my medical degree, I scrubbed the dishes and waited the tables in a Berlin restaurant."

Bob clucked and shook his head.

"I came here seven years ago, before the Wall came down even," she continued. "Marilyn helped make of Cleveland a home for me. She gave me a job at Chadwick-Medicon even while I studied pharmacology at night school. Bob and I followed her here to Siegel when she left Chadwick." Therese smiled up at him. "We all three of us were very close."

Bob grinned. "We used to call ourselves the Three Musketeers."

" '*Tous pour un, un pour tous!*' " Therese added, then interpreted, " 'All for one and one for all.' "

"The *Four* Musketeers, after Tiffany came along," Bob concluded.

Cal smiled and nodded. She had never seen a murder victim with so many good friends.

Therese suddenly waved her hand in a continental gesture of impatience. "Bob?"

He jumped away from the window. "Of course—I'm forgetting my manners. Would you folks like anything to drink?" He slouched over to the refrigerator, a full-size model bearing the familiar circle of yellow and black spades and an inscription: DANGER! RADIOACTIVE MATERIALS! He opened the door and scanned the contents. "Let's see— we've got apple juice, iced tea, Hi-C, and a bottle of Therese's old carrot juice with something green growing on top of it—looks like penicillin."

"I have meant to clean out the fridge." Therese's freckles turned an even deeper shade of orange. "But the time, it has been too short."

"I'd like some apple juice, please," Plato said. He was huddled on the other end of the couch with a Kleenex box perched in his lap, honking every so often and looking utterly miserable. He coughed like an end-stage consumptive.

Bob frowned worriedly while Plato finished his coughing fit, then turned to Cal. "And what would you like?"

She smiled curiously. "I'd like to know what kind of radioactive materials you folks are keeping in there."

"What?" Bob glanced at the front of the refrigerator door and laughed, deep booming retorts like the cannons at the end of the 1812 Overture. "That's just to keep the security guys from stealing our stuff."

"They liked to come here late at night, make of our food the midnight snack," Therese explained, "until Marilyn caught them."

"One of the times she slept here overnight," Bob added.

"Which was perhaps every other night."

Bob grinned. "She told them the food was radioactive."

"She said we are making the experiments," said Therese. "Feeding to rats the irradiated food."

"Marilyn got the sign for us." Bob lifted his upper shoulder in a shrug. "Don't ask where."

Therese shook her head mournfully. "Most probably from a radioactive place."

They laughed together. Listening to them talk reminded Cal of watching a tennis match—except that they were both on the same side.

The two pharmacologists didn't wear rings or show any obvious affection. But they had that sense of each other's thoughts, that easy familiarity, that way of looking and talking and moving that announced they were a pair, that conveyed an absolute sense of each other and very politely shut out the rest of the world. Cal tried to remember if she and Plato had ever been that way.

"One security guard, he was sick for a week after that," Therese added. "I think he has lost perhaps thirty pounds since then. He seems to believe he has the cancer."

They laughed again, and Cal smiled with them. It seemed a little cruel, but then the security guards hadn't stolen *her* lunches.

"Marilyn kept her insulin in here, too," Bob added. He sobered suddenly. "I think that's what really pissed her off—picturing those bumbling security guards messing with her medicine, maybe breaking her vial or handling the syringes."

Therese nodded slowly, then smiled at Bob. "Maybe Chuck should get a sign for his bookcase, too—he has complained of the missing Hillerman book now for weeks."

"Good idea." He turned to Cal. "So what'll you have, Doctor Marley?"

"Just Cal is fine," she told him. "How about some iced tea?"

"Great. Therese brewed it up this morning." Bob rummaged in the cupboard for a pair of reasonably clean glasses and served the apple juice and iced tea. He smiled that sad, apologetic smile again. "I suppose we're being awfully nosy. But I saw you folks leaving Chuck's office this afternoon, and he told us why you were here—"

"And we worked the late hours tonight anyway," Therese added.

"We're putting together a submission for an NIH grant." Bob took the chair beside Therese's and stared at the tabletop. "So when we saw you—"

"We couldn't resist asking."

They both shrugged sheepishly.

Cal wondered if she should just wear a sandwich-board detailing Marilyn Abel's autopsy findings and her reasons for being suspicious. This was the fourth time she'd told the story in the last twenty-four hours. But she went ahead and explained the situation anyway. Hopefully, the couple would provide enough information to make it worthwhile.

"It sounds like Marilyn was murdered," Bob concluded, stroking the furry little mustache.

"Yes, it does," Therese agreed. She shivered a little, and Bob patted her hand. "But who would possibly want to—"

"Did you find out anything from Chuck?" Bob asked suddenly.

"Not much," Plato replied.

Bob and Therese exchanged glances. They didn't seem surprised.

"Just general things," Cal added. "He was just starting to tell us about the Patracin testing when we ran out of time."

From across the sofa, Plato caught her eye and frowned critically. She smiled back. It was only a *little* lie. Besides, it was for a good cause.

Bob's heavy eyebrows folded together. "I'm surprised he even told you the name of the drug."

"Chuck makes the big secret of it," Therese added.

"He's secretive about everything." Bob curled his lip with disdain. "He'd cut that medical student—Tiffany—out of the loop if he possibly could."

"He sounded pretty excited about the new drug," Plato lied.

Cal shot him a grateful glance. Plato was getting the hang of it.

"He sure is," Bob agreed. "From what Tiffany has said, the tests are going really well."

"This week, they finish another round of animal studies," Therese noted. She steepled her fingers and shrugged noncommittally. "We shall see. I have the doubts whether a drug so similar to streptomycin could be at all effective with the resistant tuberculosis."

"Maybe, maybe not," Bob argued. "Remember, Patracin is a very complex drug. Structurally, it's more similar to the other aminoglycosides—with 2-deoxystreptamine occupying the central position and a pair of completely unique amine sugars providing resistance against both acetylase and phosphorylase . . ."

Cal listened with half an ear while Bob and Therese lobbed molecules at each other. Her aptitude for pharmacology roughly matched Plato's anatomy expertise. She hadn't flunked the course during medical school, but she'd come pretty close. Bob and Therese might as well have been talking in German.

After a few minutes, Cal yawned and Plato coughed delicately. The two researchers glanced over as though surprised their guests were still there and then called a reluctant truce.

Bob frowned. "Anyway, we'll probably be the last to hear the results."

"At least *Marilyn* told us about the experiments," Therese observed.

"She was Chuck's exact opposite."

"Das stimmt," she agreed with a nod.

The comment about Marilyn reminded Cal of her earlier interview. "Chuck told us a funny thing today," she said. "He talked about how drug research is a very hit-or-miss thing—'especially the way Marilyn worked.' What do you suppose he meant by that?"

Therese twirled the chain of her reading glasses round and round her finger. She smiled into her lap. "He *hated* the way Marilyn did things."

"Right." Bob grimaced. "For all his laid-back Beach Boy air, he's very compulsive."

"And Marilyn wasn't?" Plato leaned forward, sounding surprised.

"No." Bob stood again, his dark eyes twinkling. "Come on and see for yourself."

He led the others out of the pharmacology lounge, back through June's rain forest, and down a short hallway with only two doors. He stood before the first door and fumbled with his key ring.

"Therese and I share the other office," he said. "Although she's supposed to get this one, if we ever clean it out."

He sounded a little dubious. Once he opened the door and flicked on the overhead light, Cal could see why.

It was even worse than Plato's office. Bookcases lined the four walls, but most of the shelves were empty, their books stacked and scattered across the desk, folding table, chairs, and floor like a spoiled child's building blocks. An ancient combination record player/eight-track cassette deck huddled between two file cabinets; LPs and eight-track cartridges were strewn around at random. Atop the desk, a bright new computer, keyboard, and mouse parted the sea of books and loose papers like Moses leading the Israelites across the Red Sea. But even the computer and monitor were sinking beneath a rising tide of floppy disks and manuals. The only other clear spot on the desk was a cookie jar, filled with a brownish substance that looked like dirt; Cal assumed it was coffee.

A thick layer of dust already coated the bookcases and file cabinets, and the room had a musty smell. No plants here, but the walls were painted a sickly greenish brown. Sort of like forest green meets acid rain, Cal thought.

Above the desk, an eight-foot computer banner spelled out the word SERENDIPITY in six-inch letters.

"We come in here every once in a while to get books and things," Bob explained.

"And to begin the mess to straighten," Therese added. "I love this office—especially the window. And the color is so pretty, besides."

Cal fluttered an eyebrow at Plato. He stifled a snort, bit the back of his hand.

"You can see why Chuck needs Tiffany," Bob said, picking his way across the floor like someone caught in a minefield. "She's the only one who knows where anything is in this office."

"What does the banner mean?" Plato asked.

"That was the difference between Chuck and Marilyn," Bob said softly.

"Chuck, he believes in the theories, the abstractions," Therese continued. She was standing just inside the doorway, leaning against one of the empty bookcases. "He loves drawing chemical formulas, making the little equations. Working out 3-D computer simulations of drug molecules and receptor sites, even for drugs we already have."

"And Marilyn believed in good old-fashioned luck," Bob added with a grin.

"Serendipity," said Therese.

Cal nodded. Many so-called scientific advances were more the product of luck than pure science. Admiral Hawkins used lemon juice against scurvy three hundred years before vitamins were discovered. Penicillin was discovered by accident—Alexander Fleming found that one of his bacterial cultures was contaminated by mold—a fungus that killed nearby bacteria. Research on mustard gas led to the development of the first anticancer drugs.

Sometimes it's a lot easier to get lucky, and leave the theories and explanations for later.

"That dirt over there—" Therese pointed to the jar be-

side the computer. "That is where Marilyn discovered the
Patracin."

"Same way a lot of other antibiotics were discovered—
cephalosporins, aminoglycosides—you know," Bob added.

Cal frowned curiously.

"Whenever Marilyn went somewhere on vacation, she
brought back some dirt, or some seawater," he continued.
"Molds growing in the soil or the sea learn to make chemicals that fight nearby bacteria. An arms race for germs.
We've learned to look for these molds, grow them, and
isolate their defensive chemicals."

"That soil came from a riverbank near Rio de Janeiro,"
said Therese. "Just downstream from a sewage plant."

"Very tough germs growing there," Bob said with a grin.
"Very smart ones."

"Mother Nature is far smarter than we," said Therese.

"So was Marilyn," Bob added sadly.

"Chuck thought she was crazy in the head," said Therese, "but it worked for her before."

"And maybe this time, too," Bob mused. "Good old-fashioned luck."

"Of course, she was not really old-fashioned at all."

"Yeah. She was crazy about that computer, for one
thing." Bob tiptoed further into the minefield and gestured
at the machine. "She did everything on it. Recorded every
stage of her research, tracked all the processing steps, made
spreadsheets to estimate manufacturing costs and timelines
long before she even knew whether a drug worked or not."

"She kept all her appointments on there," Therese added
with a smile. "Funny little songs would play when it was
time for meetings and things. We could hear them through
the wall. It made us laugh."

"She just got this machine last fall." Bob shifted some
books, sat down at the desk, and patted the computer.
"Pentium processor, all the latest software, even a built-in
fax machine." He turned to Therese. "Remember when she
faxed that dirty limerick to Dean Fairfax?"

She chuckled admiringly. "Routed it through five different phone lines so they couldn't trace where it came from."

"She made it look like Dean Symthe sent it."

"You said Marilyn had a calendar on the computer?"
Cal asked.

Bob nodded. "Yeah. You want to see it?" He turned the

computer on. "It's pretty flashy—she's got Windows, Word, some neat Lotus programs . . ."

The edges of the monitor were feathered with at least two dozen sticky notes; it looked like an ungainly ostrich displaying its flat yellow plumage, or an impossibly fat eagle ready to spring into the air.

They watched the screen brighten with some glitzy wallpaper and an array of icons. Bob grabbed the mouse and clicked on an icon shaped like a tiny notebook. The program instantly loaded, filling the screen with a full-size datebook open to the current date. No appointments were listed, of course. Bob leafed back in time to December. The once empty pages were filled with notes and appointments and little stylized icons representing meetings, dinner dates, and holidays.

Cal saw that the week after Marilyn's death held just as many appointments as the week before. Unfinished business. It gave her a little creepy feeling, raised the hackles on the back of her neck. You just never know.

"How about if I print a copy of Marilyn's calendar for the week of the thirteenth?" Bob suggested.

"The week Marilyn died," Therese said softly.

Cal nodded and stepped closer to the desk.

Bob moved the mouse around and clicked on the printer icon. "Marilyn showed me how the program worked. I think I'm going to get my own copy sometime."

"Not that it helped her get organized," Therese observed, glancing around the office.

"She *was* organized," Bob protested. "She was just *messy.*"

Waiting for the printer to finish, Cal noticed one of the sticky notes pasted to the corner of the monitor. She picked it up and read: "Call: Candice Erdmann, Leonard Reiss." She showed it to Bob and Therese. "Do you know who these people are?"

"Candice Erdmann is a vice president at Valdemar Pharmaceuticals," Therese explained. "Their company has an affiliation with the medical school—with our department. Valdemar gives us some reasearch lab space and we help them with some of their clinical testing."

"Free slave labor," Bob said. "Namely, us."

"How about Leonard Reiss?" Cal asked.

Still standing in the doorway, Plato answered. "I think he's a writer for the *Plain Dealer.*"

"I don't know why Marilyn would be calling *him*," Therese said, puzzled. "But she could have many reasons to call Candice. For one thing, Marilyn had rented some equipment from Valdemar to develop her drug."

Bob pulled the stack of finished sheets from the printer and showed them to Cal and Plato. They looked just like pages from an ordinary datebook, only neater.

He looked over their shoulders and pointed to the entries. "Nothing much out of the ordinary, considering it was finals week."

Cal tapped an entry for Tuesday morning, December 14th. "HSIII, huh? She met with Dean Smythe that day?"

"Yeah," Bob replied. "She was really upset that Tiffany flunked anatomy. She tried to put in a good word for her, but Smythe wouldn't listen. He wanted to flunk her out altogether. He said that was his policy."

Cal caught Plato's eye. He gave her a little nod—Smythe really *had* planned to expel the failing students.

"The saga continued," Bob said. He pointed to another entry—a meeting with "TC" Thursday morning of the same week. "Marilyn met with Tiffany later that week. The morning before Marilyn died. They had a real knock-down, drag-out fight. Tiffany was convinced that she was going to be kicked out of medical school, and that it was Marilyn's fault."

"Why?" asked Plato. "I thought Marilyn was trying to help."

"Tiffany is very independent," Therese noted.

"That wasn't all of it." Bob shook his head. He seemed embarrassed. "I heard the whole thing—these walls are paper-thin. I guess Tiffany found out she was on the chopping block, so she had met with Smythe on Wednesday. The dean claimed that he wanted to give Tiffany another chance, but that Marilyn had given her a poor recommendation."

"I guess I'd have been upset, too," Cal conceded. She was a little surprised at how Smythe had twisted things around. The dean was often afraid to face the students with bad news; he generally delegated it to others. But his about-faces were rarely so blatant.

On the other hand, with his promising political career in the balance, Smythe probably didn't want to damage his popularity with the students. And maybe Tiffany Cramer had some sort of connections—with the student leadership, or perhaps with someone from the Cleveland political scene. "Did Tiffany and Marilyn get along well otherwise?"

"*Very* well," Therese replied. She glanced over at Bob, who nodded slightly. "Tiffany made the mistakes sometimes. But Marilyn called her a good-luck charm."

"Tiffany mixed up the reagents when Marilyn was first trying to purify Patracin," Bob told them. "Ended up with an extra amine group on the hexose nucleus. Marilyn tried it anyway, and the drug turned out twice as effective."

"That is why Marilyn kept close track of everything. I think she sometimes *hoped* for the mistakes." ·

"Serendipity." Bob eyed the banner strung above Marilyn's desk.

Cal glanced through the pages again. One more appointment was listed—for seven o'clock Thursday evening. " 'A. Welkins.' Who's that?"

"Arnold Welkins." Therese spat the name like poison. "One of the owners at Chadwick-Medicon."

"The drug company where we all used to work," Bob said.

"He was also Marilyn's ex-husband," Plato added from the doorway.

"Do you know why she was meeting him that day?" Cal asked. She hadn't realized that Marilyn had been married. She'd pictured her as a career woman, without much of a private life.

Bob and Therese just exchanged empty looks and shrugged.

An ex-husband, Cal mused. And Marilyn had met with him on the night she died. As if things weren't complicated enough. Cal rummaged in her pocket for a business card. It gave her title as deputy coroner, and listed the Cuyahoga County Morgue as her business address. "Look—if you folks find out anything important when you're going through Marilyn's papers, just give me a call. Okay?"

"Sure thing." Bob looked around the office and grinned. " 'Course, we may not finish cleaning this place for another year or so."

Cal just nodded. The way things were going, they might not have the case solved before then, anyway.

Then again, maybe they'd get lucky. She glanced down at the jar of dirt. Maybe a little of Marilyn Abel's serendipity would come their way.

Chapter 10

Early the next morning, Plato lay in bed wondering if anyone had ever died from a head cold. He had just made up his mind to be the first, to write up his own case history so it could be published postmortem in the *New England Journal,* when Cal rolled over and opened her eyes.

"Gaak!" She bounded across the bed in a single flying leap—a three-foot broad jump from a supine position, something Plato had never witnessed before or even believed possible. She squinted at her husband in the darkness. "Plato? Is that *you*?"

He smiled reassuringly, or tried to, then remembered the wad of Kleenex taped to his upper lip and nose—a sort of compression bandage for his sinuses. He'd gone through at least half a box of tissues during the night before finally calling it quits and sealing his nostrils shut. He tore away the wad of surgical tape and Kleenex and smiled again. "See? That's not so scary, is it?"

"That's not what startled me." She fumbled under the covers, extracted a small squarish object, and brandished it to Plato. "*This* is."

"Hmm. I wonder where that came from." He took the ice pack from her and frowned. "Oh, yes. I had a headache last night."

"Haven't you ever heard of Tylenol, Plato? Does 'acetaminophen' ring a bell? Or how about 'ibuprofen'?"

"I tried them. They didn't work." He was still regarding the ice pack like a foreign object, a meteorite that had crashed into their bed. He had vague memories of cuddling the pack to his aching forehead and finally falling asleep in the wee hours. "I think it was wrapped in a towel, before."

"It was." Cal mined the covers again, pulled out a sodden something and tossed it onto Plato's face. "A *wet* towel." She pulled the blankets up to her chin and shivered. "Have you thought about seeing a doctor for this?"

Plato pulled the rag from his face and sniffed. "I *am* a doctor."

"They have these neat things now," Cal continued. "Antibiotics, I think they're called. Bloodletting is passé. So are ice packs. *Especially* in bed."

"Oh." He nodded thoughtfully. "I see."

"Are we clear on this?" Her tone was sharp as a new dissecting scalpel.

"Yes, dear." An angry Cal was an awesome thing. Wondrous and terrifying—sort of like the tornado looming on the horizon in *The Wizard of Oz.* Plato pressed the Kleenex against his nose again and tried to look a little terrifying, too, but Cal had already switched on the bedside light.

She squinted at him critically, then softened. "Poor dear. Your nose looks like a beefsteak tomato."

"It *feels* like a beefsteak tomato," he agreed. "A big swollen mushy one that's been sitting in the sun too long."

"Ugh." She crinkled her nose in distaste and edged away. "Maybe you should call in sick, go and see Nathan today. Maybe he'd prescribe some antibiotics for you."

"Antibiotics don't work with viruses." Plato sat up, tipping his head back and waiting for the flood. But nothing happened. His nose was finally stopped up tight—a worthless, purposeless organ, like an appendix. "Anyway, I can't just call in sick—you know that. I've got too much to do."

"Like what?" Cal challenged. She sat up, hugged her red flannel pajamas closer about her small waist, and scowled at him.

"Like seeing Jonathan Ebbings, for one. Marilyn's brother—remember? He had a nasty fall over the weekend, and he doesn't feel up to coming to the office. I promised him I'd go out there on a home visit today."

"Oh." Cal's eyes lit with curiosity, and her protests about Plato's cold suddenly died away. "Are you going to talk to him about Marilyn?"

"Should I?" he asked innocently. "It's not like I have any official standing in the case."

"You were Marilyn's doctor," Cal pointed out. She moved closer. "That's official enough for me. Anyway, Homer told us to look things over for him, remember?"

Plato remembered. And he wasn't about to pass up an

opportunity to find out more about Marilyn's death. But Cal didn't have to know that.

He shrugged reluctantly. "Okay, you've convinced me." He pressed the towel to his forehead, closed his eyes, and gave a little moan. "Except I feel so lousy, maybe I *should* take today off, and go see Nathan."

Cal jumped from the bed and hurried out, returning with a glass of water and some Tylenol. "Here—take this. You'll feel better."

Plato swallowed the tablets and smiled weakly. "Maybe you're right." He slumped down under the covers. "Maybe if I had something to eat, too... You know what they say—'starve a cold'—"

It was Plato's morning to make breakfast, of course. One of their New Year's resolutions—up early, and no more candy bars in the morning. Cal frowned, studied his face closely, and saw not a trace of malingering. Only innocent suffering. She turned on her heel. "Okay, I'll bring up some cereal and—"

"An omelet might be nice." Plato sighed wistfully. "With ham and cheddar cheese."

Cal marched over to Plato's side of the bed, and brought her face close to his. Dark whirlwinds loomed in her eyes. "Don't press your luck, mister."

He didn't.

Two hours later, Plato was on the road to Jonathan Ebbings's house in Kirtland. He had driven into town, dropped Cal off at Riverside General, picked up his black bag, and headed for the hills and forests of Cleveland's eastern suburbs.

Plato spent one morning each week making house calls. The visits were especially helpful for his geriatric patients, who sometimes didn't drive and more often *shouldn't*. Most doctors couldn't afford to make house calls because insurance companies didn't pay for time spent on the road. But Plato was salaried by the hospital, so the lost time wasn't as much of a problem.

Even so, he tried to limit his house calls to patients living within a short distance of the hospital. He'd made an exception in Marilyn's case, back when she had her first bad flare-up. Jonathan had been impressed by Plato's work and signed himself up with the practice, too. He was older than Marilyn, but a good deal healthier.

It was a long drive, but Plato always loooked forward to it. He left the freeway near Willoughby and followed a string of narrow roads through rolling hills and winding river valleys, driving beneath a clear blue winter sky and a canopy of bare trees. Snow covered everything, glittering like diamond dust in the bright sunshine.

The Abel house was down in the valley, a tidy old colonial tucked into a copse of walnut and maple, perched on a spit of land that jutted into the Chagrin River. Every spring the basement flooded, and every summer Marilyn had sent her daughter out to pick plums and pears from the small orchard beside the house. She and Jonathan had always saved some for Plato.

Tricia answered the bell before Plato had a chance to start shivering. She looked better than she had at the funeral—her cheeks weren't so hollow, her soft brown eyes no longer looked likes caves, and her smile wasn't crooked or forced.

"Snow day today," she explained, gesturing him inside. "The pipes froze at the school."

Apparently she was still wearing her teacher's clothes—denim skirt, soft cotton blouse, stockings, and a pair of loafers. She caught Plato staring at the black marks on her knees and bent over to look.

"Damn! I *knew* I should have changed clothes first." She shook her head ruefully. "I've been going through Mom's papers in the basement. It's a mess down there."

She led Plato through the narrow center hallway to the back of the house. The place hadn't changed much since Marilyn's death. One wall of the huge family room was covered with floor-to-ceiling bookcases and another held Marilyn's collection of antique pharmaceutical equipment. Mortars and pestles, huge glass globes filled with blue- or green-tinted liquid, a shiny brass pill-counting device, even a few jars filled with medicinal herbs—foxglove, oleander, erythrina seeds, and white willow bark.

Opposite the doorway, a deep fireplace was framed by a pair of tall windows looking out over the Chagrin River, a crumpled ribbon of piled gray ice and drifted snow. A month from now the crews would start dynamiting it again, but it wouldn't help the Abels escape the spring melt. They were too low, too close to the river.

Tricia told him that Jonathan would be downstairs in a minute, and ran off to change her stockings. Plato slumped into a club chair before the fireplace, a red leather monstrosity that swallowed him up like a giant callused hand. Every house should have a chair like this, he thought. Part of the building code, maybe with a sign—EMERGENCY USE ONLY. He leaned his head back against the cushion, closed his eyes, and tried to ignore the pounding in his sinuses.

He could hear Tricia skittering around upstairs like a mouse in the rafters, could hear Jonathan's slow and measured steps down the stairway, could almost hear the sound of Marilyn's voice out in the hallway, the squeak of her wheelchair as she wove through the furniture to greet him and tell him how much she'd improved since his last visit.

He opened his eyes with a start, and saw Jonathan Ebbings sitting in the chair across from him.

"Don't mind me," he said, chuckling. "You were having such a good snooze there, I hated to wake you." He roared with laughter, then leaned forward to pat Plato's knee. "How're you doing, Doctor Marley? Kind of tired, huh?"

Plato started to protest, to deny falling asleep, but realized that Jonathan was probably right. He grinned. "Caught me red-handed. I guess I didn't get enough sleep last night."

"You don't look so good, Doc." He leaned forward and stared at him with Marilyn's pale blue eyes. "Your nose looks like a beefsteak tomato. You sound like a frog trying to yodel. You had your flu shot this year?"

"No," Plato admitted.

"Could be flu then, or maybe you need some antibiotics." He rubbed his chin thoughtfully. Except for the eyes, Jonathan bore little resemblance to his sister. Where Marilyn had been short and delicate, Jonathan was tall—taller than Plato—with the shoulders of a longshoreman, which he wasn't, and the flattened nose and ham hands of a long-ago boxer, which he was. His long head was crowned with a shock of brilliant white hair that would have made a punk rocker jealous. Beneath it, his face was cragged and seamy with sun and age. His thin lips pressed together in a tight line, and his forehead wrinkled with concern.

"It's just a cold," Plato assured him. That was the problem with geriatric patients—they were always older than you, at least until you were ready to retire. And until then, they often treated their doctors like their own sons or daughters.

"A cold?" Jonathan leaned forward eagerly. "Then you just wait here—I've got the perfect thing for it."

He eased himself from the chair and hobbled over to the kitchen. Despite his rough looks, Jonathan had spent his life working as a research chemist for a paint company. According to Marilyn, though, he had always wanted to be a doctor.

Apparently Plato was to be his first patient. Jonathan returned from the kitchen with a tall glass and handed it to him. Inside it, golden liquid bubbled and fizzed.

"My special remedy," the old chemist announced proudly. "Marilyn's not the only one in the family with medical talent."

"What's in it?" Plato peered into the glass warily.

"Honey, bitter lemon, tonic water, nutmeg, and a couple of secret ingredients." Jonathan waved the secret ingredients away casually. "You'll want to drink it quick, though. All in one gulp—that works best."

"Nothing poisonous?"

Jonathan looked insulted, so Plato tipped his head back and drained the glass.

He knew what at least *one* of the secret ingredients was. The oldest remedy in the book, the cure for what ails you, the heart of a thousand tonics. Plato wondered if he'd be legal to drive home and wondered what the police officer would say if he told him the truth.

"Your eyes are watering," Jonathan observed. "That's good—that's the red pepper."

"Thanks," Plato gasped. His throat felt like it was being fired in a kiln. "That's much better."

"Uncle Jonathan!" Tricia was standing in the doorway in a pair of jeans and a huge Kent State sweatshirt that hung down to her knees. "Don't tell me you gave Doctor Marley some of that awful concoction of yours." She rushed to Plato's side and rolled her eyes. "He made me take some of that once, back when I was a kid. I ended up in the hospital the next day."

"You had tonsillitis," Jonathan protested. "My 'concoction' can't cure tonsillitis."

"Did you tell him about your arm?" Tricia asked, dragging a chair over to join the group. "No? I didn't think so."

"It doesn't hurt much." He rubbed his left forearm gingerly, but kept it carefully hidden under the long sleeve of his sweater. "I think it's just about better now."

Plato stood and staggered over to Jonathan's side, his head whirling with the cold remedy gumbo he'd taken this morning and the fifth of bourbon the old chemist had hidden in his concoction. He pulled Jonathan's sleeve up over the huge purplish-brown bruise that covered most of his forearm.

"I kind of banged it when I fell down," he confessed, wincing slightly as Plato probed for broken bones.

"How did you fall?"

It was an accident, Jonathan explained, a misstep on the ladder when he was taking the Christmas lights down outside. Plato made sure that Jonathan hadn't blacked out, suffered a temporary stroke or anything similarly serious, and finally assured him that he hadn't broken any bones and didn't need to go to the hospital. He took care of the routine things then—a blood pressure check and quick physical exam, and made sure his patient didn't need any prescriptions—then slumped back into his chair.

"See?" Jonathan asked. "You look better already. Your color's improved, anyway."

"He's flushed from the bourbon," Tricia observed critically.

"Anyway, I appreciate your coming out here, Doctor Marley." Jonathan suddenly sobered. "I've been meaning to give you a call, to thank you for coming to the funeral. And for everything you did for Marilyn—"

"We both wanted to thank you," Tricia said. "I know it meant a lot to her, having you to turn to."

Plato fussed with a tissue, embarrassed. He shrugged. "She was a great lady. I enjoyed taking care of her."

Jonathan coughed and stared at his big empty hands. "Your wife called us yesterday. She told us about the new autopsy results. I wondered if you'd heard anything more . . ."

Plato had been waiting for him to ask. Many patients held their biggest concerns until the end of the visit, spilling them just as Plato was about to leave. This time, though, he didn't mind. It saved him the awkwardness of broaching the subject himself.

Plato shook his head slowly. "Cal is still trying to pinpoint something that could tell her for sure one way or the other."

"She hasn't found anything definite?" Tricia asked. "Then maybe Mom died a natural death after all."

"I don't—" Plato began, but Jonathan interrupted him.

"Marilyn sure was acting *strange* that week," the chemist said. "Especially that last day."

"You saw her on Thursday?" Plato asked eagerly.

"Of course, she'd been excited for the couple of weeks before," Jonathan began, ignoring the question. He sat back in the chair, steepled his fingers, and stared up at the ceiling fan whirring slowly and silently. "Ever since those drug tests came out so well."

"That's right." Tricia nodded. "The rat studies—she was happier than I'd ever seen her."

"Until that last Tuesday—when she had that big flap with the dean out there. What was his name? Wythe or Blythe or something."

"Smythe," Tricia said.

"That's right." Jonathan nodded. "She told us about the whole thing. She was so mad she cried—it took the wind right out of her sails."

"She was pretty down after that," Tricia agreed.

"He treated her like dirt—just marched her right out of his office. If I were twenty years younger, I'd have clobbered him." His lips formed a thin red line and then disappeared completely, his face purpled, and the boxer's hands clenched into fists. Beads of sweat broke out on his forehead.

Plato realized he'd better change the subject. Somewhere beneath the surface, Jonathan seemed to blame Randolph Smythe the Third for Marilyn's death. As though the humiliating experience might have taxed her strength and caused the heart attack. Knowing Marilyn, though, Plato doubted it. She would have just fought back, stronger than ever.

"That's a state-funded school—I had half a mind to call my congressman and complain," Jonathan griped.

Little did he know—next year, Randolph Smythe might *be* his congressman. Ironically, Smythe was running on a law-and-order ticket. More money for prisons, more police in the streets, or some such thing. Maybe the dean would help them catch Marilyn's murderer—*that* would win him a few votes.

"You said you saw Marilyn on Thursday?" Plato asked.

"Thursday afternoon. We were going to see *Miss Saigon* downtown—Tricia had tickets."

"I got them so Mom and I could celebrate her new drug," she explained. "But I had to cancel that morning—I gave my ticket to Uncle Jonathan."

"And I drove all the way downtown to the medical school." His tall forehead creased. "But Marilyn said she changed her mind—said she had an appointment and couldn't go after all."

"I don't know why he's making such a big deal out of it," Tricia said.

"What time did you see her?" Plato asked. Jonathan Ebbings was probably the last person to see his sister alive.

"I got to Siegel around five o'clock," he replied. He gave a thin smile. "She was happier than she'd been all week—happier even than she was after those drug tests went so well. So I asked her why she wasn't going, and she said she had some business to take care of out at the college."

"Did she say what kind of business?"

Jonathan shrugged. "Couldn't have been anything serious. She kept *giggling* when she talked about it. I hadn't heard her giggle in fifty years—I thought she had the hiccups. Can you imagine Marilyn giggling?"

Plato and Tricia both shook their heads.

"I thought maybe her blood sugar was too high, but she said she'd taken her morning insulin, like always."

"Maybe she was just happy because the semester was over," Tricia suggested.

"I doubt it." He waved a hand in the air. "She was giddy as a schoolgirl. I asked her what I should do, since I didn't plan on going to the theater by myself, and she shoved a book at me, told me to take it home and read it."

"I don't know why he's making such a big deal about it," Tricia repeated.

"A *mystery* book," he continued. "I haven't read a work of fiction since high school. Do I strike you as a mystery reader, Doctor Marley?"

Plato shook his head.

"I should hope not." Jonathan sighed, relieved.

Plato had a sudden thought. "What was the name of the book?"

"I haven't the foggiest notion. Someting about the circus, I think." He gestured to the bookcase. "It's over there, on the far shelf. Next to the *National Geographics.*"

Tricia jumped to her feet and darted to the bookcase. "Hillerman's *Sacred Clowns.* I've read this one." She opened the book, glanced at the inside cover, and closed it quickly. "I don't understand it."

She started to replace it on the shelf, but Plato reached a hand out. "May I see that, please?"

Tricia hesitated, then handed it to him. He opened it and saw Chuck Albright's name on the flyleaf.

"I figured I'd return it myself," Tricia explained quickly. "I'm going into town this afternoon."

"Don't worry about it," Plato answered. He opened his black bag and dropped the book inside. "I'm heading over to the medical school right now—I'll save you the trip across the river."

She started to protest, then just shrugged.

"A *mystery* book," Jonathan mused. "Crazy."

They both saw Plato to the door and thanked him for coming. He smiled politely, hiding his excitement until he got into the Rabbit, backed out of the driveway, and pulled over on the shoulder of the road a mile from the house. With shaking hands, he lifted the edge of the dust jacket on the inside back cover of the book.

Taped inside the back flap was the thin square object he'd felt when Tricia had handed him the book. A black plastic object, three and one-half inches across, with a sliding metal window at the top.

A computer disk. Plato couldn't wait to tell Cal.

Chapter 11

"I tried to open the file on Marilyn's computer," Plato told Cal later that evening. "It wouldn't come up on any of her programs."

He piloted the Rabbit up the steep freeway entrance ramp and onto I-77 south. They were heading home from Siegel's anatomy lab, having spent a long session reviewing the nerves and arteries of the head and neck. The students had gotten hopelessly lost and confused, and Plato hadn't helped much. His sneezing and coughing fits had destroyed everyone's concentration, including his own, but at least he'd gotten some sympathy from the students. Tiffany Cramer had even suggested that Plato should stay home and rest tomorrow evening, but Cal vetoed it.

That afternoon, instead of boning up for the tutoring session, he had headed over to Siegel's pharmacology department. June had let him into Marilyn's office after Plato explained what he needed. Plato had copied the disk before turning the original over to Homer, always holding it by the edges in case fingerprints were an issue. Unfortunately, his cousin wasn't impressed by the find.

Neither was Cal.

"It's probably Albright's disk," she muttered, squinting through the tiny circle of clear windshield directly above the defrost vent. She grabbed a MasterCard from her purse and scraped away at the frost. "But even if it was Marilyn's, what difference does it make?"

She handed him the credit card and steered while he cleared his side of the windshield. On nights this cold, the Rabbit's puny heater wouldn't melt the frost until they were almost home. It wasn't worth waiting.

"Don't you see?" he asked. "Marilyn sent that disk home with her brother because—"

"Because she knew she was going to be killed?" Cal chuckled. "Come on, Plato. *Now* who's being dramatic?"

"The file was created on Thursday, December sixteenth." He handed the credit card back. "One of these days, we'll have to buy a scraper."

"Let's save our money and just buy a new car." She dropped the credit card back into her purse. "You say the file was made on the day Marilyn died?"

"Yeah. At twelve-thirty P.M."

She sighed. "Maybe it's worth looking into. What was the file name, anyway?"

Plato spelled it out. "R-E-C-O-R-D—dot—F-X-exclamation point."

Cal frowned—or *seemed* to, since only her eyes were visible. They were both swaddled in scarves, woolly ski hats, heavy parkas, and boots. Cal had worn a ski bib to work every day since New Year's.

" 'RECORD.FX!'?" she repeated. "That doesn't tell us much—it could be anything."

"I know."

"You tried pulling it up on her word processor?"

"Yeah. It comes out looking like hieroglyphics." He groaned. "I tried every single program on her machine— even *Harvard Graphics*. Most of them wouldn't even *try* to open the file."

A white panel truck was passing them, spattering the Rabbit with chunks of frozen gray slush. Plato eased the car closer to the shoulder. The snow was falling again, and only two lanes were clear.

"Homer will find out what's on the disk," Cal said confidently.

"I doubt it." Plato sighed. "Homer hates computers. He'll probably lose it in his desk."

The panel truck bore a familiar logo on its side: a Caduceus centered in an outline of Ohio. Beneath the insignia was written SIEGEL MEDICAL COLLEGE—RESEARCH DIVISION. The truck passed them and swung back into the right lane.

"Anyway, I've got a copy of the disk," he added. "I'm going to try it on the computer at home, see if the file will open up on one of our programs."

"Like what—*Flight Simulator*?" Cal snickered. "You think Marilyn was killed because she beat someone at *BattleChess*?"

"That's hitting below the belt, Cally. You got me those games for Christmas."

"After you *begged* me for them."

"I did not beg," Plato huffed. "I put them on my Christmas list."

"Right." Cal sighed. "In big red letters. And hung the list on the refrigerator door."

"I was afraid you'd miss it." He glanced ahead at the panel truck and grimaced. "Look at that—the idiot left his door up."

The rear door of the truck was wide open. Cal touched Plato's arm. "You'd better drop back a little, in case anything falls out."

Plato nodded. "No wonder the college is short on funds." He slowed and let the gap widen between the Rabbit and the truck. From the breast pocket of his parka, he pulled a 3½-inch computer disk and waved it at Cal. "I've got a couple of older graphics programs at home—I thought I'd try opening this on them."

"Maybe you should talk with Dave Winchell—the computer geek at Siegel."

"Yeah." He rubbed his beard thoughtfully. "I didn't think of that."

"He should know about most of the programs at the college." She pulled the scarf down to her chin and blew on her gloved hands. "Maybe he'll recognize the file format from the name. But 'FX!'—that doesn't sound like anything I've ever heard of."

"Me neither." Plato glanced quickly at the truck again. He'd imagined he saw some movement near the back door, but decided his eyes were playing tricks on him. He needed some rest—or another dose of Jonathan's concoction.

"Did you find out anything else from Marilyn's brother?" Cal asked, seeming to read his thoughts.

"Not really." Earlier, Plato had told her how Jonathan had been given the book and disk on the afternoon of Marilyn's death. "I guess he was the last person to see his sister alive."

"No, he wasn't. Homer did a little checking of his own today," she explained. "He sent Jeremy Ames down to Siegel this morning to ask a few questions."

"Sounds like you've got Homer convinced." Plato's cousin would never involve the sheriff's office unless he was absolutely certain something was up. "Who did Jeremy talk to?"

"Tiffany Cramer, for one. She admitted to seeing Marilyn around five-thirty Thursday evening—the night she died."

"Probably just after Jonathan left."

"Right. Tiffany says she went back to talk with Marilyn and apologize—for the fight they'd had earlier that day. According to Tiffany, Marilyn said she was having dinner at the medical school and meeting with someone later that evening."

"Probably her ex-husband—Arnold Welkins."

"Could be," Cal agreed. "Jeremy hasn't talked with him yet. Anyway, a security guard saw Marilyn in the cafeteria later that evening—he figures it was about quarter to seven. And that was the last time anyone saw her."

Plato had a sudden idea. "Speaking of security—maybe Jeremy Ames should go over the sign-out sheets at Siegel for that day. He could find out who was still at the medical school when Marilyn died."

"It wouldn't help." Cal sighed. "You know how their security is. Half the people forget to sign out when they leave. Besides, the security log shows that the side door near the pharmacology department was opened at eight-fifteen that evening. Security was late locking the doors that night, but it set off a silent alarm. The guard checked it out, but he didn't find anything unusual."

"So the door wasn't locked. The killer could have been anyone—even someone off the street."

"Right." Cal took a deep breath. "But Jeremy's especially interested in Tiffany Cramer."

"You're kidding." Plato raised an eyebrow skeptically. He'd thought the detective was smarter than that.

"Jeremy heard about the big fight between Tiffany and Marilyn that day. He doesn't think Tiffany went back to apologize. He doesn't believe she met with Marilyn at all that evening. Until she killed her."

"What possible reason would Tiffany have?"

"She expected to get kicked out of medical school, and she thought it was Marilyn's fault."

Plato snorted. "That's nonsense—what good would killing Marilyn do?"

"I don't know." Cal shrugged. "Anyway, that's not the worst of it. Tiffany's alibi is all wrong."

"What do you mean?"

"Jeremy talked to the librarian who was working that evening. She swears Tiffany was never there."

Plato was astounded. He was sure Tiffany Cramer had nothing to do with Marilyn's death. After all, hadn't Tiffany suggested that Plato stay home tomorrow night and nurse his cold? Clearly, she had the makings of an excellent and compassionate physician—he was sure of that.

But why would she tell the police she had been in the library, when she obviously hadn't?

The snow was coming down harder, and finally melting on the windshield. Plato flipped on the wipers. Up ahead, the panel truck was still cruising along, the driver oblivious to his open rear door. Again, Plato glimpsed some movement in the shadows from the corner of his eye. Another trick of his vision.

But maybe not. Curious now, he stepped on the gas and closed the gap between the Rabbit and the truck. He turned to Cal. "Did you get any results from those lab tests you ordered?"

"The routine tox screen was completely negative," Cal reminded him. "We're still waiting on the special tests for neuromuscular blockers. Luckily, we had enough fluid for—" She broke off suddenly, gawking at the truck in front of them. "What on earth is *that*?"

Plato stared ahead. In the glare of the Rabbit's headlights, something moved. Something white, perched atop the truck's rear bumper.

"Do you see it?" Cal asked.

"Yeah." Plato rubbed his eyes. The object looked like a snowball with a tail. "Probably just a piece of ice or something."

"It's *moving*."

Another snowball appeared on the bumper, and a third. One by one, they crept to the edge of the bumper and tumbled off onto the shoulder of the road. Like a line of prisoners walking the plank.

Or rats deserting a sinking ship.

"Those are rats, Cal. White laboratory rats."

"I know." She peered out the side window and cringed. "They roll an awfully long time."

"The truck's doing sixty. But I wouldn't be surprised if the rats survive—they're tough little things."

Cal shuddered, locked the door, and slid over beside Plato—as though a tumbling rat might just leap up, pull the car door open, and drag her outside.

"Maybe I should try to pass, to wave him over," Plato suggested.

"Maybe." She curled her lip and swallowed hard.

Plato edged into the left lane just as the truck's right turn signal flashed. The driver swerved down onto the I–480 exit ramp. By the time Plato recovered, they were past the exit and over the bridge.

"We can't turn around for another mile," he said. "He'll be long gone by the time we get back here."

"Forget it. We can call the college and report it when we get home." She sounded relieved. "It's probably nothing important—I think Siegel sells healthy rats to some of the hospitals for experiments."

But Cal was wrong. At home, they called the medical school and explained the situation. The security guard promised to call the Dean of Research—Randolph Smythe the Third—and report the incident.

He didn't have to. The story made the eleven o'clock news. A breathless Wilma Smith announced that a shipment of laboratory rats had escaped en route from Siegel Medical College to Valdemar Pharmaceuticals. The rats were on their way to be sacrificed and studied.

Apparently, the extra safety locks had been left off several cage doors. The cages had popped open during the bumpy freeway ride. At least a dozen rats, test subjects for an experimental drug, were believed to be scattered across Cleveland's south side in the vicinity of Interstate 77. All of them were infected with a virulent and highly drug-resistant strain of tuberculosis.

Marilyn Abel's luck had apparently run out.

Chapter 12

The next morning, Cal was sure her own luck had run out as well. She was trapped in Randolph Smythe the Third's office at Siegel, a victim of a long lecture on medicine, politics, and Smythe's life story.

"I've got a confession to make, Cally. Can I call you Cally?" Smythe leaned across his desk and wrinkled his brow thoughtfully. The dean was somewhere between middle aged and elderly, but still quite handsome—aquiline nose, strong honest chin, sympathetic gray eyes. All crowned by a cap of wavy brown hair that looked almost natural. Part movie star, part revivalist preacher, part caring healer—Big Brother with a stethoscope.

Cal shrugged. "That's fine."

During their meeting, she had studied his style with no little fascination. Smythe was a politician for the '90s—hiding all his skills, smoothness, and savvy beneath a thick veneer of hometown simplicity.

You wanted to trust him. Some instinct deep inside told you that Smythe was an Honest Man, a Man Who Could Get Things Done.

"Maybe you think Randolph Smythe the Third had the world handed to him on a silver platter," he was saying. He gave a deprecating smile. "Well, I'll tell you something about my family. I never even met Randolph Smythe the First—he was a hobo and a drunken hellraiser who left my grandmother two years after they got married. Randolph Smythe the Second was a coal miner on weekdays and a Bible-thumping Baptist minister on Sundays."

He grinned and spread his hands. "I hope I'm a little more like my father than my grandfather. But I've got parts of both in me—I won't be afraid to raise a little hell when I get to Washington." He tossed his head back and laughed with a sound like a donkey choking on a thistle—"Gaw-HAW! Gaw-HAW! Gaw-HAW!"

Cal chuckled politely, though she'd heard the speech on television before. Word for word, it was part of one of his ads.

"The March primary is critical, absolutely critical," he repeated for the tenth time. "I'm counting on your vote, of course."

Cal just nodded. She didn't have the heart to tell him that she was registered as an Independent.

"In fact, I have to leave for a fund-raising luncheon in"— Smythe glanced at his Rolex—"in twenty minutes. So we haven't got much time to discuss the students' progress. Speaking of which, how is Tiffany Cramer doing?"

"Reasonably well," Cal said. "The other students—"

"I should *hope* so." He nodded, satisfied. "Her father is Judge Cramer. *The* Judge Cramer. He's going to be at the luncheon today—I'll tell him you said Tiffany's doing much better."

Cal shook her head warily. "I'm not making any guarantees . . ."

"That's all right." He waved off her concern with a blithe smile. "I know she'll do just fine. She's a very capable student, very bright. I'd like you to make sure she gets every opportunity to pass this exam. *Every* opportunity."

"I see."

Cal could see it all—now that Smythe had mentioned Judge Cramer. The judge was very influential in local party politics—a sort of Grand Vizier to the party chairman. That probably explained Smythe's abrupt about-face with Tiffany last December. When the dean had met with Marilyn and refused to give Tiffany another chance, he couldn't have known about Tiffany's political connections. He must have realized his blunder pretty quickly, though. Later that week, when he met with Tiffany herself, Smythe had given the impression that he was on the girl's side, and that *Marilyn* was responsible for her imminent expulsion. He'd been only too willing to have Cal tutor the students and offer a retest—an uncommon bit of leniency for Randolph Smythe the Third.

But then, Smythe was definitely trying to bolster his image. The bumper stickers and posters hanging beside his diplomas and degrees bore warm, fuzzy, four-color photos—pictures of Randolph in his white coat and stethoscope holding babies, listening to the heartbeat of a child's teddy bear, squeezing the shoulder of an elderly patient in the intensive care unit, a doctor's care and concern reflected in his steel gray eyes.

Not that Randolph Smythe the Third had ever practiced medicine—he was too ambitious. He'd earned his medical degree and then picked up a doctorate while working in a research fellowship on the East Coast. After hitching his name to a few influential papers, he had come back to Siegel and concentrated on administration, bobbing from one position to another and rising in status until he finally became dean of research—and Harlow Fairfax's imminent successor as provost.

His office matched his position—a huge corner suite with walnut paneling, plush pile carpeting, and a desk that could double as a Ping-Pong table if Smythe ever bothered to add a net. He was sitting back, his chair swiveled halfway toward the corner where the two window walls met. As he spoke, he gazed wistfully at the sprawl of Cleveland—a modern-day Napoleon plotting his advance into Prussia.

"You could talk to Judge Cramer yourself tomorrow night," he mused. "He's going to be there, you know."

"Where?"

"At my house party." He turned back to Cal, lifted an eyebrow. "Didn't you get an invitation?"

"No." Cal didn't really want one, either.

"I'll see that my secretary gives you a map." He turned back to the windows. "It's just a small reception to honor the researchers at Siegel—and draw some *favorable* attention to the college."

And draw some favorable attention to himself as well, Cal suspected. The college was getting a lot of negative publicity lately. And so, by reflection, was Randolph Smythe.

"Back when I was a researcher at the NIH," he said, sighing, "it was a different world out there. Issues of status, publication, grant support—were all secondary to the goal of discovery. Of finding that test, that drug, that trait that could unlock the door to a whole new vista of opportunity. Researchers *still* feel that way, underneath all the paperwork. I want to salute that pioneering spirit—and give credit where credit is due."

"That sounds wonderful," Cal said. She shifted restlessly. "But getting back to the students, I think they're making excellent progress. Even so, I was hoping we might move the exam back a couple of—"

"Ah, Olivia." The dean looked up. The door behind Cal had opened and Smythe's secretary wheeled a cart across the floor. Cal hadn't heard her approach. The deep pile carpeting muffled all sound, both inside and outside the room. Smythe waved Olivia over to his desk, lifted the lid from a carafe and sniffed.

"Outstanding, my dear. As usual." He beamed at Cal. "Olivia's coffee is fantastic. I don't know how she does it."

"It's an *automatic* coffeemaker, sir." The secretary, a petite brunette with a shy smile and a lisp, poured a cup and handed it to Smythe. She turned to Cal. "Decaf or regular?"

"Regular, please."

Smythe stirred in some cream and sugar. "Last month, when I was presenting at a conference in Oslo, I had Olivia make three thermoses for me. That was the only coffee I drank during the entire three days." He took a sip and lifted his eyes heavenward. "Someday, Olivia, I may just marry you so I can have this on weekends. Gaw-HAW!"

Olivia blushed. After all, Smythe *had* married one of his secretaries, after the death of his first wife.

He was right about the coffee—it was quite good. Better than the mud that came from their well water at home, anyway. Cal drained her cup quickly; she needed a jolt. Plato's coughing and sneezing and wheezing had kept her awake half the night, until she finally crept downstairs and slept on the couch. It was maddening—despite all the noise Plato made, he never woke up. This morning, he had gushed about feeling rested and refreshed, after the best night's sleep he'd had all week. And *Cal* was miserable.

"Leonard Reiss called again." Olivia pursed her lips and refilled both their cups. "That reporter from the *Plain Dealer*."

"I know, I know." He frowned at Olivia. "Were you able to stall him again?"

She nodded. "I told him you were performing an operation at Riverside."

"An *operation*! Gaw-HAW!" Smythe grinned approvingly. "That'll keep him off our trail for a while." He glanced at Cal. "Nothing wrong with a little dissimulation where the press is concerned. This Reiss fellow has been pestering me about the rat business. They'll get the whole story soon enough."

"Did you figure out what happened yet?" Cal asked.

"I couldn't *believe* it when that security guard called me last night." He sighed. "Thank you, Olivia." He nodded his dismissal at the secretary, waited for her to step out, and lowered his voice. "Albright claims it was Tiffany Cramer's fault—can you believe it? I think that guy has it in for her, don't ask me why. Anyway, he says she didn't put the permanent locks on half of the cages."

"The back door of the truck was open," Cal noted. "I don't think *that* was Tiffany's fault."

"We talked with the truck driver about that." Smythe shrugged helplessly. "But he's union, so what can you do? Anyway, I think Albright's full of crap about it being Tiffany's fault. Someone should have double-checked. She's a student—she's supposed to be *learning* back there, not doing scut work for Albright."

Cal nodded, impressed. Maybe some of Smythe's honesty wasn't an act after all. Then again, maybe he just wanted Judge Cramer's support.

"Of course, the most important issue is reassuring the public," he continued. "We can sort out the blame later. Our first press release stressed the fact that the rats are probably not contagious. The health risk is practically nonexistent. As you know, TB is spread by airborne transmission or by eating—and how many people eat rats or let them cough in their faces?" He nodded firmly, seeming to convince himself. "And besides, in this cold weather, the infected rats probably died very quickly."

Cal didn't bother asking about rat bites. She also didn't point out that a search of Interstate 77 and the surrounding area had failed to produce any rats, dead or alive.

"I'm not worried so much about the *public* health as I am about the health of the college," he concluded sadly.

And rightly so, Cal reflected. Last year, the governor had slashed state funding for Siegel, and he was hinting that more cuts might follow as the November elections approached. On the other hand, if Dean Smythe won a congressional seat, he might be able to bring some federal money into Siegel's coffers. And the governor's attitude might change as well.

Smythe glanced at his watch again, put his hands to his face and smoothed the gloom away. He stood and donned his white coat, wrapping the stethoscope across his neck. With his costume and his grave, sympathetic expression, the administrator looked like he'd just stepped away from the bedside of a dying patient.

He led Cal to the door and stopped, touching his finger to his lips. "One more thing. I saw a pretty disturbing article in this morning's paper."

"Really?"

"The *Plain Dealer* says that the coroner's office is looking into Marilyn Abel's death." He eyed her from beneath a shelf of lowered brows. "There was some suspicion of foul play—that she might have been poisoned or something?"

Cal nodded. "That's right."

"It's hard to believe—it sounds pretty sensational. I *hope* there's no truth in it." Smythe grimaced. "Marilyn's death was a loss for us all. And I want you to find out the truth— get to the bottom of this. But I hope you can use your influence at the coroner's office to have this investigation handled quietly. We're not really ready for any more bad press."

"I can't argue with that," Cal agreed noncommittally.

He stood silently for another moment, then squinted at Cal thoughtfully. "I'm not sure if you're aware of it, but we have an assistant deanship opening up at the college. A half-time position in academic affairs."

"I'd heard about it," Cal said. The Siegel trustees were already interviewing applicants, some from across the country. Mostly medical college administrators like Smythe, along with a few regular teaching faculty, researchers, and clinicians.

"I'd like you to apply for the post, if you're interested," he said. "I've heard some of your lectures for the anatomy department, and I understand that your group of failing students is improving. Your opinions at the academic board meetings are quite sound. I know I've mentioned having you chair the board, but I think you should set your sights a little higher. You'd make an excellent candidate for the position."

"Th-thank you, Dean Smythe." Cal didn't quite know what to say. She was wary of Smythe's motives, but still enormously flattered. The idea of applying for the assistant dean's post had never occurred to her.

"It's just an idea," Smythe cautioned. "I can't make any guarantees, of course."

"I understand."

Smythe turned away briskly, swung the heavy oak door to and led her over to his secretary's desk.

"Doctor Marley will need a copy of the map, Olivia. Please run one off for her."

"The machine is broken again, sir." The secretary sighed. "The repair people can't send anyone out until Monday."

Smythe groaned. "That machine is *always* broken." He thought for a moment, then snapped his fingers. "What about that guy down in maintenance? That weaselly little fellow?"

"Schwartz?"

"Yeah. He fixed it last time—see what he can do." He grinned at her. "We can't have you running over to accounting every time you need a copy made. And don't forget to sweep."

Olivia nodded and turned to Cal. "We have some extra invitations in the storage closet—I can pull one for you."

Smythe picked up his briefcase. "I hope to see you and Plato there tomorrow evening, Cal."

She nodded, surprised at herself. "We'll try to make it."

Walking down the hallway, he added, "Be sure to pick up some bumper stickers on your way out."

Cal's opinion of Smythe had improved some, but not that much. She hadn't put a bumper sticker on her car since the days of John Anderson.

Olivia led her to the storage closet, opened the door quickly and braced herself for an avalanche. The closet was jammed floor to ceiling with boxes of campaign paraphernalia—bumper stickers, posters, banners, little American flags, buttons, and even some toy stethoscopes bearing one of Smythe's campaign slogans: *Randolph Smythe—Taking the Pulse of Cleveland.* Jammed into the corner was a small upright Hoover.

The secretary opened one of the smaller boxes, pulled out an invitation and handed it to Cal. It was printed on heavy rag stationery and embossed in gold with the college's seal.

"There's a map in the envelope," she explained.

Cal thanked her, pointed to the vacuum cleaner and grinned. "Dean Smythe has you doing a little light housekeeping on the side, huh?"

"Sometimes." She shook her head and reached for the Hoover. "He's a dear, but he's very compulsive."

Cal helped Olivia pull the vacuum cleaner out of the closet and followed the secretary over to Smythe's office door. Olivia gestured at the heavy pile carpet. A pair of tracks led from the doorway to the edge of the dean's desk and back.

"Coffee cart," Olivia explained. "Dean Smythe makes me vacuum out the track marks. He's pretty fussy."

Cal's reply was cut off by the bleating of her pager. She reached into her pocket and read the display: the toxicology lab at the morgue.

"Can I borrow your phone?" she asked.

"What's the number?" Olivia led Cal to her desk and dialed.

Cal waited anxiously for the call to go through. The phone was picked up on the first ring by Mike Kim, the Ph.D. who headed the county's toxicology lab.

"I ran the mass spec analysis on that vitreous sample you gave me." Mike was usually unflappable, but today he sounded almost breathless. "We've got some *very* interesting results. You might want to come down here and see for yourself."

"I'll be right over." Cal set the phone down, thanked Olivia, and hurried out to her car.

Chapter 13

"*d*-Tubocurarine," Cal told Plato later that evening. "The purified alkaloid of curare. A neuromuscular blocker—a potent paralyzing agent."

They were standing in the empty anatomy lab, talking in hoarse whispers while they unwrapped the victim's body. Cal glanced down at Marilyn's distorted, half-dissected face. She smoothed the gray hair, patted the gnarled, ropy hand, and stared into the clouding blue eye. At least now the truth would be known.

"I revised Marilyn's death certificate," she continued. "I listed the manner of death as suffocation following poisoning, and the cause of death as willful homicide."

She heard Plato take a deep breath. This whole thing was hitting him pretty hard. Marilyn had been one of his favorite patients—he had admired her strong will, her intelligence, her perseverance in the face of crippling multiple sclerosis.

Marilyn's death, just before the holidays, had saddened him. But Plato had long ago learned to accept the inevitability of his patients' deaths. Geriatricians care for many of the oldest and sickest people. The better ones learn to accept their own limitations, to view death as an inescapable process—something to be faced and accepted. The final consultation.

But murder was an entirely different story. Despite Plato's apparent interest in the case and his efforts to unravel the web of Marilyn's life and death, Cal was sure he never really believed his patient had been murdered. She had feared the news would depress him all over again.

But she was wrong. His gloved fists were clenched, his jaw was set, and his lips were pressed to a tight line. He glared up at her with anger flaring in his pale green eyes.

"We have to find out who did it, Cally." He stared down

at Marilyn's body and bit his lip. "I don't care what Homer says. I want to *know*."

"Plato, I—"

"What the hell kind of a way is that to kill someone? To *paralyze* her?" He laughed bitterly. "She was half-paralyzed already."

Cal shook her head, struck by the irony. She had rarely seen Plato so angry.

"And it still didn't work," he raved, gloved hands waving, white coat flapping wildly. "So she had to lay there, fully conscious, fully aware, while some nutcase jammed a pillow down her throat and smothered her to death."

"I know how you must feel, Plato—"

"She was my *patient,* Cally." He stared up into the bright dissecting lamp. "And my friend."

The sudden silence was interrupted by the clatter of lockers and the chatter of voices in the hall. The four failing students wandered into the lab together and shouted greetings across the coffin rows like battle-weary soldiers returning from a sortie.

"We're spent the whole afternoon upstairs in the library," Samantha explained.

"Reviewing the head and neck," Raj continued. He pushed his glasses up and smiled. "We figured we're all in this together, so we're all going to pass together, too. Help one another out."

"Yeah—the Four Musketeers," Blair agreed. "Right, Tiffany?"

Tiffany Cramer smiled weakly. She was hugging herself, staring at Marilyn Abel's body. Her eyes shined wetly.

"Was it something I said?" Blair asked.

"It's okay," Raj answered. He stepped to her side and squeezed her hand. "She's just had a bad couple of days."

"Her old man again, huh?" Blair frowned sympathetically, but Raj just shrugged.

Cal decided to change the subject.

"How about if we get started?" she asked brightly. The others turned to her and she continued. "Anyone going to Boston Mills tonight?"

"We all are," Samantha answered.

"If we finish up here in time," Blair added.

The January ski outing at Boston Mills was an annual tradition at Siegel Medical College. A chance for students to unwind together, to break the ice with some of their instructors, to leave the textbooks and cadavers far behind. The small ski resort sat atop a tall ridge overlooking the Cuyahoga River, about twenty miles south of the city.

Cal had dragged Plato along on the outing last year, coached him to snowplow on the bunny slope, coaxed him over to the more difficult hills, tutored him on turning and stopping, and finally helped carry his stretcher down to their car. It was only a hairline ankle fracture, but he swore he would never ski again.

He was wrong, of course, but she hadn't argued the point.

"We'll try to make this a short session," she told them. "That should be easy, if you've reviewed the material as well as you claim."

"Are you and Plato going?" Samantha asked.

"I'm not much of a skier," Plato replied. He gave a whistly little cough, a wheezy bark that was starting to get on Cal's nerves. "And besides, I'm still pretty sick."

"You look a lot better than you did yesterday." Cal turned to the others. "Doesn't he?"

Tiffany shrugged, and the other nodded dubiously.

"I got our tickets this morning," Cal said. She reached beneath the table and retrieved the model of the skull, carefully avoiding Plato's gaze. "How about if we work on the head again today?"

"The dread skull." Raj sighed. He took the model from Cal and stared into its eye sockets. "Alas! poor Yorick. Where be your jibes, your gambols, your fossa and foramina?"

"Good question." Cal lifted the lid and extracted the brain. "How about finding Yorick's hypophyseal fossa?"

Raj instantly pointed to the saddle-shaped depression on the floor of the skull, near the front. Cal passed the skull around the circle, asking about the various holes and fissures, quizzing them on names and functions, asking which arteries or nerves passed through which outlets, even doubling back and trying to trip them up with trick questions.

But after a full hour of interrogation, she hadn't succeeded. The four students had made a lot of progress since Monday—in both knowledge and self-confidence.

"All right," Cal finally said. "One last question. Which artery passes through the foramen ovale?" She poked her dissecting probe through the small oval-shaped hole near the center of the skull.

"No artery does," Raj answered quickly.

"The foramen ovale transmits two parts of the trigeminal nerve," Tiffany recited.

"And the lesser petrosal," Blair added.

Cal smiled and nodded. "And it perforates the lesser wing of the sphenoid—right, Samantha?"

"Wrong." Samantha grinned. "That's the *greater* wing of the sphenoid."

"Really?" Plato asked. He frowned at Samantha. "Are you *sure*?"

During the sessions, Plato had usually sided with the students, nudging them toward the right answers, dropping hints and pointing them in the right direction when they made mistakes. This time, though, Samantha was right.

She stared at Plato in confusion, studied the model of the skull again, and considered her answer carefully. The others held their breaths and stared at the ceiling. Raj hummed at few bars of the *Jeopardy!* theme song. Finally, Samantha gave a firm nod. "Yes, I'm sure. It's the greater wing of the sphenoid."

They all clapped and cheered.

Cal slipped Yorick back under the table. "You win, guys. Drive safely, and don't break any bones."

"You mean we're finished for today?" Samantha asked.

Cal nodded. "You're all doing just great. Keep this up and you'll pass the makeup exam with flying colors."

She reached down and eased the shroud over Marilyn's face. The students all rushed to help bundle the cadaver away for the night. Just as they swung the doors shut, a raucous clatter sounded from across the lab, somewhere off in the darkness. A rhythmic clanging like a crowbar hammering a flagpole.

"Wh-what's *that*?" Cal nearly jumped out of her skin. She darted down the aisle toward the sound and Plato rushed after her. The racket was coming from the cooler—the refrigerated room where new cadavers were stored.

Behind them, the students were chuckling.

Blair Phillips called after them. "Cal, Plato—it's okay. That's just the condenser coils in the cooler."

"They do that all the time," Samantha added.

All the same, Cal crept to the metal door of the cooler

and eased it open. The clamor was almost deafening. She
reached around the doorway and switched the light on. Inside, ranks of naked cadavers hung from pairs of heavy
metal ear hooks, zipped into clear plastic bags, their faces
masks of surprise or drowsy stupor or plain indifference,
frozen snapshots of their rendezvous with death. A steel
gurney was parked beside the door, a naked blue cadaver-
to-be stretched upon its surface, grinning up at Cal. Probably a late arrival that the Giraffe hadn't prepared yet. In
the corner opposite the door, a huge refrigerating unit
hissed and rattled and clanged with a clamor like an irate
cadaver trying to break free of its metal coffin.

Cal shuddered and turned away, swinging the door shut
behind her. She hurried back up the aisle, puzzled by her
sudden jitters. Dead bodies had certainly never bothered
her before.

She rejoined the group and forced a smile. "That's all
for today, folks. Just make sure you keep studying over
the weekend. And don't forget there'll be a practice exam
on Tuesday."

They all groaned together. As the group wandered out
to the sinks, Cal stopped Tiffany and pulled her aside. They
were standing in the lab foyer near the x-ray viewers, their
faces ghostly white in the pale glow of the screens.

Marilyn's former lab assistant looked downright hag-
gard—unkempt hair, dark circles under bloodshot eyes, and
not a trace of makeup. She was wearing a ragged T-shirt
and a pair of surgical scrub pants, and no jewelry besides
the small diamond solitaire ring cinched to the drawstring
of the surgical scrubs.

"Sorry I didn't answer much today," Tiffany said halt-
ingly. "I was up a lot last night—couldn't sleep."

She was staring at the CT scans on the screens while she
talked. The films showed an entire human body in a series
of slices, from head to toes. Above the illuminated screens
and lining all four walls of the lab foyer were Sergei Malenkov's greatest accomplishment—an entire human being,
sliced in dozens of inch-thick sections which precisely
matched those of the CT scans. The sections were mounted
in hunks of clear urethane plastic like giant square paper-
weights, and bore precise labels pointing to blood vessels,
nerves, muscles, and major organs.

CT scans showed the body in cross-sections, like salami

slices. Understanding the body from such a perspective was often difficult, especially for medical students. Sergei's project was a fascinating and useful piece of work, but it always made Cal feel a little queasy.

Tiffany seemed to feel the same way. She shivered a little and turned back to Cal. "I guess I have a lot on my mind."

"I guess so," Cal agreed. She took a deep breath. "I just wanted to let you know that Jeremy Ames is a good friend of mine, and—"

She stopped talking. Tiffany had winced at the sound of Jeremy's name.

"Are you all right?" Cal asked.

"Yes." Tiffany fingered the ring at her waist. "Yes."

"I just wanted you to know that Jeremy is a good friend of ours," Cal repeated. She squeezed Tiffany's arm, looked into her eyes. "Whatever the problem is—*whatever* it is—you can trust Jeremy. But you've got to tell him the truth."

For a moment, a glimmer of hope shone in Tiffany's pale blue eyes. But it quickly flickered out. "I don't know what you mean," she said hollowly. "I *have* told him the truth."

She glanced out at Raj for an instant, then back at Cal. Raj was standing in the hall, scrubbing his hands and watching Tiffany closely.

Cal slipped her gloves off and pulled a scrap of paper from her hip pocket. She scribbled their home phone number on the back and handed it to Tiffany. "Here. If there's something you want to talk about—anything at all—just give us a call. We'll be home this weekend."

"*I* won't be home." Tiffany sighed. Again her eyes flicked over to Raj. "I'll be in Marilyn's office most of the time. Bob Stahl is paying me to go through her things, to get her notes and papers sorted out."

Still, she stuffed the slip of paper into her pocket. "Thanks anyway."

Raj dried his hands and hurried over. He shot Cal a curious glance and turned to Tiffany. "You'd better wash up in a hurry. Blair's taking us all down to Boston Mills in his van."

Tiffany got cleaned up and the students—the new Four Musketeers—drifted off toward the stairs. Cal hurried to the sink and started scrubbing her hands, trying to wash away her sudden misgivings as well.

Beside her, Plato was just finishing up. "I can't wait till

we get home. A whole weekend with no call, no pager, and no cadavers." He sighed happily. "I think I'll go to bed early tonight."

"Not *too* early, I hope. I wanted to get at least a couple of hours in on the slopes."

He reached for a paper towel and froze. "What? Don't tell me you really bought tickets. How *could* you—after what happened to me last year?"

"You don't have to be embarrassed." She smiled reassuringly. "No one will remember you."

"I'm not worried about being embarrassed." He grimaced. "I'm worried about being *killed*."

"Nonsense." She rinsed and grabbed a paper towel. "You just need some practice."

"I need some sleep." He gave that wheezy, whistly cough again. Like a croupy hyena. "A nice warm bed, a cup of hot chocolate, and that new *Fletch* novel."

"You can sit in the ski lodge with your novel," Cal pointed out. "They've got a huge fireplace, and their hot chocolate is great."

"I can't exactly sleep there, you know." Plato's eyes drooped. "Maybe you should go without me."

"Tomorrow's Saturday—you can sleep in. Besides, I want to talk to some people there." She raised an eyebrow at him. "Valdemar Pharmaceuticals is sponsoring the trip, so Candice Erdmann will probably be there. Remember—she was the one Marilyn was going to call when she—"

"I know, I know," Plato grumbled. He flung the paper towel at the wastebasket and missed. "All right. But I'm staying in the lodge. I'm not going outside, and I'm *not* putting skis on."

He retrieved the paper towel, took another shot, missed again, and finally dropped it into the wastebasket.

"Fine." Cal smiled to herself. Last week, Plato had been less than enthusiastic when she told him about an upcoming medical conference out in Aspen. But Cal was sure he'd come around. Like the students, he just needed a little prodding. And a little self-confidence.

Chapter 14

As it turned out, Plato's self-confidence got an unexpected boost that evening. When they got to the ski lodge at Boston Mills, Cal led him to the main reception area, a drafty room with dark-stained pine walls, a lofty ceiling, and huge windows facing the lighted slopes. A few frumpy deans' wives were parked in the corners like discarded furniture, but most of the faculty and students were outside. A cheery blaze crackled in the fireplace, casting enough warmth to melt the snow on the benches nearby. Cal helped her husband pull a bench closer to the fire, then unfolded a thick wool blanket and tucked him in with his cough drops, hot chocolate, and novel.

Feeling a little guilty, she buckled up her ski boots. "You're sure you'll be all right?"

"I'll be fine." He barked the hyena cough and honked into a Kleenex. "You just enjoy yourself. Don't worry about me."

But she did worry, at least a little. Enough to return an hour later to check on him. And find that she needn't have bothered. Even from across the room, Cal could see that Plato was feeling much better—the best he had in days. As if by magic, he was breathing more easily, his nose had faded from red to a dull pink glow, and he'd tucked the blanket and novel away beneath the bench.

Plato wasn't alone. He had fallen under a spell.

A dark-haired, dark-eyed, fair-skinned witch was nestled beside him on the bench, staring deep into his eyes, hanging on his every word, acknowledging his cleverness with little giggles and nudges and admiring glances, and generally hypnotizing him.

Plato wasn't doing a thing about it. He seemed to be enjoying himself.

He turned away from the witch, saw Cal approaching, and gave her a vapid smile. "Hi."

"Hi."

She stood there, watching Plato shift uncomfortably beneath her glare. The idiot smile slowly drained away. The distance between him and his companion magically grew.

The witch squinted up at Cal, cocked her head and gave a curious cough.

Plato blinked once, twice, then finally snapped out of the spell. He jumped to his feet, grinning at Cal and tossing his arm over her shoulder like they were old drinking buddies. He smiled down at the woman on the bench. "Candice? I'd like you to meet my wife, Cal Marley. Cal, this is Candice Erdmann. The senior vice president of Valdemar Pharmaceuticals—they're sponsoring the ski trip."

Cal smiled, relieved. Plato had probably been pumping her for information about Marilyn Abel. "Nice to meet you."

"My pleasure." The witch's lips parted to show a perfect set of brilliant white teeth—probably all capped. Still sitting, she presented a hand palm-down, as though Cal should kiss it. They shook instead.

"Plato has been keeping me company heah," the drug executive drawled. "Ah'm not much of a skier."

Her soft Southern lilt was full of warm breezes and cherry blossoms and contrived courtesy. "You're a lucky woman," she continued. "He's an extra-*ord*-inaruh gentleman."

She flashed those big dark eyes up at Plato and smiled.

His ears reddened and he shuffled his feet. "Candice was just telling me that the ski outing was actually her idea. They started sponsoring it years and years ago, back when she was a drug rep for Valdemar."

Candice gave him an icy smile and flapped her eyelashes. "Not *so* many years ago."

At least a couple of decades, Cal guessed, studying the executive's face more closely. The fire's dim glow cast flickering shadows across her flawless skin, alternately hiding and revealing the tracery of wrinkles at the corners of her eyes and mouth. From a distance, she might have been even younger than Cal. But a closer look showed the wear and tear that plastic surgery couldn't quite hide.

With characteristic tact, Plato protested, "But this ski

outing's been going on since the seventies. So it's probably been twenty—"

Cal stomped on her husband's foot to cut him off.

A spark of anger flashed in Candice's dark eyes, and the perfect facade almost crumbled. But the plaster smile's cracks were quickly smoothed over. She tossed her head back and tittered, wiping the laughter away with the back of her hand. "I guess the years just have a way of slipping by, don't they?"

"Anyway, the ski trip is a great idea," Plato added lamely.

"I think so, too." Samantha Ricci had clomped over to their group, cheeks rosy with windburn, melted snow dripping from her Nordica ski boots. She stood beside Plato, nodding her head. "They're having a slalom race over on the North Bowl slope. Open to people from Siegel. Anyone want to come along?"

"How about you, dear?" Candice leaned forward and patted Cal's hand. "Plato tells me that you're an extra-*ord*-inaruh skier."

"I haven't skied much since we got married," Cal hinted, turning to Plato. "You're looking better. Maybe you should come out and try a few runs."

"Oh, *would* you?" Candice jumped to her feet and stood in front of Plato, squeezing his arm and gazing up into his eyes. Trying to get that spell working again. "Ah'm just a beginnuh, never got past the bunny slopes. Maybe you could *teach* me a few things."

Cal doubted it. Candice seemed to have all the moves down pat.

Plato's beard split into a broad smiile. "I *am* feeling a little better." He turned to Cal. "Maybe I could do a little skiing, see how I feel."

Cal's respect for Candice's magic grew. Aside from the smile and the voice, and that subtle way of flouncing her hair and shoulders and touching people without seeming to, she had remarkable healing powers. This was the first time all week that Plato had stopped whining about his cold and was showing a little enthusiasm. And for *skiing,* of all things.

"Maybe we could all go out together," Plato continued.

The witch's face fell. She stared out the window at the near-vertical face of the slalom slope and took her hand away from Plato's arm. "Ah'm not exactly up to running time trials yet, dear."

Cal took the hint. "How about if I check out the slalom course with Samantha? You can give Candice some lessons on the bunny slope." Like how to fall down—Plato was really great at that. "We can all meet back here later on."

She took Samantha's arm and hurried off before her husband could protest.

Waiting in line for the lifts, Samantha smiled at her. "You sure are mellow, Cal. A lot of women would have been jealous."

Cal chuckled. "Candice Erdmann is almost old enough to be Plato's mother."

"So what's a couple of dozen years? My husband ran off with one of his high school students." Samantha shrugged. She was looking up the hill, studying the slalom course through the haze of wind-whipped snow. "He was pushing forty. Age didn't make any difference to *them*."

"I'm sorry." Cal glanced at the student. She didn't know what to say.

"*I'm* not sorry," she replied, finally turning her gaze to Cal. "Bruce was pretty traditional—he hated it when I got my nursing degree. He'd have never let me go to medical school."

Cal shook her head sympathetically. They skated onto the pad and waited for the lift chair to swing round and scoop them up.

Lurching into the sky, Cal mused, "Anyway, I don't think Candice Erdmann is exactly Plato's type."

"Oh, I don't think so either." Samantha grinned. "Did you see how he looked when we walked off? Sort of like a mouse that just got cornered by a cat."

Cal laughed. "More like a mouse that got cornered by a Bengal tiger."

"Yeah." Looking forward, Samantha nodded. "Now *there's* a well-matched couple."

She was watching the lift chair two places ahead of them. A tall blonde was sitting there alone. No—a child was sitting beside her, his dark hair barely visible over the top of the chair.

Cal looked closer and saw that it wasn't a child at all. It was Raj Prasad. And Tiffany Cramer.

"I've kind of gathered that they're an item," she observed.

"More than an item," Samantha countered. "They're *engaged*. But don't tell anyone I said so. Nobody's supposed to know."

Cal remembered the ring hanging from Tiffany's necklace during anatomy lab. "Why the big secret?"

"Tiffany's father hates Raj." Samantha lifted her skis, tapped her poles against the bindings and watched the clumps of snow float lazily down onto the snowy path below. "He hates anyone who can't trace their lineage back to the Mayflower. So he refused to let her see him."

"That's pretty awful." Up ahead, the couple was horsing around, tickling and poking each other, setting the chair lift swaying on its cable. Raj's booming laughter and Tiffany's shrill giggles floated back to them across the treetops. "Isn't she old enough to make her own decisions?"

Samantha nodded. "Tiffany hasn't let it stop her, of course." She frowned down at her ski gloves. "But lately the judge has threatened to cut her off, stop paying for medical school."

The ski lift suddenly ground to a halt. At the crest of the hill, a clump of skiers had toppled like dominoes on the off-ramp. The lift operator left his booth to untangle them and clear the runway.

"You sure know a lot about Tiffany," Cal observed. "You two must be very close."

Samantha nodded. "We're roommates. Theoretically."

Cal didn't bother asking what "theoretically" meant. But she guessed it had something to do with Tiffany's lack of an alibi for the night of Marilyn's death.

"Funny thing is, Tiffany wouldn't care much if the judge cut her off. She never really wanted to be a doctor anyway."

Cal gave a puzzled frown. "Then why is she in medical school?"

"Her father pushed her into it. After college, Tiffany really didn't know what she wanted to do." The lift started up with a lurch. "But lately, she decided she wants to be a pharmacologist."

"You're kidding."

"Not at all." She shook her head. "Tiffany's a wizard at biochemistry. All those chemical structures are mapped in-

side her brain—I think she has a photographic memory."
Samantha read the doubt in Cal's face. "You're wondering
why she flunked anatomy, huh? I wondered about that, too.
I think part of it was to get back at the judge. In the library
this afternoon, she knew every name on every page of the
atlas." She smiled at the memory. "We'd show her a page
for just a few seconds and then cover the names, and she
got them right every time. It was like watching David Cop-
perfield or something. Tiffany acted like she thought everyone could do that."

"But why is she so interested in pharmacology?" Cal
asked.

"It was that Marilyn Abel lady," Samantha began. "Tiffany started out kind of rebellious this fall—never studying,
hardly ever going to class. I don't know *what* she was doing
all day, but she wasn't at school." She rolled her eyes.
"And at night, she always had the television on. Watching
those crappy network movies." Samantha shrugged. "I kept
telling her she was going to flunk out, and she kept telling
me she didn't care."

Up ahead, Tiffany and Raj slipped off their lift chair and
down the ramp in perfect tandem, like a pair of sparrows
winging across the snow.

"She took the lab assistant's job for the money—so she
didn't have to hit the judge up every time she wanted to
see a movie." A touch of awe crept into Samantha's voice.
"I don't know what Marilyn Abel did, but she got Tiffany
hooked on that lab work. Marilyn made her go to the
classes and study for the tests, but any free time Tiffany
had, she either spent with Raj or down in the pharmacology lab."

"Then I'm surprised she still failed anatomy," Cal said.

"She'd been working on Marilyn's latest project the
whole weekend before the exam," Samantha explained.
"She could have passed it easily, but she only studied for
a couple of hours."

Cal nodded. That explained why Marilyn had been so
anxious to intercede with Randolph Smythe. She had probably felt responsible for Tiffany's failure.

"Only two hours of studying, and she still almost passed
the anatomy final. I'd give just about anything to have a
brain like hers." Samantha leaned forward and they both
sprang from their chairs onto the exit ramp. As they skied

over to the crest of North Bowl, she continued, "Medicine or pharmacology or whatever, Tiffany Cramer is going to *be* somebody—you just watch."

She led the way across the hilltop to the North Bowl—the steepest hill at Boston Mills. The slope was deeply concave near the top and leveled off about two-thirds of the way down, like a soup bowl tipped on its side. Up here, the wind blew fiercely, whipping the assembled skiers with gusts of powdery snow. Flurries danced and swirled beneath the bright lights dangling from the lift poles on the hill. Far below, the ski lodge was faintly visible through the churning snow; off in the distance, Cal could see the inky black trail of the Cuyahoga River snaking through the valley.

Cal and Samantha pulled up at the edge and studied the course together. The slalom sticks were tightly bunched at the top and bottom of the slope—the more level areas—but the gaps widened in the speedy central portion. Boston Mills wasn't anywhere near the league of Colorado or even Wisconsin, but the course looked challenging and fun. Cal had been a member of her high school ski club back in Chicago. The sight of the gates brought back memories and a familiar tingle of anticipation.

Cal skied over and registered, tied number "13" outside her ski jacket, and joined the group of rowdy medical students clustered near the starting gate. Every minute or so, another racer was launched down the hill. Many were decent skiers, but most had obviously never tried slalom before. Even the better ones carried too much speed into the tighter gates or were too tentative and slow and ended up walking through the finish line. But most of the skiers missed gates or simply crashed off the course, pinwheeling down the steepest part of the Bowl, their trail marked by a blur of color and wild blasts of snow at the impact points.

Resort personnel were kept busy replacing downed gates and smoothing out the turns.

Standing near the starting gate, Cal was pelted in the rear by a well-aimed snowball. She turned and spotted Raj standing across the clearing, leaning over to scoop up another snowball. Cal dug into the packed snow and shot first, scoring on the top of his head. He looked up and grinned, teeth showing brightly in his dark face. He and Tiffany fired back, but both shots were long and carried into the crowd of innocent bystanders gathered near the gate.

Retaliation was swift and merciless. In seconds, the top of North Bowl was a battleground of flying snow and ice. The fight was still raging when Cal's number was called.

She herringboned up to the starting gate, crouched into a tuck and ran through the course again in her mind. At the signal, she jumped onto the course.

The hill was shorter than the ones she was accustomed to, from those ski trips to Wisconsin, but Cal didn't notice the difference. She hadn't raced slalom in years, not since high school. Not since her mother was alive. Twisting through the first tight gates and cruising into the steepest part of the hill, Cal imagined she heard her mother's crazed cheers again: *Come on, make that turn! Faster, Cally!*

But it wasn't her imagination after all, or even a woman's voice. It was Plato, parked halfway down the steepest slope at Boston Mills, hopping up and down on those ultrashort beginner's skis, shaking a *cowbell,* for heaven's sake, and grinning like an idiot. Cal couldn't imagine how he had gotten there—probably climbed up from the bottom, on his hands and knees.

She was so surprised to see him that she almost missed a gate, cutting her skis just in time and spraying a rooster tail of snow and ice over toward Plato as she pivoted back into the track. Two more turns and she was back into the flat, crouching low with skis riding close and parallel to avoid bleeding any speed. She rode the rest of the hill in a tuck, rising just enough to make the last few turns, then poling her way to the finish line.

The clock-keeper sang out her time and a cheer rose from the crowd of students and faculty clustered nearby. Blair Phillips skied over and shook her hand.

"That's five seconds better than the next-best time," he told her.

"Really?" Cal was surprised. She hadn't thought she was *that* fast. "Whose time was that?"

"Mine." Blair grinned and swayed to an impossible angle, the skis holding him upright. He barely missed spilling beer from the paper cup he held, emblazoned with the Valdemar logo. "Want some?"

"No, thanks." Cal turned away and looked up the slope. The next skier had just left the starting gate. He was quick and smooth, flicking through the turns with the slightest of movements.

"I'm conducting an experiment," Blair announced in a voice three times louder than necessary. He gave a crooked grin. "On the effects of alcohol on skiing."

Cal eyed him critically. She'd have to make sure one of the other students drove Blair's van home tonight. "You probably would have done even better if you were sober."

"I don't think so. I probably wouldn't have tried it at all." He glanced up the slope and swallowed heavily. "I'm afraid of heights. But after a couple of beers, I wanted to give it a try."

"You've never slalomed before?" Cal was amazed.

"I never even *skied* until this winter." He sipped the beer and smacked his lips. "Snow-skied, anyway. I grew up in Texas, on the Gulf. Did a lot of waterskiing."

"I hear the motions are similar." Cal smiled. Blair wasn't quite as drunk as he acted. His voice had fallen back to normal, and he'd stopped swaying.

"Yeah." He eyed the slope again. "Except there aren't any *hills* in waterskiing."

The racer whipped through the final gate and skated to a stop. His ski jacket and pants looked familiar, but heavy ski goggles masked his face.

The clock-keeper announced the time—nearly a full second faster than Cal's. The skier pulled off his—*her*—goggles. It was Samanatha Ricci.

By now, Plato had picked his way down the slope, snowplowing or walking or sliding on the seat of his pants until he finally reached Cal and Blair.

"Radical skiing, Plato," Blair commented admiringly. He held out his beer. "Want some?"

"Sure." Plato took the beer, tipped his head back and drained the cup. "Thanks."

Blair mournfully contemplated his empty cup, then glanced up as Samantha joined the group. "You were awesome, Sammy."

"I hear you did pretty well yourself, Blair." Samantha grinned. "You, too, Cal."

"Where'd you learn to ski like that?" Plato asked her.

"I grew up in Denver. I used to teach skiing out in Aspen."

"Aspen," Cal breathed, as though the name itself were sacred.

"Okay, okay." Plato smiled at her. "Maybe we'll go out to that conference after all. If I don't kill myself first."

They watched the last of the skiers race, but the trio's times held. Samantha won a fifty-dollar gift certificate from a local ski shop, Cal was given a pair of Thinsulate ski gloves branded with the Valdemar logo, and Blair received a long pink GastroBid ski hat colored to resemble a human stomach and trailing small intestine, complete with ulcer.

He put it on his head and tucked his long brown hair up into the knitted duodenum, which dangled nearly to his waist. He coiled the trailing loops of intestine around his hand and showed the bundle to Samantha. "Okay, what's the blood supply?"

"That's easy." She patted the upper loops, near the stomach. "The upper half is supplied by the superior pancreaticoduodenal artery, a branch of the gastroduodenal, which comes off of the hepatic, which is a branch of the celiac. The lower half—"

"All right, already." He snatched the intestine away and adjusted his hat. "*Yeesh!* You need to lighten up a little, Samantha. How about some beer?" He held up his cup, realized it was empty, then shrugged. "Maybe we should go celebrate at the lodge."

"Great idea," Plato agreed. He was huddled next to Cal, shivering in his huge coat, teeth chattering loudly. "This time, I'm buying."

Skiing over to the lodge, Cal turned to Plato. "Where's your girlfriend?"

"She got kind of bored with me." He sighed. "I fell down even more often than she did. And some snow got in her hair—she got really pissed about that. Said it was my fault."

"Poor thing."

Tiffany and Raj were waiting for them near the bar. Raj handed beers around and admired Blair's ski hat. Tiffany seemed far more relaxed; she even cracked a smile when Raj donned the pink stomach.

"You look a little like the Cat in the Hat," she told him.

"I'm afraid this thing's going to digest my hair." He handed the cap back to Blair, who carefully replaced it on his head.

An eclectic blend of music was blasting through the wall

speakers—rap, hip-hop, a little Counting Crows, and some Guns n' Roses-style screeching.

Beside her, Plato stirred restively. "Whatever happened to music?" he griped. "You know—songs with meaning, lyrics that made sense, melodies that were pretty? Remember the Allman Brothers? Remember the Beatles?"

"You're getting old," Cal chided. She liked most of the newer music. It really wasn't *that* much different. Just variations on a theme.

"Old? You call thirty-three *old*? You should see some of my patients." He snorted. "How old do you think Paul McCartney is?"

"Old," Cal said. "*Really* old."

"The granddaddy of rock 'n' roll," Blair commented.

"I thought Chuck Berry was the granddaddy of rock 'n' roll," Plato muttered.

Blair frowned. "Who's Chuck Berry?"

Sipping her beer, Cal saw that Candice Erdmann was again holding court by the fire. Several male faculty were bunched nearby, pretending to warm their hands at the fire, tossing offhanded remarks her way, grinning like a bunch of schoolboys.

Chuck Albright had the place of honor, though. This time, Candice was holding *his* hand and gazing into his eyes and flouncing her shoulders in time with that gaily musical laugh of hers as though the chairman of pharmacology were really Robin Williams in disguise.

Plato nudged Cal's arm. She turned in time to see Samantha Ricci raising her beer cup in a toast.

"Here's to Plato and Cal," she pronounced. "Our wonderfully patient anatomy tutors."

"Hear, hear!" Blair Phillips tipped his glass back.

"We owe you guys a lot," Raj said soberly.

Samantha sipped her beer and nodded. "You two are different from most of the other faculty at Siegel."

"What do you mean?" Cal asked.

"Oh, I don't know." Samantha shrugged and scuffed her heavy ski boots on the scarred wooden floor. "It's sort of like you're *interested*. In us, I mean." She looked around at the others for help.

"You care about what happens to us," Tiffany said. She studied Cal closely. "Or at least, you *seem* to."

"Of course we do," Cal agreed. "We were students ourselves, and not so very long ago."

"Most of the faculty just care about numbers and statistics," Blair pointed out. "They want to keep the state dollars coming in, so they worry about National Board scores and dropout rates, and pushing people into primary care."

"I think you're selling the college short," Cal said. "I don't think Siegel is any worse than most medical schools, and quite a bit better than many. A lot of the faculty and administrators are *very* concerned about the students."

"Some are," Samantha conceded.

"And some just *act* like they are." Blair nodded at Randolph Smythe the Third, who was crossing the room just then. He spotted Candice Erdmann and swung over to her orbit like a comet plummeting toward the sun. The drug executive stood and planted a kiss on his cheek.

"You should have seen Smythe during our physiology final," Blair continued. "Walking around the lab and wishing everybody a Merry Christmas. What a fake."

Cal shrugged. She wasn't quite so willing to write Smythe off.

Candice walked away with Smythe, leaving Chuck Albright and the other faculty behind. The crowd slowly dispersed.

"I heard Doctor Albright was going to fire you," Samantha murmured to Tiffany. She looked a question. "Because of that thing with the laboratory rats."

"Nobody's going to be fired, but he's pretty upset. And not just because of the rats escaping." Tiffany shrugged. "All of a sudden, Marilyn's new drug isn't working. All the rats are dying of tuberculosis."

"The *treated* rats?" Plato frowned. "I thought that new drug was supposed to be the best thing since penicillin."

"That's what we thought, too," she agreed. "But this latest round of tests is showing exactly the opposite. We might as well not be treating them at all."

Blair bit a fingernail and squinted at Tiffany. "The rats on the van—the ones that escaped? Those were the control rats, right? The ones that weren't treated?"

"Right. We were sending all the rats to Valdemar Pharmaceuticals to be sacrificed." She frowned. "The van wasn't big enough for all the cages, so we sent the untreated rats first. We were going to send the treated rats on a second trip. Now we may not bother, since they're all dying anyway."

Cal frowned. Marilyn's wonder drug was apparently a flop after all.

But Blair adjusted the GastroBid ski cap and continued. "Could you have labeled them wrong? What if you sent the healthy, *treated* rats on the van?"

"That's impossible," Tiffany scoffed. "We labeled the solutions clearly—the treated rats received Solution A, which was Marilyn's new drug. The control rats received Solution B, which was just saline. Their cages were labeled the same way. I sent the B rats on the van to Valdemar."

"Did you prepare the solution in advance?" Raj asked.

"Y-Yes." A hint of doubt crept into her voice. "We made a huge batch to keep it standardized, to leave less room for error. So we kept both solutions in the refrigerator."

"And if you mislabeled them when you first prepared the solution?" Blair began.

"Then Marilyn's drug might work after all!" Tiffany flushed with excitement. Her cloud of depression lifted for the moment.

"And if the solutions were mixed up, then only *treated* rats escaped," Samantha pointed out. "So they would be free of tuberculosis."

"And so would southern Cleveland," Blair noted wryly.

Tiffany gave a quick nod, considering. "You may be right. We can test the solutions to be sure. I'll try it tomorrow."

"It's just the kind of mistake Tiffany would make," Raj chided. He elbowed his fiancée gently and grinned.

"Serendipity." Cal glanced at Tiffany, and the student smiled back. *Now* Cal understood why Marilyn had liked having Tiffany around.

Chapter 15

"So what did you find out from Candice last night?" Cal asked Plato.

They were sitting at the oldest bar in Cleveland, sipping mugs of Burning River Ale and waiting for Homer Marley and Jeremy Ames to meet them for lunch. The Great Lakes Brewing Company was a nostalgic restoration of the Old Market Tavern, which sat across from the West Side Market. Just up the street from Riverside General, it was a favorite hangout of the hospital crowd, and a place for young downtown execs to roll up their sleeves and relax.

It had also been a favorite hangout of Elliott Ness, back in the '40s when he was Cleveland's safety director. Plato gazed at the two bulletholes visible in the mirror frame and pillar behind the long mahogany bar; legend claimed the shots had been fired at Ness. The more credible version traced the bullets to the 1950s, when the Old Market Tavern had gone to seed and become a hangout for roughnecks and rowdies. But Plato still preferred the Ness legend.

"Can't stop daydreaming about her, huh?" Cal was wrinkling her nose at him.

"Daydreaming about who?" Plato asked innocently.

"I was asking you about Candice Erdmann," she repeated. "What did you find out last night?"

"Umm." His conversations with the drug executive last night hadn't gone exactly according to plan. He frowned thoughtfully, dredging his memory for an intelligent answer. But he came up empty.

"Umm," he said again. "She likes jazz—especially the big acts they get over at Rhythms. She grew up in Memphis. And she has a fifty-nine Cadillac Convertible, hardtop, that's faster than anything the state troopers can put on the road. She says Elvis had one."

"A little background—that's all right." Cal tilted her head expectantly. "What else?"

"She makes a mean burrito." He took another sip of ale and wiped the foam on his sleeve. "Or so she says."

Cal frowned into her mug and pinched the bridge of her nose. "Did you find out anything important? Anything we can use?"

"She has this extra-*ord*-inaruh condominium down in Beachwood," Plato continued doggedly. "She just *has* to have me over for a visit sometime."

"For one of her mean burritos."

"Yeah."

"That's *really* helpful." Cal swiveled, propped an elbow on the bar, and glared at him. "Maybe you can seduce her over a dish of refried beans. Hide a tape recorder in the guacamole dip and get her to confess."

"No way—I turned her down." He reached out and squeezed Cal's hand. "After all, I've got this simply extra-*ord*-inaruh wife . . ."

She grimaced. "Who can't make a burrito, even a *friendly* burrito, to save her life."

"That's okay." He slid his arm around her waist and leaned over to whisper in her ear. "You've got a lot of other, mmm, *compensations.*"

"So do you," Cal purred. She turned and cocked an eyebrow at him. "Unfortunately, spying isn't one of them. But maybe you'll do a little better with Candice tonight. I heard she's going to be at Smythe's party."

"Tonight? Smythe's party?" Plato shook his head. Cal was obviously confused. "We're playing poker at Jeremy's, remember? What does that have to do with—"

His question was cut off by a sudden slap on his shoulder, a grizzly bear's love tap that spun his stool completely around. Plato glanced up to see his cousin's broad, grinning face.

"You folks ready for some lunch?" Homer Marley reached a paw inside the pocket of his black leather jacket, yanked out a lottery ticket, and brandished it under Plato's nose. "I just hit on the instant. A hundred bucks—can you even believe it? So I'm picking up the tab today."

"That'll be a first." Behind him, Detective Lieutenant Jeremy Ames was pacing back and forth like a nervous Dachshund with a cigarette. He reached up and grabbed

Homer's arm. "Lemme see that." His thin eyebrows rose. "*Whew*—he's not kidding. It's really a winner."

"Of course it is." Homer sniffed indignantly and stuffed the ticket in his wallet.

"Who knows—maybe he'll really pay for lunch today. For once." The homicide detective shrugged at Plato and Cal. "God knows, Homer owes us all a few meals." He reached out a thin hand and patted the lawyer's ample waistline. "I think about half of this came from my refrigerator."

"And the other half came from ours," Plato said.

Jeremy grinned. Clad in a dapper gray suit, silk tie, and scuffed shoes, the sheriff's lieutenant was a stark contrast to Plato's huge, easygoing, slow-moving cousin. Ames was small and quick, with a long thin snout, bulging eyes, gray brush-cut hair, and nerves wound tight as guitar strings.

"How you doing, Cal?" Jeremy asked, giving her a nip on the cheek. He turned back to Plato. "You look *awful.*"

"Thanks." Plato took a deep breath and hacked; the insides of his lungs burst into flame. Tears welled up in his eyes.

"You sound like an old smoker." Jeremy frowned and took another quick puff from his cigarette. "It's bad for your health, you know."

"Especially secondhand smoke," Plato hinted.

"He's got a cold," Cal explained.

"*And* she dragged me out skiing last night," Plato complained. "I'm probaby going to die of pneumonia."

"No kidding." Jeremy frowned sympathetically and stubbed his cigarette out in the ashtray on the bar. "Leave me your golf clubs, would you? That Ping set Cal got you last Christmas. They're too small for your cousin. Right, Homer?"

"That's okay," the lawyer chuckled. "I drew up their will—he's leaving me his baseball card collection."

Jeremy glanced at his watch—a jerky twitch like a puppy listening at a mousehole—and snapped his head toward the tables. "Let's eat before Homer spends all his money."

After the waiter had taken their orders, Jeremy flipped open his notebook and turned to Cal. "You get the final results on that eyeball juice?"

Cal dug in her purse and tossed a copy of the revised

death certificate across the table. "*d*-Tubocurarine. The purified version of curare."

"Curare?" Jeremy repeated. He cocked his head. "Then she really *was* poisoned?"

"Definitely." She nodded firmly. "But the cause of death was suffocation."

"What?" He scratched his ear and frowned. "You'd better back up—you've lost me there."

Plato listened as Cal explained her theory about the murder method again. Marilyn hadn't received enough curare to kill her—even with the weakness from her multiple sclerosis. Maybe the killer had counted too much on that weakness, underestimating Marilyn's stamina. Whatever the reason, he or she had needed to use a pillow to finish the job. One of the pillows from the sofa in the pharmacology lounge.

"Then the fibers match?" Jeremy guessed.

"Right." Cal nodded. "The forensics lab compared them with a piece of fabric from one of the pillows."

"That's pretty raw," Homer commented. He shook his head like a dazed grizzly bear. "Poor lady couldn't even fight back."

"There's lots of worse ways to die." Jeremy shrugged it off and tore into his Brewmaster's Pie. "With that poison in her, she probably wasn't even awake."

"Yes, she was," Plato countered. "They've given curare to volunteers, to find out how the drug works. It doesn't affect the brain at all."

"Then how does it paralyze people?" Jeremy asked between mouthfuls.

"By blocking the connections between nerves and muscles." Plato riffled his pockets for a tattered piece of paper. "I copied this page yesterday—it's from *Goodman and Gilman*—one of the top pharmacology texts."

He had highlighted the passage on curare; he handed it around the table for the others to read:

"The onset of effects is very rapid. Slight dizziness and a sensation of warmth are first experienced. Difficulty in focusing and weakness in the jaw muscles are then observed ... Relaxation of the small muscles of the middle ear improves acuity of hearing for low tones. The limbs feel heavy ... Respiratory movements become more dia-

phragmatic as the intercostal muscles are involved ...
The accumulation of unswallowed saliva ... causes the
sensation of choking. Throughout the stage of complete
muscular paralysis, consciousness and sensorium remain
entirely undisturbed. The experience is definitely
unpleasant."

" 'Definitely unpleasant,' huh?" Homer grunted, then
handed the paper back. "I bet *that's* a big understatement."

"You got it." Plato grimaced. "When she started getting
weak, Marilyn probably figured her disease was suddenly
getting worse. Or maybe she even guessed that it was curare—she was pretty sharp. But there wasn't anything she
could do about it except lay there, hoping it would go
away."

"Like a stunned fly waiting for the spider to come
home," Cal added.

Jeremy Ames dropped his fork and shuddered. "Okay—
you've made your point. What I don't get is, how did the
killer slip her the poison?" He gnawed his lip thoughtfully.
"Was it in something she ate, or did he have to stick her
with a needle? And if he did, why didn't he just give her
some more when he saw it wasn't working?"

"I've been thinking about that," Cal said. She shook her
head. "Tubocurarine would have to be injected—it's harmless if eaten. But you can't just give someone a shot without
their knowledge. And if she knew about it, why didn't she
struggle, or try to get help? She would have had a minute
or two before an injection would start working."

"I've been thinking about it, too." Plato pushed his chair
back and stroked his beard. "I think she didn't know she
was injected, because she did it herself."

Homer slowly looked up from his chili and frowned.
"What do you mean, injected herself? Suicide?"

"Yeah," Jeremy jeered. "And she stuffed a pillow down
her throat when the curare didn't work."

"She didn't think she was injecting *curare*," Plato explained patiently. He folded and refolded his napkin. "She
thought she was injecting insulin."

Cal paused, then nodded suddenly. "Why didn't *I* think
of that?"

"Because you're not her doctor," he told her. "I was. I
looked back over her medical chart yesterday, just to be

sure. She was taking thirty units of insulin at dinnertime every evening—that's about three-tenths of a milliliter. Injecting it subcutaneously, under the skin."

"And somebody switched her insulin for curare." Homer lowered his huge head and slurped a spoonful of chili. "Could they do that?"

"Sure." Plato shrugged. "Marilyn's insulin came in bottles; she only used part of a bottle in any given day. The killer could have drawn some insulin out of the bottle and replaced it with tubocurarine. The drug is colorless in solution; she'd have never known."

"How much would she have gotten?" Cal asked.

"Depends how much the killer put in her bottle," Plato answered. "Insulin has a milky-white color, and tubocurarine is white powder. The murderer could have added quite a bit of poison without worrying about whether all the powder dissolved."

"Could she have gotten enough to kill her?" Homer asked skeptically.

"She could have easily taken five milligrams," Plato replied. "Ten is lethal for most people. Less would have done the job for Marilyn, because of her MS. And if she had been drawing up a bigger dose of insulin, like she gets in the morning, she probably would have died outright from the paralysis."

"The killer wouldn't have had to finish the job," Jeremy murmured. His bulging eyes drooped.

"And I would have never found the broken cartilage," said Cal.

The table fell silent for a time. Jeremy picked at his Brewmaster's Pie, Homer moved on to his crab cakes, and Cal munched her sub sandwich thoughtfully. Plato was still leaning back in his chair; he hadn't touched his burger yet.

Homer washed his lunch down with a swig of root beer and eyed Plato. "All this is fine for you—you're her doctor. But what about the killer? How did *he* know Marilyn was going to take insulin that particular evening?"

"Maybe he didn't." Cal shrugged. "It didn't matter. She kept her insulin in the fridge in the pharmacology lounge. And she took her insulin every day. She'd have taken the curare eventually."

Jeremy drummed his fingers on the tabletop. "But he

had to check back, and get rid of the phony insulin bottle, right?"

"Right," Cal agreed. "That's probably how the killer found out that she wasn't dead. And that he had to finish her."

"He couldn't just pop up in her office every morning and evening to check if the poison worked," Jeremy pointed out. "So either he or she *knew* Marilyn Abel was staying late that night, or the killer was there most of the time anyway. That would fit with her assistants, or that medical student—Tiffany Cramer. And they also knew about the victim's habits. That narrows our field a little."

"So does finding out who could have gotten their hands on tubocurarine," Homer added. He cocked an eyebrow at Plato. "It's not like running down to Revco for a bottle of aspirin, right?"

"Not quite," he agreed. "But I'm almost certain they have some tubocurarine out at the medical school."

"What for?" Jeremy asked.

"Animal experiments, mostly." Plato grimaced. "We used it a lot in dog lab, back when I was a student."

"More and more, it sounds certain the killer was someone at Siegel," Jeremy mused.

"You could check and see who had access to the drug," Homer told the detective. "See if anything was missing, if any locks were forced. Find out if anyone was spotted in a place where they weren't supposed to be."

"We could look through the security records at Siegel," Ames agreed. "But the drug was taken almost two months ago—maybe more, if the killer was planning ahead. We need to find out who had access and opportunity."

Homer nodded. "Someone familiar with her habits, maybe someone with a key to the drug cabinet."

"And someone with an ax to grind." Jeremy finished his Brewmaster's Pie and wiped the plate clean with a hunk of sourdough bread. He gnawed the crust and nodded briskly. "Everything fits with that Tiffany kid—the lab assistant. Judge's daughter or no, she—"

"Why do you keep picking on Tiffany Cramer?" Cal asked suddenly.

Plato sighed. Jeremy Ames might have looked like a Dachshund, but he was as narrow-minded as a pit bull. He tended to grab suspects in his jaws and shake them, dropping them only when their innocence was obvious—in a kind of disappointed way, like he was giving up a thick, juicy steak. The simplest solution was almost always the right one, Jeremy liked to say. And he was usually right. Like medicine, detective work was a ton of routine and paperwork and monotony, punctuated by bursts of activity, bizarre events, and stress. But the monotony usually won out.

"Tiffany Cramer had a motive, and she probably had the method—access to that insulin bottle," Jeremy pointed out. "*And* she could get the poison, right? She worked in pharmacology."

"They don't necessarily keep tubocurarine in the pharmacology department." Cal sighed. "It's a research lab, not a drugstore. They probably keep it near the animal lab."

Jeremy shrugged, stroked his forehead with those long, thin fingers and shot Cal an apologetic glance. "I know you don't think she did this, Cally, but how do you explain that bogus alibi of hers? The librarian was absolutely certain that she wasn't there that night. Even her *roommate* says she wasn't home that night."

"I think I know where she was," Cal said.

"Where?"

"Just give me a chance to talk to her." She looked away. "I don't think it had anything to do with the murder."

The detective snorted. "So you think Tiffany Cramer isn't hiding anything?"

"I'm not saying that." She raised her hands. "I just don't think she was involved in the murder. She and Marilyn were too close, for one thing. And besides, there are a lot of other people to consider."

"Anyone in particular?" Homer asked slowly.

"How about Chuck Albright?" Cal suggested. "He knew Marilyn's habits. And I'll bet he had easy access to the poison. A lot easier than Tiffany Cramer. Remember, she's just a student."

"But he had no motive, as far as I can tell." Jeremy set his fork down and pushed the plate away. A waiter hurried over to clean their table. "Marilyn Abel was the shining star in his department, right?"

"Even more than that." Cal waved the dessert menu away and paused until the waiter moved out of earshot. "Albright had an interest in Marilyn's new drug—Patracin.

I talked with a friend of mine in the legal department over at Siegel yesterday, off the record. Marilyn had a much better arrangement with Siegel than she had at Chadwick-Medicon. Her contract said she was to get four-fifths of the profits for any drug she developed at Siegel. The college and Albright split the other twenty percent."

"So why kill her?" Homer asked, his round face a puzzle of wrinkles. "She was the goose with the golden—"

"The golden egg?" Cal asked. "But she'd *laid* it already. And according to her contract, the rights to any unpatented works reverted to Albright and the college when she died. A fifty-fifty split between the department chairman and Siegel. Since Patracin hasn't been patented yet, the college is considering it to be an unfinished piece of work. And Albright sure isn't complaining."

"But the drug is practically ready for clinical trials," Plato pointed out. "It may not be patented, but it *is* a completed piece of work. Marilyn's family could contest that in court."

"And maybe they'd win." Cal crossed her arms. "But Albright doesn't know that. As it stands right now, Marilyn's death multiplied his profits by a factor of five."

Plato nodded. Now he understood why Albright was reluctant to talk about Marilyn's new drug. He recalled the department chairman's words—*The drug was in very rough, preliminary stages.* If Albright admitted that Patracin was nearly ready for patenting and clinical trials, he stood to lose a large stake in the profits.

Maybe that explained why he was blaming Tiffany Cramer for the Great Rat Escape. An effort to discredit her, since she knew exactly how little Albright had contributed toward the development of Patracin.

"I didn't think TB was around anymore," Homer said.

"It is," Plato replied. "It's making a big comeback. And it's harder to treat than ever."

"Is the money such a big deal, though?" Jeremy asked. He pushed his chair back and lit a cigarette. "I mean, we're not talking about a million dollars or anything, are we?"

"For a safe, nontoxic, highly effective drug to fight TB?" Cal asked. "The profits could amount to *several* million— and the patent rights could be worth several hundred thousand dollars, or even a million."

Homer whistled. "Albright could claim half of that—half a million dollars."

"The pharmaceutical jackpot," Plato murmured to himself.

"Huh. Even *ten* percent of a mil isn't chicken feed." Jeremy blew smoke rings at the ceiling. "Then again, maybe he really *needed* the extra dough. We could look into that."

"And maybe Marilyn wasn't going to sell Patracin at all, or not right away," Cal pointed out. "The longer she held onto it, and the farther along Patracin made it toward FDA approval, the more money she could get once she sold the patent."

"Maybe Albright wanted to sell the drug to Valdemar, but Marilyn didn't." Plato told them about Albright's interest in Candice Erdmann last night. Perhaps the department chairman was trying to make a sale.

"Or maybe Marilyn wanted to sell it to that Arnold Welkins guy instead," Jeremy guessed. "He *owns* a drug company, right? I wonder if he'd heard about Patracin."

"I doubt it," Plato replied. "He was Marilyn's ex, remember. I don't think she'd have sold the drug to him if her life depended on it."

"Maybe it did," Cal mused.

"Albright, Erdmann, and Welkins. We need to question all three of them again, now that we know about this new drug." Homer sighed. "This is getting complicated."

"Don't worry—Plato'll take care of interviewing Candice Erdmann." Cal gave a wry smile. "He and Candice are pretty tight; she's invited him over to her condo for burritos."

Homer frowned slowly, squinting at Cal and then at Plato. "You'd better watch your step," he warned his cousin. "Or we just might have *two* homicides on our hands."

Beneath the table, Cal kicked the lawyer's shin. He grunted.

"It's perfectly innocent," she insisted. "We're going to a party tonight—Candice Erdmann and Albright both should be there. Plato's taking advantage of Candice's weakness for ski pros."

Jeremy squinted at him, impressed. "I thought you were a *terrible* skier, Plato."

"I am." Plato scratched his head, bewildered. "Cal—"

"Too bad about tonight," Homer muttered. "Fourth Saturday of the month—I guess you two forgot it's poker night."

"We didn't." Plato shook his head. *"Cally—"*

"We'll just deal Nina in," Jeremy said. He smiled proudly. "I've taught her a lot of American card games lately—she's getting to be pretty good."

Nina Ames was the detective's fifth—and probably final—wife. Final because she was the first one who could actually tolerate his idiosyncrasies, his long hours as a homicide detective, his insane devotion to Tai Chi. All that, plus a stunning northern Italian face and figure, an off-beat European sense of humor, and a talent with pasta, threatened to tame even Jeremy Ames. Rumor had it that the homicide detective was cutting back to a sixty-hour work week.

He gave a smug grin. "She's making *Manicotti al forno*—Plato's favorite."

"More for us," Homer said happily.

"Cally—" Plato cried.

She reached out and patted his hand. "Plato doesn't mind, really. We're going to a fund-raiser for Randolph Smythe the Third."

"That old windbag?" Jeremy hooted. He pulled out a fresh cigarette and puffed it to life with the embers of the first. "I didn't think he was your type."

"He's dragging a lot of the Siegel faculty there. Didn't I tell you, Plato?"

"No," he muttered sullenly. Desperate, he sniffed loudly, let his eyelids droop, and hacked. "You know, this might be a good night for me to stay home and catch up on my sleep. I think this cold's getting worse . . ."

Homer winked at Jeremy. Across the table, they grinned and chuckled together.

"I've heard this excuse somewhere before, Plato," Cal teased. "Anyway, Candice would be *so* disappointed if you weren't there. I bet there'll be lots of great food."

"Yeah, right. Smythe's probably a vegetarian."

Jeremy cocked his head and glanced at his watch. He sprang to his feet. "Hey—I've got to fly. I'm giving a self-defense lesson at the YMCA at four o'clock." He grinned. "And I promised I'd be home early to taste the manicotti."

Homer pushed his plate away. "I'll get there early, too. You might need a second opinion."

They both shrugged their coats on. Homer patted Plato's shoulder. "You have fun at that party, okay?"

"But be careful," Jeremy warned as they walked away. "I've heard Smythe's parties can be pretty wild. You just might *die* from overexcitement."

"Thanks, guys." Plato was so depressed that he didn't even notice Homer's unpaid check on the table.

Chapter 16

Randolph Smythe the Third's home was an estate in the traditional sense—a sprawling manor house nestled among dozens of acres of fir and pine, orchards and pastures, even a stable and barn, in an exclusive little corner of Olmsted Falls. The quiet, pastoral feel of the meadows and woodlands was shattered every few minutes by a low-flying jet; Cleveland Hopkins Airport was just up the road from Smythe's home.

A wide ribbon of black asphalt pierced the wrought-iron gate and wound through the forest and fields toward the main compound, where dozens of imported cars dozed in the chilly moonlight and awaited their owners' return. At the front entrance, a valet was tugging a mink-wrapped package from a BMW, then running around to nab the keys from her husband.

"I *hate* parties like this," Plato grumbled. "Full of snobby rich people trying to impress one another with their houses and clothes and cars."

He flipped the old Rabbit into gear and followed the BMW to an empty stretch of driveway beside the house. The valet parked, waved Plato on into the next space, and trotted back toward the house.

"Just give me a television, a bag of Doritos, and a case of beer." He backed the car into the empty space and set the parking brake. "*That's* a party."

"You're *so* cultivated, Plato." Beside him, Cal was staring out the window at the frozen duck pond and smoothing the pleats in her red taffeta dress.

"Just practical," he replied, unruffled. "And don't tell me most of the people in there don't feel exactly the same way. We're all going to be bored stiff."

He killed the engine and pocketed the keys.

"Hey!" Cal grabbed the keys from his pocket and switched the ignition back on. The radio roared to life again with the sound of a cheering crowd. "What'd you do that for?"

The Cavs were leading New York by just two points, with ninety seconds left in the game. Plato grinned at his wife and settled back in his seat to listen. "You're *so* cultivated, Cal."

"Just practical." She reached for his hand and stared out the window again. "Isn't this romantic?"

"A frozen Rabbit, a Cavs game, and Thou."

"No, really." She squeezed his hand. "The moonlight, the trees, the pond—I bet they get geese in the summer."

"Messy things," Plato muttered.

They listened as the Knicks pulled ahead, then fouled themselves out of the game when Brad Daugherty converted on a three-point play. The final buzzer sounded.

Cal switched the radio off and sighed. "Maybe *we* could have a pond someday."

"We have one now—in our basement. I could buy you a rubber duck."

"Thanks anyways. I'll wait." She buttoned up her coat and opened the door, leaning into the blast of cold wind. She turned and poked her head back inside. "You coming?"

Plato grabbed his keys and they hurried along the driveway.

"What are all these rich people doing here anyway?" Plato asked suddenly. "I thought this party was to honor the researchers at Siegel."

"I think it's really to honor the *Dean* of Research—Randolph Smythe the Third," Cal replied. "An exclusive little gathering, probably to fill the future congressman's war chest."

"At Siegel's expense," Plato muttered. They turned the corner and he glanced up at the floodlit front of the house. Stone, stucco, and dark-stained wood planks. Tudor on a grand scale—a David Winter cottage all grown up and brought to life. "But then, why are *we* here?"

Cal shrugged. "We've both published a few research papers. And maybe he wants to show off a token female faculty member."

She didn't sound entirely displeased. Plato had heard about the assistant deanship, and Smythe's suggestion that she should apply. Cal didn't seem sure whether to take it seriously, and neither was Plato. But he would probably urge her to go ahead and try.

On the other hand, if Siegel's deans were required to entertain on Smythe's grand scale, Cal didn't stand a chance. The valet ushered them through the front door and slunk back out into the cold like the family dog leaving for the dreaded winter walk.

Randolph Smythe the Third's foyer could have been a grand ballroom, or the set for an MGM dance number. Plato half-expected two dozen tuxedoed gents to strut down the double stairway and burst into song, sweeping Ginger Rogers off the wide landing and tossing her down into Astaire's arms. The floor was a chessboard for giants—alternating panels of black and pale pink marble polished to a mirror sheen—with an archipelago of Persian rugs scattered at random intervals. Four marble columns, each thicker than Homer's waist, stretched up to the ceiling to support a crossed arch. From its center, an enormous chandelier floated like an impending Close Encounter.

A handsome young man wearing a gray tuxedo and an English accent rushed up to take their coats. "Very good, ma'am. Excellent, sir, excellent."

The coats disappeared like a conjurer's trick.

"Well, *that* went rather well," Plato said happily, tugging his suit jacket into place. "He liked how I took my coat off."

"See?" Cal asked. "This isn't so hard, is it?"

As if in response to a radio signal, Randolph Smythe cut himself loose from a gaggle of chittering older women and glided across the floor to his latest guests. He shook their hands warmly and flashed a smile at Cal.

"So *glad* you could make it tonight. And this is your husband? Plato, is it?" He tilted his head and thought, finger on his lips. "Yes, I remember you from your days at Siegel. Quite a promising niche you've carved for yourself. Geriatrics—definitely an up-and-coming field."

Before Plato could respond, Smythe continued.

"I'd like you to meet my wife, Valerie." On perfect cue, an attractive woman hardly older than Cal appeared at Smythe's elbow and smiled. "Valerie, this is Plato and Cal Marley. Plato's a Siegel grad, teaching geriatrics at Riverside. Cal is a forensic pathologist—and one of our best guest lecturers in the anatomy department."

Valerie shook their hands. "I'm very pleased to meet you. Welcome to our home."

Mrs. Smythe had apparently studied at the Jacqueline Kennedy Onassis School for Politicians' Wives—she had the same soft voice, the same bright smile, the same lamb-like innocence. A woman the public could trust.

But her hair was blond, her face was even prettier, and she had a pouty mouth that looked a little tired at the corners, a smile that seemed rather brittle. Her manner toward Cal was downright chilly. She clutched her husband's elbow possessively, gazing down her nose with a sour look.

But the moment passed, and her smile thawed again.

"Ahh—here are some more guests," her husband announced. An elderly couple with a cane, a walker, two attendants, and a pile of gold jewelry had just hobbled through the door. Smythe turned back to Plato and Cal and smiled broadly. "Please do enjoy yourselves; we have a number of refreshments available in the library."

The host and hostess hurried off to greet their new guests and usher them into the foyer. That task complete, they flitted from group to group like honeybees, spreading the pollen of Smythe's political message and gathering the nectar of financial support. Plato recognized a few faces from the hospital. Mostly subspecialists—fabulously wealthy doctors interested in maintaining the status quo. Not exactly Plato and Cal's crowd.

"You're staring," Cal observed.

"At the bear," Plato replied. "He's dead—he won't mind."

Across the room, at the landing where the two staircases joined to form the stem of a Y, a bearskin was splayed across the wall with a pair of crossed muskets gleaming above his snarling mouth. Plato had heard that Smythe was a hunter and collector; this was apparently one of his prizes. The grizzly looked like a victim of a steamroller accident.

Cal tugged his elbow and led him across the floor to the library, a vast room lined with leather-bound books, dark walnut paneling, and huge windows facing out over the frozen pond. Bob Stahl was slouching near one of the windows; he brightened when Plato and Cal approached.

"So Dean Smythe roped you folks in too, did he?" Bob

looked comfortable in a double-breasted sport jacket, open-
collar cotton shirt, and Dockers.

Plato tugged on the knot of his tie and wished Cal had
eased up on the dress code tonight. "We got a last-minute
invitation," he explained.

They shook hands and Bob gestured to a vacant wing
chair nearby. "I've saved a place for you, Cal." He
shrugged. "Actually, Therese was sitting there, but she
abandoned me for some Austrian heiress. They're off in the
trophy room, admiring Smythe's dead animal collection."

"I saw Chuck Albright out in the foyer," Cal said as she
sat down. "Looks like the whole pharmacology department
is here."

Bob gave a funny twitch of his crooked mustache.
"Smythe's got us on display, because of that lab rat thing.
Wants to show the public that we're not a bunch of
morons."

"I heard they found some of the rats this afternoon,"
Plato said. Channel Five had interrupted a college basketball game to deliver the late-breaking news bulletin: seven
of the escaped convicts had been trapped in the basement
of a bakery near the freeway. Six were captured alive and
unharmed; a cop had winged the seventh in the tail when
it jumped into a wedding cake.

"Not a trace of TB in any of them." Bob grinned. "We
measured Patracin levels on them this afternoon. Tiffany
was right—it was the *treated* rats that escaped."

"A lucky mistake," Cal observed.

"She makes a lot of them. *Good* mistakes. Marilyn would
be proud." He gestured toward the bar. "Hey—how about
if Plato and I round up some drinks?"

Cal settled deeper in the wing chair. "I'll take white
wine, if they have it. Beer if they don't."

Plato and Bob threaded their way through the crowd,
past a grand piano and over to the bar. Waiting their turn,
they watched the piano player do a snappy improvisation
on "Just One of Those Things," trickling over and under
the melody, leaping down the scales with the grace of a
ballerina, shadowing the rhythm with flashy counterpoint
melody, and finally whirling into a sharp, breathless ending.
Several people in the room clapped.

"That's Smythe's son, you know," Bob told Plato. "Randolph Smythe the Fourth."

"You're kidding." Plato peered through the crowd and caught another glimpse of the piano player. He could see the family resemblance, but Junior was in his twenties—not much younger than Valerie Smythe. "I take it Mrs. Smythe isn't—"

"Isn't his mother? Right." Bob turned and pointed to a small portrait hanging over one corner of the bar, half hidden between the bookcases. A stern but beautiful woman sat in a chair with a ten-year-old boy standing stiffly beside her. "Smythe's first wife. Killed by a burglar when the dean was out of town at a conference."

"Wow ... How awful." Plato studied the portrait, then glanced back at the piano player. Randolph the Fourth was launching into that haunting prelude to "Stardust." "I guess that's why Smythe is so focused on the anticrime legislation."

Bob flapped a hand and twitched his mustache again. "He plays it up in the press a lot—see the poor victim and all that. But I hear he wasn't that close to his first wife. Mostly it's just for PR."

Uncomfortable with Bob's cynicism, Plato turned his attention back to the music, listening as the melody swelled. "That kid is awfully good."

"He does classical, too. He's guested with the Cleveland Orchestra."

"No kidding." Plato studied Smythe's son as the music wound down to its melancholy ending. Surely the technique wasn't much of a strain for him; the arrangement was relatively simple. But his long, handsome face was etched with lines of intense concentration, a mask of pain and pleasure both. The expression seemed to flow from his face and hands straight into the music, a purity of emotion that transcended the medium. Randolph Smythe the Fourth was an artist.

They joined the thunderous applause this time, then turned away to lean on the bar, a long stretch of walnut curving across the corner of the library. As they moved closer to the center of the bar, Bob suddenly jumped back and grinned. "Hey—get a load of this."

Plato stepped over and looked. At the midpoint of the bar, the two wings of polished wood and brass met at a window of clear Plexiglas: a hundred-gallon aquarium built into the bar's surface. Oddly beautiful fish with colorful bodies and bright spiky plumage circled among the plants and carved rocks like bizarre birds of prey hovering in a watery sky.

The bartender, a hulking specimen with brooding eyes and no neck at all, took their orders and grinned. "Don't lean too hard on the Plexiglas," he warned. "Those are lionfish—every single one of those spines is poisonous. The venom can kill you."

"So can alcohol, Frank. Different deaths for different people." Behind them, Smythe was chuckling at his joke. He clapped Plato and Bob on the shoulders. "Though I think alcohol's the better way to go. I got stung by one of these years ago, when I was scuba diving near Baja. Hurt like hell; nearly killed me. How are you enjoying the party?"

Bob gave a tight smile. "Very well, Dean Smythe."

"Glad to hear it." Hands in his pockets, Smythe rocked back on his heels and grinned. "Did you catch my son playing over there?"

They both nodded.

"I've never heard anything like it," Plato said, and meant it. "You must be very proud."

"I am. Believe me, I am." The perpetual smile grew as Smythe glanced over at his son for a long moment. Finally he turned back to Bob. "Say—there's a fellow here from the *Plain Dealer* I'd like you to meet. Guy named Leonard Reiss. He had some questions about that fiasco with the lab rats. How about if I send him your way next time he corners me?"

"Sure." Bob shrugged. "Glad to help."

"Great." Smythe clapped him on the back, then drifted away to rub elbows with more of his guests.

"I guess that explains why Therese and I were invited," Bob mused. "Everyone else here is either a department chairman or one of Smythe's rich friends."

"Except Cal and me," Plato noted. "I still can't figure out why *we're* here."

"Maybe it's her connection with the coroner's department," Bob joked. "Smythe could be trying for the cemetery vote."

"The way his ratings are soaring, I don't think he'll need it."

Bob sipped his single-malt whiskey and smacked his lips.

"I don't mind running interference for him. Therese is having fun, and the drinks aren't bad."

While Plato waited for his beer and Cal's chardonnay, Bob nudged his elbow and gestured across the room. "You'd better hurry up. I think someone's trying to move in on your lady."

Plato glanced toward the windows. A short man with a bad toupee and a rodent face was standing beside Cal's chair, talking and smiling broadly.

"Arnold Welkins." Bob's lip twisted. "He's a woman-chaser, a leech. We'd better pry him away from Cal, or he'll stick to her all evening."

Plato picked up the drinks and they hurried through the crowd. But halfway across the room, Bob Stahl was stopped by a plump, red-cheeked fellow with starched blond hair and a shabby suit.

"Doctor Stahl? Nice to meet you." He bobbed his head, the blond mane moving like a papier-mâché sculpture. "I'm Leonard Reiss—Dean Smythe suggested that I have a word with you."

Bob turned to Plato and shrugged apologetically, then followed the reporter to an empty corner of the library.

Over near the windows, the rodent had moved even closer to Cal; he was practically sitting on her lap. As Plato approached, she turned to him and smiled politely.

"Thank you *ever* so much, dear." She took a sip of her wine and giggled. "I *really* shouldn't have any more of this, but it tastes so yummy and it makes my nose tickle."

She giggled again. Plato gawked as though an alien had taken control of her body.

"Cal?" He sounded worried.

"Plato, you *must* meet Arnie—Arnie Welkins. It *is* okay if I call you Arnie, isn't it?" Her voice was pitched up to a mouselike squeak. She leaned forward, tugged the sleeve of the ferret's tuxedo jacket, and batted her brown eyes up at him.

Welkins blushed, plump purple lips curving in a shy smile, pointy nose twitching happily. "Of course, my dear. Of course. I feel like I've known you all my life."

"Oh, you're *so* right. I feel *just* the same way." She turned to her husband. "Plato, darling, you really *must* see Randolph's trophy room. Arnie says it's the most *amazing* thing. All sorts of animal heads from all around the world.

I'd go there myself, but—" she giggled and hiccuped, then covered her mouth shyly, "I'm afraid I'd be ever so *frightened.*"

"Cal?" Plato peered into her eyes worriedly. "Are you feeling all right?"

She turned toward him, giving Arnie a profile, and flashed a horrid wink with the eye the Chadwick executive couldn't see.

"I'll be just *fine* here with Arnie," she squeaked. "He's been telling me all about his research over at Chadwick."

"Er—oh, I see." Plato didn't quite see, exactly, but he took the hint and wandered off into the crowd.

Cal watched him leave, then turned her attention back to Arnie. "Did you hear about those laboratory rats escaping on the freeway? What a *frightful* thing." She gazed up at him admiringly. "But then, owning part of a big drug company like Chadwick-Medicon, I suppose you know *all* about it."

"Actually, my dear, I wasn't a bit surprised." Welkins drew himself up self-righteously. "Valdemar Pharmaceuticals has a *reputation* for that sort of carelessness."

Arnold Welkins was a colossal bore. Cal wondered how a fascinating person like Marilyn Abel had ever fallen for such a pinhead. It certainly wasn't his looks—Welkins was a flail-chested, round-shouldered scarecrow of a man, his matted black toupee plastered atop his gray hair like so much straw, his shy little chin almost eclipsed by those huge purple lips, his pinched features and pointy nose twitching like a groundhog testing the first spring air. Or maybe a laboratory rat picking his way through a maze, sniffing for the piece of cheese at the end.

Marilyn couldn't have fallen for his personality, either. Summoning all her patience, Cal sat back and listened to a diatribe about Chadwick-Medicon's chief local competition. According to Welkins, both manufacturers specialized in antibiotics, but Valdemar's drugs tended to be less safe, less effective, and more expensive. Arnold had personally overseen the development of several new cephalosporin antibiotics during his tenure at Chadwick; the profits from two of the later drugs had allowed him to buy a large share of the company. Of course, he didn't see fit to display his wealth as ostentatiously as their hosts, but he owned a perfectly *lovely* yacht and enjoyed weekend sails to the Bass Islands. Perhaps Cal would like to—

"Then *your* company didn't have a stake in that new anti-TB drug?" Cal asked innocently. "Someone at Siegel told me it's a big breakthrough, going to make a pile of money."

"Of course, if you listen to *talk*, every new drug is a big breakthrough." He sniffed. "But as far as financial interest goes, neither Chadwick nor Valdemar have purchased the patent rights yet. The drug is actually being developed by researchers at Siegel Medical College—they're only leasing equipment and space from Valdemar. For that matter, the chief developer was a woman who used to work for me at Chadwick."

Cal's jaw dropped. "Really? How *fascinating!*"

She patted the arm of the chair invitingly.

He perched beside Cal and nodded slowly. "In fact, we have reason to believe that the groundwork for the new drug was performed at Chadwick. Before Ms. Abel was fired."

"She was *fired*? And then she stole secrets from you?" Cal frowned sympathetically. "How dreadfully *dishonest.*"

"Well, not exactly *fired*," Arnold temporized. "Let's just say that she wasn't being a team player anymore."

"But to steal company secrets and try to profit from them . . . Have you told the police about that?"

"Er—actually, uh—no." Welkins's head hunkered down between his shoulders. "The allegations, if they *are* allegations, are rather difficult to substantiate. As to their potential basis in fact, I really couldn't—"

"I heard that researcher lady was killed—*murdered.*" Cal shivered daintly. "Could that have had anything to do with the drug she was working on?"

A panicky look crossed the drug executive's face—a laboratory rat suddenly strapped into the guillotine, waiting for the blade to fall. He drew away from Cal. "*What* sort of work did you say you do?"

"I'm with the coroner's office. *Fascinating* stuff." She giggled innocently, leaned closer and whispered, "I probably shouldn't be telling you this. But the police think you met with her that night—the night she died."

"Rubbish!" He stood and backed away, beady eyes widening, nose twitching violently. The bit of cheese at the end of the maze had turned into a great big cat. "I've explained it to the police—Marilyn reached me on my car phone and canceled the appointment, after I had already left the office. So I went downtown. I've got three friends who'll attest to that."

"You have *three* friends, Arnold? However did you manage that?" Candice Erdmann had appeared suddenly behind him. She patted Welkins's shoulder and turned to Cal. "You needn't worry about Arnold, dear. He isn't *capable* of murder. In fact, he isn't capable of a *lot* of things. Are you, Arnold?"

Welkins scowled at her and hunched lower, but his face reddened. He shifted his glare to Plato, who was standing beside the Valdemar executive.

"Besides, what would his motive be?" Candice continued. She had a look of ageless beauty tonight in her black velvet dress, pearl necklace and earrings, dark hair pulled up in a crown, face painted so perfectly that even the tiniest wrinkles and flaws were hidden. Snow White's evil stepmother, still determined to be the fairest of them all. She smiled at Cal. "Arnold hasn't a chance of acquiring Patracin, even with Marilyn out of the way. His company has been operating in the red for two years now—I don't think they could buy the rights to manufacture *aspirin*."

"But *you* certainly had something to gain," Welkins snarled. "Marilyn didn't want to sell Patracin to Valdemar. But now that she's gone, Chuck Albright has made you a number of very *interesting* offers. Hasn't he?"

"Certainly more interesting than anything *you* could offer, Arnold." Candice held her ground, staring down her nose at Welkins until he finally mumbled something and slunk away. She turned to Plato and Cal with an apologetic shrug. "I'm *dreadfully* sorry. That man has the most *amazing* way of bringing out the worst in a girl."

Candice smiled and touched Plato's arm. "If you'll excuse me—"

She turned on her heel and strolled away with that hip-rolling walk of hers.

"No love lost between those two," Plato grunted.

Cal finally noticed that he was holding two plates loaded with goodies from the buffet table. He brandished them and grinned.

"They specialize in California Boutique here—red and

purple and orange lettuce, alfalfa sprouts, weird beans, and those disgusting miniature vegetables. But they've got a few wings and baby back ribs." He passed her plate over with a proud smile. "*And* I nabbed the last of the Swedish meatballs."

"Good work." Cal dove into her meal with reckless abandon. Still standing, Plato studied her warily.

"Is it really you again, Cally? Some space-alien took over your body a while back, turned you into a short Marilyn Monroe."

"Who, me?" She giggled into her hand, raising her voice half an octave again. "It's just that *wine,* Plato dear. And Arnie—he was *ever* so sweet, really he was."

"Egads." His face screwed up and he made a funny sound, like a cat with a stubborn furball. "I think I'm going to be sick."

"Don't worry," she assured him between bites. "Aliens haven't stolen my brain. I was just pumping Arnold for a little information."

"Thank goodness," he sighed. "What did you find out?"

They finished their dinners while Cal recounted her conversation with Arnold Welkins.

"So he thinks Marilyn stole Patracin when she left Chadwick-Medicon?" Plato asked, amazed.

"Not really," Cal replied. "He backed off pretty quickly when I asked him about it. But he certainly seems interested in acquiring the drug. If he can."

Plato grinned. "That was quite a scene there, wasn't it? We ought to get those two together more often."

"Like two wet cats in a sack." Cal wrinkled her nose. "I think they'd make a *lovely* couple."

"A truly extra-*ord*-inaruh idea."

"Speaking of which, did you learn anything new from Candice?"

"Not really. She says she didn't meet with Marilyn at all that week. But she had a great deal of *respect* for Marilyn. Acted like she was Marilyn's biggest fan."

"Then I wonder why Marilyn was set against selling Patracin to Candice's company," Cal said.

"Me, too. I didn't ask Candice about that." He collected the plates and set them on a nearby table. A waitress shimmered over and instantly whisked them away. Plato perched on the arm of Cal's chair and lowered his voice. "But I *did* have a fascinating talk with Sergei Malenkov."

"Is he here?" Cal asked eagerly. "I'd love to see him."

Plato shook his head. "He left already, said he had to pick up some papers at the medical school." He glanced around. "The party's breaking up pretty early, isn't it? Anyway, Sergei let me in on an interesting little piece of information. He said he worked late at the medical school on the night Marilyn died."

"Really? I'm surprised he didn't mention that to the police."

"Nobody asked him. Anyway, he didn't think it was really important." He raised an eyebrow at Cal. "And I don't think he wanted to point fingers at anyone. Especially a department chairman."

Cal sucked it a deep breath. "I bet I know what you're going to say."

He nodded. "Sergei's office is right under the pharmacology lab. He says he heard a sound like rolling thunder outside, around nine o'clock that night. He has a window that faces out on the parking lot—just about at ground level. He looked out and saw a red Corvette tearing out of the parking lot."

"Just about the time Marilyn was killed," Cal observed.

"Uh-huh."

"And I'll bet only one person at Siegel owns a red Corvette."

"Right again."

"Chuck Albright," Cal guessed.

"You're batting a thousand."

She frowned. "I think we'd better have a little talk with Homer tomorrow."

Chapter 17

"Plato?"

Cal's voice floated up to the observatory from somewhere in the house below.

"Plato?"

He didn't answer. Staring at the computer screen, a jumbled maze of numbers, letters, and nonsense characters, Plato hardly heard her. An idea had come to him during the long drive home from Smythe's house. Cal had pledged to stay awake and keep him company but, as usual, she'd reclined the passenger seat and promptly fallen asleep, leaving him alone with his thoughts. Which had mainly focused on Marilyn's computer disk, and the mysterious file it contained: "RECORD.FX!"

Obviously a record of some sort, but Plato had no idea what the "FX" stood for. In mathematics, Fx meant "function." Still, that made no sense—"record function"? And what did the exclamation point mean?

Plato had seen file names with exclamation points before. Piloting the Rabbit down Interstate 77, he tried to remember where.

Something to do with program disks ... most new programs seemed to have files with exclamation points. Why?

And then, just as the Rabbit was getting squeezed between a tractor-trailer and a guardrail, the answer hit him. File compression—encoding data in a certain way so that it would fit in a smaller space. With the increasing size and complexity of the newer graphics-based computer programs, software companies were saving money by packaging their programs as compressed files. A new computer program that might have required fourteen floppy disks to install now only needed seven.

Was the file on Marilyn's disk just a pirated software

program, then? Plato hoped not—it certainly wouldn't be much help in finding the murderer.

But what if it were a data file—one that was simply too big to fit on a single floppy disk? What if the file had been compressed, to make it fit?

Plato could hardly wait to get home and try it out. Almost before the Rabbit skidded to a stop in their driveway, he had dashed into the house and up three flights of stairs, to the old observatory that now served as their study. One of their computer programs had a disk-compression utility, which Plato hoped could make some sense of Marilyn's file. He had flipped the machine on, started the program, loaded Marilyn's disk, and ordered the computer to decompress the file.

But the machine had balked.

"Foreign File Format," it had complained. Rather ethnocentrically, Plato thought. "Decompression Halted."

So Plato had tried to fool the compression/decompression program, by changing the file name to one the program might recognize. This time, the computer didn't balk. Instead, it eagerly sank its teeth in, chewing on the file for several minutes before finally vomiting a torrent of meaningless gibberish and locking up completely.

Evidently, Plato had poisoned it. Every time he pressed any key whatever, the computer answered with an annoying and insistent "BLEEP!"

"Just Leave Me Alone," it seemed to be saying. "Go Away. BLEEP!"

The computer seemed quite upset with him.

Plato's only recourse was to turn the machine off and try again. But before he did, footsteps sounded in the stairwell below.

"Plato?"

He finally turned away from the accursed device.

Cal was standing just inside the doorway, in her slinky satin nightgown, arms folded across her chest, shivering. The observatory was dark except for a shaft of moonlight streaming down through the cupola overhead. The light fell across her cream-colored nightgown, making her look like a wraith—the Ghost of the Observatory. "What are you doing?"

Plato admired the subtle messages his wife could convey, just by her tone of voice. In only four words, she had managed to express her disbelief that anyone could be so foolish as to sit in a frigidly cold study at midnight on a Saturday, poring over a screenful of gibberish, and her conviction that if anyone *could* be that idiotic, it would have to be Plato, her husband, to whom she had—perhaps regretfully, now—vowed to stand by in sickness and in health, even if that sickness involved psychiatric problems, and a resignation to stand by that vow, even if it killed her.

"I was—I was just—uhh . . ." Plato tapped a few keys.

"BLEEP! BLEEP! BLEEP!" Even the computer seemed to scorn him.

"I was—umm—"

"You're trying to decode that stupid file of Marilyn's again." This time, no subtle messages were needed. But Cal's frown suddenly turned to puzzlement and concern—for the computer. She rushed across the room, dodging the spiral stairway leading up to the cupola, and squinted at the machine. "Why is it making that noise? Is it broken?"

"No. It just crashed." He switched the computer off and on again. The screen blanked, then flickered back to life. "I had an idea. I thought Marilyn's file might have been compressed."

Quickly, he filled Cal in on his theory, and his failed attempts to decode the file.

She didn't seem impressed. "If it didn't work, why are you turning the computer on again?"

"I thought maybe I'd—uh—try something else." Actually, Plato wanted to make sure he hadn't broken the damn thing. Cal would surely kill him.

Not that she had much use for it; she still banged out her autopsy reports on the morgue's ancient manual Underwood, carbons and all, wearing her right index finger down to a nub. But Plato had talked her into spending a couple of thousand dollars on a home computer and, to Cal, an investment was an investment.

Even if it was a stupid male toy.

Experimentally, Plato tapped a few keys and started the Windows program. No BLEEP!s. All was forgiven.

Cal swiveled Plato's chair around and sat on his lap. She peered at the monitor, her features soft and shadowy in the screen's dim glow. Deep brown eyes, turned-up nose, lips like newly opened rose petals. And slightly pointed ears, not quite hidden beneath the shoulder-length fall of blond hair. Small as she was, Cal could almost be an elf. An attractive little she-elf.

She had looked *very* attractive tonight, in the red taffeta dress. With all the fuss at Smythe's party, Plato had never gotten around to saying so.

Anyway, in the nightgown and the moonlight, she looked even prettier now.

Cal tossed her head and tugged her hair back over the pointy ears. "If Marilyn compressed the file, shouldn't you use *her* computer to decompress it? The file wouldn't be foreign to Marilyn's computer program, right?"

"Right." Except that Plato didn't want to wait until Monday. He had hoped to unlock the puzzle tonight. Disappointed, he slid the mouse around on its pad and pointed the cursor at Marilyn's file. Maybe if he tried changing the file name again . . .

"Anyway, I can't believe that this file of Marilyn's means *anything*," Cal continued. "It's just too pat, too easy."

"You just don't want a murder case to be solved by some computer nerd sitting at a keyboard," Plato complained. More than anything, Cal believed in good, honest detective work. Whether it was done on the streets of Cleveland or in the autopsy suite.

"If Marilyn knew something important, something that could kill her, why would she hide it on a computer disk that her brother would never have found? And in a silly code that no one else can crack?" She grinned. "Why not just send a *note* home with Jonathan—one that says, 'If I am killed today, Chuck Albright did it.' "

Plato frowned. "Why Chuck Albright?"

"Or whoever." Cal crinkled her nose in annoyance. Apparently, she had tipped her hand.

"But you suspect Chuck Albright, huh?" Plato persisted.

"Why not? He had motive, means, and opportunity. How else do you explain the red Corvette that Sergei saw screaming out of the parking lot? I wouldn't be surprised if Jeremy Ames rustles up a warrant for Albright tomorrow morning—after I tell him about what Sergei said." She shrugged. "I wish I could talk with Tiffany Cramer first— I'd like to know what she thinks of Albright."

"Oh, by the way." He jerked a thumb over at the answering machine sitting beside the desk. "She called and left some messages while we were at Smythe's party. I saved them."

"Tiffany called?" Cal sounded pleased. "What did she say?"

"The first message was about those lab rats they captured—how they were healthy and full of Patracin. So Marilyn's drug seems to work. She sounded pretty excited." Plato frowned. "She left two or three more messages after that. Really vague ones, just saying she'd try back again later."

"I'd better call her in the morning," Cal said. "She may know something about Albright."

"You're really fixed on him," Plato observed, then shook his head. "I have trouble picturing Chuck Albright as a murderer."

She patted Plato's hand. "Just last month, Homer convicted a sweet little old lady on a first-degree charge. She killed her husband for a two-thousand-dollar life insurance policy. She knitted booties for her granddaughter during the trial." Cal sighed patiently. "Anyway, Chuck Albright had the most to gain from Marilyn's death, as far as I can tell." She turned and locked gazes with Plato. "Wouldn't *you* bump off somebody for half a mil?"

"Depends who it is, I guess." Plato considered. "That window salesman that keeps calling at dinnertime, no problem. Or that obnoxious surgeon who's always sidling up to you at staff meetings."

"The one that pinched me?"

Plato nodded.

"Me, too," Cal agreed.

"Why not Randolph Smythe?" Plato asked suddenly.

"Why not bump him off?" She paused. "He *is* pretty annoying, but—"

"No, no. Why couldn't *he* haved killed Marilyn Abel?"

Cal's lip curled. "What on *earth* are you talking about?"

"Have you seen his aquarium?" Plato asked. When Cal shook her head, he told her about the lionfish and its deadly venom. "Maybe he got some of that lionfish poison and—"

"Lionfish venom doesn't *paralyze* people," Cal pointed out. "Anway, the test was positive for tubocurarine, not fish venom. Remember?"

Plato's face fell. "Oh, yeah."

"Besides, what *possible* reason could Smythe have for bumping off Marilyn Abel?"

He fumbled for words. "That argument with Tiffany Cramer—"

"Oh, right. He didn't like Marilyn speaking up for her student, so he killed her." Cal shook her head pityingly. "You'd better quit trying to reason this out, and just stick with your computer disk."

"It was just an idea," Plato said glumly.

"And a very *interesting* and *unusual* idea. I applaud your creativity." She leaned over and gave his shoulders a squeeze. "A *stimulating* mental exercise. But I've noticed that your cold seems much better today." She hitched herself closer and nuzzled his neck, lowered her voice to a breathy whisper. "And I was kind of wondering if you maybe had recovered enough to endure some stimulating *physical* exercise."

Plato reached for the computer and put the machine to sleep.

He woke up two hours later, in the cold heart of the night. As usual, Cal had stolen all the covers and cocooned herself up like a silkworm, leaving him with a handkerchief-sized corner of sheet and few tassels from the knit comforter. Their bedroom was in the northwest corner of the house, the only treeless area on the property. The wind howled in the eaves and sang its chilly winter song. Frost lined the insides of the windows. This far from the furnace, the draft from the heating vents wouldn't stir a match flame.

Plato shivered violently. Before finally falling asleep, Cal had snugged herself up to his side, murmured something about how *deliciously* warm he was.

Now he knew why. He'd been a fool to go skiing last night. He should have checked into a hospital instead.

The dryness in Plato's throat, the funny wooziness in his head, the way his skin was hot to the touch even though his insides felt as cold as a dip in Lake Erie, all explained why he'd seemed so deliciously warm to Cal. He slid out of bed, hopped over to the bathroom and took three Advils and two Tylenols without even bothering to check a temperature.

And donned another pair of sweats before climbing back into bed. And another. And another.

And finally drifted off to sleep again, clinging to the corner of the sheet.

Not much later, the telephone rang. Through a haze of sleep, Plato heard Cal unraveling, worming free of her cocoon, fumbling for the phone in the half-light of dawn, and finally picking it up. Her voice was gravelly. She sounded surprised.

Plato came wide awake when he heard Cal's sharp intake of breath, that funny little gasp—the same noise she'd made another morning almost a year ago now, when a voice on the phone had told her that Plato's uncle Matt was dead.

He sat up and slid over to her side of the bed. She was nodding, concentrating.

"Yes, yes," she was saying. "I'll get there as soon as I can."

She cradled the phone and turned to Plato, eyes wide and bright and fearful. Like a deer caught in the headlights of a car.

"That was Raj. Tiffany Cramer is in the hospital." Cal swallowed and turned her eyes to the floor. "Somebody tried to kill her last night."

Chapter 18

Cal didn't reach the hospital until much later that morning. Hanging up after Raj's phone call, she had noticed Plato's flushed cheeks, sunken eyes, and rapid breathing, but she hadn't thought much of it until he staggered out of bed for more Advil and collapsed to the floor.

"Plato? *Plato?*" Half dressed, she had rushed to his side. He wasn't unconscious, just light-headed and a little confused. And *hot*—like the Little Engine That Could, huffing and puffing away on the floor, arms and legs pinwheeling as he struggled to get back on his feet.

Cal helped him up and tucked him back into bed with a thermometer and a dozen or so blankets, then watched the mercury swell all the way up to a hundred and four before finally slowing down. She sat with Plato for an hour after dosing him with Advil and Tylenol, waiting for the fever to break.

It did—all the way down to a hundred and three. So she poured a cool bath and plunged his complaining body into it, half expecting a gout of steam when his fiery skin touched the water.

After a few minutes of shivering in the chilly bath, he managed a weak grin. "Next time our basement floods, I'll use a rubber raft. This cold water stuff is getting kind of old."

"You should take better care of yourself," Cal clucked.

"I think I caught a chill in the anatomy lab," Plato complained. "Or maybe it happened out on the ski slope Friday night."

"You didn't *have* to come outside. If Candice Erdmann hadn't—" But Cal stopped talking when she saw that Plato's little shivers had grown to convulsive tremors. She helped him out of the tub, swaddled him in four towels and his biggest, fluffiest robe, then trotted him back to bed.

A hundred and one.

"I feel all right now," he insisted. "Really, I do."

She gave him a dubious frown, and felt his forehead.

"You need to go and find out how Tiffany's doing," Plato pointed out. "Raj must be crazy with worry."

Cal grabbed her pager from the bedside table and flicked it on. She pulled the phone over to Plato's side of the bed and lifted the receiver to make sure it was working. "If you start feeling funny again, or if the fever gets worse, page me. Okay?"

Beneath the mountain of blankets, Plato nodded solemnly.

"I want you to stay in bed today. And take your temperature every hour. And—"

"And I want *you* to quit worrying. I'll be *fine*." He reached for his book, an old John Irving novel he'd somehow missed, flipped it open and started reading. He glanced over the top of the cover. "You still here?"

"All right, all right." She had gotten up then, brandishing the beeper. "You *page* me if you start feeling crummy. Understand?"

"Yes, Mom."

Standing in Riverside General's lobby, Cal felt a sudden twinge of guilt. After all, she *had* forced him to come to the tutoring sessions, to the ski outing, to Smythe's party. But how was she to know he was really sick? Plato was always whining about colds, or headaches, or upset stomachs. All men did. She had imagined it was just more of the same.

Next time he started complaining, she would just pop the thermometer into his mouth. That would shut him up, one way or another.

She trotted off toward the elevators and rode up to the third floor, to the SICU—the Surgical Intensive Care Unit. Where the sickest patients in the hospital stayed. Where the mortality rate was the highest. Where Tiffany Cramer lay in a bed like any other patient, her fate just a roll of the dice, for all Cal knew.

Jeremy Ames was pacing the hallway just outside the elevator. His head jerked up when the door opened, and his face broke into a wide smile when he spotted Cal. He seemed relieved.

"Hey, Cally. What gives?"

"What are *you* doing here, Jeremy? This isn't a homicide case." Cal's throat choked with sudden fear. "*Is* it?"

He shook his head and rushed over to squeeze her shoulder. "No, kiddo. Nothing like that." His bulging eyes squinted curiously. "I was just wondering if what happened last night might be connected with the Abel case. But it doesn't seem to be. Unless you know something I don't."

"I don't know anything yet," Cal sighed. "What happened?"

Ignoring the NO SMOKING signs plastered all over the walls, Jeremy lit a cigarette.

"Looks like she got mugged, just outside Siegel." He shrugged and slumped into one of the orange plastic chairs propped against the wall, and waited for Cal to sit beside him. "She was working late at Siegel last night. In the pharmacology lab. I guess she does that a lot?"

Cal nodded.

Jeremy flashed that curious squint again—like a Dachshund with a speck of dust in its eye. "You knew her pretty well?"

"I was tutoring her." Cal sighed. "We were—*are*—getting to be good friends. Her boyfriend called me at home this morning."

The detective grunted. "It's a bummer, but it could have been a lot worse. She got clocked over the head somewhere in Siegel's parking lot. The guard says he heard something out there around one o'clock—just after the Cramer girl had walked out the door. A screech of tires, he thinks. Or maybe a scream. But he didn't see anything through the security office windows." Jeremy rolled his eyes. "Most of the parking lot is screened from those windows. He didn't even leave the office to take a look. Some security."

"Siegel's finest." Actually, Cal didn't much blame the guard. Who would want to venture outside in that neighborhood late at night?

"Some bag lady found her in an alley. Totally out of it, head bleeding all over the place." He took a long drag, stared at his cigarette like he was surprised to find it in his hands, then shrugged. "She called nine-one-one."

"Nice bag lady."

"The girl's purse was missing, so they brought her in as a Jane Doe. The hospital got the ID when an intern recognized her as a Siegel student. Down in the ER." Hands in his lap, he stared at the spotless steel elevator doors. "Cleveland Police are handling the investigation. The cop in charge says they've had a lot of muggings in that neighborhood lately. Lots of crackhouses around there. They found a piece of iron pipe in the weeds near the parking lot. Same blood type, same blond hair."

Cal winced. "How'd she end up in an alley?"

"From the trail of blood, they figure she blacked out, then woke up and wandered into that alley where the bag lady found her," Ames explained. "The investigating officer's calling it a smash-and-grab that went haywire."

Jeremy didn't sound convinced.

"But you came here anyway," Cal pointed out.

He nodded and turned slowly to face her. "What do you think?"

Cal took a deep breath. "I think Tiffany Cramer knew something. I think she's lucky to be alive."

Jeremy's face hardened, and his mouth drew to a thin line. He nodded again. "I was afraid of that."

"She left a couple of messages on the answering machine last night, while we were at Smythe's party." Cal frowned. "She wanted to talk to me about something. Something she didn't want to leave on the machine. She sounded sort of scared, but sort of excited. I wish I'd been home. Maybe I could have—"

"And maybe I could have solved this damn case before someone else got hurt." He patted her arm. "Enough with the *mea culpa*'s—we've both got a good case of the guilts. Let's do something about it."

Cal nodded.

"How about if you start by finding out how Tiffany is?" Ames jerked a thumb at the swing doors to the SICU. "There's a crotchety old nurse in there—won't let me into the family waiting room, won't let me talk to anyone." He scowled. "She wouldn't even give me Tiffany's condition. Her mouth's buttoned tight as a—well, very tightly."

Cal smiled. "Okay. And maybe I can get a word in with her boyfriend, or her family. Maybe she told them something worthwhile."

But that hope was dashed as soon as Cal met Judge Cramer. He was standing just inside the swing doors, at the entrance to the family waiting room. He grabbed Cal's elbow as she came by.

Raj was nowhere to be seen. He was probably hiding from the judge.

"You a nurse here?" Cramer snarled.

"I'm a doctor." Cal looked down at his hand. "And you're holding my arm."

Reluctantly, he loosened his grip and let his hand fall back to his side. "I'm Judge Cramer. My daughter's in Bed Three."

The judge wasn't anything like Cal had expected. She had pictured a tall man. Thin, with silvery hair and a distinguished manner. Someone very judgelike, very dignified.

Tiffany's father was just the opposite. Almost as short as Cal, and almost as wide as the doorway. A fringe of Grecian Formula circled his great globe of a head, with a few wispy strands painted over the north pole. A bulbous nose marked the equator, and red and purple veins stood out like so many rivers and streams.

Cal instantly disliked him. She tried to cut him some slack, to think of him as a distraught parent, Tiffany Cramer's father.

But it didn't work.

"I *demand* to see the neurosurgeon in charge." He reached for the collar of his judge's robe, realized he wasn't wearing one, and scratched his flabby neck instead.

Apparently, Judge Cramer didn't realize that nobody *demands* to see neurosurgeons—it wouldn't do them any good. In the hospital hierarchy, neurosurgeons were one step below God. Few would admit to it, though.

"I've been waiting here for *fifteen* minutes," Cramer continued. He checked his wristwatch. "I'm a *very* busy man."

Cal frowned. Judge Cramer wasn't up for reelection this year, and court cases weren't heard on Sunday. He certainly wasn't late for a date on the golf course. Maybe he had tickets for the Cavs game this afternoon. Or a date with his tailor—Cramer's flashy suit fit him like a sausage skin.

Bottling her temper, Cal managed a tight smile. "I'll see what I can do."

The nursing station was a short walk up the hall: a broad circle of plastic and steel and glass that reminded Cal of the bridge on the Starship Enterprise. Monitor screens glowed with electrocardiogram traces, blood pressures, heart and breathing rates, data flowing across their screens as smoothly as rain. Beneath the hushed lighting, residents, nurses, and ward clerks quietly studied charts or tapped away at keypads. Two bright red crash carts were drawn up like sentries at opposite sides of the station, charging themselves for the next crisis. Hanging from one of the chart racks, a pilfered sign read OPEN 24 HOURS—WE NEVER CLOSE. At the far end of the circle, a computer sat in majestic splendor beneath a single floodlight, awaiting orders to calculate medication drip rates, ventilator settings, or the price of a take-out order from Shooter's.

Surrounding the bridge was a curving bank of windows showing neither Klingon warships nor streaking stars but very sick humans. Few of the privacy curtains were drawn; most of the patients were too ill to care about privacy. Tiffany Cramer was out in plain view, in a bed close to one of the crash carts. Not a good sign.

She wasn't breathing on her own, either. Tiffany and most of the other SICU patients were hooked up to ventilators, their chests rising and falling in measured cadence with the huffs of the machines: an orchestra of sighs. Moving closer, Cal could see that Tiffany's long blond hair—what was left—was thatched and matted with blood. Her eyes were almost swollen shut and framed by dark circles: the raccoon's mask of severe head injury. A central intravenous line snaked up the sleeve of her gown to enter the subclavian vein. A spiderweb of wires and cables relayed information to the monitor hanging over her bed along with its twin out at the nursing station.

"Can I *help* you, Doctor?" A nurse was hovering at Cal's elbow, studying her name badge and frowning with disapproval. Cal didn't blame her—in the rush to leave this morning, she'd mistakenly donned the ID tag from the Cuyahoga County Morgue.

She riffled through her pockets, found the Riverside General tag, and made the switch. "I'm a friend of Tiffany Cramer's. Can you tell me who is her attending physician?"

The nurse scowled. She was gray-haired and stern, with the sturdy build of a Sherman tank. Probably the same lady who had stiff-armed Jeremy. She stood for several seconds, stretching her chins a little and peering down her nose. Like Cal was some exotic bug, and she wasn't sure if it was poisonous.

But then she glanced up over Cal's shoulder and her face cracked into a sudden smile. "Doctor Veravada! This woman here is—"

"Cal Marley!" the voice boomed behind her.

Cal whirled and saw a familiar face. "Teddy! Thank goodness."

"Why thank goodness? Virtue is its own reward!" Teddy Veravada's plump brown jowls crinkled into a smile. "You are friends with this medical student, Tiffany Cramer, yes?"

Cal nodded and shot a worried glance toward Tiffany's cubicle.

"Then come!" His voice boomed out across the quiet unit. At the nursing station, heads lifted from charts and keyboards, then quickly turned away when the neurosurgeon was recognized. "I'm taking care of her. We must have a talk."

She followed him down the curved hallway leading to the step-down unit. Halfway there, Teddy keyed open a door and flicked on the lights. It was a typical conference room, with a long Formica table, comfortable swivel chairs, and a couple of fake potted plants. Here in the center of the hospital, the fake plants enjoyed fake sunlight streaming from two fake windows on the far wall. The artificial windows were expensive, but this was the place where doctors met families to discuss the outlook for their loved ones in the SICU. The little room needed all the atmosphere it could get.

Teddy sprang into one of the swivel chairs and propped his Hush Puppies on the long plastic table. When Cal entered and sat down, Teddy was still smiling.

Not that Teddy was his real name. Cal had seen it once, printed on one of the pathology forms. Well, most of it, anyways. It was too long to fit on the forms, far too long for most people to pronounce or remember.

The neurosurgeon preferred "Teddy," and so did everyone else. For one thing, the name fit. With his chubby brown cheeks, furry black beard, and plump middle, Veravada resembled an overstuffed and overly energetic teddy bear.

With a personality to match. Teddy Veravada was an exceptional neurosurgeon, and a sweetheart. Though he was Riverside's best, he still treated his patients and colleagues with respect. Especially Cal. Whenever he was working on a difficult surgery, he asked specifically for Dr. Marley to analyze the frozen sections—the specimens that were collected during surgery and often determined how he would handle the rest of the operation. Cal had taken an extra year of neuropathology before branching off into forensics. Teddy knew that. He trusted her implicitly. He owed her many favors.

He smiled again. "I have good news for you, I think!"

Cal's ears rang. To Teddy, the entire world needed hearing aids. Or they would, soon enough. But she smiled back. "Good news about Tiffany?"

"Yes." He took a pen from his pocket and tapped it against the bridge of his nose. "You are familiar with much of the clinical picture? Or should I start at the beginning?"

"The beginning, I think." Cal hadn't looked over Tiffany's chart yet.

"She reached the emergency room at three o'clock this morning. Comatose, of course." Tap, tap, tap went the pen. He took a deep breath. "She did not look good, but looks are not everything, are they? The resident was convinced that she had an epidural hematoma. When I asked him what we should do, he said perhaps we should trephine her skull. Can you believe it?"

Cal shuddered. Trephining—one of the oldest medical treatments in history. The ancient Romans carried small hand drills in their medical kits—useful for releasing evil spirits from the head. In modern times, a trephining instrument—a sort of tiny circle-cutting saw—was very rarely used to release accumulated blood and relieve the pressure on the brain. But the procedure carried some risk.

"She has an epidural hematoma?" Cal asked, feeling sick. Things were looking worse for Tiffany.

"No! The emergency CT was clear. She is very hard-headed—the follow-up MRI just showed a very mild brain contusion and a hairline fracture of the temporal bone. *Trephining!*" Teddy spat in amazement. "We didn't *need* the CT anyway—all we had to do was check her reflexes. This younger generation, all they want to do is scan, scan, scan. Cover their asses against malpractice, instead of using this." He tapped his forehead.

"She has reflexes?" Cal asked hopefully.

"Excellent reflexes. Excellent! As normal as yours or mine. And shortly after I examined her in Emergency, she began moving." Teddy's laugh was like a thunderclap. "The resident nearly fainted. Over the course of the day, Tiffany's coma has progressed to a semicoma. And now she is showing signs of genuine alertness."

"Looking at her, I thought she was still in a coma," Cal mused. Talking to Teddy was like riding a roller coaster. She had thought Tiffany's outlook was grim, but the neurosurgeon acted like she might be home in time for dinner.

"A *semicoma*," Teddy corrected. "With an injury like hers—a sharp, blunt blow to the left side of the head, apparently followed by a fall, the young lady *should* be unconscious. The brain is just doing a little repair job, see? Closed for inventory."

"She's still on a respirator," Cal pointed out. "Is she breathing on her own at all?"

"Of course." Teddy flapped a heavily jeweled hand, unconcerned. "A simple precaution, to maintain oxygenation. As her recovery progresses, we'll start weaning her from the ventilator. With luck, we will extubate her tonight. Or perhaps sometime tomorrow. Barring any complications, she should be able to speak tomorrow, and perhaps move to the step-down unit."

"That's *wonderful*." Cal felt the tension draining away.

"Of course, we must observe her very closely for development of intracranial hemorrhage—especially subarachnoid. And the MRI scan *did* show the hairline fracture, the mild confusion." He grinned. "But I think she will recover quite nicely. *Without* the trephining."

A discreet knock sounded, and the conference room door swung slowly open. The nurse who had confronted Cal peered around the edge of the door. Facing Teddy, she looked less like a Sherman tank and more like a shy old Volkswagen.

"Doctor Veravada?" Her voice was soft as suede. "Judge Cramer would like to speak to you about his daughter. I tried to tell him you were—"

"Yes, yes. Of course." Teddy stood. "So you see, Cal, we're not out of the woods yet. But there's quite a bit of sunlight, and the forest seems to be thinning."

"Thank you, Teddy."

They walked back to the unit together.

"She is a student of yours?" he asked.

"Yes. A very promising one." Cal thought of Tiffany's

"photographic" memory, the lectures down in the anatomy lab—Tiffany Cramer was gathering some firsthand experience of the anatomy of the skull. And Cal remembered Samantha's conviction that Tiffany Cramer would *be* somebody someday. Cal just hoped she would get the chance.

They stopped outside the family waiting room; Judge Cramer was barring the doorway. Raj Prasad was trapped behind him, peering past his bulk. Compared to the judge, Raj looked like a starved waif.

"You!" Cramer glared at Cal. "I thought you were going to get my daughter's doctor."

Ignoring Teddy, the judge stepped aside and turned, pointing a shaking finger at Raj. "And I will *not* tolerate this young gentleman's presence here. This is a *family* waiting room, for members of the immediate family. Not for—"

"Raj!" Teddy's face lit up with sudden recognition. He squeezed past Judge Cramer and shook Raj's hand warmly. *"Namaste! Kem cho, bhai?"*

The room was filled with a sudden torrent of Gujarati. Apparently, Teddy and Raj knew each other very well. Apparently, they had a lot of catching up to do.

From Raj's face, Teddy might have been a cousin, or an uncle: Perhaps he was.

"Another one!" Cramer fumed. He huffed at Teddy, rolled his eyes, and looked to Cal for sympathy. "Who *is* he, anyway?"

"Doctor Veravada," Cal replied. "He's your daughter's neurosurgeon."

She decided to go talk things over with Jeremy, and leave the trio to sort things out themselves.

Chapter 19

Plato made his infamous Code Blue Chili whenever he had a cold. Lying in bed alone with his novel after Cal had finally left, he realized that was his problem. With all the tutoring and skiing and partying this week, he hadn't had time to make his favorite meal. A cure-all that worked better than anything Jonathan Ebbings could devise—and one that wouldn't give him a hangover, either.

So he pulled on a pair of sweats and his latest James Taylor T-shirt, stepped into his woolly moccasin slippers, and padded downstairs to the kitchen. He rummaged through the pantry for tomato sauce and kidney beans and canned plum tomatoes, found a few reasonably healthy onions lurking underneath the sink, and dragged out the big can of olive oil. As usual, all the pilots were out on the old stove; he nearly singed his beard off trying to get the burner lit.

The shredded beef was sizzling in the olive oil and Plato was crying over the diced onions when the telephone rang. It was Homer.

"You smelled it, huh?" Plato asked.

"Smelled what?" Homer's voice was thick with sleep. "Hey, Cally left a message on my machine this morning. Said she wanted to talk over the Abel case with me."

"Right." Plato drained the beef and tossed the onions in. Pivoting around and under the telephone wire, he found a lid for the pan and turned the flame down.

"So I thought maybe it would be better if I came over. So we could talk face-to-face."

"Your TV broken again?"

"Not *again*," Homer said. "*Still*. It never came out of the shop. How'd you know?"

"There's a Cavs game this afternoon." Plato glanced at the stove clock. "It starts in exactly forty-five minutes. You live forty minutes away. That just gives you time to roll your lazy lawyer self out of bed, get dressed, hop in your car, and make it down here in time for the tip-off."

"You should be a detective."

"My intellectual powers would be seriously wasted."

"La-de-da. Hey—you got any of that chili you made last New Year's? Remember how you were going to freeze some?"

Plato could almost swear he heard Homer *sniff.*

"You could get a job finding truffles," he told his cousin.

"Huh?"

"Nothing." He stuck a can of plum tomatoes into the can opener and turned it on. From out of nowhere, Dante sprang to the counter, slid past the can opener, and flopped onto the floor again, nearly breaking his neck. He arched his back and walked away haughtily. "We ate the chili already. A couple of weeks ago."

"Oh." Homer sounded hurt. "Then maybe I should just bring a pizza."

"Forget it." Plato bent down to get their biggest soup pot from an undersink cabinet. Standing again, he staggered a little and almost lost his balance. The room went yellow for a second, then cleared. "Forget it. I'm making some more right now."

"More chili?"

"Yeah." Plato heard a sharp *-click-.* "Homer? Homer?"

He hung up the phone. Behind him came the slow snickety-snick of claws on linoleum, like the drumroll at an execution. Blind Foley was hobbling across the kitchen floor. He sat and licked Plato's hand. His reactions were a little slower than Dante's.

"Foley the Wonderdog," Plato said fondly. "Sorry, buddy. It isn't dog food, either."

Foley licked his chops and stared up at Plato with those sad, cloudy eyes. Foley *had* been a Wonderdog, years ago. Back when Plato was in college, he had taught the dog to play basketball, of a sort. The Australian shepherd would leap after passes or rebounds or dribbles, sacrificing his body to knock the ball off its trajectory. His jumping abilities were phenomenal for such a short-legged dog. Plato always played shirts and skins, so his dog could tell what the sides were. Foley had won many bets and helped win more than his share of pickup games for Plato and his friends.

Now, even Dante didn't tease him anymore. The cat was curled up beside the heating vent, blocking most of the airflow with his puffy orange fur, staring at Foley with bland distaste.

"I think we need to find someone for Homer," Plato told his dog.

Foley nodded encouragingly, tongue lolling from the corner of his mouth.

"Someone who can cook." He shivered. God, it was *cold* all of a sudden. "My cousin is going to eat us into the poorhouse."

Foley licked his hand again.

"You're right. That's uncharitable." Plato chopped the plum tomatoes in the blender and added them to the monstrous soup pot, along with the tomato sauce, shredded beef, and onions. He opened the kidney beans and stirred them in, too, fiddling with the burner flame until it was just perfect.

The room went yellow again. For an instant, the flame seemed to flare, roiling up and engulfing the pot. Plato blinked and it was gone. He rubbed his eyes. "Sheesh!"

He thought about his cousin again. "On the other hand, Homer does more than his share of the work around here. He deserves a free lunch once in a while."

"Right," Foley replied.

Plato glanced down, astonished. Foley's bark had sounded just like human speech. The dog could be on Letterman.

"Think the Cavs will take it all this year?" Plato asked his dog.

Foley said nothing.

"Me neither," Plato agreed, relieved. He opened the spice cupboard and pulled out the cumin, red pepper, garlic, paprika, rosemary, black pepper, and cinnamon. At least, he *thought* it was cinnamon. He had a little trouble reading the label. Maybe he'd try a little nutmeg this time. And vanilla, and ginger. He was feeling generous. "Think they'll make the playoffs?"

"They've had too many injuries," Dante meowed from across the room.

Plato nodded absently. He'd expected that kind of pessimism from the cat. Dante was smart, but he always looked at the bad side of things.

Shaking the spices into the bubbling cauldron, Plato realized that something was very wrong. Deep down, he knew that even the smartest of cats had trouble speaking in complete sentences.

He pressed his hand to his face. His cheeks felt even hotter than the chili. In fact, if the pilot went out again, he wouldn't need a match. He could probably light the flame just by pressing his forehead to the burner.

Taking stock, Plato realized that he felt terrible again. Barely able to stand. He slumped over to one of the kitchen chairs. His throat was nearly swollen shut, his sinuses were about to burst, and his head thrummed like a boiler ready to blow. He cleared his throat and launched a horrible coughing fit.

Foley padded over and lay on his feet, glancing up at him with concern.

"I think I need some medicine," Plato told him.

Happily, the dog didn't reply.

Plato tottered across the kitchen to the medicine cupboard. One Dimetapp, two Sudafeds, two Tylenols, and three Advils. He peered at the colorful mound of pills in his hand and decided that wasn't enough. It was time for the heavy artillery. Time for an antibiotic.

Plato added an amoxicillin capsule to the pile. One of the big five-hundred-milligram jobs. It looked like a horse pill. He coughed gingerly, realizing that he might have trouble swallowing so many pills. He pressed beneath his chin. Tender lymph nodes stuck out like marbles at the angle of his jaw and down the sides of his neck. Probably strep.

How ironic it would be if Cal came home to find that he'd choked to death on an antibiotic pill.

He couldn't have that. So he rinsed out the blender and whipped up an icy cold milk shake, tossing the pills in and hearing them snap and gronkle into tiny swallowable pieces. Pretty colors swirled through the shake when Plato finally stopped the blender. He took a quick taste.

"Needs more amoxicillin, I think." He tossed in a couple of more capsules and flipped the blender on again. He needed a loading dose anyway.

For good measure, he tossed a few amoxicillin capsules

into the chili, too. Their shiny red coats glistened and bubbled as they sank below the surface.

The doorbell rang just as Plato was downing the last of his shake. He walked to the door, licking foam from his lips. He felt better already.

Homer stamped the snow from his thigh-high hiking boots and ducked inside. Unzipping his leather jacket, he paused for a sniff. A blissful smile crossed his face. "That smells *great,* Plato. One of these days, you'll have to give me your recipe."

"I never use a recipe," Plato answered. "It's a little different every time."

"Forget Albright, Cally." A couple of hours later, Homer was stuffing himself with tortilla chips and salsa; Plato had insisted that the chili wasn't quite ready yet. "He's got a cast-iron alibi for last night. One that you're not going to believe."

"You're right—I'm not going to believe *any* alibi of his," she insisted. "Did Jeremy tell you what Sergei saw? The red Corvette, tearing out of the parking lot the night Marilyn died?"

"He didn't need to," Homer answered patiently. "You told me about that an hour ago."

"I did?"

In a sleepy haze, Plato watched the two argue, without quite following the gist of their conversation. The Cavs game was all but forgotten. For once, Cleveland was soundly trouncing the arch-villain Chicago Bulls by a laughable margin.

Plato was tucked into the couch beneath two blankets and an afghan, a cup of hot tea beside him. He was lucky to be downstairs at all. Arriving home, Cal had found him in the kitchen with Homer, fussing over his chili. She had shooed Homer out of the kitchen and snarled at Plato, threatening to cudgel him with a frying pan unless he got back into bed.

"I'm *fine,* Cally," he had told her. "Really I am."

He decided not to bring up his conversations with Foley and Dante. Even a pathologist would realize that something was amiss.

And so it was. The milk shake had taken much of the fever away, but Plato still felt awful. In the back of his mind, he wondered if something were seriously wrong. If his sickness was more than just strep throat.

But with the attack on Tiffany last night, the case seemed to be coming to a crisis. Plato couldn't shake the feeling that Marilyn's disk held something important. But it was obvious that nobody else thought so.

He'd get himself checked out after he deciphered the disk. Tomorrow was Monday. He had some time open in the morning; he'd run to the medical school and work on Marilyn's computer. He was certain he'd find the answer then.

"So what's the cast-iron alibi?" Cal asked Homer. She was perched in a chair by the heating vent, Dantelike, with her legs tucked up under the giant Bulls sweatshirt that she'd brought with her from Chicago. "Don't tell me—Albright was having drinks with a senator when Tiffany was attacked."

"Even better." Homer was sprawled in the old vinyl recliner, a can of beer in one hand and the television remote in the other. "He was having drinks with Tricia Abel."

"Tricia Abel?" Cal sat up and squeezed her forehead. "Wait a minute. You mean, he has the audacity to claim he was having drinks with Marilyn's daughter?"

"He claims it, Tricia Abel claims it, and the waiter at Hornblower's claims it." Homer had just gotten off the phone with Jeremy Ames. "Jeremy has already talked with all of them himself. Believe me, Cal, when you told me about that red Corvette, I was ready to pin it on Albright." He shrugged. "But I guess we were wrong."

"He was having drinks with Marilyn Abel's daughter," Cal repeated. She flopped around on the chair and gave a little gasp, like a fish washed up on the sand. She stared off at the cold fireplace and blinked several times. "He was having drinks with Marilyn Abel's daughter."

"You're repeating yourself," Homer pointed out.

Finally, Cal snapped out of it. She sat up hopefully. "This was the first time they've seen each other, right?"

"No," Plato replied from his nest. Homer and Cal glanced his way, both surprised. "At least, I don't think so. When Albright's book showed up at Jonathan's house, Tricia was very eager to return it."

"Albright and Tricia Abel have been seeing each other pretty regularly, for quite a while now," Homer said.

"Keeping it kind of secret, trying not to stir up gossip at the medical school. But Marilyn knew about it. According to Tricia, she wasn't exactly thrilled, but she didn't put up much of a fuss, either."

"He must be fifteen years older than Tricia," Plato mused.

Cal shrugged. "Maybe they were in on this together."

"No," Plato replied flatly. He thought he knew Tricia Abel well enough to rule *that* out.

"Or maybe Tiffany really *was* mugged." Cal leaned back and closed her eyes. "Then it could still be Albright."

"That's one hell of a coincidence," Plato pointed out.

"Or maybe Albright *hired* somebody to—"

"Yeah, right. He hired a hit man to bump off his medical student." Plato's lip twisted. "You're as bad as Jeremy, Cal. Has it ever occurred to you that maybe Albright *didn't* kill Marilyn Abel? That maybe he *didn't* need the money? Who knows?—maybe he's completely innocent."

"Not *completely* innocent," Homer grumbled. "He's gotten about a dozen parking tickets from Siegel security. He likes to park at that loading dock by the pharmacology office." He glanced over at Cal. "But he probably *is* innocent of murder. The night Marilyn died, he went out to dinner with Tricia Abel. She drove—picked him up after work, and dropped him off after dinner. She didn't actually *see* him get in his car and leave, but she dropped him off at around nine o'clock. He swears he never went inside."

"And the silent alarm went off at eight-fifteen," Plato pointed out.

"*If* that was the murderer," Cal argued. "*If* the clocks were right, and *if* the security guard wrote down the time right. We don't have a good time of death, remember. Marilyn was seen alive by the security guard at seven forty-five. She could have died anytime between then and early the next morning."

"Come on, Cal—"

"Okay, okay." Cal sighed. "If the killer wasn't Albright, who was it? We haven't really considered anyone else."

"*I* have," Homer answered. "Jeremy and I have talked to a couple of dozen people in the last few days." He raised a grizzly paw and ticked off the names on his fingers. "Tricia Abel. Jonathan Ebbings. Malenkov. Bob Stahl and Therese Vogel. Practically the entire damn faculty out at that medical school. Every single security guard. Those two drug execs—Erdmann and Welkins." He grinned. "Now there's a friendly couple."

"Where were *they* last night?" Cal asked suddenly.

"Who?"

"Candice Erdmann. And Arnold Welkins."

"Why? You think one of them killed Marilyn Abel so their company could get that new drug?" He chuckled. "I've heard of company loyalty, but isn't that going a little far?"

"Not for Arnold Welkins." Quickly, Cal recounted the scene with the two drug executives last night. "Welkins *owns* a big chuck of Chadwick-Medicon. If the company folds—like Candice hinted it might—he stands to lose his shirt. On the other hand, Patracin could be a gold mine for him. With Marilyn gone, he'd have half a chance of acquiring the patent." She waved a hand and glanced at her husband. "Plato's friend Candice is a high-power exec at Valdemar. She could have been just as eager to get her claws into Patracin. And maybe Marilyn wanted to hold onto the patent, or sell it to another company."

"Huh." Homer swung his gaze back to the television. The Cavs game was over, so he switched over to the public station. On the Serengeti plain, a lioness stalked a sick water buffalo, brought it down, and fed it to her young. "Neither of them have very solid alibis for the night of Marilyn Abel's death. Welkins was supposedly in his car, or at some downtown club, and the Erdmann woman was home by herself the whole evening. She says."

"I think we need to take a closer look at those two."

"So do I." He flicked across the channels and stopped at the weather. A big winter storm stretched from Chicago to Canada, swallowing Lake Erie like a giant green amoeba. It was sweeping down toward Cleveland. The weatherman was trying to hide his excitement. "Tomorrow's not too busy for me—maybe I can try to see them again."

"Mind if I come along?" Cal asked.

"Not at all. That might help." He flicked back to the lions, who were just finishing their meal, then glanced over at Plato. "My stomach's shriveled up like a dried prune. You think that chili's ready yet?"

"I don't know." Plato sighed and flapped a fevered hand over the blanket. "Maybe Cal should bring me a taste."

"Forget it." Homer levered himself up from the recliner and dropped the remote in Plato's lap. "I'll taste it myself. You want a taste, Cal?"

"Sure." She followed him into the kitchen.

Plato could hear them talking as they got the food ready. Their faraway words ran together with a sound like water gurgling over a rocky stream bed.

He closed his eyes. The burbling stream became the trickling of water in an aquarium. Smythe's aquarium. Plato was leaning on the Plexiglas, asking the bartender for another drink. The bartender was Jonathan Ebbings. He was grinning, mixing together another one of his concoctions. The liquid bubbled and fizzed, mist rising from its surface. As he handed it across the bar, Plato felt the Plexiglas crack beneath his weight. His reflexes were impossibly slow; his arms felt like lead weights were tied to his wrists. He tried to move, to struggle, but his paralyzed hands were dragged down, down into the water, down to the pretty hovering fish with its long, poisonous spines. The fish moved closer, closer.

He tried to scream, but nothing came out.

"Plato! *Plato!*" He opened his eyes to find Cal perched on the edge of the sofa near his head, shaking his shoulders. Homer was sitting on the coffee table, holding his wrists.

Frowning, his cousin finally released his hands. "You were thrashing around like a wild man. I thought you were going to give yourself a black eye."

He squinted at Plato with concern, then walked over to the recliner and dove into his bowl of chili.

"That must have been some dream," Cal said. She slid down the sofa, handed him a bowl of chili, and set her own dish in her lap.

Plato nodded. "A fever dream. I was just about to get stung by a lionfish when you woke me up."

Cal shook her head. "You and that lionfish. I don't think I'll ever get to see Cape Cod again."

"It was just a dream, Cally." Plato shrugged. "Anyway, there aren't any lionfish on the East Coast."

He glanced over at his cousin. Homer was lapping up the chili, his face only inches from the rim of the bowl, his spoon moving in a rapid blur, back and forth, back and forth. Not a drop was spilled on his favorite sweater, a bright red merino wool pullover he'd brought back from Scotland last year.

"You've got great technique, Homer," Plato told him. "You're an artist—like those Ukrainian gymnasts on the parallel bars. It looks so easy, I'd swear I could do it myself." He contemplated his dish sadly. A masterpiece of chili and shell macaroni, blanketed by a thick coat of dripping cheddar cheese. "But I don't think I can. I'm not very hungry."

Homer halted the spoon and glanced over at him with sudden concern. He turned to Cal. "You'd better get him to a doctor. He's never been *this* sick."

"I know." Cal felt his forehead and frowned. "Time for more Advil, I think."

Plato grimaced. "I'm going to burn a hole in my stomach."

"Tylenol, then." She got the bottle and dished out another two pills, watching as Plato downed them with visible effort. "First thing in the morning, I'm calling Nathan."

Nathan Simmons was one of Plato's friends from medical school. He was also their family doctor.

"You're going to see him tomorrow if I have to drag you there myself. Understand?"

"I've got a full office day scheduled," Plato protested. "Anyway, it's probably just strep. Maybe a little bronchitis."

He coughed, setting off another big spell of racking heaves. Cal pounded his back. Homer glanced at him with alarm.

"I think he's got pneumonia," the lawyer said.

"I wouldn't be a bit surprised," Cal agreed. She poked his chest. "Dan can cover for you at the office. That's what partners are for."

"I wanted to drop by Siegel and try to decompress that disk," Plato added.

"Tell your computer friend to do it." She turned to Homer. "Or maybe the police have made some progress with it."

Homer shook his head. "One of our systems guys took a look at it. He says it's not an ASCII file."

Plato groaned. "Any *idiot* can see that it's not an ASCII file."

"What's an Askey file?" Cal asked.

"A text file," Plato replied. "Just plain text, so you don't need a special computer program to decode it and read it." He scowled at Homer. "You've got some swell computer guys working for you, huh?"

"He sure is huffy today," Homer observed.

"He's sick," Cal sighed.

"No kidding." Homer brought his dish to the coffee table and reached for Plato's. "You really don't want any of this?"

Plato nodded weakly. "Really."

He was relieved when Homer finally took the food away. The sight and smell were making him queasy.

"This is great stuff, Plato." Cal set her dish down and patted his arm. "Maybe you'll want some tomorrow."

Plato didn't feel like eating anything, ever again.

"I think this is the best chili you've ever made," Homer agreed happily. Plato's bowl was nearly empty, but Homer was slowing down. The spoon's passes were almost visible.

"It's *different*, somehow." Cal turned to him and frowned. "What did you put in it, anyway?"

Plato considered. The afternoon's events were pretty muddled. "I honestly can't remember."

"Nothing poisonous, I hope?" Cal grinned.

He thought back to his conversations wtih Foley and Dante, his pharmaceutical milk shake, the amoxicillin capsules bubbling and dissolving into the chili. He shook his head slowly and smiled. "No. Just lots of things that are good for you."

"A cure for what ails you," Homer agreed, squelching a burp.

"You're so right." Plato closed his eyes and slept.

Chapter 20

Late the next morning, Cal stood at the visitors' entrance to Riverside General Hospital, peering through the swirling snow for a sign of Homer's battered black Chevy Caprice.

She had ridden to work with a friend this morning, leaving Plato home with the Rabbit so he could make it to his appointment with Nathan this afternoon. He had looked a little better this morning; his fever wasn't as high, and he was breathing easier. The antibiotic seemed to be helping.

She had woken up before Plato, snuck downstairs and called in sick for him. Plato's partner, Dan Homewood, had taken his share of sick days this year; he owed Plato a few. Luckily, Dan had a pretty light day scheduled. Mostly meetings. Easy enough to cancel. He asked that Cal call him later tonight and tell him how Plato was doing. Plato had squawked a little when he finally woke up, but he seemed secretly relieved.

Once at the hospital, her first stop had been the SICU. Tiffany Cramer was still there, and still pretty groggy, but she was far more responsive than yesterday. The resident said they expected to remove the breathing tube that afternoon. Teddy had made his rounds at six A.M. and left an illegible scribble in Tiffany's chart. It was a short note, so Cal assumed everything was going well.

A message was waiting for her when she finally reached the pathology lab. Homer had called, saying that he'd swing by the visitors' entrance at eleven-thirty, if she was still interested in talking to Erdmann and Welkins.

She was. So she stamped her feet and breathed on her hands and leaned into the bitterly cold wind while she waited for the assistant county prosecutor to arrive.

She didn't have to wait long. The rusted heap loomed through the snow, sliding to a stop just in front of Cal.

Homer leapt out and led her around to the driver's-side door.

"The other door doesn't open," he explained.

Cal kicked snow from her boots and ducked inside, sliding across the bench seat. Homer hopped in and slipped the Caprice into gear. The car fishtailed its way through the heavy snow and into the turnaround, scraping bottom as it whomped back into the street.

"Needs a new exhaust," Homer said.

"Needs a lot of new things," Cal replied. She had never ridden in Homer's car before. The smooth vinyl seat and dash were riddled with cuts and melt-holes. Homer's old girlfriend had been a smoker, Cal remembered; the car still reeked of cigarettes. The radio had been ripped off last summer; only a gaping hole and a few tattered wires remained, like the socket of some giant tooth. The floor beneath her feet had a big soft spot. Tentatively, she poked the carpet with the toe of her boot. There was nothing beneath but air. A perfectly round hole, about a foot in diameter, covered only by carpet. A Flintsone-mobile.

Nervously, she cranked the window open a little, and shut it again. At least *that* worked.

Cruising along Interstate 90 west, feeling the cushion of wind beneath her feet, Cal had to wonder. Homer wasn't married and never had been. He'd gone to a state university, so his student loans probably weren't as awful as hers or Plato's. He didn't own a house. As far as she knew, he wasn't a gambler or a drug addict.

What did he spend his money on?

"Investments," Homer said suddenly.

Cal started.

"You're wondering where all my money goes, aren't you?"

Cal shrugged. "A little."

"Investments," he repeated. "Very bad investments. I've fired three brokers, but it hasn't helped. I'm so bad at it, people at the office ask what I'm buying—so they can invest in something else."

"Oh." She gazed out the window, a little embarrassed. "We've invested in a rambling wreck of a house. I guess that wasn't the greatest decision, either."

"I know." Homer sighed. "It runs in the family."

Cal nodded slowly. She glanced down at the road map

on the seat between them. It was folded open to the western suburbs. "Who are we seeing first?"

Homer shrugged with one shoulder. He drove cop-style, one hand resting in his lap or fiddling with the heater knobs, the heel of the other hand pressed against the wheel at six o'clock, spinning it through the turns and gunning the engine at just the right moment to keep the tires on a perfect line, regardless of the terrain. Just like Plato—both their fathers had been cops. The Marley Brothers, both beat cops, terrors of the near east side back in the '50s.

Jack Marley had smoked himself into an early grave. And Homer's father was in a posh nursing home out in Avon Lake; Cal guessed that was where a lot of the lawyer's money went.

At least he didn't have to pay doctor's bills; Plato saw Uncle Leo *gratis.* Or *pro bono,* as Homer put it.

"We're heading out to Valdemar Pharmaceuticals," Homer explained, "but we don't have an appointment."

"No?"

"Both their secretaries have been stonewalling me all morning. Took me and Jeremy three days to catch up with them last week."

"Are you sure Candice Erdmann is at the office today?" Cal asked. "She spends a lot of time at Siegel, from what I've heard. I bet she's at the hospitals quite a bit, too."

Homer gave his one-shouldered shrug again. "She'll be there."

He exited the interstate at Columbia and swung north. Valdemar Pharmaceuticals was perched on the lakefront near Huntington Park, on land that had once been the summer home of a wealthy Cleveland family.

A lot of Bay Village had been that way, back in the early 1900s. Summer cottages and summer mansions strung along the sandy beaches and shallow waters where a gentler Lake Erie lapped at the shores.

It was hard to imagine, now. The area was still very residential, very affluent. But the lake was frozen into hoary sheets of ice, a rumpled gray blanket stretching to an invisible horizon. Through a thicket of bare trees, she glimpsed a white ribbon of beach—barren, forlorn, deserted.

The long driveway led to a vast parking lot, neatly scoured and salted. Off to the right stood the old Valdemar mansion, a ruinous cavern of stone and stucco from an

Edgar Allan Poe story. But apparently it was being re-
stored; scaffolding hung from the front and side walls, and
half of the slate roof had been replaced.

Ahead loomed the main facility, the International Head-
quarters of Valdemar Pharmaceuticals, according to the
black marble obelisk at the far end of the parking lot. A
sprawling structure of pink marble, stainless steel, and
curved glass. The top floor, a perfect isosceles triangle,
rested on three columns, each big enough to be office buildings themselves. One area writer had compared the structure to a monstrous slice of deep-dish pizza teetering atop
a trio of beer cans. It was an apt description.

The thought of it also made Cal hungry. It was nearly
lunchtime.

Homer parked in a visitors' slot. They trudged through
the salty slush and over to the sidewalk, a sinuous trail that
branched off to snow-covered gardens or small pavilions or
tiny covered bridges crossing fake, frozen waterfalls.

"Must be beautiful in the summer," Cal mused.

"Like a miniature golf course without the holes," Homer
replied. "I keep asking myself, where's the windmill?"

The path led to the closest beer can: Building A. The
marble-walled lobby was hushed and cool and clean, and
smelled faintly of roses. It reminded Cal of a funeral parlor.
The long, curving reception desk was covered with some
exotic red wood, varnished to a glassy finish and inlaid with
brass pen holders, like the counter at a bank. A very nice
bank.

Apparently it was lunchtime. Just one receptionist was
sitting behind the counter, filing her nails. Homer grabbed
Cal's elbow and guided her past the counter, to the bank
of elevators on the far wall.

"Can I help you?"

Behind them, the receptionist had put down her nail file
and stood. She had blond hair and blue eyes and a chilly,
pained smile, like she was holding ice chips between her
teeth.

"It is customary to register at the reception area, sir."
She picked up one of the pens and gestured. "If I could
please have your name and the party you are trying to
reach?"

"I'm Assistant District Attorney Homer Marley." Homer
walked across the lobby, took the proffered pen, and

dropped it back into its brass well with a loud *snick*. "I need to speak with Candice Erdmann. Immediately."

Her smile melted into a mild, patronizing smirk. "I'm afraid that won't be possible. You telephoned earlier, didn't you?"

"Yes."

"Ms. Erdmann is *still* in conference and cannot be disturbed. Her secretary is *still* out to lunch." She gestured to a group of chairs at the far wall. "Perhaps you would like to have a seat. I could telephone her again once her conference is finished."

Homer grimaced. "And do you have any idea when that might be?"

"I'm sure I couldn't say, sir." She gave the ice-chip smile again. "As I told you, her secretary is out to lunch. Perhaps when she returns, she can help you."

"Last week, it took three days to get through to Ms. Erdmann," Homer replied. "I've been trying all morning and I haven't even reached her secretary today. I think I've been very patient."

"I'm sure you have, sir. But we have been *very* busy. I'm sure you understand. Now, if you would just take a seat over—"

"Come on, Cal." Homer whirled and hurried over to the elevators. Hanging between them, an engraved brass directory of the A building listed only twelve names. Candice Erdmann's was one of them: sixth floor. Homer pushed the Up button.

Behind them, the receptionist squawked something about calling security. She was reaching for the phone just as the elevator doors closed.

Up on the sixth floor, a perfectly round corridor stretched out on either side of the elevator. Cal followed Homer through the doors just in time to see a small, rodentlike fellow darting into the stairwell at the far end of the circle.

"Is that who I think it is?" Cal asked.

"You bet," Homer replied.

Candice Erdmann's office door was at right angles to the elevator, at three o'clock. As far as Cal could see, the entire floor housed only two offices.

"Rank hath its privileges," she observed.

Homer grunted. He knocked on the office door and gestured for Cal to open it.

The office inside was a vast semicircle, fully furnished with sofas, chairs, a fake fireplace, even a wide-screen television tucked into the wall. Three chandeliers hung from the ceiling. The walls and ceiling were paneled in dark cherry. Across the room, a small screened cubicle held a mahogany writing desk with matching chair, a personal computer and printer, and several file cabinets.

The door swung open behind them.

"Here they are." A burly security guard was blocking the doorway. "You two had better come with me."

He took Cal's arm and reached for Homer's, then thought better of it. He gestured to the hall behind him instead. The receptionist was smirking just outside the door.

"That's all right, Martin." Across the room, the cherry paneling had cracked to reveal an invisible doorway. Candice Erdmann stood there, looking slightly breathless. "I'll see them now, please."

The security guard shrugged and turned away. The receptionist's face reddened, but she retreated also.

Candice Erdmann beckoned. "Please come into my office."

They followed her into a room that was only half the size of the foyer outside. It was furnished with more of the same: leather club chairs and sofa, cherry paneling on the walls and ceiling, a pair of fine crystal chandeliers hanging over a vast mahogany desk. The chandeliers probably didn't use much electricity; the window behind her desk covered the entire rear wall of the office in a quarter-circle.

Candice caught their stares and smiled. "Yes, it's smaller than my foyer. But my guests sometimes have to wait a long time, and I like them to be comfortable. And besides, I think I have the better view."

Standing at her desk, she gestured to the window wall behind her. It had the ring of a prepared speech, the conversation starter she used for all her first-time visitors.

It worked, too. Even in the depths of winter, the lake was magnificent. Snow riffled the ice in fine patterns of white on gray, like a monstrous wave-washed sandbar at low tide. Staring at all that vast emptiness, Cal felt small and insignificant.

And with the light behind her, Candice Erdmann seemed

even more impressive. She was wearing a royal blue velvet sheath dress, pearl earrings, and a brightly colored silk scarf. She smiled at them.

"I apologize for the mix-up, Mr. Marley. As the young lady downstairs mentioned, I'm very busy today." She gestured at the two club chairs and sat behind her desk. "I hope we can make this brief."

They sat. Homer steepled his fingers and gazed out at the lake, a faraway look in his eyes. He acted like he had all the time in the world. He even spoke slowly. "You two were getting your stories straight, right?"

Candice frowned. "I'm sure I don't know what you're talking about."

"Arnold Welkins," he prompted.

When she still seemed confused, he dropped his hands and hunched forward in his chair. "Listen, Ms. Erdmann. We've had people tailing you and Arnold, off and on for most of this past week. You've met on at least four separate occasions, not counting this time."

"This time?" She seemed genuinely surprised. She pressed her hand to her scarf. "Why, I—"

"We saw him ducking into the stairwell. That makes five times altogether—twice at Chadwick, twice here, and once at the Crawford Museum." He leaned back again and crossed his legs. "All that fighting and clawing in public— that's just an act, isn't it?"

"You *followed*—" The blood slowly drained from Candice Erdmann's face. She dropped both her hands to the empty desktop. "Yes."

"You were in on this together, weren't you?"

"In on—*no*. No, it's not what you think." She bit her lip. Her fingers drummed the desktop. "Really, it isn't."

"Then what *is* it about?" Cal asked gently.

"I can't—" Candice Erdmann closed her eyes and took a deep breath. She shook her head firmly. "I can't tell you. Yet."

"Then I guess you'll cool your heels in jail until you *can* tell us." Homer slapped his hands on his thighs. "Obstruction of justice charges. You and Arnold both. Separate cells, of course."

"It's not *like* that." She made a face. Her mellow accent was hardening. "It's strictly business."

"A merger," Cal whispered. She'd seen an article in the

business section just last week. For all Candice Erdmann's disparaging talk about Chadwick-Medicon, her own company wasn't doing so well, either. A shortage of R&D."

Candice's head jerked as though she'd been slapped. Cal knew she was right. The drug executive looked at her sharply. "If I tell you, will you promise it doesn't go beyond this room?"

"We can't promise anything," Homer answered quickly. "Except that if you don't give us a good explanation, you and Welkins will both be arrested. And then your secret meetings won't be very secret anymore."

Candice closed her eyes and nodded. "Cal's right. Arnold and I have been working out the details of a merger."

She stared at her hands. "Valdemar has the cash and the distribution network, but our research division doesn't have enough brains to make a good placebo. Chadwick still has a solid research department, thanks to Marilyn Abel, but they're strapped for cash. A merger makes good sense. Arnold and I have been working as liaisons between our two companies."

"Why the big secret?" Homer asked.

"Chadwick-Medicon is a plum ripe for the plucking. All it needs is some cash to become profitable again." She shrugged, as though the answer was obvious. "But with its cash flow problems, it's also a good candidate for a hostile takeover."

She sighed. "Arnold and the other owners want to stay local, keep control and merge with us. But even Valdemar can't afford a bidding war."

"So you two had to pretend to hate each other," Cal observed. "You gave a very convincing act."

"I didn't have to *act* very much." She smiled ruefully. "Maybe I went a little too far Saturday night. It was just such a shock to see Arnold there." She primped her hair and frowned. "I was an old friend of the dean's first wife; we were roommates at Radcliffe. I have no idea why Arnold was invited. He's a rather odious person, isn't he? But business is business."

"And what about Marilyn Abel?" Homer asked. "Was that business, too?"

She looked up, focusing on the doorway behind them. "I don't understand."

"She never would have sold her drug to Valdemar," Cal

said, "if she knew that her ex-husband might profit by it. Had she found out about the merger?"

Candice's face reddened. She turned her gaze to Cal's right shoulder. "I don't appreciate your implication."

"I think you should answer the question, Ms. Erdmann," Homer said. "Had Marilyn Abel found out about the merger?"

Her jaw muscles tightened, giving her a predatory look. But her dark eyes seemed frightened. "I think perhaps I should not answer any more of your questions before consulting with my attorney."

Homer shrugged. "That's fine, Ms. Erdmann." He leaned to hand her a business card across the table. She had to stand to reach it. "That's my office number. You can make an appointment to see me this afternoon, in the company of your attorney. If we don't hear from you by five o'clock, I'll secure a warrant for your arrest as a material witness."

With her index finger, she slid the card around and around on the desktop. Behind her, the great lake seemed as impressive as ever. But Candice Erdmann suddenly seemed very small. She gave a quick nod. Her voice dropped to a whisper. "I understand."

Back outside, Homer took a deep breath. "Now, that's more like it."

Cal nodded. "She seemed pretty shaken up there, near the end."

"No kidding. I think either she did it, or she knows who did."

Cal wasn't so sure. But something Candice said had started another wheel turning in her head. Another path she hadn't even considered.

In the car, Homer glanced at his watch. "Lunchtime. No point trying to chase Welkins down until we've had a proper meal. How about if we run over to Fagan's first?"

"Sorry, Homer." Climbing in, Cal glanced at her Timex. "I'm already having lunch with someone at the medical school."

"Who?"

"Leonard Reiss. The guy whose name was pasted to Marilyn's computer monitor."

"That PD reporter? Jeremy questioned him already—he didn't know anything." Homer shook his head and started the car. "You're just wasting your time."

"So I should cancel, and come to Fagan's with you?"

"Yup."

Cal twisted in her seat and stared at him. "Homer, do you *ever* pay for lunch?"

"Not if I can help it." He frowned thoughtfully. "Maybe I can give Jeremy a call . . ."

Chapter 21

"I never met the woman." Across the table, Leonard Reiss toyed with his salad. "I never even *talked* to her. I wish I had."

Cal frowned. "But on the phone, you told me—"

"I was *supposed* to meet with her. The night she died." He stared at the ceiling, his spiky blond hair waving like a field of ripe wheat. "A Thursday, I think it was. I waited at the Rusted Penguin for over an hour, but she never showed up. That place up the street from the medical school. What a dive."

They were having lunch in Siegel's newly remodeled cafeteria. The shabby olive wallpaper and dusty fake plants had been replaced by new chartreuse wallpaper and cleaner fake plants. The new trays had little compartments like tables on sailing ships, so the food didn't slide around. The plates featured Siegel's logo in gold and blue.

The food hadn't changed. Cal picked at her vegetable lasagna. Either the flat noodles had never been cooked in the first place, or the cook had left the lasagna in the oven all night. The vegetables had melted into a gooey slush. The cheese was a thin layer of crust, like cooled volcanic lava. The tomato sauce had dried and hardened to the consistency of clotted blood.

The company wasn't any better. When Cal had called Leonard Reiss this morning, to ask why his name was mentioned on a Post-It note on a dead woman's computer, he said he wanted to talk it over with her. When she pressed, he acted evasive, merely suggesting that they meet for lunch.

She had agreed, but suggested that they have lunch on her turf—Siegel's cafeteria. With the food as bad as it was, Reiss would have nothing to distract him. He would have no choice but to tell her all he knew.

Which wasn't much.

"What time were you supposed to meet her?" Cal asked.

"Nine o'clock." Reiss lifted a brown lettuce leaf hopefully, peered underneath, then set it back down. He wasn't terribly fat, but he clearly enjoyed eating. He had bulging red cheeks, like a sunburned smuggler with a mouthful of diamonds. The buttons of his shirt were straining to hold his round little belly. His hands were chubby and soft as a little girl's. A wedding band pinched the base of his left ring finger like the string of a balloon.

"Why did she want to meet with you?" Cal asked, exasperated. Getting information from this guy was like interviewing one of the cadavers downstairs. "Did she sound nervous when she called? Or upset?"

"I don't have the faintest notion." He pushed his salad plate away and unwrapped the slice of chocolate cake. A safe bet; almost no cafeteria can screw up chocolate cake. "I was out on a story when her call came in. A kid in the newsroom took her message. She just told him who she was, and said that she had some information I might find interesting, that might be worth a story. I called her office here at Siegel a couple of times that morning, but I couldn't get hold of her."

"Then how did you set up the meeting?"

"She was in and out all day—I guess it was final exam week." The cake was vanishing quickly. His cheeks bulged even further. "She finally left a message with her secretary, asking me to meet her at the Rusted Penguin at nine that evening. I said okay, but she never showed up."

"And you have no idea what it was about?" Cal had trouble hiding her disbelief.

"No." He shook his head. "I honestly wish I did. I'm sure there was a story in it. I assume it may have had something to do with her death."

"But you never volunteered the information to the police?"

"Why should I have?" He shrugged. "No one knew she'd been murdered until last week. A fellow from the sheriff's office called me Saturday afternoon, and I told him everything." He spread his plump little hands. He seemed just as frustrated as Cal. "Believe me, I would have told someone if I had anything worthwhile. I've been poking around a little, here at the medical school and out at those two drug companies. But I can't get interviews with any of the players. I'm not a science writer, so this isn't exactly my home turf."

Cal sighed. "I suppose not."

"I *did* cover that escaping rat business, though." He brushed a hand across the wheat field and smiled proudly. "Mostly because I happened to be out here, looking into the Abel story." He glanced at Cal and his pale eyebrows drew together. "Didn't I see you at Dean Smythe's party Saturday night? Talking with Arnold Welkins?"

"Yes." Cal was staring at the petrified lasagna and losing interest in the conversation. If Leonard Reiss wasn't a science writer, why had Marilyn Abel wanted to reach him?

"You're a friend of his?"

Her eyes snapped back up to the reporter's face. "Friend of whose?"

"Arnold Welkins."

"Hardly."

"Too bad." He seemed surprised. "I wanted to get some quotes from Welkins, and from that lady at Valdemar—Candice Erdmann. But I never could get in to see them."

You're not the only one, Cal mused silently. Aloud, she asked, "Why did you want to reach them?"

"My editor wants me to turn that rat escapade into another feature for the *Sunday Magazine.*" Again, his thick lips twisted in a happy smile. "That would make my second in three months. It would be about research gone awry—I could tie the rat story in with Los Alamos, genetic engineering, and get a slant on the ethics of research. Throw in something controversial, like the fetal tissue business. Maybe talk to a lawyer or two about the legality of regulation." He squinted at her more closely. "You're *sure* you aren't friends with Welkins?"

"I'm positive."

"Huh." His shoulders slumped. "I need someone who can put me in touch with those people. Like that medical student who got mugged—what was her name?"

"I have no idea," Cal lied.

"We could feature you in a little sidebar, if you'd like." He finished his cake and pushed the plate away. "A little op-ed piece. LOCAL PHYSICIAN TAKES STAND ON MEDICAL RESEARCH. Something like that."

"I'm not a researcher. Sorry."

Reiss's face deflated. Even his cheeks shrank a little.

But Cal hardly noticed. She was too busy thinking. Leonard Reiss wasn't a science writer, it was true. But she had suddenly remembered what kind of writer he was. She even remembered the *Sunday Magazine* feature he had written, though she hadn't noticed his byline at the time.

As they walked out of the cafeteria, Reiss pulled a yellow slip of paper from his pocket and grimaced. "You ever get a speeding ticket in a parking lot before?"

"No."

"Some security they've got here." He showed her the ticket. "One faculty member killed last month, a student assaulted yesterday morning. And all these bozos can do is ticket people for doing twelve in a five-mile-per-hour zone. Can you believe it?"

Cal made sympathetic noises.

"Last week, I got another one. For parking in that handicapped space near the front door. How was I supposed to know?—the sign was covered with snow."

She studied the ticket carefully. Typical carbonless paper. At its edge, red letters specified that this was the MOTORIST'S COPY. She handed it back and led him to the front door of the college.

"Hey—if you get any leads on the Abel story, give me a call." He handed her a business card. "Okay?"

"Sure." Cal tucked the card in her pocket and hurried away. If her hunches were right, she had several leads already.

Her first stop was Siegel's medical library. Luckily, they kept back issues of the *Plain Dealer* for a couple of months before discarding them. But they probably wouldn't discard Leonard Reiss's *Sunday Magazine* piece for quite a while. If ever. The librarian had kept the copy behind her desk, handed it over reverently, and told Cal how they planned to make an engraving and display it on the wall.

She read the article carefully again, searching for some hint, some clue. She didn't find it.

Next, she stopped at the security office and checked over the parking ticket records. Sure enough, the security guards had been quite diligent on the night of Marilyn Abel's death.

Finally, she walked outside and checked the handicapped

slot where Leonard Reiss had received his ticket. The slot was near the main entrance, but the wheelchair ramp led to another door farther along to the right. A special handicapped-access door. She entered and followed the logical path to Marilyn's office in the pharmacology department.

It all made perfect sense. Except Cal still didn't understand why.

Chapter 22

Monday afternoon, Plato took a little detour on his way to Nathan's office at Riverside General. He had promised Cal that he would spend the morning in bed, and he had. He had promised her that he would go to his three o'clock appointment with Nathan. And he would.

He had just left home a little bit early. And seeing that he had an extra half hour to kill, Plato decided that he might as well run over to the pharmacology department at Siegel and try to decompress Marilyn's disk. After all, it wasn't like he was dying of pneumonia.

All the same, Plato knew that Cal was supposed to be at Siegel this afternoon, meeting with a reporter or attending a committee meeting or something. So he left his car parked near the loading dock and snuck in the back way. Just to be safe.

He wouldn't want Cal to get upset.

He was slipping down the hallway toward the pharmacology office, trying to dream up a way to access Marilyn's computer again without having to answer too many questions, when Bob Stahl approached from the other end of the hall. The gangly pharmacologist greeted him like an old friend.

"Plato!" They shook hands just outside the office door. "Good to see you again!"

"How're you doing, Bob?"

"Better than you." He patted Plato's shoulder and his tall forehead creased with concern. "You look like you've just run a marathon."

Plato's winter coat was unzipped, but his sport shirt was damp, and beads of sweat trickled down his temples. He was already breathing hard after the short walk up the stairs from the loading dock.

He mopped the sweat away with his sleeve and grinned.

"I just ran up from the back entrance. I'm hoping to make it outside again before Security tickets my car."

"I've gotten a few of them myself. Still haven't paid yet, either."

Plato leaned against the wall to catch his breath.

Bob frowned. "You sure you're not sick or something?" He opened the office door and gestured to Plato. "How about taking a rest in the lounge, maybe having something to drink? You don't look so good."

"It's just this cold of mine." Plato considered for a moment, then decided to tell Bob the truth. He trusted him. "Actually, I was just hoping to borrow Marilyn's computer for a few minutes."

He told Bob about the disk, his attempts to decode the file, and his theory that the data might have been compressed.

"I bet you're right." Bob nodded. "Marilyn used to compress *all* her files, big or small—with some obscure program that no one else had. For security, she said." He shook his head. "She'd give us some data on a disk, or a report, and we always had to borrow her machine to decompress the files."

He led Plato to Marilyn's office, opened the door, and switched on the light. Little had changed—the SERENDIPITY sign still hung across the far wall, the jar of dirt still sat beside the computer, and the piles of books and records were just as tall as ever. But someone—probably Tiffany— had started sorting through the papers. Three file boxes were stacked beside the door. A fourth one, half full, sat on the sofa beside several heaps of papers and manila folders.

Bob flipped the machine on. "You want me to pull the file up for you?"

"Maybe you could just get me started." Plato grabbed the disk from his jacket pocket. Fortunately, it hadn't gotten wet. "You've probably got better things to do."

"No problem." He slid the disk into the computer's drive. "Actually, I'm done for the afternoon. I just turned in my questions for tomorrow's practice exam—the first test of the quarter."

Plato remembered the practice exams. A couple of weeks into each quarter, a day was set aside for practice exams. It was a way to keep students from slacking off during that long stretch before midterms. A wakeup call for procrastinators like Plato.

He wondered how Blair and Samantha and Raj would do on the anatomy practice exam. Their makeup test wasn't for another week, but doing well on this week's practice exam could build their confidence, and put them on the right track.

"After Therese finishes up, we're going over to the hospital," Bob continued. "To visit Tiffany."

"I heard she's doing better," Plato said.

"Yeah." He swiveled away from the computer for a moment and waved his arm around the room. "She was working on this stuff before she left Saturday evening. I wondered if maybe she found something in Marilyn's papers, and that's why she got jumped. So I looked around a little." He raked his hand through his hair. "No dice. I couldn't find a thing."

"You don't buy the police's line that it was a random purse-snatching, huh?"

"No. Do you?"

"No," Plato replied.

"I guess that's part of why we're here." Bob swiveled back to the keyboard. He typed a series of commands, started the decompression program, and set it to work on the disk. He sat back. "So you think this file might have something to do with Marilyn's getting killed?"

"I really don't know." Plato shrugged. "But the file was created on the day she died. I can't help thinking it had *something* to do with it."

In seconds, the computer finished its work.

"DECOMPRESSION COMPLETE," it announced. "COMPRESS/DECOMPRESS ANOTHER FILE, Y/N?"

Bob typed "N," and closed the program. He handed the floppy disk to Plato. "I put a copy of the decompressed file on Marilyn's hard drive. It's too big to fit on this floppy, so I left it alone. What next?"

"Can we try running some of Marilyn's programs to see if any of them recognize the file?" He glanced at his watch. "I have an appointment at Riverside, but I still have a few minutes."

"Fine. It shouldn't take long." One after another, Bob ran each of Marilyn's programs—her word processor, spreadsheet, database, statistical number cruncher, a few graphics and paint programs, the personal organizer, and even a couple of computer games. But none of them recognized the file.

"That's strange," Bob muttered. "It doesn't seem like a text *or* a graphics file."

Plato shook his head, disappointed. "Sorry about this. I guess it was just a waste of time after all. Maybe the file came from some other computer."

"I doubt it." Bob peered into the screen and stroked his crooked mustache. "No one else around here has that compression program of hers, I'm sure of it. The file *must* have come from here. It doesn't make any sense."

"I know." Plato glanced at his watch again. "I've got to run. I might come back later and try running through the programs one more time. Can you clear it with your secretary?"

"Don't worry about it. I'll probably still be here." Bob was still squinting at the screen, brow furrowed, tongue pressed between his lips. "I'm going to keep working on this. Now you've got me curious."

Plato scribbled his pager number on one of Marilyn's Post-It notes and stuck it to the edge of the monitor. "Here. Give me a page if you figure it out."

"Sure." Still frowning at the monitor, Bob didn't even look up as Plato turned to leave.

"Plato, Plato, Plato." Nathan Simmons was stuffing tobacco into his pipe and shaking his head. "You should have come sooner. *Much* sooner. You look terrible."

They were standing in Nathan's office at the Riverside Family Health Center, just a floor below Plato's office in the geriatrics area. The room itself was a clone of Plato's office: four square walls, a window looking out over the snow-covered nurses' dorm across the street, a creaky steel door, ratty carpeting, even the same kind of sheet-metal desk. But while Plato's office was merely a glorified closet, a place to hurl his coat and boots and mail, Nathan's office was more like a miniature art gallery.

Paintings and prints and tapestries covered the walls—everything from impressionist through postmodernist and back to the primitive dabblings of some hermit friend of Nathan's living on an island in the Caribbean. The immaculate top of his desk was adorned with a brass sculpture of some ancient Greek gods wrestling or making love or whatever it is ancient Greek gods do. Resting on his walnut coffee table was his latest prize, a more modern carving in alabaster or pale marble—the face of a marvelously beautiful woman superimposed on the jutting, angular peaks of a city skyline. As the sculpture was rotated, the face grew older and more haglike and the buildings more prominent, until finally the face was gone and only the city remained. The sculptor called it "Urban Development."

An air filter/humidifier unit was tucked in a corner of the room, and an extra pair of deadbolts were installed on the door. The sculptures and paintings were gifts from Nathan's wife, and worth a small fortune. Leah Simmons was a subspecialist, a dermatologist. Working only part-time, taking no night or weekend call, she made more money than Plato and Cal combined.

Nathan walked over to his desk and picked up the telephone. "Terry? How about sending a wheelchair over to my office. I think we'll need it for transport. Great."

"Nathan—" Plato began.

"Sit down, Plato." Puffing on the unlit pipe, he came over and stared up at his patient. "I'm surprised you're still *alive*, let alone breathing. You're swaying like a palm tree in a hurricane. Sit down, for Chrissakes. You make me nervous."

Plato sat on the arm of the sofa. "A *wheelchair*? You've got to be kidding."

Nathan Simmons always took things too seriously. Even in medical school, he had been very cautious, very careful. He had never had to cram for tests; he studied for exactly three hours every night, and went to bed at eleven P.M. precisely. At twenty-three years of age, he had always brought his own lunches to school, insisting that the cafeteria food was too high in sodium and saturated fats. He had driven a beat-up old Mercedes-Benz, a vast tank of a thing, on the premise that surrounding himself with steel was the best defense against accident-related injuries.

He married Leah Burkowitz because she had strong bones and healthy teeth, and long-lived grandparents on both sides of her family.

For all his caution and fastidious ways, Nathan had fallen into the pipe-smoking habit early in his medical career.

When their first child was born, he hadn't been able to quit. He had just stopped lighting the tobacco.

He pulled his chair over from his desk, squinted at Plato's face and reached for his neck. His hands were cool and dry and gentle, but the nodes were still tender. "Have you looked in a mirror lately, Plato?"

"I try to avoid it."

"That's obvious. Here, open wide." As he peered into Plato's mouth, Nathan's tiny dark eyes widened. His bushy eyebrows fluttered. "Yech. Strep at the very least. I think they're building condominiums in there."

"Feels like high-rise apartments."

"I'm surprised you can still breathe." He gagged Plato with a culture swab, slid his chair away, and crossed his arms. Staring at his patient, he gave that funny little wiggle of his brown toupee, like he always did when he was annoyed.

Nathan had bought the toupee in his senior year of medical school, after attending a seminar on skin cancer. When Plato gently pointed out that the toupee didn't fit very well and didn't even match his original black hair color, Nathan countered that he only wore it for protection from the deadly rays of the sun.

Plato suspected that his friend had grown rather attached to the toupee, so to speak. Certainly his wife, the dermatologist, could fix him up with hair transplants for free. But such a concession to vanity didn't fit with Nathan's nature. And he wouldn't be able to wiggle it at his patients, as he was now doing with Plato.

"Strep doesn't explain your sunken eyes, your rapid breathing, your persistent high fever after a full day of amoxicillin." He frowned at Plato. "You *are* a physician, aren't you?"

"You sat beside me at graduation, remember?"

"Yes. You had a rubber model of the human brain hidden under your mortarboard. You kept tipping your hat to people. It was embarrassing." He slid closer again, unslung the stethoscope from his neck and slid the bell inside Plato's shirt. "Doctors make the worst patients. Why did I ever accept you in my practice?"

"Because you love me?"

"Be quiet." Nathan listened to Plato's heart and lungs, then swiveled around and listened to Plato's back, where the lung sounds are much clearer. Eyes closed and head bowed, he listened again. Finally, he had Plato remove his shirt. He walked the stethoscope down Plato's back a third time and nodded. "You need a chest X ray."

"Are you kidding? Nathan, I'm *fine*." Plato shrugged his shirt back on and suffered another coughing fit. A few more of those, and he'd turn completely inside out. Eyes watering, he asked, "Are you going to put me in an exam room?"

"I don't need to. Lay down on that couch." Nathan walked over to his desk and picked up a prescription pad. He scribbled an order on the pad, tore it off, and handed it to Plato.

"Chest X ray, PA and Lateral," the note said. "Wet reading, please."

"Any first-year resident could tell that you're seriously ill," Nathan continued. "At least bronchitis, more likely pneumonia."

"But Cal listened to my lungs last night," Plato protested. He stood up. "She just heard a few rustles. Otherwise I was clear as a bell."

"You're also dry as a bell. You're dehydrated." Nathan wasn't much taller than Cal, but he pushed Plato back into the couch with his index finger. "Your lungs are too dry to make much sound. You're blue around the gills—we may have to put you on oxygen. Your eyes look like a pair of green marbles, and your skin reminds me of something from a wax museum. I've seen dead people who looked healthier than you."

A knock sounded at the door, and Nathan's nurse poked her head in. "Doctor Simmons? We've got a wheelchair for Doctor Marley."

"Thanks, Cynthia." He walked over and opened the door, then helped Plato into the wheelchair. He turned to Cynthia. "Can you arrange to transport this wretch over to radiology?"

"Sure thing, Doctor."

He slanted his eyes down at Plato skeptically. "You may want to put some leather restraints on this thing and tie him down. I don't want him wandering off."

Two hours later, Plato was back in Nathan's office, still in the wheelchair. They hadn't tied him down with restraints, but Cynthia had found a particularly tough-looking orderly to wheel Plato over to radiology. On the ride across and back, he had pushed the chair with one hand, kept the other on Plato's shoulder, and regaled him with stories about his days as a prison guard down in Lima. During the one-hour wait before Plato's X ray, he had watched *All My Children* and filled Plato in on the story lines.

He had finally left after dropping Plato back at Nathan's office, safe and sound. Minus his shirt—the radiology department had swiped it, leaving him with a flimsy hospital gown that tied with two strings in the back and protected him from drafts about as well as a paper napkin. Sitting in the wheelchair, Plato felt exposed and vulnerable. He also felt tired. It was barely five o'clock, but Plato felt like he could sleep for days. Outside Nathan's window, the streetlights were already coming on. Baseball-sized gobs of snow floated from the sky like the fallout from some giant angel-food bomb. Night was falling, and the big storm was tuning its instruments, starting the overture.

Plato climbed out of the chair and hobbled over to the couch. Lying down, pulling his coat up to use as a blanket, he heard the familiar screech of his pager, muffled inside his coat pocket.

It was a Siegel number. Plato stumbled over to Nathan's desk, picked up the phone, and dialed.

Bob Stahl answered the phone. "Plato?"

"Yes, Bob." Having just walked all the way across the room, Plato had trouble catching his breath and hiding his fatigue in his voice.

"Sorry to bother you, but I thought you'd want to know. I figured out what kind of file that was."

"You did?" Plato slid to the floor and leaned against Nathan's desk. Through the flimsy gown, the sheet metal felt like a giant ice cube. "That's fantastic."

"You may not think so, once you hear what it is." Over the phone, Bob's voice held a smile. "There was one kind of program we didn't think of checking out."

"On Marilyn's computer?" Plato frowned. "I thought we tried all her software."

"Except the telecommunications program." Bob sighed. "It was a *fax*, Plato. I don't know why we didn't think of that."

"Yeah." Plato scratched his head. "I guess the letters 'FX' should have tipped us off, huh?"

"Exactly. That's what finally made me think of the fax program—seeing those letters over and over again. I opened Marilyn's fax viewer and pulled up the file. There is was, simple as pie."

"So what was it?" Plato squirmed left and right, twisted his back around, and pulled the sides of the gown together, but it didn't help. He was freezing.

"Nothing important. Just another one of Marilyn's practical jokes, I think. Here, let me pull it up again." A shower of keypad clicks crackled over the line. "It's a speeding ticket. I guess they nailed Randolph Smythe for doing sixty-four in a fifty-five zone. On that stretch of I–480 out near Hopkins Airport."

Plato groaned. "Great. My wonderful piece of evidence, and it turns out to be a prank."

"I bet Marilyn's having a good laugh right now, wherever she is. She was probably going to stick copies on the bulletin boards around the school. The fax came from Smythe's office—she must have snuck in and sent it." Bob paused. "You know, it's a funny thing. I thought that stretch of freeway was a sixty-five zone."

Plato frowned. He was right. Unless— "What's the date on that ticket, Bob?"

"Oh, yeah. They upped the speed limit about five years ago, didn't they? Lemme check." Another fusillade of clicks sounded in the background. "It's handwritten, kind of scribbly. I'm reading it right off the screen—I've got to zoom in. Oh, yeah—here it is. Eighty-six. November eighth, nineteen eighty-six."

"That's pretty obscure," Plato observed. "If that's the only ticket Smythe's had in the past ten years, he's a better driver than me."

"Better than me, too. Hey, I've got to run. You want me to make a copy of this, have June send it over to your office?"

"I guess not. Thanks anyways." What was the point? "I'll just tell Cal about it—she'll have a good laugh."

Plato hung up the phone, crawled back over to the couch, and curled up under his coat. If only he could get some rest . . .

He had just drifted off to sleep when a knock sounded at the door. Cynthia poked her head into the darkened room, light streaming in from the hallway behind her.

"Doctor Marley? Your wife is on the phone out here. And Doctor Simmons says he'll be with you shortly. He's been tied up with another emergency."

Another emergency? Plato wondered. What was the first one?

Cynthia helped him climb into the wheelchair and pushed him down the hallway. The telephone was waiting at the combination lab and charting station.

"This phone line doesn't go into Doctor Simmons's office," Cynthia explained. "We could have her call you back on the other line—"

"This is fine, Cynthia. Thanks." He took the phone and watched her walk down the hall and into one of the exam rooms. "Hello, Cal?"

"Plato! Are you all right?" Over the line, she sounded breathless, too. "You've been there *forever*. I tried calling home but there wasn't any answer."

"That's because I was still here."

"I know. I was worried. What's going on? Are they admitting you to the hospital or something?"

Plato chuckled bravely. "Nothing to worry about, Cal. Nathan and I have just been shooting the breeze. You know, catching up on old times, griping about hospital politics."

"For *two hours*? Are you sure there's nothing wrong?"

"Positive." He glanced down at the countertop. His own chart was sitting there, atop the lab reports and the "wet reading" from his chest X ray—a preliminary report by the radiologist, made just after the film was taken. Seeing his chart and lab work gave him a queasy, disoriented feeling. Like an out-of-body experience, or reading his own gravestone in a dream. "I'm fine. Just strep throat, and a little bronchitis."

He slid the radiologist's wet reading out from beneath his chart. At the top of the green sheet of paper were his name and patient number. Below was typed Nathan's name as the attending physician, and a request to "rule out bronchopulmonary pneumonia." After that was a paragraph of esoterica dictated by the radiologist—terms like streaky infiltrates, fluffy opacities, atelectatic changes, clinical dehydration per attending. Finally, at the bottom was the radiologist's impression: "Probable bronchopulmonary pneumonia."

"Just a little bronchitis," Plato repeated. "Nathan's switching me to a cephalosporin. I'll probably have to take a couple of days off."

"That's a relief." Cal sighed. "For a while last night, I was afraid you had pneumonia."

"I was clear when you listened to me, right?"

"Pretty clear." She still sounded a little doubtful. "Is Nathan there?"

"He's in with a patient." Plato decided it was time to change the subject. "How did your trip with Homer go? Did you find out anything from Erdmann and Welkins?"

"Nothing worthwhile," Cal replied. But she didn't sound very disappointed.

"That's too bad. Sounds like we struck out all around."

"What do you mean?"

"I had Bob Stahl check out that file of Marilyn's, on her computer."

"You went to Siegel today?" Her voice hardened. "I thought I told you to—"

"Just for a minute, Cal. Anyway, he decompressed the file and was finally able to read it."

"And?" She sounded annoyed.

"And it was nothing. A ten-year-old speeding ticket, from that stretch of freeway over by Hopkins. I guess Dean Smythe was in a hurry to catch a plane."

"Dean Smythe?" Cal's breath caught. "*How* old did you say that speeding ticket was?"

"Ten years."

"Do you remember the date?"

"Let's see. November eighth, I think. Yeah. November eighth, nineteen eighty-six." Plato frowned. "What possible difference does it make?"

"All the difference in the world." Quickly, Cal explained to Plato how she had spent her afternoon—the talk with Leonard Reiss, the visit to security and the parking lot at Siegel, the all-important *Sunday Magazine* article.

"So you were right after all," she concluded.

When she finished, Plato's mind was whirling with the implications. Everything fit together, everything made sense. Even the motive, now. "Are you going to call Jeremy and Homer?"

"I'd rather tell them in person," she replied. "You think you could get a copy of that ticket for us?"

"No problem. I'll give Bob a call and run right over. We can drive to the courthouse together—Homer should still be there."

She sighed. "You're really okay, Plato? I'm worried about you."

"I'm fine. Believe me, I'm fine. Nathan practically laughed me out of his office. Kept teasing me about my medical degree."

"Okay. I'll meet you up in the lobby."

She hung up. Plato finally let loose with a terrible coughing fit. This time, he almost blacked out before it was over. Maybe he really *did* need some oxygen.

He waited for his head to clear, caught his breath, and flipped open his medical chart. He read the final entry with a smile. Nathan Simmons would never change. The good doctor had written a typical Subjective-Objective-Assessment-Plan (SOAP) note, just like they had learned in medical school:

SUBJECTIVE:

The patient, a 33-year-old male physician, complains of cough, shortness of breath, high fevers, chills, loss of appetite, and lethargy. Illness began with typical symptoms of upper respiratory infection six days ago—mild fever, cough, pharyngitis, sinus drainage—but worsened significantly over the past three days. Fever documented by patient to over one hundred four Fahrenheit, productive cough, episodic delirium and/or loss of consciousness, shortness of breath on exertion, chills and sweats, all despite twenty-four hours of oral amoxicillin therapy, taken without this physician's recommendation or knowledge.

Vintange Nathan, Plato thought. Covering his behind. He kept reading:

OBJECTIVE:

Temperature: 103. Pulse: 98. Blood pressure: 105/58, no orthostatic changes. Respiratory rate: 36 per minute at rest. Labs: CBC shows markedly increased white blood cell count with dramatic left shift. Blood chemistries all within normal limits. Chest X ray consistent with bronchopulmonary pneumonia (see report per radiologist). Throat culture results pending.

ASSESSMENT:

1. Bronchopulmonary pneumonia, probably bacterial in origin.
2. Posssible sepsis.
3. Probable strep pharyngitis.
4. Denial, high potential for noncompliance.

PLAN:

1. Sputum studies for isolation of causative organism.
2. Admit patient to hospital for intravenous therapy with empirical antibiotics, pending identification of causative organism for pneumonia. Once sensitivities identified, will switch to appropriate, specific antibiotic therapy.
3. Blood cultures x2 for documentation of sepsis and identification of causative organism if sputum studies fail.
4. Contact patient's spouse to ensure that patient follows through with treatment regimen and complies with hospitalization and medical advice.

Up the hall, Nathan was entering another patient's room. He grinned to Plato and signaled that he'd only be another minute, that Plato should go back to the office and wait. Plato nodded.

Quickly, quietly, stealthily, Plato crept back to Nathan's office, donned his coat, and slipped away down the back stairwell.

Chapter 23

Hanging up the anatomy lab phone, Cal felt prickles on the back of her neck. Like she was being watched.

Even now, after years of autopsies and dissections and crime scene investigations, she still got that fluttery little feeling in the presence of death. She was surrounded by cadavers. She felt like one of them was staring at her.

She couldn't help turning around and glancing behind her. "Sergei?"

Randolph Smythe was standing in the doorway of the lab, a sad, fatherly frown painted on his handsome face. The frown of a politician announcing a natural disaster. The frown of a father whose daughter has betrayed him.

"Sorry, Cal. Sergei's gone for the day."

Cal had come down to the anatomy lab to talk with Sergei Malenkov. To ask whether he'd seen another car whipping out of the parking lot on the night of Marilyn Abel's death. To ask whether he'd seen Dean Smythe's car.

But the anatomy lab was closed and locked in preparation for tomorrow's practice exam. She had needed to use her key to get in.

Apparently, Sergei had already gone home after readying the cadavers for the practical. All the steel coffins were open. Each body bore colorful little plastic flags attached to pins. Tomorrow's exam would cover the abdomen. On the cadaver nearest Cal, red and blue and yellow flags were stuck into the common bile duct, splenic artery, and the portal vein.

Failing to find Sergei, she had telephoned Plato at Nathan's office to tell him what she had discovered.

"Is there anything I can help you with?" Smythe smiled sadly. His arms were crossed. In his glowing white lab coat, with his perfect hair and his perfect face, he looked like a movie angel. Or maybe Saint Peter, standing at the gate. "The lab is supposed to be sealed and locked, you know."

"I know. I just wanted to talk with Sergei." Cal's mind was racing. Her heart thrashed in her chest like a squirrel in a cage. How much had Smythe heard? How much did he know? "I wanted to ask him about Chuck Albright. He saw Chuck's car racing out of the parking lot on the night of Marilyn's death. Did you know that?"

The dean shook his head gravely. "That will hardly do, Cal."

"I'm sorry. I don't understand."

"You will." Dean Smythe strolled into the lab and leaned against the edge of the bone table. Cal was standing on the other side of the table, near the lab's telephone. Between them lay the disassembled human skeleton, bones gleaming bright beneath the fluorescent lights, naked skull grinning up at the ceiling.

"I'm a very sensitive person, Cal. That's why I couldn't help noticing the strange way you were looking at me during our committee meeting today." His head was bowed, eyes turned toward the skeleton. His fingers slid over the radius and ulna, caressed the bare metacarpals of the hand. "Your glances were furtive, almost guilty. Appraising." He looked up at Cal. "I worried that perhaps someone had seen me with Tiffany the other night, that perhaps an arrest was imminent. So I followed you after the meeting, followed you down here. And heard some of your extremely illuminating telephone conversation."

Cal felt the blood drain from her face. The sticky linoleum seemed to lurch under her feet. She grabbed the edge of the table and held on.

"I must admit that I was quite impressed," he continued. He brushed his hand through his perfect hair and grinned. "You see? I was right about that assistant deanship, wasn't I? You certainly have the intellect to do the job."

"Thank you." Cal's voice was rusty, raspy. Like she hadn't used it in a year or two.

"I *am* rather curious, though." He slipped his hands into the deep pockets of the white lab coat. "I believe I covered every conceivable loose end. How did you figure it out?"

Apparently, Smythe hadn't heard Cal's entire conversation with Plato. Maybe she could bluff him, or stall him.

Keep him talking until help arrived. After all, he was a budding politician.

But then she realized that help wasn't going to arrive. The lab was sealed until the exam tomorrow morning. She couldn't keep him talking *that* long.

"A lot of little things," Cal finally replied. Her voice still quivered and rasped. "A comment one of the students made—about how you showed up in the physiology lab during the final exam, wishing everyone a Merry Christmas."

"That *was* rather awkward," he admitted.

"I checked and found out that the tubocurarine is kept in an office at the back of the physiology lab. For the dog studies. I'm surprised no one saw you taking the drug."

"I didn't realize the lab was being used at that hour." He shrugged. "I came back later and took the drug, when the lab was empty."

"I kept that little fact in the back of my mind," Cal continued, "but I didn't know what to do with it. I also heard that Marilyn Abel disliked you—especially after what happened with Tiffany—but so did a lot of people. You can't kill people just for disliking you."

"It would probably make winning elections much easier," he joked.

"It certainly would." Oddly enough, Cal was beginning to relax. She didn't feel like she was talking with a murderer. She just felt like she was talking with Dean Smythe, about an issue that had little to do with either of them. "The use of tubocurarine itself narrowed the field. The murderer had to be someone with medical expertise."

"That limits it to ten or twenty thousand people in the metropolitan area," he observed.

"He also had to be familiar with Marilyn Abel's diabetic problem. And her habit of working late, eating dinner, and taking her evening insulin dose here at Siegel."

"Ah, yes. That narrows the field considerably."

"The three members of the pharmacology department were obvious suspects. So were her ex-husband, Arnold Welkins, and maybe Candice Erdmann as well. So was anyone who had access to Marilyn's medical records, who knew she took insulin twice a day. You were familiar with Marilyn's medical condition—you probably saw a copy of her employment physical."

He nodded slowly, a smile playing at the corners of his mouth. He seemed to be enjoying Cal's narrative.

"And you knew that Marilyn often worked late or stayed overnight."

"Certainly." He straightened the lapel of his lab coat. "Of course, I couldn't *count* on it that evening."

"So I suppose you offered to meet with her, to talk things over with her and explain everything?" Cal guessed. "After her evening dose of insulin, of course."

"Scientists can be very naive. And even Marilyn was unwilling to believe the implications of what she had learned."

"Anyway, I still didn't have any real reason to suspect you." Cal stared at the floor, but she couldn't keep the bitterness from her voice. "Even when you tried to bribe me with the assistant deanship if I would suppress the investigation. I thought you were just trying to avoid bad press for the school."

"I was trying to do neither," he protested. "I honestly felt—*feel*—that you are the best person for the job." The little smile reappeared. "Unfortunately, I'm afraid you would have to be appointed postmortem. Is that the proper word?"

"Posthumously," Cal corrected mechanically.

"Posthumously, then."

He had the unshakable certainty of a prophet or a madman. Cal swallowed heavily. "Anyway, we concentrated our attention on the other suspects."

"To my great relief."

"But during our investigation last week, we left out one small detail. Marilyn Abel had the name of a reporter stuck to her computer monitor." She shook her head. "The police interviewed him, but he couldn't tell them anything worthwhile. I talked to him also, at lunch today, but he wasn't much help."

"She didn't have time to meet with a reporter. I watched her van that entire day. She never left the college." Smythe's face reddened, and clouded with sudden anxiety. "Unless she telephoned him . . ."

"She may have," Cal lied. "He may not be giving us the whole story. He may be holding onto it."

"Not likely." The dean's face cleared. "He would have splashed it all over the papers by now, if he had anything."

Cal shrugged. She had planted a few seeds of doubt,

anyway. "I asked myself, why would a pharmacologist have the name of a *Plain Dealer* political writer stuck to her computer monitor? Surely, if Marilyn wanted to make some announcement about her new drug or about her research, she would contact a science writer."

"Exactly," Smythe rumbled.

"But then, at lunch today, the reporter mentioned his *Sunday Magazine* article from last month. I thought I remembered the article, but I wasn't sure. So I looked it up." She met Smythe's eyes. "The feature article was about you, Dean Smythe. Your entire life story, laid out in full color for all the voters to see."

"I sent Reiss a case of Scotch for that story." His nose wrinkled. "He sent it back. He says he doesn't drink."

"I figured Marilyn had seen the article, and that was why she planned to call Reiss." Telling the story, Cal's mind was split. One part was keeping up the narrative, trying to make it interesting, to keep Smythe distracted. The other part was trying to think of some way out of this mess. Using the telephone would take too long. Even the fire alarm was too far away. "It seemed that Marilyn had some information about you, but I had no idea what it was."

"Ah, yes. Now we reach the heart of the matter." He rubbed the side of his nose. "Come to think of it, I really don't know whether you have that information. And if you do have it, I *still* have no idea how you got it. I made a thorough search of Marilyn's office and found nothing."

Cal resisted the temptation to jump ahead and explain. It would speed things up too much. She desperately needed to buy some time. So she took up where she had left off. "I was lucky to stumble on to the link connecting Marilyn, Reiss, and you. But another lucky thing happened during lunch."

"The chef had a heart attack," he guessed.

"No." Cal didn't even crack a smile. "But Leonard Reiss mentioned getting a parking ticket—for parking in the handicapped space near the front entrance. That made me think about Marilyn and her wheelchair. She always parked in that handicapped space, didn't she?"

"Of course. I could see it from my office window. She was very proud of her independence."

"I walked outside after lunch today. I noticed that the handicapped entrance is separate from the main lobby. The handicapped-access door opens onto the administration foyer. And a small corridor leads through administration back to the pharmacology area. A shortcut.''

"Marilyn was always tracking snow and water through the halls," he complained. "I scolded her about it several times."

"I'm sure you did. The shortcut leads right past the back door of your office." She spread her hands. "I don't understand how, but Marilyn must have overheard a conversation that incriminated you in some way."

"I couldn't understand it either," he confessed. He scratched his chin thoughtfully. "I've been over it a thousand times, and I think I've figured it out. The maid always forgets to latch the back door to my office. And whenever someone opens the handicapped-access entrance, the wind pushes my door ajar. That must have happened when Jack was there that morning."

"Who's Jack?" Cal asked quickly.

"A police officer, and a friend of mine." He rolled his eyes. "He had stolen something and had foolishly brought it to me at the college, demanding payment. A piece of paper I had completely forgotten about. Marilyn Abel was extraordinarily lucky to come by at that particular moment."

"Serendipity," Cal said.

"What?"

"Nothing."

While Smythe was talking, Cal had sent her eyes around the room. No windows penetrated the anatomy lab proper. Up the hall, Sergei's office was half a floor higher than the lab, but it was still mostly below ground. Even Sergei's window was hardly large enough to crawl through.

Not that she'd ever get that far. Smythe was much bigger than Cal. And he was much closer to the only door out of the cadaver lab.

"Perhaps I should have burned the item right then, right in my office. Much of this could have been avoided." He shrugged. "But I was concerned that a smoke detector would sound, or that my secretary would walk in, or that any number of other unfortunate occurrences might call attention to the item. Besides, I had nothing to fear. So I locked the item in my desk drawer."

Cal wasn't surprised that Marilyn's myriad skills included lock-picking.

"Later that day, after a luncheon meeting, I found that someone had meddled with the papers on my desk." He sounded indignant. "I called in my secretary, but she insisted that she hadn't been into my office. Then I noticed that the back door was ajar."

He smiled proudly, hooked a thumb in the buttonhole of the lab coat and rocked on his heels. "And, doing my own little piece of detective work, I realized that it was Marilyn Abel."

"Because of the wheelchair marks in the heavy pile carpet." Cal couldn't resist stealing his thunder. After all, he was going to kill her anyway. Or try to. "Your secretary vacuums the track marks away after bringing in the coffee cart. Marilyn's wheelchair marks were probably just as obvious."

"Even more so," he agreed.

Cal was amazed that he admitted to all of her accusations, without a glimmer of protest. But then she remembered Smythe's unwavering conviction that she would have to receive her deanship posthumously.

She glanced down at the skeleton on the table, and it finally hit her. A primitive solution. One of the oldest in history. Wasn't there something in the Bible about the jawbone of an ass?

"And that was all the evidence you had?" the dean asked suddenly. He seemed suspicious, and more than a little disappointed.

"Oh—Leonard Reiss's parking ticket also reminded me how diligent our security force is about ticketing cars." As Cal talked, she inched her hand closer and closer to the skeleton's right femur. The mandible was far too small to be effective. "They're even brash enough to ticket a dean's car, on the night he's busy committing murder."

"I knew I should have broken in and destroyed their copy." He shook his head ruefully. "But I never got a chance—they never leave that damned office."

"You parked your car near the loading dock earlier that day, finished Marilyn off, and left through the side door. No one saw you leaving, though an alarm signal went out." Her fingers slowly closed on the leg bone. Her hands were shaking; she feared the bone would rattle against the steel table like a drum. "But Security had already ticketed your car."

"I *really* must make sure I destroy their copy," he mused. "Perhaps I could—"

While he talked, Cal clenched her fingers, willed all her energy into her brachioradialis and triceps and biceps and deltoid and latissimus dorsi, and whirled the human femur around in a wide arc that ended at Dean Randolph Smythe the Third's head. Or would have, if he hadn't ducked. For a man in late middle age, his reflexes were fabulous. Cal was thinking this even as she felt the leg bone bounce off the top of his head and spin her completely around. She dropped the femur on the floor and dashed around the table.

And felt Randolph Smythe's hand like an anchor on her elbow, nearly yanking her arm from its socket as she sprinted by.

He pulled her around and back like a child's rag doll. She stopped struggling when she saw the snub-nosed thirty-eight-caliber revolver pointed at her chest.

Cal hated guns. They inspired in her an absolute, rabid terror. A mind-numbing fear. Her legs turned to pudding. She sagged against Smythe.

Her mother had been killed with a gun, when Cal was just fifteen. Supposedly a suicide, though Cal would never believe it. She had been in the house, had heard the shot. One minute, her mother was alive, cheerful, full of the beauty of life. The next, she was a horrible specter, a gruesome testimony to the absolute finality of death.

Even now, Cal preferred to have the other deputy coroners handle the gunshot victims, if she had a choice.

"Y-you don't need that," she pleaded. She couldn't take her eyes off the gun. It was old and heavy-looking. The barrel was tarnished with splotches of rust. Bullet noses gleamed from the cylinder, like the teeth of a snarling Rottweiler. The muzzle was a black, endless pit. Like a black hole—the gateway to another universe, an alternate reality. A reality Cal wasn't ready to face.

"Naturally, I'm opposed to all forms of gun control," Smythe said conversationally. Holding most of Cal's weight, he wasn't even breathing hard. "I picked this up in a pawn shop a few months ago, no questions asked. For protection—after all those muggings started around the school. I could use it now, and toss it in the river. The ballistics would never be traced to me. I know that from past experience."

Cal knew it, too. Somewhere—at the bottom of Lake Erie, maybe—was a similar revolver. It had been rusting there for ten years now.

"You don't have to. Really you don't." Cal's legs were shaking now. "I won't say anything. I won't tell anyone. *Please.*"

"But your husband will." He shrugged. "A pity you had to tell him about me. Another loose end to tie up. I was quite relieved when you decided not to telephone the police."

"P-Plato was going to," she lied. Her voice cracked.

"No. I distinctly heard you say you wanted to tell them personally." His eyes closed for a moment, then he gave a quick nod. "Perhaps I could use you to get to Plato. Perhaps you should page him, tell him you're at my house. Tell him to come alone."

He pulled the hammer back until it clicked. The revolver turned slightly, the Rottweiler licking its chops.

"I c-couldn't do that." Plato *would* come alone, she knew. "Please don't ask me to."

Two floors above, twenty-four granite steps up, a door clattered and squeaked open. A jangling of keys and a familiar whistle announced that one of Seigel's finest was making his rounds.

Here comes the cavalry, Cal thought. She would never poke fun at Seigel's security again.

Now Randolph Smythe was trapped. The hunter had become the prey. His eyes widened, frantically darting about the room for some avenue of escape. There was none; the only way out was up the long stairwell, past the security guard.

His gaze suddenly fixed on the gleaming metal wall across the room. He pressed the revolver into Cal's back.

"The cooler," he whispered harshly. He pulled her along toward the big steel door. "Get into it. Now."

Chapter 24

"Doctor Marley?" The security guard was staring at Plato with concern. "Pardon me, sir, but you look *terrible*. If you'll excuse my saying so."

"Quite all right," Plato answered agreeably. "People have been telling me that all week."

He was sitting on a bench in Siegel Medical College's main lobby. The guard was peering at Plato through the grubby window of the security office. Between them was about thirty feet of linoleum. Even from that distance, the security guard could see that Plato was seriously ill.

"Your lips are blue," he observed. "In fact, your whole *face* is blue."

Plato just nodded. Talking had become something of a strain.

"Is there anyone I should call?" The guard was tall, blond, earnest-looking, and very young. He tugged at his lower lip and cast a quick glance at the telephone beside him. "An ambulance, maybe?"

"No," Plato finally answered. He shrugged, pulling his coat collar up to hide the hospital gown. "I'm just waiting for my wife."

"Doctor *Cal* Marley?" He frowned, reached a hand out through the window and grabbed the clipboard. "Let's see. She signed in at twelve-thirty, and she hasn't signed out yet. She must still be here."

"I know. I'm waiting for her." Plato caught his breath, then continued. "She said to meet her in the lobby."

"But, sir." The security guard sounded quite puzzled. He glanced at his watch and back at Plato. "You've been sitting there for forty minutes now."

"Forty minutes?" Plato asked, surprised. "Has it been that long?"

"You fell asleep a couple of times. At least, I *think* you

fell asleep." He tugged his lip again. "You didn't close your eyes; they just kind of glazed over. You know?"

"Yes." Plato sat up, shook his head sharply and tried to think. Forty minutes! Bob had given him a copy of the fax on his way out; Plato had been sitting ever since. Where *was* Cal, anyway? Was she in trouble? Had she gone to see Jeremy and Homer on her own? Was she still back in one of the offices, working out the final details of the case?

"I guess I'd better go look for her," Plato muttered.

"What's that?" the guard asked.

"Cal." Standing wasn't as hard as he'd expected. But staying on his feet was pretty tricky. The floor seemed to heave and wiggle beneath his shoes, like an ocean of Jell-O. "I need to find Cal."

He staggered across the linoleum and finally braced himself on the counter—a tiny island in the rolling sea. He stared down at the guard. The poor boy was even younger than Plato had thought. His shirt looked brand-new; a straight pin was still stuck in the collar. Plato stared at the boy's name tag: "Douglas Douglas."

"Okay, Douglas Douglas, just point me toward the pharmacology department. Maybe she stopped there."

"Maybe I'd better go with you," the boy answered. With a jangle of keys, he stood and trotted out through the security office door, locking it carefully behind him. He took Plato's arm and led him to the main corridor. "I need to make rounds every hour anyway. It's almost time."

"That's awfully nice, Douglas Douglas." Plato leaned on the boy's arm. The heaving floor steadied a little.

"Actually, my name is Henry Douglas," he answered. He pointed to his name tag. "See? H. Douglas."

With some difficulty, Plato focused on the badge. The two images blurred and merged into one. Double vision. He was sicker than he'd realized. "Oh. Quite right. Sorry, Henry."

"That's okay, sir."

"Just call me Plato."

"Plato?" The boy seemed surprised. "Is that really your name? I mean, my uncle's name was Plato. I didn't realize anyone else was named Plato."

"Not in this millennium," Plato muttered.

"Wasn't Plato a philosopher or something?"

"Actually, he was a physician," Plato replied. "Discovered pneumonia."

"I thought that was Galen," the security guard muttered. When Plato glanced sharply at him, he shrugged. "I'm going to Cleveland State, part-time. Working on a history degree. It's just my first quarter, though."

"Oh. I don't know much about Galen. But Plato was a Greek philosopher. Student of Socrates. I made up the part about pneumonia."

They reached the pharmacology department. The door was locked. Henry knocked, but no one answered.

"I'll try my key," he suggested.

The outer office was dark, except for a pair of ultraviolet lights shining on some cacti near the windows. They checked the offices and the lounge, but the rooms were all dark and empty.

Out in the hallway again, Plato shrugged. "Maybe the anatomy lab."

He was feeling better. The floor had slowed its heaving. He didn't need to lean on Henry anymore. But he still had to stop every few paces to catch his breath.

"Maybe." Henry shrugged. "But I bet she already left. I haven't seen a single person here at the college besides you in the last hour or so. Everyone's home studying for exams."

At the door to the anatomy lab stairwell, the security guard pulled out his keys and frowned. A large plastic sign announced in bold red letters that the anatomy lab was sealed until tomorrow's exam. But the door wasn't locked, and the latch was not quite engaged.

"Funny," he said. "I came through here about an hour ago. I was *sure* I locked it."

Plato followed him into the stairwell. "Cal's probably down here—she must have forgotten to lock the door behind her."

"Could be." Descending the steps in front of Plato, the guard nodded. "I turned the lights off on my way out, and now they're on again."

"She's probably checking over the practice exam." Plato reached for Henry's shoulder. The granite steps were quivering beneath his feet.

He made it down the last few steps and breathed a sigh of relief. Henry hurried on through the corridor and stopped at the entrance to the lab itself.

"Doctor Marley?" he called, poking his head into the lab. "Is anybody here?"

Plato caught up with hm and started inside, but Henry shook his head. The security guard's face had a greenish cast, like old copper. "If you don't mind, I'd rather wait out here."

"No problem." Plato shuffled slowly into the lab and looked around. The sight made him feel just as queasy as Henry.

The ranks of cadavers were lined up like a military parade, lying stiffly at attention in their open steel boxes, eyes right, feet shoulder-width apart, hands clutched in the final salute of death. Their body parts were marked with colorful little flags. A stack of examination forms rested on a table in the center of the room, like a time bomb waiting to explode.

The rush of unpleasant memories, the sudden wave of remembered anxiety, the renewed heaving of the floor, the fever in his head, all gave Plato a feeling of seasickness, of wanting to vomit.

He staggered across the room, leaned against one of the walls, and caught his breath. Glancing down, he saw the half-dissected face of Marilyn Abel, winking crookedly at him.

Hang in there, she seemed to be saying. *Just a little longer. Don't give up.*

Plato looked away quickly. The way he felt, it wouldn't be long before he hallucinated Marilyn back to life.

A high-pitched wail shattered the stillness.

Plato reached down to the pager on his belt. Who would be paging him today? Not the hospital; he was supposedly home recovering from his illness. Maybe it was Cal, calling from the courthouse, or the sheriff's office.

The telephone was back by the door. Plato navigated through the cadaver platoon again, lifted the receiver, and dialed.

A familiar voice answered. It wasn't Cal.

"Plato? Plato Marley?" The voice was calm, self-satisfied, gloating. "Awfully good of you to call."

"Dean Smythe?"

"Yes." He took a deep breath. "I'm sorry to be disturbing you at the dinner hour. Are you at the medical school?"

"Yes." Plato closed his eyes and tried to sort his scattered thoughts. Dean Smythe was the very last person he had expected to hear on the other end of the line.

"I assume you're looking for your wife. You won't find her there."

Plato's heart sank into his shoes.

"I do hope you haven't contacted the authorities yet. For Cal's sake."

"Dean Smythe?" Plato tried to think. It was hard, with all the clattering in the background. "Please speak up. I'm down in the lab, and it's pretty noisy."

"That's the compressor," Smythe answered quickly. "It makes a terrible racket. We really must have it fixed."

Plato remembered now. Friday night's tutoring session. Cal had thought someone was trapped inside the cooler, and that was just how it had sounded.

He put a finger in his other ear and concentrated. "What do you want? Where's Cal?"

"She's here, at my house. Perfectly safe. I want you to come here, alone. Without contacting the authorities. I need to talk with you." The dean sighed, a mournful whistling sound. "Please don't bring the police. Or else, *till death do us part* will come quite soon for you and Cal. Do you understand?"

"I understand." Plato slowly cradled the phone, turned, and shuffled back toward the door. He almost tripped over the human femur leaning against the wall. Mechanically, he picked it up and placed it in the right spot on the bone table.

Careless students.

"Was that your wife?" Henry asked.

"No," Plato replied. "But I know where she is now."

The guard eyed him with renewed concern. "You look like you've just seen a ghost."

"I have." Plato thought of Marilyn Abel, lying there and winking at him. And he thought of Smythe's gloating voice, his certainty that Plato would come, alone.

He was right.

Walking back to the stairs, the security guard shuddered. "That cooler gives me the creeps, you know?"

"I know," Plato replied. "Sounds just like someone's in there, doesn't it?"

Chapter 25

Pulling into Randolph Smythe the Third's long driveway, Plato told himself that he was being a fool. At the very least, he should have called his cousin. Homer would have known what to do. Surely the police, the sheriff's office, had some kind of protocol for situations like this.

Right. Chapter 37, subparagraph 6 of the *Police Officer's Weird Situations Manual:* HANDLING HOMICIDAL MEDICAL SCHOOL DEANS WHO HAVE TAKEN HOSTAGES. It would probably mean going in there with guns blazing, trying to take Smythe unawares in his own home. And acting surprised when the Dean of Death took the life of his hostage.

Plato would have balked at telling the police, so Homer would have insisted on coming along. Or worse yet, he would have followed Plato to Smythe's house, hoping to surprise the dean and overpower him.

It wouldn't work. Plato thought of the bear plastered to Smythe's wall, the garish collection of game trophies, Smythe's gun collection. Sneaking up on the Great White Hunter would be next to impossible. He didn't want Homer to try. No sense getting all three of them killed, when two would do just as well.

He had little hope that Smythe would hold up his end of the bargain. And in his present condition, Plato was hardly capable of overpowering one of his nursing home patients, let alone Randolph Smythe the Third. But he didn't want Cal to be alone.

So he was being a fool. Who cared?

He pulled into the turnaround, parked the car in front of the lofty porch, and mounted the stone stairs. It was nearly seven o'clock. The snow was falling heavy and soft now, blanketing the world in silence. Even the jet passing overhead sounded muffled. In the deep white quiet, Plato's harsh breathing sounded like a death rattle.

Each step was agony. Plato felt like he was carrying a sack of sand on each shoulder, and three on top of his head. His neck kept buckling under his head; his chin kept knocking into his chest. Each drink of the cold, crisp air was a strain; his breaths were coming faster and faster. His lungs were filling with fluid from the infection. It was like trying to breathe maple syrup.

A Venturi oxygen mask would feel nice about now, Plato reflected. With about 60% O_2.

The door swung open just as Plato reached for the bell. Randolph Smythe the Third was beaming at him with the identical smile he had given his guests just two days earlier.

"Plato Marley! Good to see you again." He stepped back from the doorway and waved Plato inside. "Come in, come in."

He was wearing a brilliant white lab coat over his suit. A stethoscope hung around his neck. He took Plato's coat and tossed it onto a chair beside the door. "I'm afraid Valerie couldn't be here tonight. She's attending a benefit concert. My son is performing with a chamber orchestra downtown. Raising money for the burn unit."

Plato slowly panned his eyes around the foyer. The Spielberg chandelier hovering overhead was only putting out half its power, so the room was bathed in twilight. But aside from the pillars and paintings and fancy rugs, the foyer looked empty.

He turned to Smythe. "Where's Cal?"

"Don't worry." Smythe chuckled. He patted Plato on the back. "You'll be joining her shortly."

He led Plato across the giant chessboard floor and over to the library. He stopped in the doorway and waited for his guest to join him. "My, you're walking awfully slowly today." As they moved into the brightly lit library, he cocked his head at Plato. "Dear me. You look terribly ill, Doctor Marley. Pale, almost cyanotic."

"A touch of pneumonia," Plato croaked.

"How very unfortunate for you," he clucked. He rubbed his chin thoughtfully. "But it does give me an idea—"

From somewhere in the house, a telephone rang faintly.

"Please excuse me," the dean said. He gestured toward the bar. "Perhaps you should fix yourself a drink. I'll be back in a moment." He strode off, but stopped at the doorway. "Oh. And please don't try anything foolish. For Cal's sake."

Plato nodded slowly and slumped farther into the room. The furniture hadn't been moved since the party. He closed his eyes to slits and tried to imagine that it was still Saturday night, that everything since then had been just a dream. A very bad dream.

The room slowly filled with voices and music and a milling herd of Smythe's wealthy friends. Over by the window, Cal was doing her dumb blonde impression for Arnold Welkins. At the piano, Smythe's son was weaving over and under the melody of "The Very Thought of You." And Bob Stahl was standing beside the bar, listening to Smythe's story about the lionfish.

Except Dean Smythe was right beside Plato, at his elbow. Plato blinked, and the room was empty once more.

"That didn't take long." Smythe was rubbing his hands together, looking rather pleased with himself. "You're sure you won't have a drink?"

Plato shrugged. He was still looking at the bar. The memories had faded, but the portrait of Smythe's first wife still hung in the corner.

He walked closer and stared up at the painting. "Why did you kill her?"

"Kill who?" Smythe sounded alarmed. But he followed Plato's gaze and glanced up at the portrait. "Oh. You mean Dolores."

"Yes." Who *else* could he have meant?

"That's rather a personal question, isn't it?" When Plato didn't answer, Smythe just shrugged. "But I suppose, under the circumstances, you deserve an answer."

Plato turned and leaned on the bar. With glazed eyes, he stared at the dean. Or rather, the *deans*—there were two of them now. Plato was too weak to focus. Too tired from the effort of breathing, of trying to control his shivering as another feverish spell took hold.

"Our marriage was doomed from the start. Just one of those things." The twin Smythes took a deep breath and turned away from the portrait. "Two different worlds. Dolores was an Easterner—a Radcliffe debutante, born into a wealthy family. Power and prestige. Veddy, veddy conscious of her position on the social ladder." In Plato's eyes, the two Smythes slowly merged into one again. He stared at the floor and scratched his head. "I was a coal miner's son from Scranton. A poor young physician limping along on a research fellowship. I think she married me just to spite her father."

He glanced up at Plato. The lines in his face deepened. "It was a match made in hell. We grew to hate each other. She finally asked me for a divorce, but I wouldn't agree to the terms."

"You wanted the money," Plato guessed.

"Hardly." Smythe laughed bitterly. He swept his arms about. "I told her she could have *everything*. The house, the cars, the money. Half of everything I earned for the rest of my life—she laughed at that, of course." Fists clenching and unclenching, he twisted his gaze up to the portrait. His voice dropped to a whisper. "No. She wanted Randy. She wanted my son.

"And she was going to get him, too."

Plato looked up at the picture. The mother's possessive hand on her son's shoulder, a faint smile on her lips. Even in death, she seemed to be mocking Smythe.

"So you killed her," Plato said. "Ten years ago last November. You were supposedly at a conference in Chicago."

"I *was* at a conference in Chicago," he replied. "But I took a seven o'clock flight home and broke into the house. Randy was at a friend's house that night—I made sure of that before I left." His gaze softened. "I begged, *pleaded* with her. But she wanted the boy all to herself. When I pulled the gun out, she laughed. She dared me to use it."

His voice cracked. He stared at the floor again. "It was all very easy, really. I stole most of her jewelry, dumped the gun and jewels into Lake Erie, and took the red-eye back to Chicago. No one at the conference realized I had ever left."

"But you got a speeding ticket that night. On your way to the airport."

"Yes." He glanced up sharply. "And I have been wondering how you two found about about it. I searched Marilyn's office—*twice*—and couldn't find a thing."

"She faxed it," Plato replied. "Your copying machine breaks down a lot, doesn't it?"

Smythe nodded. "But why couldn't I find her fax?"

"She faxed it to her computer, and never printed it. She

put the file on a disk and sent it home with her brother that afternoon. A sort of insurance policy."

He started. "Then her brother knows, too?"

"No." Plato didn't want Jonathan involved in this. Enough was enough. "He gave the disk to me. He had no idea what was on it."

Smythe sighed, relieved. "Then I've closed the loop."

"What do you mean?" Plato asked. "Other people know about it. Tiffany Cramer probably—"

"Tiffany Cramer," Smythe interrupted, "is going to have a small accident tonight." He sighed. "A pity. She really was a fine student."

"An accident wouldn't do you any good," Plato told him. "Tiffany's breathing tube was supposed to be pulled this afternoon. She's probably told her story to the police by now. I assume you were the person who attacked her Saturday night?"

"Of course." He shook his head, smiled ruefully. "Poor Tiffany had the audacity to call me—*here*—during the party Saturday. She planned to expose my little secret. Apparently, like your wife, she had seen the *Sunday Magazine* article, and she somehow caught a glimpse of my speeding ticket. Probably on Marilyn's computer screen, if what you say is true—though I don't see how she could have remembered the date a month after she saw it. Unless she has a photographic memory or something." He shuddered at the recollection. "It was quite a shock. I told her she didn't know what she was talking about, and threatened her with immediate expulsion. To buy some time."

"That's why the party broke up early," Plato said.

"I dropped hints here and there. That Valerie wasn't feeling well, that I was tired from campaigning. I thought the last guests would *never* leave." He took a deep breath. "Luckily, I made it to the parking lot just as Tiffany was leaving Siegel."

Plato was confused. "But she *must* have told the police by now."

"She hasn't been extubated yet." The dean smiled and jerked a thumb over his shoulder. "That was the senior SICU resident—a graduate of Siegel. I had called earlier today, asking about poor Tiffany's condition. He promised to call me back as soon as sign-out was over. He just told me that they're playing it safe and keeping Tiffany on the ventilator until tomorrow morning." He spread his hands. "Until then, of course, she can't talk. And she's presumably under some sedation, so she won't be writing any messages either."

Smythe was right. But Plato still didn't understand. "Then she'll talk tomorrow morning. Are you going to skip the country between now and then?"

"No." He fingered the stethoscope dangling from his neck and frowned. "I'm afraid Tiffany Cramer is going to have a rather disastrous complication during the night. A massive intracranial hemorrhage." He nodded thoughtfully. "They've been experimenting with that anticlotting drug at the medical school. It's used for heart attacks. You've heard of TPA?"

"Yes."

"I'm becoming quite a regular customer at the physiology department's drug cabinet." He shrugged. "Generally, the drug is quite safe, unless you have some fragile, damaged blood vessels. Like Tiffany has."

Plato felt ill. The TPA would dissolve the wispy, friable clots healing the damaged arteries and veins inside Tiffany's skull. At the very least, she would suffer a major stroke. More probably, she would simply die.

Smythe was insane. Some little screw must have come loose when he killed his first wife.

But on the other hand, it was a brilliant solution. They would never learn that Tiffany's hemorrhage was intentional. After she died, who would think to run a test for an anticlotting drug?

Cal would.

But Smythe was certain he had closed the loop.

"Where's Cal?" Plato asked again. He wasn't sure he wanted an answer.

The dean smiled slowly. He raised both hands in a placating gesture. "Don't worry, Plato. I said you'd be joining her soon, didn't I?"

Plato finally brought himself to say what he'd suspected all along. To pronounce the words he hadn't wanted to believe. He forced them past the knot in his throat.

"You killed her."

"*I* didn't kill her." Dean Smythe strolled over to the sofa and picked up a soft cushion. "It's that damned cooler in the anatomy lab. Sergei has urged me to have it replaced.

He says the ventilation system doesn't work, that the lock won't open from the inside. He's afraid someone will get trapped and suffocate.

"I'm afraid he's right."

Dean Smythe raised the pillow in front of Plato's face. It was very pretty, covered with brightly colored swirls, patterns of blue and red and yellow. Primary colors, like the streamers at a birthday party.

Plato remembered his sixth birthday. All his friends were there. His father, the cop, baked a cake that looked and tasted like a brick. But Plato loved it.

He had taken a deep breath and blown out all the candles, wishing his mother could come back. But she hadn't.

He took a deep breath now, blew at the pillow. Wished Cal could come back.

But she never would.

The pillow settled on Plato's face, blocking his mouth and nose. He tried twisting his head, but his strength was gone. Plato was weak from the sickness, the fever, and the sudden shock of knowing Cal was gone. He was trapped, paralyzed. His arms and legs were so frail they could barely move at all. Smythe had won. Plato's death would look like another accident—a consequence of his pneumonia.

The dean was pressing him against the bar, bracing Plato's body in place with his knees, leaning down on Plato's chest, mashing the pillow against his face. Plato couldn't see the pretty colors anymore. Couldn't see anything but black. Couldn't move a muscle.

Just like Marilyn.

He pictured her then, alive, images flicking by with each frantic heartbeat. His favorite patient. Marilyn with her cane. Marilyn with her walker. Marilyn with her wheelchair. Always getting worse, but never giving up. Flashing that crazy grin of hers, that determined smile, that goofy wink. Telling Plato that hell would freeze over before she let some damnfool disease get the best of *her*.

Determined even in death, winking at him from the cadaver cart. Telling Plato to do the same thing now. Never give up.

But it was no use. Plato could hear the last frantic gurgles of blood in his ears.

Gurgles?

Nobody's blood *gurgled*.

Smythe leaned harder. Apparently, Plato wasn't dying fast enough. Some air was getting past the pillow. Enough to buy Plato another minute of life. The murderer leaned harder still.

And Plato heard—*felt*—a crackling beneath his head. And he realized where the gurgling was coming from. Not the rushing of blood, or his horribly labored breathing—now stopped altogether with Smythe's extra weight on the pillow.

No, it came from the aquarium just beneath his head. Just beneath the crackling Plexiglas.

And Plato finally remembered his fever dream. Slowly, incredibly slowly, Plato lifted his arms, his hands up to grasp Smythe's left elbow. Hoping for just a little bit of Marilyn's luck.

The dean ignored Plato's hands on his arm, just leaned harder.

And Plato waited, summoned all his energy for one final writhing, snakelike twist that jerked his head away from the shattering Plexiglas and plunged Dean Smythe's left hand deep into the water.

The lionfish struck almost instantly. Twice, judging from the sudden muscle spasms in Smythe's arm. The dean let out a horrible bellow and jerked his hand away from the tank.

Pushing the pillow away from his face, Plato watched Randolph Smythe the Third stumble across the carpet and sprawl along the sofa, howling in agony. Plato slid down to the floor and, with gruesome fascination, watched the dean's arm redden and swell, nearly doubling in size over the next few minutes. Finally, he summoned the strength to stand and stagger over to the sofa.

The dean's perfect hair was mussed. His perfect skin was florid. His perfect smile was a contorted grimace. His breaths were coming in quick, ragged gasps. He gazed up at the ceiling like a flagellant in prayer. Slowly, painfully, he wrenched his eyes up to Plato's.

"Where is your telephone?" Plato asked. He didn't trust himself to find it in this house. Not in time to save Dean Smythe. Or Cal.

"Trophy room," the twisted mouth breathed. "Under the python."

Plato found the telephone, dialed 911, and waited.

Chapter 26

Shivering in the cold and the dark, Cal Marley fought the urge to sleep. For the first hour or so, she had yelled and thrashed and pummeled the steel doors of the cadaver box. At least, it had *seemed* like an hour. It was hard to gauge the time in this total, utter blackness.

And then, after finally giving up, she had heard the high-pitched squeal of a pager from somewhere outside. It had sounded like *Plato's* pager. So she had shouted and screamed and banged on the lid again, rocking the box until it threatened to tip off the gurney. She'd kept it up for another hour or so. But no one had come.

Cal had wriggled around inside the box then, testing the hinges, straining against the lid. But her fingers couldn't get a grip on the cold and slippery steel. Small as Cal was, she still couldn't squirm around enough to get any leverage on the doors. She could only pry the lids apart an inch or so, poke her fingers through the slit and feel the rope Smythe had used to tie the lids together.

When the guard's footsteps had sounded in the stairwell, Smythe had forced Cal into the cooler, pulling the door nearly shut and holding his hand over her mouth, his gun at the base of her neck until the footsteps had faded away again. He had flicked on the lights then, glanced around the cooler's interior and spied the empty steel coffin. Smythe was reasonably sure that Cal couldn't escape from the cooler once the door was latched, but he didn't want to take any chances. Inside the cadaver box, Cal couldn't make too much noise, and couldn't figure out a way to open the cooler door.

Ordering her to climb onto the gurney, he had smiled and promised to come back early tomorrow morning to place her body on the floor.

"By then, you'll almost certainly have frozen to death,

or exhausted all the air in here," he told her. He swung the doors up and tied the lid shut, his voice sounding tinny through the thin steel. "Sergie *warned* me that an accident could happen in this old cooler. I suppose we'll have to replace it after tonight's tragedy."

Even with the rope cinching the handles in place, a narrow shaft of light had shone on Cal's face through the slit between the lids. But that, too, had been snuffed out when Smythe finally turned off the light, walked out of the cooler, and firmly slammed the door behind him.

Lying alone in the dark, Cal wondered if Smythe was right. How much air did the old cooler hold? She thought back to her physiology classes and tried to calculate how much oxygen was present in the small chamber, how much air the cadavers displaced and how much she consumed with each breath.

It was impossible to know. She might have enough air to last her three days or three hours. Either way, there was nothing to be gained by wasting it. Why bother making noise when anyone outside would just assume it came from the faulty compressor? Her best hope was to stay alive until Smythe returned, and try to surprise him. Cal willed herself to relax, to breathe slowly, to conserve precious oxygen.

But then the shivers started. With her usual rotten luck, Cal had chosen to wear a skirt today. Plato had teased her about it this morning, saying she'd catch her death of cold.

He was probably right. Either that, or she'd suffocate.

Cal suspected that the shivers came from fear as much as from cold. She didn't want to die. She didn't want Plato to die. She didn't want to think about the dozen or so cadavers hanging from ear hooks just outside her box.

Like Marilyn Abel, she had donated her body to science. She didn't want to think about being embalmed, about Smythe coming down to the anatomy lab to gloat during her dissection.

Cal clenched her jaw. She wouldn't let that happen. She would be alive when he came back in the morning. Cal tried to breathe slowly, to control the shivers. Tried to banish her fears, by focusing her mind on something else.

Closing her eyes, flattening herself against the cold steel, Cal thought about her life. The good things and the bad. But mostly the good things.

Mostly, she thought about Plato. How they had met in

the hospital. His first stumbling, clumsy overtures. On her first Valentine's Day at Riverside General, he had bought a carnation from the Women's Auxiliary and brought it to the lab, introducing himself. When she asked him to pin the flower on her blouse, his hands shook.

She thought back to their first date, their first kiss. The first time they made love. Their honeymoon in Antigua. Warm beaches, clear blue water. Snorkeling off the *Jolly Roger,* getting sick from the rum and the waves. Making love in the ruins of an old windmill on a deserted cane farm.

They would never have children now. She wondered what they would have been like.

Lying there in a cadaver's steel coffin, surrounded by a dozen dead bodies, she thought about the afterlife.

Would Plato be there?

Now that her shivers had finally passed, the chilly air reached its icy tendrils around her arms and legs, soothing, caressing. *Sleep now,* it seemed to say. Cal felt her breaths coming a little faster; the cooler must have held less air than she had imagined. Or maybe Sergei's formula put out some kind of poison, some chemical or gas that displaced the oxygen in the room. Maybe the cadavers themselves had used up the air in their slow process of decay.

Did it matter?

Cal surrendered to the urge to sleep. She sank down, slowly down, into cool slumber. Like falling into a fluffy snowbank. The cadaver box was impossibly comfortable. If only she didn't have to work so hard to breathe.

As she drifted out of awareness at last, a small and very unimportant voice in her mind wondered if she were dying.

Minutes or hours or days later, glorious light streamed into Cal's face. She blinked like a mole seeing the first light of spring. She blinked like a lost soul seeing the gates of heaven at last.

Above her stood a tall, blond-haired, blue-eyed kid. Dressed in pale blue. The real Saint Peter this time. Or maybe an angel.

Oh, God. She really *was* dead.

But why did Cal keep seeing angels? Wasn't she supposed to see a long blue tunnel, with a bright light at the end?

"Hello," the angel said.

"Hello," Cal answered.

"Are you Doctor Marley?" he asked.

"Yes."

He's rather stuffy for an angel, Cal thought. Don't they use first names in heaven?

"Oh." The angel kept glancing over his shoulder nervously. His face was a little green. He didn't look very comfortable. He seemed to be afraid of something. "I've met your husband. He's on his way here, you know."

"Will I get to see him?" Cal asked anxiously. She shivered. God, it was *cold* up here.

"Yes," the angel replied. He frowned, and glanced over his shoulder again. Something was definitely bothering him. "Yes, of course."

"That's *wonderful*," Cal replied. She stared up into the bright lights of heaven. "We'll still be together then. I've always wondered about that."

The angel flashed her a strange glance, looked over his shoulder once again, and swallowed heavily.

"Can we get out of here?" he asked suddenly. "This place gives me the creeps."

"Can't this thing go any faster?" Plato shouted above the din.

Homer's ancient Chevy Caprice was clattering down Interstate 71 like a steam locomotive with square wheels. The rattle-bang of the engine pounded Plato's chest. His head drummed against the ceiling like a jackhammer. Outside the road seemed to shimmer and shake with the vibration. Snowflakes streamed past the windshield like stars in a sci-fi movie. Lampposts loomed and blurred away, moving quickly enough to strobe-light the car's interior.

But they weren't moving quickly enough for Plato.

"We're doing eighty-five already." Homer was peering through a small clear patch of windshield. His wipers were long chunks of ice, pushing the snow back and forth, back and forth. His chin was resting on the dashboard. "This is as fast as she'll go."

Plato slumped lower in his seat, moved his head away from the ceiling. "Cal *has* to be alive, Homer. That cooler must hold plenty of air."

Unless the cold got to her, he thought quietly. Or unless the cadavers put out some kind of toxic gas. What was *in* Sergei's secret embalming fluid, anyway? No cyanide, Plato hoped.

"She's probably out by now," Homer said. "The dispatcher at 911 talked to the guard at Siegel himself, and explained the situation to him."

"But the guard never called back," Plato pointed out.

"No. The dispatcher tried calling Siegel again just before we left Smythe's, but there was no answer."

Maybe the guard *couldn't* answer, Plato thought. Maybe he was busy doing cardiopulmonary resuscitation on Cal.

"Drive faster, Homer."

His cousin nodded, and mashed the gas pedal a little harder. The engine's whine grew until Plato's ears crackled with the noise. The car sounded like a P–51 Mustang going into a death spiral.

Up ahead, the hood suddenly jerked open a few inches. Plato braced himself for instant death.

Homer shot him a grin, shouting, "It does that all the time. It's still latched, so it won't pop open. I think."

Plato nodded. Seconds later, he felt a sudden rush of cold air dragging at his feet. He glanced down at the floor. The bit of tattered carpet covering the hole had vanished, sucked away in the airstream.

Up ahead, the lights of the Terminal Tower glowed through the snowstorm like ghostly beacons welcoming the Ancient Mariner into port. The tower itself was hidden in the clouds, along with most of Cleveland's skyline.

They swung north into town and exited the freeway at East Ninth, Homer's wheels shuddering and shaking across patches of ice and snow and dry asphalt. Plato watched a hubcap sail into a clump of weeds as they rounded a turn near Public Square. The old Caprice was leaving pieces of itself all over Cleveland; he wondered how much would be left by the time they reached Siegel.

They crossed the Detroit-Superior bridge in a puff of snow and smoke, the Cuyahoga swallowed up in the storm far below. A few more turns, and Homer finally whomped into the driveway of the medical college, swerving up over a curb and into a NO PARKING sign when his headlights picked up the white bulk of an ambulance parked just outside the main entrance.

"Oh, God," Plato said.

"It's okay, Plato." Homer wrestled his door open,

dragged Plato out, and half carried him up to the back door of the ambulance. He peered inside and shook his head. Empty.

He stuck his shoulder back under Plato's arm and dragged him up the long stone stairway to the entrance. A pair of cops were standing just outside, smoking cigarettes. They nodded to Homer and whispered to themselves. One of them pointed at Plato and frowned. The other one opened the door.

The paramedics were stomping snow from their shoes just inside the foyer. An empty stretcher stood beside them.

Plato had seen medics waiting like that before. Outside of crime scenes, waiting for the forensics team to finish their work.

"Oh, God," Plato said again. He squinted down the long hallway for some sign of Cal. At the far end, the doorway leading down to the anatomy lab was open. It looked as far away from Plato as the finish line at the Boston Marathon. He staggered forward. "Come on, Homer. Help me get down there."

"Down where?" Homer asked. "She's right here."

Plato turned slowly. Cal was sitting just inside the door, on the same bench where he had waited earlier that evening. A blue wool blanket was slung over her shoulders. A mug of hot chocolate was steaming in her hands. She smiled at him and stood.

He stumbled across the linoleum, put his hands on her shoulders, and gazed down into her eyes.

"You look *terrible*," he told her. "Your lips are all blue."

"*You* look terrible," she replied, frowning. "Your whole *face* is blue."

"Pneumonia does that, you know." He folded her into his arms. After a long embrace, he turned and pointed toward the paramedics. "Come on. You'd better get on that stretcher."

"I've had enough gurneys for one day, thank you. For a whole lifetime." She tugged his hand and led him to the stretcher. "This one's for you. They were going to leave once they saw I was okay. But I heard you were coming, so I told them to wait."

She turned him around and pushed his shoulders, much like Nathan had. He fell onto the cart.

"I talked to Nathan just now. He told me how you snuck

away from his office." Her arms were folded and her lips were pursed. "You have pneumonia in both lungs. Every lobe. He said your chest X ray looked like you were drowning in mud."

"Oh."

"I've been worried *sick* about you." She eased him back onto the cushion, lifted his legs, and slid them under the blanket. "Afraid you wouldn't make it here. Afraid that wreck of Homer's would finally fall apart."

"It almost did." Plato fumbled for words, to say what she meant to him, how ecstatic he was to find her alive. "Cally, I—"

She put a finger over his mouth. "No more talking. You're wasting oxygen."

With her other hand, she cinched the stretcher's belt tight across his waist. She glanced up at the paramedics. "Next stop, Riverside General. And see that he doesn't get away, okay?"

"Sure." One of them cinched the belt even tighter. Plato felt like he was being cut in two.

"He's a lousy patient," Cal told them. She shrugged off her blanket, tucked it over his shoulders, and followed the stretcher outside. "The pneumonia's affecting his brain. He's wandered off from the hospital once already."

"He'll be fine, lady," the paramedic told her as they eased the cart into the ambulance. "He's going straight to the hospital. He won't get away this time."

"Just to make sure, I'm coming along." She climbed in, knelt beside Plato's bed, and clutched his hand. And watched him all the way to the hospital.

Chapter 27

A week later, Plato was home in bed, flipping through the pile of mystery and suspense and science fiction novels Cal had brought home from the library. Grazing on peanut M&M's and plain M&M's and Hershey Kisses and the occasional Nestlé's Crunch bar. Flipping through the *Plain Dealer* and reading that Randolph Smythe the Third was recovering nicely from his nasty sting, but that he was being arraigned on two counts of murder and three of attempted murder. Reading the follow-up story about Homer's appointment to the case. And enjoying the attention of his ministering angel, who had finally returned home from work but was already on the phone again.

The conversation was quickly over, though. Cal hung up and turned to Plato.

"That was Dean Fairfax." Cal's eyes were bright. She smiled happily. "He just wanted us to know that all four of our students passed the makeup exam."

"Even Tiffany Cramer?" Plato asked, surprised.

"She passed with honors."

"You're kidding. She was just discharged from the hospital Saturday."

"Raj had brought her notes and studied with her all week." Cal's smile faded a little. "I visited her Saturday, just before she was discharged. She told me she was thinking about dropping out of medical school, no matter how well she did on the test."

Plato sat up quickly. "Why?"

"To go into pharmacology." Cal shrugged. "To follow in Marilyn Abel's footsteps, I guess."

"I can think of a lot worse footsteps to follow," Plato said. He frowned. "But I doubt her father will be too pleased about it."

"I don't think it matters much," Cal said. "She'll have plenty of money of her own pretty soon."

Plato nodded. Last Tuesday, the day after Smythe surrendered to the police, Tricia Abel had received a letter from the United States Patent Office. Marilyn had applied for a patent on Patracin just before her death. The patent application, which had been approved, had listed Tiffany Cramer, Bob Stahl, and Therese Vogel as full partners in the venture. Once the patent was sold, the three of them would each get a fifth of the profits, along with Marilyn's family. Albright and the college would split the last twenty percent.

Maybe Siegel wouldn't fall into the Cuyahoga after all.

"Chuck Albright has told Tiffany that he'd love to have her as a doctoral student," Cal added.

"Why am I not surprised?"

"She wants to stay in the area, to be with Raj. So she might take Chuck's offer. Maybe get a combination M.D./Ph.D. degree."

"Not a bad idea," Plato said. "She's certainly smart enough for it."

"Tiffany's thinking it over," Cal said. "She's interested in infectious disease, just like Marilyn. I suggested she could become a specialist—develop antibiotics and get involved in the clinical trials, too."

"With a little luck," Plato mused, "she just might do it."

"Speaking of antibiotics—" Cal reached for the bedside stand and picked up a bright metallic object. "I brought your medicine."

"Aw, come on, Cal." Plato shuddered. "Can't we skip this dose? Just give them twice a day? There was a study in the *Journal of Infectious*—"

"No way." She scowled at him. "Nathan only agreed to let you come home early from the hospital if you followed the rules. Now roll over."

"Cally—"

She flicked the syringe with her fingernail, squirting the air bubble and a few drops of fluid out through the tip of the long thick needle. "Roll *over*. Or do you want this in front?"

"No, thanks." Plato complied, wincing as the needle went in. Wincing again as the medicine flowed into an already sore muscle. "I think you hit the sciatic nerve, Cal. I'm tingling all the way down my leg."

"I'm at least three inches away from it, silly. If you knew your anatomy—"

"My foot's tingling. I think it's going numb." The shot was taking forever.

"Nonsense." Cal sounded pleased with herself. "I'm getting rather good at this, aren't I?"

"Better than you are at cooking." Plato had been eating chili since he arrived home two days ago. "But that wouldn't be hard. *Ouch!*"

Cal had pulled the needle out, rather too abruptly, Plato thought. He turned over and tried not to rest his weight on the sore spot.

"Speaking of the sciatic nerve," Cal said casually, "Dean Fairfax was very impressed with our success at tutoring the anatomy students."

"*Your* success."

"He wants us to tutor another section next quarter. In March." She smoothed the pillow under his head, pulled the blanket up to his chin, and felt his forehead with the back of her hand.

"He wants *you* to tutor another section next quarter," Plato said petulantly.

"Come on, Plato. We make a great team." She put the needle on the nightstand and slipped her hand under the sheet. "Don't you think?"

"Nuh-uh. You're not going to get off that easy this time." He pushed her hand away. "No means no. I don't have time. I have a full schedule in March. Four new lectures to prepare. Three weekends on call."

Cal picked up the syringe again and contemplated the needle thoughtfully. "And another fifteen shots until you're switched to antibiotic pills." She glanced over at Plato. "I would hate to make a mistake with one of them. Poke a nerve or something."

Plato skittered across to the other side of the bed, eyeing Cal warily.

She waved the needle back and forth in the air. "Tick-tock, tick-tock. I could play darts with this thing. Pin the tail on the Plato. All sorts of games." She glanced over at him. "On the other hand, if I didn't have to worry about tutoring the students all by myself, I could devote my full attention to administering this medicine properly. And painlessly."

Plato sighed. "When do we start?"

Cal set the syringe down and slipped between the sheets. "Right now, I think." She placed her hands on Plato's chest, then moved them slowly lower, lower. "Now. The pudendal nerve has three rather important branches. Did you know that?"

Plato gave an involuntary quiver, swallowing hard. "No."

"The perineal nerve goes down *here*." She looked up quickly. "Are you listening?"

He took a deep breath, gave a shaky nod.

"Good." She moved away a little, glanced up at him and smiled. "I'll bet you never realized anatomy could be so interesting, did you?"

"No." He pulled her close again. "But I'm willing to learn."

Author's Note

An estimated 250,000 to 350,000 Americans have multiple sclerosis. The disease affects the central nervous system—the brain and spinal cord—by "short circuiting" the nerve fibers that carry signals from the brain to the body and back. In healthy people, special myelin sheaths cover and insulate the fibers, dramatically speeding the transmission of nerve impulses. But in multiple sclerosis, these myelin sheaths deteriorate and disappear in random fashion, forming scattered patches that interfere with nerve signals throughout the brain and spinal cord. People with MS can therefore suffer from a bewildering variety of symptoms ranging from mild weakness or dizziness to blindness, paralysis, and extreme disability.

The long-term outcome of multiple sclerosis is just as variable. The disease tends to cause waves of attacks and remissions. After each attack, the individual may recover some, all, or no function. Over a period of years, though, many people suffer a gradual and progressive deterioration.

Researchers have explored a variety of possible causes for multiple sclerosis—including viral infection and immune problems—but the exact cause is still unclear. Therapy is aimed at helping patients through each attack, preventing further attacks, and controlling symptoms. No cure has yet been found, but recent developments such as the FDA approval of a beta-interferon drug which regulates the immune system offer hope for still more effective treatments in the near future.

Equally important are efforts by the Multiple Sclerosis Society, a national organization dedicated to educating the public about multiple sclerosis, fostering continued research, and providing support to patients and their families. For more information or assistance, call the Multiple Sclerosis Society's toll-free number at: 1-800-FIGHT-MS (1-800-344-4867), or write: The Multiple Sclerosis Society, 733 Third Avenue, New York, NY 10017.

Turn the page for
a sneak look
at the next
Cal & Plato Marley Mystery:
SKELETONS
IN THE CLOSET

Chapter 1

"It's hideous, Cally." Plato Marley took another bite from his sandwich and grimaced at his wife. "It's killing my appetite."

Cal smiled fondly at the object parked between the sugar and the ketchup bottle. "Pretty accurate, isn't it?"

"Pretty loathsome." Plato swallowed heavily and forced his gaze away from the table. He stared across the Cuyahoga River instead, watching the ponderous mass of an iron ore barge slowly blot out his view of Cleveland's skyline. They were lunching at Shooter's today, celebrating Cal's promotion to Assistant Professor of Anatomy at the medical college.

Despite the warmth of the late October afternoon, the restaurant's vast outdoor deck was all but deserted. The only other diners were an older couple seated at the opposite end of the pavillion. The waiter had offered the pair a table nearby, with a better view of the river, but they had glimpsed Cal's prize and politely declined. They were huddled over their table near the door, whispering and darting occasional glances at the grisly object.

Cal speared a radish into her mouth, hefting the human head with her free hand and demonstrating its virtues for Plato while she crunched away at her salad. "I'm testing it for a company in Maine. Three guys—a sculptor, an anatomist, and a plastics engineer."

Half of the skin was already peeled away, exposing a tapestry of muscles and nerves. A marvelously realistic eyeball rested atop the A.1 bottle, glaring down at Plato's chocolate mousse pie. Cal peeled the other skin away, along with the ear and most of the tousled brown hair, and handed the mess across the table.

"Feel that," she urged. "They call it Plaskin. Just like the real thing, huh?"

Reluctantly, Plato slid his fingers over the flayed latex. Cal was right. He could feel little surface irregularities, a few wrinkles in the skin of the forehead, and he could *swear* he felt a five o'clock shadow. His stomach flip-flopped. "God! How do they *do* that?"

"Don't ask me." Cal draped the skin over the sugar bowl and started peeling muscles away. "They tried explaining it, but I don't understand it all myself. They start with a cast of someone's face." She gestured at the head. "This one's based on Harold Hawkins, the president of the company. Handsome guy, when he's got all his skin on. Anyway, they use some kind of computer modeling to get the proper surface textures for different kinds of skin, for the surfaces of organs, muscles, brain, whatever."

She detached Harold's temporalis muscle and handed it across to Plato—a limp scallop-shaped piece of tissue with the look and feel of raw flank steak. After handing it back, Plato instinctively wiped his fingers on his napkin.

"A lot of companies make peel-away models," Cal continued. "But these Plaskin models feel just like the real thing. It's that plastics engineer—he's got this stuff down to a science."

She undid a pair of hidden catches and started to swing the now-bare skull open at the midline, affording Plato a glimpse of the dura mater, the outer covering of the brain. He quickly grabbed her arm and showed her his watch.

"Sorry, dear." He feigned disappointment. "I'd love to see more, but I've got to make rounds at the hospital this afternoon."

Cal glanced at the watch and sucked in her breath. "And *I've* got to lecture in the anatomy lab in half an hour." She swung the skull closed again and pressed a salivary gland into place, then paused. "But what about our desserts?"

"Let's take them home," Plato suggested. "We can have them tonight."

The waiter boxed their desserts and handled their check with record speed. Reassembling the model took much longer. When Cal finished, she still wasn't satisfied. "Only problem with this stuff," she observed as she pressed the half-nose into place, "is that it just doesn't stay *on* very well. There! How's that?"

Plato frowned as the nose slipped away again, revealing the septum and ruddy turbinates of the nasal passages. The tousled brown hair was askew, as though trimmed by an astigmatic barber. The eyeballs stared in opposing directions. The tongue wouldn't quite fit inside the mouth.

All in all, the model looked far more like the victim of some horrific crime than an anatomy lab teaching aid.

"I think Harold could use a little Velcro," Plato observed.

"You may be right," Cal clucked. She gently slid the head into an oversized Ziploc sack and stuffed it into her canvas bookbag, then handed him the dessert box. "You can carry this. We'd better hurry."

Luckily, Siegel Medical College wasn't far away, but just up the road on the west bank of the Cuyahoga. Plato swung the ancient Rabbit into the parking lot with ten minutes to spare, pulled up to the curb, and reached across to open Cal's door.

She treated him to a long, lingering kiss, then frowned.

"What's the matter?" Plato asked.

"I wish you had time to walk me up to the door," she sighed. "I get so tired of being ogled."

"Ogled? Someone is ogling you?"

Cal pointed to the sidewalk leading from the parking lot to the entrance. Siegel Medical College had finally raised enough money for a much-needed research wing, along with repairs to the crumbling back half of the building. A barbed wire fence lined the edge of the sidewalk. Beyond lay a vast rectangular pit, roughly the size of a football field. The construction area was populated with equipment from a sandbox of dreams: excavators, backhoes, cranes, dump trucks, a cement mixer or two, all bearing the familiar Windsor Construction Company logo.

"The female medical students call it 'running the gauntlet,'" Cal explained. "Every time a woman staffer or student walks in from the parking lot, those construction workers start whistling and hooting, carrying on like a pack of lovesick coyotes."

Plato rolled his eyes. "You're kidding."

"They're always drooling over my legs," she continued, smoothing her tan slacks. "That's why I haven't worn any skirts to work for the past couple of weeks."

He switched off the motor and set the parking brake. "Come on, I'll walk in with you. I've got a few minutes to spare."

Not that it was likely to do much good, Plato knew. Even if his presence kept the workers quiet today, he couldn't escort Cal inside very time she came to lecture at the college. Maybe they could complain to the administration—Dean Fairfax owed them a favor or two.

But as they passed the building site, Plato saw no sign of the construction workers.

"Maybe they're at lunch," he guessed.

"No such luck," Cal replied. "They eat on-site. Otherwise the women could sneak in and out. See? There they are."

Cal pointed past the barbed wire fence to the far side of the enormous hole. An excavator was down in the trench, its shovel resting on the lip of the ditch. A crowd of yellow hard hats was clustered around the scoop.

Up ahead, one of Siegel's security officers was hurrying out of the main entrance. He spotted Cal and jogged over.

"Doctor Marley, thank goodness you're here." Henry Douglas smiled with relief.

"Why?" Cal asked. "What's wrong?"

"I don't know." The young security guard tapped the heels of his shoes together nervously like Dorothy in the *Wizard of Oz*. The finely polished leather glinted almost as brightly as the ruby slippers. "I just got a call from the building foreman. Their shovel hit something—he thinks it's a bone."

"Bone?" Cal frowned. "Human?"

Henry shrugged. "Don't know. I had no idea who to call. This isn't exactly covered in the Security Officer's Handbook, you know. I tried the anatomy lab, but there was no answer."

Plato nodded approvingly. Not many people would have thought of contacting Anatomy, but Henry was pretty bright. He'd helped Cal out of a tight situation once before.

"Let's go." Cal turned on her heel and marched toward the gate. Plato and Henry followed close behind.

At the gate, the construction foreman opened the door and shot a questioning glance at Henry.

"This is Doctor Marley," Henry explained. "One of our anatomy professors."

The foreman wasn't much taller than Cal, but he was a foot or two wider. He grinned broadly and shook hands with Plato. "Nice to have you along, Doctor. This little lady your assistant?"

He shot a wide smile at Cal, touring his eyes over her honey-blond hair and trim figure, then frowning at her slacks.

Plato shook his head and pointed to his wife, pretending he wasn't a physician himself. *"That's* Doctor Marley."

The construction foreman gave a wide-eyed grunt, like he'd just caught a wrecking ball in the solar plexus. He slowly lifted his gaze to Cal's face. "Oh. Uhh, sorry, lady."

He recovered quickly, turning to the security guard. "Don't you think maybe we ought to call the police in on this or something? Get somebody *official* involved here?"

"Doctor Marley is also a deputy coroner," Henry explained. "That's about as official as you can get."

The foreman shrugged dubiously. "It's your call, buddy."

"So where's this bone?" Cal asked.

"Over here." The foreman sighed, pointing back toward the excavator. "But you'd better get some hats on first."

He led Cal and Plato to a rack of hard hats beside the gate, then walked them around the back edge of the crater. Henry had headed back to the security office, but a dozen construction workers followed the trio. The foreman stopped at the excavator scoop. The rest of the machine was still down in the pit, its long arm outstretched like a giant fiddler crab about to heave itself free of the ocean.

Standing several feet away from the scoop, the foreman pointed to a dirty white shaft poking up from the fresh clay. "See it?"

Cal set her bag down, pulled the bone free and gave it a cursory glance, then passed it over to Plato. "Fibula."

Plato glanced at the long thin bone. He, too, recognized it as a leg bone. But he hadn't the foggiest notion whether it came from a human or hippopotamus. The foreman backed away quickly when Plato offered him a look.

"I can see it just fine from here," he said. "Looks like a cow bone. We get a lot of those. Found a whole cow skeleton last year, when we were digging for a new wing at Case Western."

"Could be," Cal agreed. "The fibula isn't very distinctive—it could be from a cow, or a deer, or maybe even a bear. Are there any more?"

"You'd have to look down in the hole." He waved his

arms in front of him, palms out. "We stopped digging when Jamahl hit this. Didn't want to mess up the investigation."

"Didn't want to mess up your hands," one of the workers teased, then grinned at Cal. "Don't let Ernie fool you—he almost lost his lunch when we found that cow skeleton last year."

"That's bullshit, Jamahl." The foreman's face lit up like pink neon. "And you know it."

"Sure, Ernie. Sure." The tall black man shook his head and chuckled. "Whatever you say."

"I want to climb down there and take a look," Cal said. "Do you have a small shovel I can poke around with?"

"Yeah," Ernie replied. He jerked a thumb back to a large steel box perched on the rim of the excavation. "But it's too deep for climbing—you'll have to go down in the cage. I'd better go down with you."

"Better stay in line, boss," Jamahl cautioned.

The foreman whirled around. "Don't you have some work to do?"

"Nope." He grinned broadly. "This is my excavator, remember?"

Cal frowned down at the huge excavator scoop. It was full of clay. "There could be some more bones in here too, I suppose."

"Sure could, ma'am," Jamahl agreed. "How about if I get another shovel and check through it?"

"That would be wonderful." She turned to Plato. "Would you mind helping him while I check down below?"

"No problem." Plato nodded eagerly. Hospital rounds would run late today, but he didn't mind. For once, he was just as curious as Cal.

He and Jamahl spent a good half hour sifting through the clay with their hand shovels, gently prodding the soil, shaking and slicing it into tiny pieces, and finding nothing but rocks. While they worked, Jamahl filled Plato in on his boss.

"Ernie's a pinhead. But he's the owner's nephew or second cousin or some such thing." He gathered another shovelful of clay and squinted at it. "He's worse than usual today, though."

"Why is that?" Plato squinted at a wristbone for several seconds before deciding it was a rock.

"We had the whole foundation dug and ready for pouring, all on schedule," Jamahl explained. "Then this morning, the building inspector comes and says the ground is still too soft here by the river. Says we need to dig down another two feet. I thought Ernie was going to kill him."

"Why'd you tell him to stay in line?" Plato asked.

The construction worker chuckled. "Ernie gets out of line a lot. Thinks he's God's gift to women—can't keep his hands to himself. But if she's really a doctor, she just might burn his ass to the ground." He glanced at Plato. "I wouldn't mind seeing that. I'm next in line for his job."

"She's really a doctor," Plato assured him. "And you're right, he'd better not mess with her."

"You know her pretty well, huh?"

"You could say that. She's my wife—" Just then, Plato's shovel struck something hard. "Hey, I think I've got something here."

Together, they probed the boundaries of the object, carefully lifted the surrounding block of clay free, and placed it on the ground. Using their fingers, they scooped dirt away until Plato got a firm handhold on the bone. Jamahl wrestled the last of the clinging clay away as Plato plucked the bone free and held it aloft. Camped around the edge of the pit, the other workers saw it and cheered.

"Distal femur," Cal pronounced from behind him. She took the bone from Plato and studied it carefully. The bone was large and straight, but the jagged edge of the shaft suggested that the other half was still buried somewhere in the pit.

"Did you have any luck down there?" he asked.

"Not much." She reached into her sack and pulled out a familiar-looking bone. "Nothing but the other fibula. Not that it matters, now. We'll have to get a crew from the coroner's office to come and dig up the rest of the skeleton, very carefully."

"What do you mean, 'rest of the skeleton?'" Ernie squeezed between Plato and Cal, using his vast abdominal girth as a sort of flying wedge. "I'm not going to let you throw this whole project off schedule over a stupid cow skeleton."

"It's not a cow skeleton," Cal assured him calmly.

"Deer, bear, whatever. The point is, you can't—"

"The *point,* Ernie"—Cal jabbed the flying wedge with her finger—"is that this is a *human* skeleton."

The foreman backed off and massaged his paunch. "You can't possibly be sure of that. You just said—"

"I said I couldn't tell for sure from the fibula," Cal admitted. She brandished Plato's find under the foreman's nose. "But the *femur*—now, that's a whole different story."

Plato had to grin as Cal adopted her lecturing tone and led the crowd of construction workers over to the flat edge of the scoop. "Aside from the skull, the distal femur—or thigh bone—is one of the most distinctive bones of the human body."

She propped the base of the bone on the flat surface. Rather than standing perfectly vertical, the long shaft took a thirty-degree angle to the left.

"It's all a question of mechanics," Cal began. She tapped the level surface of the scoop. "Pretend this is the top of the tibia, the lower leg bone. It's flat in all animals, like a shelf. Has to be, or the thigh bone would slide off, right?"

A dozen hard hats nodded.

"Now think about the back legs of a cow, or a deer, or a horse. They come down straight from the pelvis, don't they? Their thighs are like two pillars, dropping basically straight from the hips to the ground." She angled the thigh bone so it stood perfectly vertical. "Like this, so they can support the weight of the body. That's the way it is with four-legged animals. Same thing with bears—they have a very wide stance, right? Their feet are about the same width apart as their hip joints."

The audience nodded again. Like the medical students, Cal had them hooked.

"Of course, bears don't move very fast when they're standing. Having their feet so far apart means they have to swing their hips each time they take a step. So if a bear wants to move fast, he drops down to all fours."

"She's right," someone in the crowd agreed. "Last time I went hunting in the Alleghenies, I—"

Someone shushed him.

But Ernie was growing impatient. "So get to the point. What's all this got to do with human bones?"

Cal rested the edge of the femur flat again, so the shaft angled away from vertical. "In humans, the feet are placed closer together than the pelvis. The lower leg bones rise pretty straight, but the upper leg bones have to angle outward to meet the pelvis at the hip joint. We're the only animals that have an angled femur—that's how we can run fast on two legs."

Most of the workers nodded their understanding, but Ernie wasn't convinced. "I still don't see how you can tell all that from one little bone."

A younger fellow near the front spoke up. He placed his feet together and pointed to his hips, smiling earnestly. "See, Ernie, the thigh bone angles out like this, so—"

"I know *that,* Jimmy." The foreman rolled his eyes in disgust. "I'm not a *complete* idiot. I'm just saying, maybe this came from a girl bear—girls have bigger hips, right? Or maybe it came from a gorilla, or a cow that broke its leg."

"There are other indications," Cal persisted. "The lateral edge of the patellar groove, for instance—"

"My point is," Ernie interrupted, "I'm not going to shut down this job site until I get some kind of official word."

Cal's voice hardened. "I assure you I'm the only official you need. As Deputy Coroner for Cuyahoga County—"

"Listen, lady." Ernie gave a patronizing smile. "I enjoyed your little talk, but we've got a job to do here. I can't let some hysterical female march in and close things down without getting some kind of backing." He turned to Jamahl and jerked a thumb at the excavator. "Get digging again. We've wasted half the afternoon as it is."

Jamahl shook his head slowly. None of the other workers moved either.

Plato saw Cal reach into her coat pocket for her ID badge from the coroner's office, then change her mind. A faint smile played at the corners of her mouth.

"I have other proof that these are human bones," Cal said quietly.

"Forget it." Ernie sneered. "I'm not interested in another lecture."

"This proof speaks for itself," she assured him. "I hadn't wanted to bring this up, but since you insist—" She yanked a familiar Ziploc pouch from her booksack and pressed it into Ernie's grasp. Before he looked down, she continued. "I dug it up down there while you were waiting in the cage. It's remarkably well-preserved. Sure, a little bit of the skin has peeled away, and that nose keeps falling off, but—"

Realization of the bag's contents slowly dawned on the foreman. He stared at Harold's head with a sick, horrified fascination. Like a center fielder realizing he's just caught a live hand grenade instead of a baseball.

A greenish pallor spread over his face as he swiveled his gaze up to Cal, swallowed heavily, and dropped the sack. It landed with a ghastly *squish*. Legs shaking, the foreman tottered off to the trailer parked in the corner of the building site. He didn't quite make it.

"Ernie always did have a weak stomach," someone muttered. The others chuckled.

Cal retrieved the bag, dusted it off, and dropped it back into her booksack. "I'm going to give Harold the highest recommendation I can. An absolutely splendid reproduction."

Plato grinned. "That wasn't very nice, Cally."

"It wasn't meant to be." She rubbed the back of her coat. "Silly bastard *pinched* me—twice. In the cage. I told him if he did it again, I'd cut his fingers off."

She patted her breast pocket, which Plato knew held several dissecting scalpels, then turned to the other workers. "As Deputy County Coroner, I'm closing this construction site for today. I need you all to get your things and step outside the fence. The police will be here soon and they'll let you know what to expect."

As the hardhats shuffled off, several flashed admiring glances at Cal. She drifted off toward Ernie's trailer.

Standing beside Plato, Jamahl grinned. "That's one *fine* woman you got there."

"I know."

They both watched Cal approach the trailer. In response to her knock, Ernie reluctantly poked his head out the door. As Cal talked, the foreman nodded vigorously, eagerly, to her every suggestion.

"Bet she keeps you in line, though."

Plato sighed. "You got that right."